Dog Days
Forever

Dog Days Forever

A NOVEL

SHANNON RICHARD

AVON

An Imprint of HarperCollinsPublishers

P.S.™ is a trademark of HarperCollins Publishers.

DOG DAYS FOREVER. Copyright © 2023 by Shannon Richard. All rights reserved. Printed in the United States of America. No part of this book may be used or reproduced in any manner whatsoever without written permission except in the case of brief quotations embodied in critical articles and reviews. For information, address HarperCollins Publishers, 195 Broadway, New York, NY 10007.

HarperCollins books may be purchased for educational, business, or sales promotional use. For information, please email the Special Markets Department at SPsales@harpercollins.com.

FIRST EDITION

Designed by Diahann Sturge
Title page and chapter opener image © Anna Hoychuk / Shutterstock

Library of Congress Cataloging-in-Publication Data has been applied for.

ISBN 978-0-06-323561-8

23 24 25 26 27 LBC 5 4 3 2 1

For Nicole Fischer

You becoming my editor was a dream that
took a decade to become reality.
Thank you for seeing my potential all those years ago.
Thank you for fighting so hard to work with me.
Thank you for fighting so hard for this book.
Thank you for being you.

Dog Days Forever

Prologue
The Last Summer

The rain had been coming down for hours. A summer storm had rolled in over the little town of Cruickshank, North Carolina, settling down between the mountains and getting comfortable for the night. It didn't want to go anywhere, and there was no one who understood that feeling better than Maximillian Abbott.

Everything was perfect. The queen mattress beneath him was like a cloud, the cotton sheets soft on his bare skin, and he was wrapped around the love of his life. He knew he could circle the globe, but his favorite place to travel was the distance between Caroline Buchanan's collarbone up to the hollow behind her ear.

Max pressed a kiss to her skin before trailing his nose along the slope of her neck, inhaling her the whole journey up. She always wore citrusy scents, and these days it was grapefruit. He'd have sworn he could get drunk on it as the sweet scent filled his lungs.

She did something to him, something he didn't understand, something that was too powerful and perfect to be explained by man or God.

Thirteen years had passed since Caro had walked into Max's life, and things hadn't been the same since. It had been his first summer in Cruickshank, and everything had been new to him besides his grandparents.

He didn't do well with change either.

Max hadn't been familiar with the massive Victorian house that Martin and Ava had just moved into. It was so different from the brownstone in Boston where they'd lived for the first six years of his life, the one where he'd spent every Christmas and summer vacation so far. His favorite pizza place had been a couple of blocks to the left, and a park with a swing set was a few blocks to the right.

No, their new house had creaky floors, two staircases that never led him to the place he wanted to go, and a massive, scary tree outside his window that scratched at the glass during storms.

Forty-eight hours into his summer vacation, and he had hated it . . . until he met her.

"Caro?" Max whispered before lightly biting her earlobe.

"Mmm," she hummed, her body stirring against his. Her legs swished against the sheets as she pressed back against him, skin to skin.

He moved his hand across her stomach and to her side, gently tracing his fingers over her ribs as he kissed her bare shoulder. "Do you remember the first time we met?"

She shifted again, rolling over in his arms so their faces were mere inches apart. There were a few candles lighting up the space in her little loft apartment, and he wasn't sure if the glow in her hazel-gray eyes was from the flickering flames around them or if it was coming from inside her.

"Like it was yesterday." The warmth and vibrance of her smile seemed to add to the limited light.

For as long as he lived, Max would never forget the first time he saw her. It was imprinted on his brain, a permanent photograph, never to be erased.

Caro and her mother, Rachel, had shown up on a particularly rainy Monday morning. Rachel had been hired to help his grandparents around the house. She was their assistant, cook, gardener, whatever needed to be done.

Max had watched the two newcomers in the kitchen, peeking out from his safe place behind the door that led to the living room. Even then he'd known there was something almost otherworldly about Caro. She reminded him of the fairies and forest nymphs that he read about in his storybooks.

She'd caught him watching her, and the second her eyes locked with his, her mouth split into a giant grin that somehow lit up her entire face . . . like it was doing right now.

Six-year-old Max had felt a jump in his stomach somewhere behind his navel, a feeling he always associated with roller coasters and Caro . . . a feeling he was experiencing in the present moment.

"You were wearing a hot pink tutu and bright yellow rain boots that made you look so tiny." His hand was at her back, his fingertips tapping gently across her spine like he was playing a piano. "Though you're still tiny."

"Hey!" She playfully pinched his side, making him squirm against her until he grabbed her hand. "It's not my fault I reached five foot two and stopped growing while you just *had* to get to six feet."

"It doesn't matter." Max pulled her hand to his mouth and kissed her knuckles. "We still fit together."

"We've always fit together."

It was true, even from the start. He'd been a painfully shy child who had trouble stringing a sentence together, and she'd been a bouncing ball of energy who could have an entertaining conversation with a brick wall. And yet they'd fit.

Max leaned in close to Caro, brushing his lips against hers. "Always."

It was Caro who pushed in for the kiss, opening her mouth. Her tongue found his as her leg slid up and over his thigh, showing just how well they fit together.

They hadn't finished making love that long ago, and yet he needed her again. But he always needed her—*would* always need her.

Max forced himself to break the kiss, pressing his forehead to hers as their uneven breaths mixed in the space between their mouths. "Do you remember the first thing you said to me?"

Caro pulled back from him, settling her head against his arm so she could look at his face, her smile firmly back in place. "I asked you if you liked chocolate chips in your pancakes and whipped cream on top. It's still the best breakfast."

"Oh, without a doubt," Max agreed as he pushed a strand of her dark brown hair out of her face. "Do you remember what you told me after that?"

Her smile grew. "That Max was a good pirate name, and we should go on an adventure after the rain stopped."

"And we've gone on so many adventures since then," Max said as he started to wrap the strand of hair gently around his finger.

"So many."

"Caro, I know we're young. And I know that our relationship has been mostly long distance . . ."

Max had lived in New York his whole life, up until a year ago when he'd moved down to North Carolina to go to UNC–Chapel Hill. Four hours was much more manageable than eleven, but they'd still never been in the same place for longer than three months.

"And I know that us being together full-time has been delayed another year . . ."

Caro's face fell at those words, her expression sad. The plan had always been for her to join him at UNC after finishing high school. But those plans had changed when her mother was diagnosed with cancer. She'd decided to stay home for the year and help take care of Rachel and the rest of her family.

"But this summer has given us other gifts."

She'd moved into the loft above her parents' garage, giving them some sort of privacy when he was in town that summer. They didn't have to sneak around, didn't have to set alarms to wake up early and creep back into their own beds as if they'd been there the whole time.

"I've gotten to go to sleep with you in my arms every night, gotten to wake up next to you. It's been . . . perfect."

"It really has been." Caro started to blink rapidly, her eyes brimming with moisture. "I love having you here, Max. All mine."

"All yours." Max moved his hand up, gently wiping away the tears that were now on her cheeks. "Caro, I knew the first time I met you that I would follow you anywhere. That I'd be up for whatever adventures you wanted. And nothing has changed. It won't, a year from now, or five, or fifteen."

"It won't," Caro echoed on an unsteady breath, tears now freely streaming down her face as her eyes searched his.

"Marry me."

"Yes," she said, without a moment of hesitation.

The word was barely past her lips when Max crushed his mouth to hers. He rolled so she was beneath him, her arms wrapping around his back. She was holding him so tightly he'd have sworn she wanted to disappear into him as much as he wanted to disappear into her.

But there was one last thing that needed to happen before that.

For the second time that night, Max made himself break the kiss. It took a force of will that was stronger than he realized he possessed.

"Max." His name was a plea. "I need you."

"I know. I *know*. I just . . . I have to do something first." He sat up, kneeling on the bed as he reached for the nightstand drawer next to him, pulling it open and grabbing a little blue velvet box.

Caro sat up, her eyes moving from his hands to his face. She was beaming, biting her bottom lip in the way that always signaled she was so happy she could barely contain it.

He could barely contain his happiness either. Not wanting to wait a second longer to make it official, Max opened the box and pulled out the ring. He held out his hand, and Caro lifted hers into the air, placing her palm against his.

With one gentle slide, the ring was in place on the third finger of her left hand. He'd gotten the antique ring from his grandmother Ava. It was intricate white gold, a halo of tiny diamonds, and one big, round stone in the middle. And on the inside was an inscription.

To a lifetime of adventures.

Chapter One
Out of Sight, Out of Mind

Fifteen years later

The Manhattan rooftop ballroom was filled with more than two hundred people. There were celebrities, politicians, a few Nobel Prize winners, and even a couple of lower members of the British monarchy. The women were wearing thousand-dollar ballgowns in every color imaginable, while the men were sporting tuxes that were black, white, or a mix of the two.

Well, most of the tuxes. There were a handful of fashion-forward men who'd embraced the trend of colors, and one of them happened to be Maximillian Abbott. Tonight, he had on an emerald-green brocade tuxedo jacket. He'd been tempted to wear his vintage red velvet one, but it was supposed to rain that evening. As that jacket had been given to him by his late grandfather, he didn't want to take the chance of ruining it.

Max took a sip of scotch as he looked around the packed room. Massive arrangements of white flowers stretched up from every table, getting close to the gold and crystal chandeliers that hung from the elaborately painted ceiling. Freddie Mercury in Retrograde—a decent Queen cover band—was playing "A Kind of Magic" on stage.

Everyone in that ballroom was there to celebrate Hugh Hennings's seventieth birthday. He was half of Bergen and Hennings, a multibillion-dollar alternative asset management company where Max had worked for the last six years. Or maybe he should say he'd *lived* there for the last six years, since he typically pulled eighty-hour workweeks and spent more time in his office than he did in his own apartment.

Hell, he'd barely been in New York the last couple of months. He'd been in Europe scouting locations. Jumping around from Scotland to France to Italy and, finally, to Germany.

Max traveled all over the world finding abandoned or forgotten buildings to be brought back to life in the form of apartments, restaurants, boutique hotels, and many other things. Sometimes it was for a specific client, other times it was for Bergen and Hennings. He was the first step in transforming churches, old schools, sprawling mansions, warehouses, and even an old ocean liner.

He often wished he could be part of the renovations themselves, that he'd get to choose the marble that would be in the entryway or find the perfect artist to do the stained-glass windows in the lobby. He wanted to be there until the end. Whenever he toured the renovated properties, he couldn't help but make a mental list of all the things he would've done differently.

But that wasn't his job. As he'd been told many times, he had the eye. He could see the potential where others couldn't. If he was busy with renovations, he wouldn't be available to find new projects, new investments, new ways to make Bergen and Hennings more money.

His last deal had been a completely new kind of acquisition for both him and the company. It had been the most excitement he'd had in a long time. An excitement he hadn't found in Manhattan. An excitement that couldn't be found in that ballroom.

He always felt out of place at events like this, but as it was his boss's birthday, he'd thought it was important to make an appearance. Besides, it wasn't like he had anything to go back to at his empty apartment . . . or his even emptier bed.

His romantic life had taken a back seat the past couple of months. Actually, it had taken a back seat for over a year. He couldn't remember the last time he'd been on a date. Maybe a little social interaction would be good for him. They were only halfway through the cocktail hour, so there was still plenty of time left for him to mingle, something he should be doing anyway.

There was an opening for a senior associate, a position Max was in the running for. There was also the question of who was going to take over the real assets division in London. A lot of ass-kissing was going on, most of the employees putting on a show for the higher-ups.

But the whole night was a show; all events like this were. No one knew that better than Hugh's wife, Adrienne Bergen, the other half of Bergen and Hennings.

Hugh's marriage to the English heiress had been more of a business merger. Adrienne had just as much of a hand in building the Bergen and Hennings empire to what it was today. Her shrewd intellect and wit contributed to their success just as much as Hugh's know-how and drive.

The power couple stood side by side, Hugh's loud laugh punching through the music, while Adrienne was her usual charismatic self. She was wearing a form-fitting black dress that was covered in crystals. There were so many diamonds on her throat, wrists, and fingers that one would think she'd just emerged from a bath of snow, the flakes sticking to her like frost. She was fifty-nine, but she could easily have passed for a woman twenty years younger.

"Maximillian," someone said to his left.

Max would have known that husky voice anywhere. He'd spent many evenings listening to it whisper dirty things into his ear. He turned to find Kendall Margaret Ashley Campbell at his side, one of Manhattan's top divorce attorneys and his on-again-off-again girlfriend for the last four years.

They were currently off. Though their last run had been the longest yet, making it all the way to the nine-month mark. They'd even gotten to the point where they'd each left a toothbrush at the other's apartment. If that wasn't progress, Max didn't know what was.

Kendall was wearing a red dress that looked like it had been painted onto her svelte frame, and her dark blond hair was curled around her bare shoulders.

"Kendall." He couldn't help but smile. His chances of not going home alone had just shot up exponentially. "I didn't know you'd be here. I'm glad you found me in this crowd." He leaned in, pressing a kiss to her cheek.

"I spotted you immediately. You and your jackets," she said fondly as she smoothed a hand down his arm. "You just *have* to stand out, don't you?"

"Well, you know how I like to make a fashion statement. And

you're one to talk." He made a small movement with the hand holding the scotch, indicating her dress as he gave her a slow—very slow—look up and down.

"Oh, no. Don't start making that sexy face of yours." She frowned. "I won't be fooled."

"What are you talking about? It's just my face."

"Mmm-hmm." She turned to get the attention of a waiter carrying a tray of champagne flutes. She grabbed a glass, bringing it to her bright red lips and taking a slow, steady drink of the golden bubbles.

"How's it been?" Max asked, thinking about the feel of her lips pressed against his own.

"Busy as usual. I wasn't sure if I'd make it tonight. I had a last-minute meeting."

Much like Max, Kendall was also a workaholic. Their shared drive and determination kept bringing them together . . . but it was also what ultimately drove them apart. It was hard to make a relationship work when it wasn't ever the focus for either party.

And yet the Bergen and Hennings marriage worked . . .

Another of Hugh's loud laughs rent the air, and Max turned to glance at the couple. Adrienne looked at her husband with a practiced smile, not an ounce of warmth in her eyes. They were probably a foot apart, but they might as well have been on different sides of an ocean, which was the case more often than not, since Adrienne ran the London office.

"Getting a flash of what your life is going to be like in thirty years?"

Max gave an exaggerated flinch as he took a couple of steps back. "You wound me."

Kendall rolled her eyes, giving her head a small shake. "Oh, come on. Nothing gets through this." She reached up, patting the spot over his heart.

"Some things get through." He covered her hand with his, holding it to his chest.

"Oh, Max," she whispered as she slowly shook her head at him.

"I've missed you, Kendall." He gave her a warm smile, the one he knew could turn her hot in an instant if given the opening.

But there wasn't an opening.

"It's only because I'm right here in front of you, Max." There was no mistaking the sadness that flickered in Kendall's golden-brown eyes. But there was more than that. There was something in her expression that almost looked . . . pitying.

"What?" His grin faltered.

"With you, it's out of sight, out of mind."

Max didn't take his eyes from hers as he pulled her hand from his chest and started to run his thumb across her knuckles. "That's not true, Kendall. I think about you whenever I walk by the little jazz club on Fortieth Street, or when I get the crab Rangoon at Lucy Cho's, or when—"

It was then that the pad of his thumb bumped up against something hard and sharp. He looked down and saw the giant rock on the ring finger of her left hand. The diamond sparkled, the lights from the room seeming to hit it at every angle.

A memory flashed in Max's brain, one of a candlelit room and of sliding an engagement ring onto a hand he'd thought he'd never have to let go of. But Max pushed the memory away, focusing on the moment . . . focusing on Kendall . . . who was standing in front of him . . . engaged. He wasn't sure how this revelation should make him feel—or what his first thought should be—but he was pretty sure it should be something more profound than *oh*.

For the second time that night, Max took a moment to bring his eyes back to Kendall's. He needed a second to put the charming mask back in place, his mouth forming an easy smile.

"Who's the lucky guy?" he asked as he let go of her hand.

Kendall hesitated before nodding over Max's shoulder. "Silas Bloomfield."

He turned in that direction to see two guys in deep discussion. As the shorter of the two men was the mayor of New York, Kendall's fiancé had to be the tall guy with brown hair. He was a little lean and lanky, but he had a bit of a Clark Kent thing going on.

"What's he do?"

"He's a professor at NYU. He teaches quantum physics."

"Impressive."

"I think so." She nodded.

"Congratulations, Kendall." Surprisingly enough, the sentiment was genuine. He *was* happy for her.

Kendall grabbed Max's arm, squeezing tightly before letting go. "Thanks, Max." She took a deep breath, letting it out in a huff as her shoulders relaxed.

"You look relieved. Did you think I was going to be a jerk about it?"

"No, it wasn't that." She shook her head. "I just . . . I don't know. It feels weird. I just always thought we'd work out someday. That we'd find our way back, and it would finally *fit*."

There were times when Max had thought something similar. It wasn't that he thought they'd finally *fit* together—more that they'd finally figure out a way to live around each other.

"Why do you think we didn't?"

"Because we would've ended up like them." Kendall waved to where Hugh and Adrienne were still making the rounds.

"You think so?"

"We never loved each other. Hell, we didn't even believe it existed."

"And you believe in it now?"

"I do. Anyways, I just wanted you to find out about the engagement from me. I need to get back to Silas." Kendall grabbed his arm again, stretching up to place a kiss on his cheek. "I hope you find someone who makes you believe in love too."

"Goodbye, Kendall."

"Goodbye, Max."

He watched her walk away, her parting words unsettling him. The thing was, Max *did* believe love existed. He'd had it once. Given his heart away . . . and then he'd had it handed right back to him. It was why he avoided love at all costs now.

There were memories circling at the edges of his mind. Memories of hazel-gray eyes and a smile that had made him weak in the knees. Memories of stolen kisses and a soft laugh lingering in his ears. Memories of being young and foolish. Memories of a naive boy who no longer existed.

Memories he knew *exactly* how to handle. He lifted his glass of scotch and downed the last of it before heading back to the bar for a refill.

"Another Balvenie please."

Alfred, Lord Tennyson, had gotten it wrong when he said, *'Tis better to have loved and lost than never to have loved at all.* Yeah, that was the biggest line of bullshit Max had ever heard in his life. A lost love didn't give you anything but emptiness.

It was a lost love that had fucked up his views on love.

Well, she was just part of those fucked-up views. There were other people who had had a hand in turning his heart cold. And as Max grabbed his new drink and turned around, he spotted them across the room.

Vanessa Winthrop and Kenneth Bergstrom—aka his mother and stepfather.

His mother was wearing a striking blue ball gown, a canary diamond hanging from her neck, and her platinum blond hair was in some sort of complicated twist, not a strand out of place.

There never was. His mother was always the model of perfection.

His stepfather was wearing an expertly tailored black Armani suit—Kenneth only wore Armani—and his brown hair was combed in such a way as to attempt to hide that it was thinning.

They might live in the same city, but Max didn't see them often. He used to try, but he'd been stood up too many times because of their "busy schedules." They hadn't had time for him as a child, and they sure as hell didn't have time for him as an adult.

They were both doctors with God complexes; it wasn't a new or original story.

They were only a few feet away, deep in conversation with an older couple Max didn't recognize. As he'd had no idea they'd even been invited to the party, and he hadn't mentally prepared himself for an encounter with them, he wondered if he could make a quick getaway—

Too late. He'd hesitated too long. His mother turned, and her icy blue eyes landed on him.

Max glanced down at the amber liquid in his glass, wishing he'd ordered a double. Taking a big sip of scotch, he crossed the distance to them just as Freddie Mercury in Retrograde started to play "I Want to Break Free."

"Maxie," Vanessa said as she bumped her bony jaw against his. She always called him that—which he hated—but there wasn't an ounce of affection in the moniker. It was more her constant need to make him feel like a child.

Kenneth didn't say anything as he shook Max's hand in his usual no-nonsense fashion, like he was greeting a stranger for the first time.

Vanessa took a step back, waving to the couple next to her. "Maxie—"

He gritted his teeth.

"This is Raphael and Esther Vandenberg. They're charitable donors at Precipice."

Ah, that was why they were here tonight. Money for the hospital.

"This is my son, Maxie."

Max cleared his throat, holding out his hand to Raphael and Esther in turn. "Max Abbott," he corrected before looking to his mother. "I had no idea you guys would be here."

Vanessa's face tightened, her blue eyes getting even colder. "We're just as surprised to see you here. Though I don't know how I didn't spot you as soon as I walked in." She took in the emerald-green brocade of his jacket, her lips pursed like she'd just sucked on a lemon. "I don't know what it is with you and those ridiculous things."

There was no point in responding to that particular crack about his fashion, so Max moved on. "Hugh Hennings is my boss. Why are you so surprised I'd be here?"

Vanessa waved off his remark, letting out a casual laugh as if this was an oversight that could happen to anyone. "Bergen and

Hennings has hundreds of employees in New York alone. How were we to know you'd merit an invitation?"

"Oh, you work for Bergen and Hennings?" Esther asked with genuine curiosity.

But before Max could answer, Kenneth spoke, his tone full of the derision Max had come to expect whenever his stepfather talked about his career. "Yes, my stepson gets to play with building blocks all day. It must be fun to have such a carefree profession."

Max's father, Landon, had died in a car accident when Max was four years old. Kenneth had come into the picture three years later. In the twenty-six years that he'd been Max's stepfather, he'd never once referred to Max as his son. He'd never acted like a father, never claimed him, never respected him.

"Actually, I don't really *build* anything," Max clarified. "I'm an associate in the real assets division. I find old and unused buildings or properties for us to renovate."

"Oh." Raphael's eyes widened with interest. "Have you had any projects in New York?"

Max told them about the school in Queens that was turned into an apartment building, the three-hundred-year-old church in Brooklyn that was now a two-star Michelin restaurant, the warehouse that was an off-Broadway theater currently housing a play that was always sold out.

"My favorite is the Chantilly Hotel. It was an old lace warehouse in Midtown."

"Oh," Esther gasped excitedly. "My granddaughter and her husband stayed there the last time they were visiting. We went to the rooftop restaurant, and the view was incredible, especially at sunset. What was the name of it?"

"Eyelet," Max answered, feeling more than a small bit of pride at her praise. He'd spotted the FOR SALE sign in the window a few years ago. The building had been through a number of unsuccessful businesses, until he came along.

"It's really the perfect location," Raphael said, impressed. "And the lobby is spectacular. Esther could spend an entire day staring at that massive glass fountain in the center."

That fountain was made of hundreds of different colors of glass that all looked like different pieces of lace. They flowed down as if they were pouring out of the roof. It changed colors depending on where the sun from the skylight hit it.

"I really could." Esther turned to Vanessa and Kenneth, her eyes alight. "Have you seen it?"

Kenneth shook his head, his expression clearly saying, *Like I have the time for that.*

"No," his mother said through a strained smile. "We haven't gotten around to it. When did that one finish up?" she asked, trying to appear as if she actually cared.

"Three years ago."

It was clear that Esther and Raphael were shocked by this—and maybe slightly disgusted. But it didn't surprise Max; they hadn't seen *any* of his projects.

A gentle squeeze on Max's forearm had him looking down to see a freshly manicured hand, belonging to none other than Adrienne Bergen.

"Hello." She looked around, her smile highlighted by her signature dark red lipstick.

"Mrs. Bergen." Max moved to allow her space into the circle. "You've met my mother and stepfather." He waved at them in turn.

As Bergen and Hennings was a huge donor at Precipice Hospital—they each had a wing named after them—their paths had crossed before.

"Dr. Winthrop, Dr. Bergstrom." She shook both of their hands. "And Mr. and Mrs. Vandenberg," she said as she moved her focus to the other couple, shaking their hands in turn too. "I'm so glad that you all could make it tonight."

"Nowhere else I'd rather be." Kenneth smiled at her.

"The event of the season," Vanessa agreed.

"Max was just telling us what he does for Bergen and Hennings. We had no idea the Chantilly was one of your properties," Esther said.

"Yes, Max is one of our rising stars." Adrienne gave him a look of pride that he'd never seen on either Vanessa's or Kenneth's face. "He's been doing a lot of work with me in Europe over the last few months. He just acquired us a fifteenth-century castle in Germany. It's going to be a new jewel in our boutique hotel collection."

"Ohh, where in Germany?" Raphael asked.

Max spent the next couple of minutes telling Raphael and Esther all about the project, Adrienne interjecting here and there to brag about him and his expert eye. Vanessa and Kenneth didn't say a single word. In fact, they were clearly bored.

"Anyway," Adrienne said to the group, "I need to steal Max away and have a word with him before this evening gets more hectic. If you will excuse us."

"Absolutely," Raphael said.

Max looked over to the Vandenbergs. "It was lovely to meet you both."

"You as well." Esther nodded.

"We're going to have to go check out that church turned restaurant you told us about. What was the name of it?" Raphael asked.

"The Pulpit. And if you have any problems getting a reservation, just call my office," Max said before he focused on Vanessa and Kenneth. "I'll . . . see you."

Kenneth gave a noncommittal shrug as he took a sip of his drink.

"Bye, Maxie." Vanessa waved her fingers at him and turned to start talking to the Vandenbergs again. They both appeared way less enthusiastic about the conversation now.

Just what he needed, for his boss to hear that stupid nickname, but Adrienne didn't say anything as they stepped away.

"I need another drink." She led him toward the bar.

"Me too," Max said as he finished the last of his scotch.

"Two Balvenies," she told the bartender. "Max-a-million." She emphasized every syllable with her English accent. "You lived up to your name this week."

"I live up to my name *every day*, Mrs. Bergen."

"That you do." Her blue eyes narrowed on him in that penetrating gaze that would have made a lesser man squirm. "And how many times do I have to tell you to call me Adrienne?"

"At least one more time, Mrs. Bergen."

She rolled her eyes, and a small smile broke her stern red mouth. It was something that often happened when he was around her. For as long as Max had worked at Bergen and Hennings, he'd always had a better relationship with Adrienne. They had a fun banter that never crossed the professional line, even if they did toe it occasionally.

Their bartender was back in front of them now, sliding two glasses across the bar. Max picked up both and handed one to Adrienne.

"To castles in Germany." Adrienne held her glass in the air.

"And many more to come." Max clinked his glass against hers, and they both took a sip.

"So, you figure out your next big deal yet?"

"I've got a top three." Max nodded.

"You're not going to give me any more details than that?"

"Not here." He shook his head. "There are way too many eager ears at this party. I don't want a deal stolen right out from under my nose."

"I bet those eager ears belong to the same people who've had their lips pressed against my husband's ass all night."

It took everything in Max not to spit out the scotch he'd just taken a sip of.

"Not that it will do them much good."

"You've picked the new senior associate?" he asked once he was able to swallow.

"We've got a top three." She gave him a sly smile as she threw his words back at him. "I'm curious as to what your opinion is on the selection, though."

"Really?" Max was all ears, mainly because this felt like a lead-up to Adrienne telling him *he* was in the top three. "And why is that?"

"Because they'll be your liaison here when you take over real assets in London."

For the second time that night, Adrienne had said something that almost made Max choke on his scotch. "When *I* take over the London office?" *Holy. Shit.*

"Why, Max, you seem surprised." She tilted her head as that sly smile of hers grew.

Because he *was* fucking surprised. "I didn't know I was in the running for that position."

"Everyone is in the running for *every* position. Can *you* handle it?"

"Without question." This promotion was a number of steps higher than the senior associate position he'd been aiming for, but he could do it.

"Good." She gave him a little nod. "It was one of the few things Hugh and I agreed on. I'd hate for *both* of us to be wrong about something."

"Neither of you will be wrong about this."

"I didn't think so." She shook her head. "You've spent some time in London before." It wasn't a question; she was fully aware of exactly when he'd been there, and for how long.

"A summer in undergrad"—right after his life had fallen apart— "and then a year when I was getting my MBA."

"A joint degree with Columbia University and the London School of Economics, if I remember correctly."

Of course she remembered correctly, but Max nodded anyway.

"Well, it will be just like going home for you, won't it? Your promotion will be announced on Monday. You start July third."

"July? That's—" He counted in his head. "Seven weeks away."

"Yes, when was the last time you took a vacation?"

"I was just in Europe."

"And you worked almost the entire time. I mean a *vacation*. Sleeping in, binge-watching some show, going fishing. *Re-lax-ing*. You do remember what that is, don't you?"

"Vaguely."

"Exactly. If you keep working the way you do, you'll burn out. Take a vacation."

"I don't need—" But he stopped talking when she gave him a stern look.

"Take the time off, Max. You've earned it. I'll send you an email with those candidates to choose from for the senior associate position."

"Okay."

"Good. And, Max? Congratulations."

"Thank you, Mrs. Bergen."

Adrienne clinked her glass to his again before turning around and walking across the room, leaving him alone.

London. He'd gotten London. In less than two months, he was going to be picking up his life in Manhattan and moving across the Atlantic Ocean. And, as was made perfectly clear tonight, there wasn't anything holding him here.

As if the universe was proving just how wrong he was, the phone in his breast pocket vibrated against his chest. He reached inside his jacket and pulled it out, looking at the screen. A picture of his grandparents flashed before him, one of the two of them from their fiftieth wedding anniversary, a picture he hadn't been able to change after Martin's death nine months ago.

Max moved through the crowd, his focus on the doors at the back of the ballroom. He slid his finger across the screen and put the phone to his ear. "Hey, Ava, hold on one second."

His grandparents had never had cutesy nicknames. They never wanted to be called Grams or Pops, Mama or Granddad. They'd always been Martin and Ava . . . though now it was just Ava.

Max pushed the glass door open, stepping out onto the less crowded balcony. There were a dozen people out there, either needing a quick cigarette, a private word, or both. None of them had ventured out beyond the overhang, not wanting to get wet as a light drizzle had started up.

"All right, I'm good now," Max said as he leaned against the wall behind him, staring out at the rain and the bright lights of the city.

"Oh, if you're busy, I can call you back later."

"Never too busy for you." He recognized the lie the second it left his mouth. The only time he'd seen her since Martin's death was when she came up for Thanksgiving. He'd said he'd go to Cruickshank for Christmas, but that trip had gotten canceled when he'd had to stay in New York for work. So had his trip in February . . . and April.

He couldn't remember the last time he'd called her either . . . Probably when he'd canceled the trip in April. And now he was moving across the Atlantic, so it wasn't like there was going to be a lot of opportunity to visit in the future.

"I could use some good conversation and a little fresh air." Though the latter wasn't exactly a reality. The air was thick and heavy around him.

"I just don't want to bother you with this if you're busy . . ." She trailed off, her hesitation to continue clear.

"Ava, I'm good. I promise. Hit me with it." It was a night for unexpected conversations. Sure, what happened with Kendall had been a little weird, and then he'd had to deal with his mother and stepfather, which was never pleasant, but he'd also just gotten a huge promotion. He could handle whatever his grandmother was about to throw at him.

"I'm selling the house."

Okay, maybe not.

Max pushed off the wall, his back going straight. "You're . . . you're selling the house?"

"It's time for me to downsize. This place is just too big for me,

Max. I'm tired of rattling around this old house alone. It's lonely here without Martin." Her voice didn't break, but her sadness was palpable, something that seemed to be amplified as the storm settled in, the rain coming down harder around him.

A wave of guilt rolled through Max. He owed her a visit. He'd promised her he'd come down to help sort through everything Martin had left behind.

"Anyways." Her voice picked back up to its usual upbeat tone. "I called because I wanted to ask if there was anything here that you wanted. I'd hate to give away or sell something that you were particularly attached to."

His past was attached to the whole damn house. A past he had zero desire to revisit.

But if Ava was going to sell, he needed to help her, especially before he packed up his life and moved to another continent. Looked like he'd be spending his summer in Cruickshank, North Carolina, a place he'd avoided as much as possible for the last fourteen years.

Not that he'd left himself much of a choice.

Chapter Two

Everything Is Just Peachy

The snip, snip, snip of the pruning shears filled Caro's ears. She was standing in the mudroom of Ava's house, the stems and leaves of the fresh flowers slowly piling up in the basin of the porcelain sink. She and Ava had spent all morning in the various flower beds in the backyard, cutting flowers, pulling weeds, laying fertilizer, and planting seeds.

Caro had questioned Ava's desire to plant new seeds, as she most likely wouldn't even be here to enjoy them bloom in the fall.

"Well, first of all, I already bought the seeds, and I'm not wasting them. They deserve a chance to bloom just like everyone else." Ava waved her dirt-covered gloved hands at the expansive gardens. "Second of all, even after I move out, part of me will still be here." She smiled widely. "And third of all, the new owners will get to see her in all of her fall glory," she finished as she nodded to the three-story brick house behind Caro.

It was still hard to believe that Ava was selling the beautiful Victorian that had pretty much been Caro's second home since she was five years old.

God. The very thought of Ava not being there made Caro's chest ache. She had to stop herself from reaching up to rub the spot, mainly because she would've stabbed herself with a particularly thorny rose or, even worse, the pruning shears.

Caro was just going to have to appreciate this summer, and whatever time she had with Ava in this house. Besides, it wasn't like Ava was leaving Cruickshank; she was just going to move into a smaller home. Probably a cozy cottage with a white picket fence. Something low-maintenance, and without two winding staircases to navigate through multiple floors. She was still getting around just fine, but she was almost eighty-five.

Caro looked up from her flower cutting and out into the backyard, scanning for Ava's yellow sunhat in a sea of colors. It was a lost cause, so instead she started to search for one of the two four-legged, furry friends that she knew were running around the backyard.

Ava's rescue dog, Beauregard, was never far from her side, his long, fluffy tail usually wagging a mile a minute. Somewhere behind him would be Caro's current foster dog, Tibbett, a basset hound with floppy ears and sad eyes.

It took a couple of minutes to find the trio, but Caro finally spotted them on the other side of the sunroom.

"What in the world?"

The woman was standing at the top of a ladder, leaning precariously and reaching for the trellis on the side of the house. Caro dropped the shears and flowers into the sink before practically sprinting out the back door and across the lawn.

"Ava! What are you doing up there?"

"Pruning my jasmine," Ava said calmly, not even turning around.

Oh, the exasperating woman. "I can see that! Get down from there!"

"It's fine, Caro."

Beau whined at Caro's side, clearly not agreeing that everything was *fine*, while an unbothered Tibbett stuck his head in a nearby bush and quite literally smelled the flowers.

"No, it's not! Let me do it!" Caro yelled up at her as she grabbed the ladder, making sure it was steady.

"Why? Do you think you can do it better?"

"No, I think that if you fall, you will shatter into a million pieces."

Ava paused and turned to look down at Caro. "And what happens if *you* fall?"

"I'll bounce. Now, for the last time, get down from there."

"Fine." Ava carefully stepped down the ladder until she was standing in front of Caro. "How are you going to reach the top?" she asked as her eyebrows climbed high above her sunglasses. "You know I've got five inches on you, right?"

"I'm fully aware that you are taller than me, thank you. I will manage just fine." She held out her hand for the shears before she started to climb up the ladder.

"Well, while you're up there, you might as well fix that loose piece of the trellis that needs to be nailed in. It's just above the window."

Caro spotted the piece, seeing that a nail had fallen out. "If you go get me the hammer and the nails, I can fix it."

"Perfect." Ava's voice chimed up at her before footsteps faded off. "Come on, boys," she called out as two barks filled the air.

Picking up where Ava left off, Caro continued moving up the

jasmine plant, cutting it back where it needed. She was doing just fine too, reaching every area . . . except for a little patch in the top right corner. Looking around, she spotted the ledge of the porch, a ledge she'd used many times before, back in the day when she'd been climbing in and out of Max's bedroom window.

Her hands paused for a second as she stared up to that room, remembering those long summer nights.

For the second time that afternoon, a sharp pang made her chest ache. But she forced herself to push past it. It wasn't like it was the first time she'd had painful memories from this place. This house might be Caro's second home, but it also held a whole hell of a lot of ghosts for her.

Stepping one foot off the ladder, she stretched her leg out, the tip of her red sneaker just finding purchase—

"Who's up there this time?"

The sound of *that* voice had the exact same effect on Caro as being doused with a bucket of ice water. For a split second, she thought she might be *hearing* those ghosts, but as she turned her head, she had only a second to register Max looking up at her before her foot slipped and she was falling . . .

Right. On. Top. Of. Him.

There were two crashes. One was Caro and Max hitting the ground in a tangle of limbs, shouts, and grunts. The other was the ladder that she'd knocked over on her way down, the metal slamming into the brick wall of the house.

Max had taken the brunt of the fall, landing on his back in the grass, while she was sprawled across his long, hard body. Her face was pressed into his chest—*Was it this solid fourteen years ago?*—

and when she breathed in, she got a hit of Maximillian Abbott. Herby, lightly spicy, a little salty, and all him.

It took everything in her not to bury her face in the fabric of his shirt and breathe in deeper. Instead, she looked up, her gaze meeting his. There was a moment, a fraction of a second where something like longing flickered in those blue eyes. But then that fraction of a second passed, and it was gone.

"Do you plan on staying here all day?"

"I . . . No . . . sorry." She put her hands on his chest and pushed, trying to lift herself up. Unfortunately, she was again so surprised by the sheer amount of muscle beneath her palms—

Seriously, was he this big fourteen years ago?

—that she slipped and fell back into him. Not wanting to be sprawled all over him for a third time, she shifted to the left. Her legs fell to the side so that she was now straddling one of his thighs, a position that seemed much worse. When she tried to move this time, she managed to knee him in the crotch.

"*Ooomph,*" Max grunted before both of his hands landed on her upper arms and he easily moved her off him.

Caro scrambled to her feet, spinning around and watching him get slowly to his. He was wearing dark denim jeans and a gray T-shirt that hugged his biceps and chest—his stupid *too*-large chest— but hung loose around his waist.

"I'm sorry," she said again. "Did I hurt you?" She glanced down, unable to help herself as she awkwardly waved at his crotch.

His face tightened before he looked away from her, brushing the grass and dirt from his clothes. "I've had worse."

The *from you* was silent, but she heard it loud and clear. Her brain flashed to fourteen years ago . . . being in his apartment in Chapel Hill . . . and handing him back the engagement ring.

"What are you doing here?" His tone wasn't rude or mean, but he clearly wasn't happy to see her.

"You know I still work for Ava, right?" She'd started when her mom had gotten sick. "I always come on Tuesdays and Fridays, or whenever she needs me, really."

"Oh, yeah." He nodded. "I forgot." Except there was something about his expression that made her think he didn't know that she still came here regularly. But there were a lot of things they didn't know about each other anymore.

He no doubt had secrets; *she sure did*, one that she'd been keeping from him for the last eight years.

"I didn't know you were visiting; otherwise, I wouldn't have been here."

"It's fine, Caro. If you're here that much, we're going to have to figure out a way to be around each other the next few weeks."

His words were slow to process in her brain. "The next . . . few weeks?"

"I'm here through the end of June. Didn't Ava tell you?"

Wait, what month are we in now? She racked her brain. It was hard to think through the fog in her head, and the scent of him that still lingered in her nose. *It's . . . it's the middle of May. No, no, no, no, no, no, no! Nooooooo!*

"No, she didn't mention it. The end of *June*?" she repeated, a little hoarse.

"Caro, who are you talking to?" Ava's voice trailed from around the house. She came into view a few seconds later—Beau and Tibbett right behind her—but stopped in her tracks when she saw the new arrival. "Max! You're here!" she cried out, throwing her hands in the air—a hammer in one and a box of nails in the other. Ava set the stuff down on the patio table by the pool before she closed the distance to her grandson. "Give me some love!" She planted a kiss on his clean-shaven, square jaw before pulling him in for a hug.

When she let go, she took a step back, her eyes moving from Caro to the ladder that was now on the ground and then over to Max.

"What happened?"

"I lost my balance and fell on Max." Caro was still eyeing Ava. How had she not warned her? They never talked about Max, but a little heads-up would've been nice. Some time to prepare herself.

Who was she kidding? There was no preparing for Max. Nothing that would stop her hands from sweating. Nothing that could slow the erratic beat of her heart, which was currently trying to make a break from her chest.

"Really," Ava said as she looked over to her grandson. "Did she bounce?"

Max's eyebrows bunched together in confusion. "What?"

"Did Caro bounce? She made me get down from the ladder, because she said if I fell, I'd shatter into a million pieces, whereas if she fell, she would bounce. So did she?"

"Not even a little bit." Max laughed as he shook his head.

It was the smallest of laughs, but it made Caro's chest ache.

"You know, your concern for the situation is absolutely overwhelming me, Ava." Caro's words were a little sharper than intended, maybe because it felt like she was being stabbed in the chest. She needed to find an escape hatch, or pull a rip cord, something—*anything*—to get the hell out of there.

Ava bit her bottom lip, clearly trying to hide a smile. "I'm sorry. Are you hurt?"

"No, Max took the brunt of it."

"Well." Ava patted him on the chest. "He always was a safe place to land," she said, before giving Caro a meaningful look.

And on that note, I am out.

"I'm going to go. I didn't finish with the flowers in the mudroom. And since Max is here now"—she waved a hand at him—"he can help with the trellis situation."

"Ava, when did you get another dog?" Max asked as he dropped down to pet Tibbett and Beau, who were both circling around and sniffing his shoes.

"I didn't. Tibbett is Caro's foster dog."

He looked up, still giving both dogs a good head scratch. "Foster dog? I wouldn't think Sweet Pea would put up with sharing you."

And there was another painful slice through Caro's chest. Sweet Pea had been her mother's buff-colored cocker spaniel mix. She'd had the softest ears and the sweetest freckled face. When her mother had died, Sweet Pea had become incredibly attached to Caro, and Caro to her.

"Sweet Pea died three years ago," Caro said, like it was no big deal.

Except it was. She'd loved that dog so damn much. Sweet Pea dying had been another loss in her life, another thing that had broken her heart. Something else she'd had to learn to live without . . . much like the man standing in front of her. After Sweet Pea died, Caro had been unable to get another dog permanently. It was why she fostered now.

Sadness flickered across Max's face. He stood up—his mouth

opening slowly—but Caro cut him off. She didn't want to hear what he had to say.

She couldn't bear it.

"I'm going to head out," she repeated. "I'll see you later. Come on, Tibbett, let's go." She patted her thigh, turning around and heading for the house, praying the dog would follow.

She had to get away from Max as fast as her legs could carry her.

* * *

MAX WATCHED CARO walk away, his head a jumble of emotions he didn't understand, didn't *want* to understand. There was also the fact that something in his chest felt . . . out of place. He wasn't sure why it had surprised him so much that Sweet Pea had died. If he'd thought about how old she must have been, it probably would've occurred to him.

He remembered the night Sweet Pea had joined the family like it was yesterday. It had been Rachel's birthday, the last normal one she'd had before her diagnosis. The living room had been filled with pink and gold streamers that he, Caro, and Caro's sister, Lucy, had spent hours artfully stringing up. Caro had excitedly pulled him upstairs to show him the tiny sleeping puppy that she'd rescued that afternoon.

God, that was sixteen years ago.

He hadn't known that Sweet Pea was gone. It wasn't like he hadn't seen Caro since, but the last time had been at Martin's funeral nine months ago. It hadn't exactly been the best time for a chat. Though they hadn't had a long conversation in ages.

This was the most they'd spoken in fourteen years. It was a lot harder to walk away when she was lying on top of him. He was still thinking about the press of her body into his and her soft brown hair in his face. The only thing grounding him was the ache in his balls.

Though that pretty much summed up how he felt whenever he saw her. Today had definitely been worse, especially with the lingering scent of her still in his head.

She still smelled like citrus . . . It had been something lemony that afternoon.

Max didn't take his eyes off her until all five foot two of her disappeared around the corner, Tibbett the basset hound right on her heels. She walked fast for someone so short.

Max let out a frustrated breath. That wasn't the homecoming he'd been hoping for. He would've been happy putting off seeing Caro for as long as possible. Instead, she was the first person he saw . . . and she'd literally fallen on top of him.

"You hungry?" Ava asked, next to him, like *nothing* had just happened.

Max turned to his grandmother, his eyebrows bunching together. "Did you do that on purpose?"

"Do what?" she asked innocently, her green eyes going wide.

"Have her here when I got here?"

"Caro is always here on Tuesdays. She still works for me, Max."

"Yeah, she said that. She also didn't know I was coming. I don't think she would've been here had she known."

"Honey." Ava stepped forward, giving him a sweet—yet somehow stern—smile as she placed her hand on his chest. "If I changed my plans based off of when you *tell* me you're coming I'd be changing my plans a lot."

Well, that was a not-so-subtle dig. "Okay, fair point. But this wasn't me just *saying* I would visit; I sent you my flight itinerary two days ago. You *knew* I would be here."

"I must've missed the email." She shrugged.

She must've missed the email? She checked her email every morning while she drank her coffee. Really, though, he should probably just let this one go . . . He didn't exactly have the higher ground here.

"What's the trellis situation Caro was talking about?"

"There's a loose piece right there." She pointed up to the spot above the window.

"Let me fix that and then we can go in for lunch."

"That should give us enough time to make sure Caro's left before we go inside." She winked before she went to grab the hammer and nails from the patio table.

Let the goading begin. It was going to be a long summer.

Max shook his head as he moved to grab the ladder and pull it upright.

Once the trellis was fixed, he went to put the ladder away while Ava headed inside to get lunch started. Beau was by her side, long, fluffy tail wagging.

When he closed the shed doors, he looked around the backyard and decided to do a loop to see how things had been kept up. The house was on a little more than three acres of land, so it wasn't like it was a small area to maintain.

Upon first glance, the greenhouse and carriage house were fine, but he'd take a closer look later. The pool was in good shape, the water crystal clear and ready for someone to dive in. He'd be taking full advantage of it this summer. It had been a while since he'd had the freedom to swim laps whenever he wanted. Sure, his apartment building had an indoor pool, but he couldn't exactly work while underwater. But he *could* get a lot of business done during a spin on his exercise bike, or easily pause during a run or a weight-lifting session to answer an email.

The lawn was a little high and should probably be mowed, but there wasn't a weed in sight, and the flower beds were blooming like crazy. The rose garden was filled with an assortment of white, pink, red, and yellow; the daisy corner was bursting with purple and white; and a patch of reddish orange tulips was still holding strong even though it was May. The line of dogwood trees had all fully blossomed, and they set a nice backdrop to the garden.

He saved the best for last and headed for the orchard at the back of the yard. A dozen peach trees were filled with fruit that was probably a month away from being ripe enough to eat. His mouth started to water as he thought about peach jam slathered onto a piece of warm, freshly baked bread. That jam was Ava's number one specialty, and it really couldn't be rivaled.

That patch of trees offered up a plethora of memories that spanned almost half of his life. Memories of Caro and him running back and forth between the trunks and acting like they were escaping from aliens or tigers or enemy pirates. Of spreading out blankets and eating packed picnic lunches, before lying down and finding shapes in the clouds. Of the warm summer evenings, as they'd gotten older, when they'd lie beneath the stars and make love in secret.

But all those memories were in the past now, which was a place he didn't need to linger.

As he made his way back up to the house, a bright red bird

floated down from the sky before landing in the birdbath. Cardinals loved that backyard, and as he searched the trees, he saw three more flitting around. He always thought of Ava when he saw them.

He passed under the massive oak that sat almost dead center in the yard and glanced up to the middle of its trunk, where an old treehouse was perfectly nestled among the branches. Martin, along with Caro's dad, Wes, had built it during the third summer he'd spent here. He was surprised it still looked as good as it did, considering it was twenty-six years old.

He was tempted to climb up there and check it out, but Ava was waiting for him inside. Plus, it was just another place that was full of memories. When they were children, he'd spent countless hours up there with Caro, acting out some adventure or planning the next one. When they'd been teenagers, they'd snuck up there to have other adventures. Max had lost his virginity in that treehouse.

Yeah, there was no need to deal with any of *that* today. He hadn't even been back an hour, and he'd already had enough.

At the house, Max opened the back door and walked through the mudroom—which was currently bursting with flower cuttings and half-filled vases—and into the kitchen. The smell of frying bacon was in the air and practically hit him in the face. His stomach gave a loud rumble, his breakfast from that morning long gone. He looked around, a moment of contentment that he hadn't experienced in a while settling in his chest.

Even with all the baggage that accompanied this place, he was home.

The kitchen had been remodeled before Ava and Martin had moved in all those years ago, but not much had changed since. The floors were still the same rough stone tile that felt familiar on the bottoms of his feet. Wooden counters stretched out across the tops of the artfully weathered white cabinets. Stainless steel appliances—which were really the only things that had been updated over the years—gleamed from their places around the kitchen. The back wall was mostly covered with copper pots and pans that hung from hooks, a large brick oven on one side, and the massive walk-in pantry on the other.

Max and Caro had spent many an afternoon sitting on the stools at the center island, watching as Caro's mother made the two of them the world's best PB and J: fluffy white bread, creamy peanut butter, homemade strawberry jam. It had been cut diagonally and paired with an ice-cold glass of milk.

Damn, Caro really was everywhere in this place. Her fingerprints were all over his memories.

"Finally!"

Ava's exasperated voice pulled Max from his thoughts, and his eyes landed on her standing next to the stove, slicing into an orange and yellow heirloom tomato.

"We're having BLTs for lunch. Wash your hands and get the bread out," she said, looking over her shoulder, her salt-and-pepper braid swaying with the movement.

"Yes, ma'am." He nodded, heading for the sink.

"What took you so long out there?"

"Just giving myself a tour of the backyard."

"You mean making sure it hadn't fallen into disrepair?" Her hand stilled as she looked over at him again, her eyebrows raised high.

"I didn't say that. I just wanted to see how close I was to some peach cobbler."

"Mmm-hmm." She shook her head before turning back to her task of thinly slicing the tomato. "Well, I will have you know that the maintenance of the backyard has long since been dealt with. *I* hired Adam Goodson to start mowing the lawn five years ago when the heat became too much for Martin, even though he refused to admit it. As for the pool, Davey Brinks has been the pool boy—pool man?—whatever, for the last nine years. And my handyman, Nathan Sanders, comes by once a week."

"You have a handyman?" Max asked as he grabbed the clean towel that was draped over her shoulder to dry his hands.

"Yes."

"Then why was Caro on a ladder that she said she had to get you down from?"

"Because I was pruning my jasmine, and that is not something I have the handyman do. That is a task I only trust with a skilled green thumb, which she is."

"She always was," he said as he draped the towel back over Ava's shoulder and headed for the pantry.

He opened the bread box to find half a loaf of sourdough. "Yes." He groaned. "It's from Browned Butter." The bakery was the best in town and better than anything he'd ever gotten in New York, Paris, or anywhere else for that matter. He held the bag to his nose, taking a big inhale as he stepped out of the pantry.

"Where else would I buy my bread?" Ava asked as she flipped the bacon. "So, about Caro . . ."

"What about her?"

"You know she's going to be around here. You better not try to scare her off."

"I wouldn't dream of it," he said as he set the loaf on the counter.

"Mmm-hmm." Ava frowned, a skeptical look on her face that said she didn't believe a word of what he'd said.

"I'm sure we'll work it out. And last I remember, Caro holds her own just fine."

"Well, as long as the two of you play nice. I'm just glad you're here, is all, and I want to enjoy the time I have with you. But, Max, I will not ask Caro not to come around."

"I wouldn't ask you to do that." He shook his head, surprised by the honesty in those words.

It was true that he didn't want to be around her. But he also knew Ava and Caro had a special relationship, a relationship that hadn't ended even when Max and Caro's had. He had no intention of disrupting things. He wasn't that much of an asshole . . . Well, not all the time.

He was just going to have to be around her. Something he had absolutely no idea how to do anymore.

Chapter Three

The Healing Power of Nachos

The scent of lemon and pine filled Caro's nose as she walked into Quigley's Irish Pub. The mahogany floors were freshly mopped, the wooden tables covered with upside-down chairs. She looked around the space, letting herself feel just a moment of comfort.

The walls were all exposed brick, old Irish art scattered around. There were numerous stained-glass panels depicting a saint or a sheep or a complicated pattern of knots; a dozen antique clocks; a few stuffed animal heads; and a shrine of paintings and pictures depicting the Quigley family going as far back as the early 1800s.

At the very center of the room hung a rather impressive chandelier that was made of a wide variety of Irish whiskey bottles. The ceiling was the same dark mahogany as the floors, and the lighting consisted of exposed iron pipes with Edison lightbulbs hanging from the ends.

Much like Ava's, Quigley's was another home away from home for Caro. She'd spent much of her childhood going in and out of that building. It was owned by the family of her best friend turned sister-in-law, Lilah. Caro had worked there two nights a week for the last twelve years. Since her brain was too full of thoughts of Max—she'd been unable to sit around and do nothing at home—she'd decided to come in early . . . two hours early.

She set her purse behind the bar before heading to the kitchen. When she pushed open the heavy door, the scent of onions, garlic, peppers, and fresh cilantro was in the air, accompanied by rock music. The two men currently prepping up a storm were Roman and Ezekiel "Zeke" Forester. They'd been working together for nine years and married for the last four.

They were an interesting pair, but somehow fit together. Zeke was just under six feet tall, had a bald head that rivaled Mr. Clean's and two beefy arms that could rip a door off the hinges—something that had in fact been demonstrated on more than one occasion. He also served as the bouncer if there was ever a problem with a rowdy customer or two.

On the other side of the coin was Roman. He was tall and lanky at six foot five and always had his long brown hair pulled up in a man bun. There were multiple piercings decorating his ears and left eyebrow, along with tattoos covering every available surface of both his arms.

Caro touched the digital screen controlling the music and turned it down a few decibels. "Hello, gentlemen."

"Hey, Caroline." Roman looked up from where he was dicing a mountain of fresh tomatoes.

"You're a little early," Zeke said as he dumped a cutting board of chopped strawberries into an already steaming pot on the stove.

"A bit. I finished up early at Ava's." She shrugged like it was no biggie. "Please tell me that your strawberry rhubarb cobbler is on the menu tonight."

"It is indeed." He nodded.

"Save me a piece?"

"Always." He grinned at her.

Zeke might seem intimidating at first glance, but he was really a teddy bear at heart. All anyone needed to do was watch him with their dogs to see that he was a total softy. Cupcake was a fluffy Pomeranian, Peanut was a pitbull mix, and both were his babies. They'd also both once been Caro's fosters.

"I just wanted you guys to know I was here. I'll be out there getting a head start"—she waved to the front of the bar—"and working up an appetite for my dinner. I hope it's good."

"Like it would be anything else?" Roman raised an eyebrow that had a bright purple hoop at the corner.

Caro smiled as she turned their music back up and pushed through the heavy wooden door to the bar. Fishing her phone out of the back pocket of her jeans, she plugged it into the stereo in the corner. Pulling up her music, she scrolled through some of her favorite artists.

"Well, if there was ever a time for *Jagged Little Pill*, it's today," she told herself as she pressed play.

The harmonica from "All I Really Want" filled the room, and Caro upped the volume to a level that might be able to drown out even her own thoughts. But as she danced around the bar—pulling the chairs down from atop the tables—her mind inevitably went to Max . . . and how good he looked. And, *damn*, did he look good.

Just because she wasn't in love with him anymore didn't mean she was blind. She had firsthand knowledge of how hard his body was these days, after she'd literally been sprawled across it. She did *not* remember him being that solid the last time she'd had an up-close-and-personal view of his chest. She wondered what the rest of his body looked like now.

Nope. Nope. Nope, nope, nope. No, you do not.

She did not need to go down that road. It was a dead end. Something she knew full well. Instead, she needed to figure out how she was going to get through the next few weeks with him in town . . . and figure out how she was going to keep her secret from him. The one thing she didn't want him to learn about.

Caro had written *The Adventures of Pumpkin and Bean* when she was twenty-five. A children's book that was based on their childhood together. Max was Bean, and she was Pumpkin.

Pumpkin had been Caro's nickname since before she was born, and it was all Jeremy's fault. Her brother was three when their mother was pregnant with her, and he'd insisted that her ever-growing belly was because of the pumpkin seeds she loved to eat. He apparently thought one had sprouted inside of Rachel's belly. The only person who really called Caro that anymore was her father, and she suspected the only person who still called Max Bean was Ava.

That first book had been a love letter to win him back, to ask for a second chance after the mistake she'd made all those years ago . . . That was until she'd gone to New York and realized she was too late.

She'd been at a coffee shop just around the corner from his apartment, working up the nerve to go knock on his door. And then he'd walked in, his arm wrapped around a beautiful blonde.

The coffee shop had two floors, and she'd been on the one above. Max hadn't seen her, but she'd had the perfect view of them. She saw it all. The way he looked at the woman. The way he touched her. The way he kissed her.

And that was when Caro had known he'd moved on. It was the thing she'd told herself when she'd gone back to Cruickshank . . . the thing she'd told herself more times than she could count over the years. At some point, it had morphed into *she'd* moved on too.

Well, she'd moved on from loving him, but she couldn't exactly run away from *all* of their past. Kind of impossible when she'd turned *The Adventures of Pumpkin and Bean* into a book series. Five of them had been published, with her sixth coming out in the fall.

As far as she knew, Max didn't know about them. Since their breakup, the only people he'd talked to in Cruickshank were Ava and Martin. They'd made a point of not telling Caro about Max and not telling Max about Caro. And as she wrote under the pen name C. E. Buchanan, it wasn't like she'd come up if he'd ever searched for Caroline Buchanan.

But with him back in town for the summer, she didn't know if those books would remain a secret or not. Not everyone knew that Max was Bean . . . and the people who did knew full well she didn't want him to know.

Maybe it was possible.

When "You Oughta Know" came on, she tried to get lost in the music. The lemon cleaner in her hand became a microphone as she bounced around from table to table wiping the tops. She felt so much better after scream-singing the lyrics that she pressed the back button on her Apple Watch and sang it all over again. She moved through the opening tasks for the next forty minutes or so, and she had her own little concert going . . . Well, until the music stopped.

Caro looked up to find Gavin Quigley standing behind the bar, his warm chocolate-brown eyes focused on her.

Gavin was Lilah's younger brother, and though Quigley's was a family affair, he was the one running the place most nights. And since his apartment was on the third floor, his entire commute to work consisted of walking down two flights of stairs.

"Alanis Morissette?" He raised his eyebrows. "Who hurt you?"

"No one," she lied.

Gavin didn't say anything, but both of his eyebrows were now high enough to be obscured by his black hair, hair that always looked like he'd just raked his fingers through it. The man was impossibly handsome, and he knew it. It didn't help his slightly inflated ego that his nickname was GQ.

And it didn't help Caro that he was still studying her, rubbing at the healthy amount of scruff on his square jaw with his thumb and pointer finger. The gesture made his biceps stretch the sleeves of his black T-shirt.

"It's a long story. Well," she amended, "it's not actually long, but it's a story."

"One you'd rather wait to tell me when Lilah gets here?"

"Yeah." She wanted to limit the retelling of that afternoon as much as possible. Every time she thought about falling on Max, she couldn't stop the head-to-toe cringe that vibrated through her entire body. She wasn't sure if it was possible to have mortified herself more.

Knowing her, probably.

"Okay." Gavin nodded before looking around. "What still needs to be done?"

"I checked the beer. All are good except the Asheville Abbey Ale." As a full keg of beer typically weighed more than 140 pounds, she didn't even bother trying to wrestle with that task.

"Well, you are a mighty mouse, but not that mighty of a mouse."

"Ha ha." Caro rolled her eyes as she tossed a set of silverware into the half-filled bin next to her. "I might be small, but I can still take you."

"I don't doubt it," Gavin said with all sincerity as he grabbed her phone to turn the music back on.

"You can pick something else out if you want." She waved a spoon in his direction.

"Nah, I'm down with Alanis." He shook his head, pressed play, and the chords to "You Learn" filled the bar. Gavin set her phone on the counter before he started to strum on an air guitar, bobbing his head and dancing around.

She didn't want to give him the satisfaction, but it was only a couple of moments before she could no longer hold back the laugh that was bubbling at the surface. The second he got the reaction he wanted, he held his hands in the air like he was the champion, jumping around to the beat of the music. He kept it up as he pushed through the wooden door that led to the kitchen.

The next thirty minutes passed much more quickly, and working with Gavin had the added effect of brightening Caro's mood.

A couple of songs later—when the first soft chords of "Ironic" came on—Gavin went full force with his powers. He used the handle of the broom as a microphone as he dramatically mouthed the lyrics. He sang the whole song, and by the end, Caro was laughing so hard her ribs hurt.

When the music stopped, it was followed by a loud round of applause. Caro and Gavin looked over to find Lilah standing behind the bar, watching the two of them with an amused expression on her face.

"I don't know what that was, but it was highly entertaining." She stopped clapping as she came out from behind the bar, her dark brown hair swaying around her shoulders.

"Thank you." Gavin made a dramatic bow. "I'll be here all night."

"Is this part of the new opening procedures?"

"Just today. There was a need for a pickup in morale." Gavin not-so-subtly bobbed his head to the left, indicating Caro.

Lilah's brown eyes narrowed on Caro. "What happened?"

"I'd like to discuss this with food . . . and alcohol."

"Sounds serious."

"Yeah." Gavin nodded. "The only clues I've got are that she came in here two hours early and was listening to Alanis."

"Hmm." Lilah's focus on Caro became almost penetrating. "Let's see if I can figure it out on my own."

Throughout their entire friendship it had been almost impossible for Caro to keep anything from Lilah. It wasn't only the fact that they never lied to each other—though that was part of it— Lilah also had a special power. She could give anyone an assessing look that felt almost like she was reading the person's mind. It was one of the reasons why Caro's brother, Jeremy, got away with next to nothing; neither did their children.

Caro used to think Lilah should be a fortune-teller, or a palm reader, and use her talents to their full extent. But she made pretty good use of them working behind the bar of Quigley's. It got her really good tips too.

The thing with Lilah's power was that eye contact was key, which was why Caro immediately looked away from her friend and was now examining her dark purple nail polish. If she was going to guess, Caro wasn't going to help her out.

"Something with your dad?"

"My dad is good." *Man, I really need to work on my cuticles.*

"Lucy okay?"

"Yup." Caro shook her head as she picked off napkin lint that was stuck to the front of her black tank top. Her younger sister was out in LA, trying to make her music/acting career happen. Caro had called to tell her about Max, but it had gone to voicemail.

"Everything good with Ava?"

Caro made an uncomfortable sound as she rubbed her hands down her thighs. Why were her hands sweating again?

"Now we're getting somewhere."

Caro forced herself to focus and made her face as blank as possible before looking up again. "Ava is perfectly fine." Though Caro needed to have a conversation with her about whatever that setup had been with Max.

Lilah's eyes narrowed for just a second before her assessing expression cleared. "Okay. Let's get that food and those drinks."

"W-what?" Caro asked, confused. Lilah's change of direction had her off-balance . . . which was another tactic.

"Wait, did you figure it out?" Gavin asked.

"Maybe." Lilah grinned.

"There's no way." Caro shook her head.

"We'll see. Besides, I think better on a full stomach, and the only thing I had for lunch was the other half of Emilia's PB and J and a few baby carrots. And since Caro got an early start, it looks like we have plenty of time to sit and eat. So how about you guys finish up"—she waved her hand around the bar—"and I'll go back and help Zeke and Roman fix us something tasty."

Caro's stomach made a long, low growl. Clearly that leftover pizza she'd eaten for lunch hadn't held up.

"Hey, since you guys weren't here last night when we tapped it, do you want to try the new Mango Tango Tangerine Wheat?" Gavin asked as he rounded the bar to finish making the base for the margaritas.

"Ohh, that sounds perfect." Lilah nodded, turning toward the kitchen.

Caro eyed the back of Lilah's head suspiciously as she disappeared behind the door. She hadn't figured it out . . . had she?

Grabbing the tray of salt and pepper shakers, she went around and set them on the tables and booths. The only thing left to do was to refill the napkin dispensers. She'd just finished with the last table when Lilah walked out of the kitchen holding a huge plate of Korean nachos.

Bulgogi, kimchi, white queso, shredded cheddar cheese, cilantro, and green onions all piled high on freshly fried wonton wrappers. There were some bowls on the side, one filled with extra queso and the other with sour cream.

Along with the typical Irish pub fare, Quigley's also served Korean food. There was always a range of kimchi options, from mild to make-you-cry hot; Korean sweet fried pancakes, served with a side of vanilla ice cream; and bulgogi, which was typically a marinated beef barbecue, though sometimes they made it with pork. It might be considered blasphemous, but Caro would have picked Korean barbecue over Carolina barbecue without hesitation. She might have been slightly biased, but for her, it was the best damn food in town.

Lilah and Gavin's parents had met at Osan Air Base in South Korea. Desmond Quigley was an airman, and Nari worked on the base teaching Korean to the servicemen and -women. They'd fallen in love, and when Desmond finished up his service, he'd come back to the States with a new bride on his arm.

"Beer poured?" Lilah asked as she made her way to the booth in the corner that had been *theirs* since they were children.

"Working on it," Gavin called out as he held a pitcher under the tap, the golden liquid slowly moving up.

Caro grabbed three plates and three sets of silverware before heading to their booth. Sliding into the seat across from Lilah, she reached for a wonton. It crunched satisfyingly in her mouth as she bit down, a moan vibrating in her throat.

"Good God, these are amazing."

"Nothing better," Lilah agreed as she popped a wonton into her mouth.

Gavin was at the booth a moment later, setting the pitcher and a stack of three glasses on the table before sliding in next to Caro.

"Nachos. Excellent choice," he said as he poured the beers.

Caro bit into another wonton, this one with kimchi covered in cheese.

"So, tell us about Max being back in town," Lilah said before she took a sip of her beer.

Caro coughed, inhaling a piece of wonton. It didn't help that the spice from the kimchi had started to take over her mouth. Apparently, Lilah had picked the make-you-cry version.

"Max?" Gavin looked between the two women in surprise. "This is about Max?"

Needing something to clear her throat, Caro took a sip of her beer. Thank God Gavin had picked a fruity wheat beer. If he'd chosen an IPA, it would've made the heat from the kimchi *so* much worse.

Caro had learned that lesson the hard way.

"How the hell did you figure it out?" Caro coughed again, grabbing a napkin.

"It was easy." Lilah shrugged, holding her right hand in the air with one finger pointing up. "Clue one: you were listening to Alanis Morissette," she said, then another finger popped up into the air. "Clue two: you're wearing the jeans that make your ass look great."

"They really do." Gavin leaned to the side, peeking down at Caro's jeans.

"Shut up." She elbowed him in the side, fighting a smile at the compliment.

"*And* you have the whole dramatic-eye thing going with your makeup, plus you're wearing your bright red lipstick. All things that you usually do when you need a confidence boost." She pointed to Caro's mouth with her left hand as a third finger popped up on her right hand. "Clue three: you balked when I said Ava's name, but you were telling the truth when you said she was fine." A fourth finger went up in the air. "And I saw him outside Ava's house when I was driving over here," she finished.

Gavin let out a bark of laughter.

Caro's mouth fell open as she sucked in an exaggerated breath of air. "*You already knew!*" The words came out scandalized, but Caro was doing her best not to laugh. Count on Lilah to be passing by at the exact moment Max was outside.

"*Yes!* And I wasn't sure *you* knew. I wanted to make sure I broke it to you like a good friend. But clearly that wasn't necessary. So, what happened? And no cutting corners. Tell us everything." She waved a wonton in Caro's direction before taking a bite.

"Yes, *everything*. This is a safe space. We're family." Gavin gently dug his elbow into her side. "And if I've learned anything about being a Quigley, it's that you burden your family with your problems as much as possible." He winked at her before reaching for the nachos, popping a wonton that was piled with everything into his mouth in one easy motion.

"Okay, fine." Caro flicked a piece of kimchi off the next wonton she grabbed, spooning a big dollop of sour cream on top before taking a bite. "But you aren't allowed to laugh at me."

"Oh, this is going to be good." Lilah grinned as she rubbed her hands together. "What did you do?"

Caro started from the beginning, and by the end of it, they were *all* laughing.

Chapter Four
Unplugged

After lunch, Ava had gone to take a nap. She'd felt guilty, since Max had just arrived, but being in the sun all morning had drained her.

"It's all good," he told her. "I need to unpack, and I want to check out the rest of the house. If you're selling, I want to make sure we get the best value for the place."

Just talking about selling had his chest tightening uncomfortably, but it was what Ava wanted, and he was going to do everything he could for her.

Ava patted his head, as if she knew what he was thinking, before heading upstairs.

And then Max got to work. It took him a couple of hours to do his first assessment, looking over the rest of the property, checking out the rooms and the condition of the house. Ava and Martin had more than maintained the beautiful old Victorian and the acres of land it sat on.

He took a walk around the block to check out how the rest of the neighborhood was doing these days. The surrounding area was a huge factor in the property value, and he quickly determined they were going to be just fine there too.

The street Ava lived on was aptly named Dogwood Drive. The trees lining both sides of the road were currently bursting with pink and white flowers, something that happened in the entire town when spring rolled around. It must've been a late spring this year because everything was in full bloom.

He appreciated them now, but they were a sight to be seen in the fall when they turned crimson and purple. That was also when the surrounding mountains went from green to gold, the leaves changing to bright oranges, reds, and yellows.

Though the winter was great too, especially Christmas, when the town practically transformed into the North Pole. All the downtown shops decked out their storefronts for the holidays. And when it snowed? It became a regular winter wonderland. Then there was summer, when the fruits were ripe, the weather was warm, and Lake Lennox became a hotspot for everyone with a bathing suit . . . and even some without. Plus, with all the rivers and lakes around, there was a plethora of options for the avid fisherman any time of year.

Really, every season in Cruickshank was beautiful to visit, *every* season was tourist season. It was a quiet little town with a big reputation. But as the closest hotel was a good fifteen miles away, a lot of visitors had to get out-of-town rooms and travel in. There was definitely a lost business opportunity here, especially because the few lodgings available were typically booked well in advance. There were cabins out at the lake, and some historical inns and cozy bed-and-breakfasts scattered around.

But it wasn't enough to keep up with demand. The town's tourism was only growing.

A handful of houses on Ava's street had already been turned into lodging, and Max thought it was likely the same fate that awaited the grand Victorian. The street was only a few blocks away from downtown and the perfect walking distance.

Plus, it had plenty of room. Five bedrooms, each with their own bathroom, an attic that could easily be remodeled into a second master suite, and a carriage house that could be turned into a private bungalow.

As much as his business mind could see the potential, he really didn't want to think of anyone but Ava in the house. This place had felt more like home than anywhere else.

The wooden floorboards creaked as he walked around the bedroom that had been his since he was six years old. Both of his suitcases lay open on the four-poster queen bed, and the antique dresser was slowly filling up as he transferred his clothes over to the drawers.

The room had seen a couple of changes since his youth. The cherrywood furniture had been rearranged, and the navy-blue linens replaced with white. The plaid curtains on either side of the bay window were gone, and white gauzy ones hung there instead. The walls were no longer light green, but a soft gray. No doubt the coat of paint had been needed to cover up the numerous tack holes from the posters he'd decorated with over the years.

Captain America had been the main guy in the beginning, but the superhero was later joined by the Boston Red Sox logo when Max had started watching games with Martin. Once he hit his teens, Nirvana, Incubus, Green Day, and Pearl Jam posters were part of the mix as well.

But all those were gone now, replaced by half a dozen framed drawings. Every room in this house was like its own little art exhibit, which was not all that surprising, since Ava lived there. Not only was she an accomplished artist in her own right, but she'd also taught art history and was a collector. Both she and Martin had been professors at Harvard for more than twenty-five years. Though Martin had been in the English department, making his own legacy.

Max wasn't sure if these drawings were his grandmother's or some other local artist's. Ava usually painted, but she dabbled with sketches here and there. He moved closer, studying the details. They were all of Cruickshank, one of the Blue Ridge Mountains, others of the downtown shops, Sweeny Park, Lake Lennox, the vineyard, and main street lined with the blooming dogwoods that Cruickshank was famous for.

It didn't take a lot of studying to figure out the artist, and his suspicions were confirmed when he spotted the little signature in the corner. He sighed as he took a step back, shaking his head.

Grabbing his bag of toiletries, Max headed to his own private bath. White hexagon tiles covered the floors and about halfway up the walls before transitioning to the same soft gray paint that was in his bedroom. There were fluffy white towels hanging from the rack on the wall, and dark gray bath mats spread out on the floor that were soft under his bare feet. The antique porcelain bathtub was still in near-perfect condition, and the hardware had been replaced with dark brushed nickel, just like it had been in every other bathroom in the house.

"This place is practically a spa retreat," Max said to himself as he took in the massive rainfall showerhead.

That might be great for some, but considering that he was

accustomed to fourteen-hour workdays and never really took a whole weekend off, he wasn't sure if he could do relaxing anymore. Case in point, he might be on vacation, but he'd answered each and every phone call, text, and email he'd gotten from his assistant. He'd taken care of everything, all while he'd been simultaneously assessing Ava's property.

Never let it be said that he didn't know how to multitask.

Max heard his phone ping, and he set his bag down on the counter before heading back into the bedroom. The battery had been low after the last call he'd taken, so he'd left it charging on the nightstand. When he looked down at the lit-up screen, he found an email from Ava.

Re: Flight Itinerary

I got your email with your flight. Since this is clearly the best way to communicate with you, what time would you like to confirm your dinner reservation for? 6:00, 6:10, 6:20, or 6:30?

Max rolled his eyes but couldn't help smiling. Leaving his phone charging on the stand, he headed downstairs to find his grandmother having her usual evening drink on the sunporch.

And what a sunporch it was. Not only was the space full of whites, buttercreams, and yellows, but the massive windows taking up three walls provided a 180-degree view of the yard. Ava was sitting back on a rather squishy sofa, her feet propped up on an ottoman and an open book in one hand. Beau was asleep on the cushion next to her, stretched out in a patch of sun.

"You get my email?" She smiled up at him sweetly, as if there weren't a passive-aggressive bone in her body.

"I sure did. Figured I'd respond in person. That a gin and tonic?" He nodded to the tumbler in her hand. There were a couple of lime slices swimming around in the clear liquid.

"I wanted something refreshing after my day in the yard."

"How about I go make one, then I'll join you and we can discuss dinner?"

"That would be perfect. I left some stuff out on the bar in case you wanted one. Everything else is in the mini fridge."

Max headed for the sitting room and the built-in bar in the corner. The glass-fronted hutch was filled with different kinds of drinking glasses on the second and third shelves, while the first had an assortment of hard liquor. The gin was on the thick oak-slab counter, right next to a cutting board with sliced limes. He opened the mini fridge under the counter to find a bucket of ice and a cold bottle of tonic water.

Once everything was in a glass, he grabbed a swizzle stick from a container on the counter and stirred it around, mixing the drink. Picking up his glass, Max rounded the bar but paused in his tracks when his eyes landed on the open double doors to Martin's office.

It was the one room in the house he hadn't gone in yet. He wasn't ready. He needed a day or two . . . and possibly a whole bottle of scotch. Good thing he had plenty of options to choose from in the bar behind him.

Letting out a little sigh, Max headed back to the sunporch. Ava closed her book and placed it on the side table next to her as he settled himself on the other end of the sofa, Beau between them. The dog lifted his head as Max sat, stretching his legs, his feet pressing into Max's thigh. He let out a huff of air before settling back down and falling asleep again. Ava scratched his belly before turning her focus to Max.

"So, is this how it's going to be the whole time you're here? The main way I can communicate with you is through your phone?" she asked before she took a sip of her drink.

"Hey, you took a nap. But I'll admit I got a little tunnel vision assessing the property."

"That's not all you were doing. I know you were working too. I thought you were on vacation."

"I am."

Her eyebrows rose high as her mouth turned down into a frown. "In what world does being on the phone all day constitute a vacation?"

"My world."

"Well, your world needs to get a realignment. Don't you have some overqualified assistant you're sleeping with who can deal with all of this stuff?"

"I have an extremely overqualified assistant who can deal with everything. Though he's a man, and while Edward *is* pretty good-looking, we've never slept together." Max shook his head as he took a sip of his drink. "Was that your not-so-subtle way of asking if I'm seeing anyone?"

Ava looked over at him with wide-eyed innocence. "I have no idea what you're talking about. Mainly because you don't ever tell me about your love life."

"Yeah, well, there is a bit of a conflict of interest there."

"Caro?"

"Who else?"

Ava's green eyes narrowed on her grandson. "Caro doesn't ask about you, Max, just like you don't ask about her. If I didn't know you guys had a past, I'd think you were perfect strangers."

"We are strangers . . ." *Now.* Since their breakup, Max knew next to nothing about her. What had he cared what she was doing? She was part of the past, and there was no point hanging around there.

Though he'd have been lying if he'd claimed there wasn't a small part of him that wanted to know if Caro was seeing anyone, but he couldn't ask that question. It would make him a raging hypocrite, considering their current conversation, so he chose not to go down that path. Besides, if he was spending a month and a half in Cruickshank, he'd find out sooner or later.

"Was there a reason you made my bedroom a gallery for her sketches?"

"Those pictures have been in that room for three years. It's not my fault you haven't noticed."

Three years? Well, he'd visited only once in that time, for Martin's funeral, and his mind had been otherwise occupied. Staying too busy to think had been a pattern he'd kept up with for the past year. And he'd stayed too busy to talk to his grandmother too. Which was why Ava didn't know anything about his love life . . . or lack thereof.

"And, just so you know, I'm not seeing anyone," he told her before taking another sip of his drink.

"So, what I'm getting from this is you have *no* good reason to be on your phone all day while you're *here*, with *me*. Not only are you *on vacation*, but there is no girlfriend to check on."

Max shifted in his seat, turning his body toward his grandmother. "Well reasoned."

"I bet you can't give up that phone for a solid week."

"What if people need to get ahold of me? Like my friends or something." Not that he'd hung out with anyone in months. His best friend from college was the only person he really kept up with these days, and he was out in San Francisco.

"Change your voicemail saying you're on vacation and tell them if it's an emergency to call your assistant." She didn't even hesitate with her solution. "And as for Vanessa and Kenneth, if they can't get ahold of you, they'll just call me."

"There isn't a high probability of that." He frowned. "I didn't tell them I was coming."

"They don't know you're here?"

"Nope." Max shook his head, bringing the glass to his lips and taking another sip of the cold, bubbly liquid. He hoped it would wash away the bitter taste that had filled his mouth.

Ava was fully aware of the strained relationship he had with his mother and stepfather. How could she not be? Since his father's death, he'd been shipped off to Cruickshank every summer so that the busy, important doctors didn't have to deal with him full-time. Hell, the second he'd been old enough, they'd sent him off to boarding school.

"Besides, they never call me. If they need to get ahold of me, they'll have one of their assistants contact my assistant like they always do. But I highly doubt that's going to happen."

Ava's eyebrows bunched together, her mouth making that angry line it always did when they talked about his mother. He knew she tried to keep her opinions to herself, or just not vocalize them to Max, but he'd always known she wasn't a fan of her former daughter-in-law.

Ava and Martin had lost their son, and Vanessa had lost her husband. But whereas Ava and Martin had loved Max harder, Vanessa had pushed him away . . . loved him less. He was pretty sure Landon's death had stopped her from loving at all.

Maybe he did have something in common with his mother. Losing the love of his life had made him incapable of falling in love again too.

Not wanting to linger on the topic anymore, Max moved back to Ava's challenge. "Okay, if I don't have a phone, what if *we* aren't together and *you* need to get ahold of me?"

Ava smiled, her expression becoming lighter with the change of subject. "You see, I've thought of that too," she said as she reached over to the table next to her. She raised her arm in the air, a black flip phone in her hand. "It's Martin's old phone. It still works."

"You never canceled his plan?"

Ava shrugged. "It's on automatic bill pay."

"All you have to do is give them a call, and they can cancel the line."

"If it bothers you so much, add it to your list of things to do while you're here. Just make sure to do it after your week of being free from your phone."

"Let's say I agree to this—and I obviously will be successful at it—what do I get?"

"Besides quality time with your grandmother?"

"Yes." He nodded. "Besides that."

"My pineapple coconut whipped dream cake."

"Deal." Max held out his hand without hesitation.

"And no emails either," she said as she put the flip phone in his palm. "Or Facebooking, Instagramming, or tweeting."

"That's not going to be a problem." Max shook his head. "I haven't been on social media in about ten years."

Max had been in college when social media had started to become a thing. He'd had accounts, but after seeing so many people mess up their careers with a stupid picture or post, he'd gotten rid of them.

"So it will be a piece of cake."

"Actually, it's going to be the whole cake," he corrected her. He'd never met a challenge he hadn't defeated.

"Well, now that that's settled, I would actually like to hear about work. Tell me more about this deal you made that got your bosses to give you so much time off."

Max hesitated, taking a sip of his drink to stall for a second. He looked out of the windows just as two cardinals dive-bombed from the oak tree before taking off into the sky.

"What?" Ava asked, poking him in the arm.

"I didn't tell you the whole truth," Max started. "I was waiting to tell you in person, but it wasn't the deal that had them giving me the time off. I got a promotion."

"You did? Congratulations!" She beamed at him. "What's the position?"

"I'll be in charge of the real assets division . . . in London."

Ava's smile faltered, and her mouth opened on an inhale. "London?"

"I start in July."

"Well." She nodded slowly. "I'm very happy for you."

Max's eyes narrowed on her. "Are you?"

"Yes." Her smile made a slow appearance as she reached over

the now-snoring dog between them, squeezing his arm. "I'm just surprised, and selfishly sad that you're moving. That's a bit of a longer flight to see you."

"I know, but we can travel around Europe when you do visit."

"There's the silver lining." She squeezed his arm again. "I'm very proud of you, Bean."

Bean, the nickname his father had given him, short for Love Bean. Ava and Martin had always used it too.

There was more love packed into that one little nickname, in that simple gesture of her touching his arm, than Max had received in months. It filled his chest with a warmth he hadn't realized how much he'd missed.

Maybe this vacation, and this time spent with Ava, was exactly what he needed . . . even with the complication that was Caro.

* * *

MAX MIGHT'VE UNDERESTIMATED his need to stay busy.

After enjoying his gin and tonic with Ava—and making a game plan for their dinner—he'd called Edward about his new vacation rules, changed his voicemail, and given his phone to his grandmother. He'd been just fine as they'd listened to Fleetwood Mac and made pasta carbonara and arugula salad—freshly picked from Ava's vegetable garden—for dinner. He'd been perfectly content as they watched a couple of episodes of *Jeopardy!* that had been stacking up on the DVR.

It was when hour three hit that he started to feel twitchy.

Maybe that was because it had been years since he'd gone more than two hours without checking his email, responding to messages from clients, or seeing what was going on with the stock market. Max might not be on social media, but he wasn't what anyone would call unplugged. And why would he be?

There was really no activity or event that prevented him from pulling out his phone. That was why there was Wi-Fi on airplanes and intermissions during plays and operas. The only thing that would've stopped him from checking would have been going to the movies. But it had probably been three or four years since he'd even set foot in a movie theater.

Who had the time?

Another reason he might be feeling twitchy was because of what they were now watching. His grandmother had put on some home makeover show that was so completely unrealistic it was insane.

There was no way these timelines were accurate. In what world could a kitchen be redone in twenty-four hours? Or an entire house get renovated in two weeks? Maybe if they were holding everything together with Scotch tape and a prayer. Also, the budget they were showing was so ridiculous he thought his head was going to spin. No decent contractor would be able to work for those prices and make a living.

Then this husband-and-wife duo took the homeowners through a store, making it seem as if *everything* could be found in one trip and acting as if they were going to get to keep the stuff they picked out. It wasn't possible that the custom leather sofa and Amish-made entertainment center were part of the four-thousand-dollar price tag shown in the cost of the living room.

"You doing okay over there?" Ava looked at him, her eyebrows raised high.

"I'm doing just fine."

"You sure? Because if you keep fidgeting with your watch like that, I think you might break it."

Max looked down to the Rolex on his wrist and realized he was flicking the clasp open and shut.

How long have I been doing that for?

"I'm sure." Max nodded, closing the clasp again before adjusting the watch on his wrist. He glanced at the face before resting his elbow down on the arm of the leather sofa. It was just after nine, which meant he was now barely into hour four.

Fuck, he was in for a *long* week.

Ava didn't say anything else, but she did give him a rather knowing smirk before turning back to the TV. When the episode ended, she set the remote on the end table between them.

"You going to bed?" he asked, looking at his watch again. It was nine thirty. How, *how* had only twenty minutes passed?

"Yeah, it's been a long day for Beau and me. We need to hit the hay."

The dog—who'd been softly snoring from the massive pillow at Ava's feet—perked his head up at the sound of his name. When Ava pushed the leg rest of her recliner in and stood, Beau pressed his chest to the floor and stuck his butt in the air, executing an exaggerated stretch. When he straightened, he headed for the doggy door in the mudroom, his long, fluffy tail wagging back and forth. He clearly knew the routine.

"You going to make it through the night?" she asked as she stretched her back out, mimicking her dog . . . Well, except for the tail wagging.

"I'll be just fine." Max repeated his earlier sentiment, but he was definitely doubting those words, especially as he didn't usually go to sleep before midnight.

Ava must've doubted those words too, because she tilted her head to the side, giving him a long, assessing look. "You know, it might do you some good to get out for a little bit. Not sure if you remember, but Quigley's is just up the street."

As Lilah Quigley was Caro's best friend, he'd been in and out of that place more times than he could count growing up. And as the Quigleys would be beyond loyal to Caro, he was sure they wouldn't be happy to see him if he showed up. Plus, he knew full well that Lilah was married to Caro's brother, Jeremy. Walking in there would be like walking into the lion's den.

Max's eyes narrowed. "I know where Quigley's is, thank you."

"Hey, I just wanted to make sure"—Ava raised her hands in surrender, keeping her voice light and innocent—"as it's been so long since you've been here."

"I haven't forgotten anything about Cruickshank, Ava. But I appreciate the concern. I'll probably just watch some more TV." He waved to the screen as the opening montage of a different home makeover show started.

"Suit yourself." She leaned over and placed a kiss on his forehead. When she pulled back, she gave him a soft smile. Her hand went to his hair, lightly ruffling it like she'd always done when he was a kid. "Night, my Love Bean."

"Night."

"I'm glad you're here."

"Me too," he told her, the words true even in his current state of unrest.

Ava's steps faded away up the stairs, and Max returned his focus to the TV, forcing himself to pay attention and doing his level best not to look at his watch. But when Beau came running into the house—the doggy door flapping behind him as he sprinted up the stairs behind Ava—Max glanced at his wrist.

Three minutes. It had been three *whole* minutes. And during those three *long* minutes, the guy on the screen was perpetuating the lie that anyone can be a do-it-yourselfer. False: a YouTube video does not make a person an expert on rewiring their house. It doesn't even make them an expert on rewiring a toaster.

"Okay, this isn't happening," he muttered to himself as he turned the TV off and got up from the sofa. His jacket was on the hook by the front door, and his shoes were on a mat to the left. He slipped everything on before grabbing the flip phone that sat on the stand near the door.

"Ava," he called out as he dropped the phone into his jacket pocket and grabbed a set of keys. "I'm going out."

It was a couple of seconds before she called back, the smile clear in her voice even from a floor away. "Have fun!"

When Max stepped outside, he was glad he'd grabbed his jacket. The night had gotten chilly, the warm seventy-degree afternoon taking a steady drop when the sun went down. It would probably get into the low fifties before all was said and done.

When Max left Ava's house, he hadn't had a set destination in mind; he'd just headed for downtown. As Cruickshank, North Carolina, encompassed a total of 5.37 square miles, it didn't typically take long to get anywhere, even on foot.

Downtown Cruickshank was built around two main roads, both cobblestone. Malcolm Lane and Alexander Avenue—named for the town's founders—were lined with brightly colored store-fronts and brick walls covered with ivy.

As Max passed the stores, he looked at the elaborate displays in the windows of Kathleen's Corner Bookstore, Browned Butter Bakery, Dancing Donkey Café, a handful of antique shops, and a couple of boutiques.

Some of those shops were new, and there were several restaurants he didn't recognize. Most were already closed for the night or in the middle of closing, a couple of them still housing a few stragglers finishing a late meal. The Dusty Floral wedding dress shop was another new place; so were Cheese Wheel & Wine and Hamish's Fine Furnishings.

Max wandered around, and before he knew it, he found himself standing outside of Quigley's, a place that was *more* than familiar to him.

The first floor was painted a bright red with black and gold detailing that made it pop even from blocks away. The second and third floors were made of brick and had big blooming flower boxes sitting beneath the windows. The building seemed to glow with the cast-iron lamppost lights that surrounded it. A beacon in the night.

Quigley's Pub was an institution, a legend, had been since 1904, when an Irishman by the name of Charles Angus Quigley built it with his bare hands. Not only had the pub made it through Prohibition and the Great Depression, but it had survived a fire that had threatened to take down the whole block.

It was smack-dab in the center of downtown, right at the corner of Malcolm Lane and Alexander Avenue. One could say it was almost the heart of Cruickshank. It was also the building that was most often referenced when giving directions to anyone who was new in town or visiting. As Cruickshank's population was roughly 4,300 people, it was easy to spot a tourist, especially if they were lost.

But Max wasn't lost . . . Or was he?

His hesitation with coming here hadn't exactly gone away, but as he looked left and right, he wasn't sure where else to go. Maybe he hadn't forgotten the old Cruickshank, but he didn't know everything that had happened in the last fourteen years. There was a new Cruickshank he had to figure out.

But besides all that, there was a voice in his head that was getting louder and louder as he stood in front of the building. That voice was saying it didn't matter if Caro had a tie to Quigley's, because so did he. And since he and Caro had broken up before his twenty-first birthday—and he'd subsequently stopped regularly visiting Cruickshank—he'd *never* had a drink at the pub. At least not legally.

Well, it was time to change that.

Chapter Five

Green Mudslides and Green-Eyed Jealousy

It didn't matter the time of year, or the night of the week, Quigley's was typically busy. That Tuesday night, they were *slammed*. The place was packed with people, a lot of them college students taking advantage of the beginning of their summer break.

Caro loved busy nights at the bar; not only did it make the hours go by in a flash, but it had the added bonus of keeping her busy and not thinking of *things*. If there was anything she needed that night, it was to not think of *things*.

"We need more tequila," Caro called out as she tossed the empty bottle into the recycling bin in the corner, the glass clanking loudly against the other bottles. "I'm running to the back. You guys need anything else?"

"Almost out of Jack." Lilah held the bottle in the air, showing that it only had about one fourth of the brown liquor left. "The group of guys in the corner keep asking for shots."

"I'll get two, then."

"Good call." She nodded before tipping the bottle over a tray of shot glasses.

"Grab another rum," Gavin said as he dumped a generous helping in the blender. "The sorority in the pink feather boas are practically swimming in these strawberry daiquiris."

Poor Gavin, there was nothing worse than making blended drinks all night long. Caro shared a commiserating look with him before pushing through the swinging door and heading into the kitchen. The Korean nachos were tonight's special, and the spicy scent on the air filled her lungs. It might be close to ten, but the guys were still cranking out order after order.

"You as busy out there as we are back here?" Roman asked as she walked by.

"Busier," Caro said as she rounded the corner.

"I don't know how that's possible," Zeke called out after her.

After punching in the code on the keypad of the supply room, Caro pushed open the door. Absolutely everything in the space was immaculately organized, a precedent that had been drilled into Desmond during his years in the air force. And it was a standard that was kept up at Quigley's too.

There was a place for everything, and everything had a place. The shelves of hard liquor were off to the left, organized by type and alphabetized by name. Grabbing an empty box by the door, Caro filled it with what they needed up front. For good measure, she grabbed a bottle of vodka, rounding off her stash before heading out of the supply room.

Caro was halfway across the kitchen when the wooden door swung open and Lilah pushed through, her soft brown eyes narrowed and her mouth pursed in concern.

"What's wrong?" Caro asked as she slowed to a stop.

Lilah reached over and took the box from Caro's hands, setting it on the counter next to them. "Max is here."

"*Seriously?*" Yeah, it was a good call that Lilah had taken the box, as it probably would've been on the floor now. Caro moved to the window, getting up on her tiptoes to peek out. She watched as Max took a seat at one of the few empty spots at the bar.

"Did he know you were working tonight?" Lilah asked from right next to Caro, getting a look through the window herself. As she'd inherited the Quigley height and was five foot nine, she didn't need to stand on tiptoes.

Caro turned to Lilah, frown firmly in place. "I don't think he knows I work here, period."

"Well, what do you want to do? You can go home if you want."

"What?" Caro waved dramatically at the front of the pub. "We're slammed out there. I'm not leaving you and Gavin with that."

"We can manage."

Caro shook her head; there was no convincing her with that lie. "I know you're trying to protect me, Lilah, but he's in town for a while. Avoiding him isn't possible, so I'm just going to have to get used to him being around."

"You sure that's possible?" Lilah asked as she grabbed the box from the counter.

"Yes." Caro straightened her shoulders. "How's my lipstick?"

"Fierce."

"Perfect." And with that, Caro pushed through the door and headed out into the bar to deal with her past . . . which had somehow become her present.

Man, was life complicated.

The second she stepped out, her eyes landed on Max. He was looking to the side, distracted by Gary Baum, who was sitting next to him and yelling at the Braves versus Dodgers game on TV.

"Oh, come on! You're practically giving them the bases!" Gary gestured wildly in the air before grabbing his beer.

Caro took the half a dozen steps and stopped in front of him. "Hello, Max. What can I get you to drink?" she asked as if he were any other patron.

Max's focus quickly moved from Gary to Caro, his eyes going wide when they landed on her. "You work here?"

"Well, it would be pretty weird for me to try serving you if I didn't." She leaned against the bar, pulling a polite smile into place. His gaze dipped to her lips for a second, confusion lingering in his blue eyes. In that moment she was even more grateful for her lipstick choice. Anything that threw this man off-kilter was all the better for her, mainly because she'd been off-kilter all damn day.

"What can I get you?" she asked again, her question forcing his gaze back to her eyes.

Max cleared his throat, giving his head a small shake. "Do you have a menu?"

"Sure." She grabbed a menu that had a dozen or so laminated pages off a shelf. "Decide what you want, and I'll be back," she said as she moved to help Theo Taylor and Oscar Belmont.

Caro's late mother had had two best friends, Juliet Taylor and Lorraine Belmont. She'd grown up with Theo and Oscar—little brothers she'd never asked for—and both men were very much aware of the whole Max and Caro saga.

The expressions on their faces made it clear just how much they were enjoying the show.

"Refills?" she asked.

"The Abbey Ale, please." Theo pushed their empty pint glasses toward Caro, a smile twitching behind the dark brown beard covering his jaw. The man had a bit of a lumberjack vibe going on, always sporting some sort of plaid shirt.

"So Max is back in town," Oscar said under his breath, a mischievous light in his eyes.

Oscar had always been trouble, but he was so much more now. He'd been a scrawny kid but had grown into his long limbs, which were now filled out with muscle. He had brown skin, golden brown eyes, and a square jaw covered in scruff that accentuated his deadly smile.

Though there were a lot of things about Oscar that were deadly. Not only was he charming as all hell, but he was also incredibly kind. He had the ability to win over humans and animals alike— that last one pretty important, as he was a veterinarian.

"He sure is." Caro nodded as she grabbed both glasses, setting them in the dirty bin before getting two fresh ones and filling them at the tap next to her.

"Everything all right over there?" Gavin asked as he made a show of shaking up the whipped cream dispenser.

"Everything is fine. Just fine." She smiled sweetly up at him.

"Lilah and I can cover if you want to go home."

The smile slid off her face in an instant. "I'm fine, Gavin. I'm not running away. I can handle this." Maybe if she said it enough times, it would be true. It wasn't like she was incapable of interacting with him . . . Things were just . . . awkward.

"*O-kay*," he said slowly, like he didn't believe a word that was coming out of her mouth. He moved his focus to Theo and Oscar, who both gave him looks of *Let it go, man.*

Well, she'd just have to show them, wouldn't she? She could be normal. She was capable.

"Where's Clint?" Caro asked about Oscar's boyfriend as she passed them fresh glasses.

Oscar's mischievous look from earlier disappeared. "We broke up. Turns out he wasn't a one-man type of guy."

Theo cleared his throat as he grabbed his glass. "You aren't the only person with man troubles."

"I don't have any man troubles." Caro shook her head.

"Sure you don't," Oscar said before he took a sip of his beer.

Caro rolled her eyes at the pair of them before she went to help a few more customers. When she moved back to Max, he was *still* flipping through the menu.

"Anything in there sound good?"

He turned another page, his gaze moving up from the menu to her. "Those strawberry daiquiris look interesting." Max pointed to the women of the bachelorette party in the corner, who all had one in their hands.

"You want a strawberry daiquiri?" Caro repeated slowly.

"I don't know yet. Do you use fresh strawberries?" He tilted his head to the side, his eyebrows making a little furrow at the question.

"Yes."

"And what kind of rum?"

"Whatever rum you want that we have." She waved her hand behind her, indicating the rum bottles lined up on a shelf on the wall.

Max stared at the options for a moment before shaking his head. "Hmm, I don't know. Maybe I don't want rum. Do you guys do frozen margaritas?"

What the hell was going on with him? Was he purposely trying to be difficult? She didn't remember him being much of a blended-drinks guy. Was this payback for her falling on him . . . and kneeing him in the crotch?

"Yes, we do. And before you ask, the mix is fresh, and it's whatever tequila you want from our selection."

He nodded, staring at the row of tequila bottles. His gaze moved back to her, and he shook his head again. "No, that's not what I want either." He glanced back down at the menu for just a moment, before looking back up at her, his lips turning up into a little smile. "I'll have the Quigley's Irish Mudslide. With the works."

"Seriously?" Oh, he *had* to be joking. That drink wasn't even on the menu!

"You guys still make it, right? I never got to have one. At least not legally," he said as he folded the menu back up and set it on the bar.

"Yeah, we still make it. Coming right up." Caro grabbed the menu from the counter and put it away before turning around and heading for the kitchen.

Of course, he ordered the most complicated thing they made. The Quigley's Irish Mudslide was the only drink that required ice cream . . . and the only non-premade drink that consisted of nine ingredients.

Ever since Gavin and Lilah had taken over running the bar at night, they'd lobbied to get the Quigley's Irish Mudslide off the menu. Desmond hadn't been happy about it, as it had been his mother's favorite. But they'd eventually reached a compromise—it would be the featured drink once a month, the entire week of Saint Patrick's, and on December 23, as that had been Grandma Quigley's birthday. And while it wasn't on the physical menus in the pub, it was a secret item on their website. So if someone ordered it, they could have it.

Grabbing the container of ice cream from the freezer and a scoop from the drawer, Caro headed back out to the bar and to the blender in the corner.

"You've got to be kidding me," Lilah said under her breath. "He ordered the mudslide?"

"He sure did," Caro said as she popped the top off the container. She dug the scoop into the carton with such force that she was surprised her whole hand didn't go into the ice cream.

This recipe was all about threes. One, two, three scoops of ice cream. A shot of Baileys, a shot of Kahlúa, and a shot of Jameson. And then one, two, three drops of green food coloring.

Pushing the lid down onto the blender, she hit the button, keeping her back to Max the entire time. She wasn't sure if he had a self-satisfied smile on his face or not, but if he did, she didn't want to see it.

Grabbing one of the tall glasses, she tipped it to the side and slowly spun as she made the intricate chocolate swirl on the inside. By the time she got to the top, the drink was done blending. It was oddly satisfying to watch the green liquid fill up the spaces, making a pretty contrast with the dark chocolate.

But that didn't stop it from being a pain in the ass to make.

Gavin was at her side again, handing over the metal whipped cream dispenser.

"Thank you." She did a fancy little flourish, covering up the bright green on top. Once the mountain of cream was sprinkled with chocolate shavings, she finished it off with a whiskey-soaked cherry.

Caro had been so focused on her drink making, and determinedly not looking at Max, that she hadn't noticed the newest party of girls who'd made their way into the bar. But she sure did notice them when she turned around with Max's drink in hand.

They were at a table next to the door, pulling up an extra seat to the eight-top to make it a nine. All of them were wearing cowboy hats and tight white T-shirts. Big block lettering across their chests read NADINE'S LAST RODEO, and there was a silhouette of a woman riding a bull while lassoing a man. Two of them were making their way to the bar, sidling up right next to Max. One of them had a maid of honor sheriff's badge pinned to her chest, the other was wearing a cow print miniskirt.

"Oh." Miniskirt's bright green eyes lit up. "What's that?" she asked, nodding to the drink Caro was setting down in front of Max.

"It's a Quigley's Irish Mudslide," Max answered.

"Is it any good?" Sheriff MOH asked.

"Let's see." Max turned back to Caro, a wicked smile on his mouth before wrapping it around the straw and taking a big drink. He closed his eyes and let out a satisfied sound, before turning back to the two women. "It's amazing."

"That's kind of a girly drink for a dude, isn't it?" Miniskirt asked with a teasing smile.

Max shrugged, taking another sip. "It's basically an alcoholic milkshake, and I have a weakness for ice cream. Best of both worlds."

Yeah, Caro knew *exactly* how much Max loved ice cream. He'd never been one to steal cookies out of the cookie jar, but he sure as hell had been one to steal an ice cream sandwich out of the freezer.

If he could order it as an appetizer, he would. It could be ten degrees outside, and he'd still want to get an ice cream cone, or a cup, or a whole damn carton.

The Max she'd known before had never, *ever* turned down ice cream. Apparently, some things hadn't changed.

"Do you have a weakness for anything else?" Miniskirt asked, her teasing smile only getting bigger.

"Beautiful blondes with green eyes."

Well, his taste in women *had* changed. Not that it mattered to Caro. He could like whoever he damn well pleased.

Miniskirt giggled while Sheriff MOH looked over to Caro, and the thing she'd been waiting for since they walked up to the bar happened.

"We'll take nine of the Quigley's Irish Mudslides. And the tab's on me," Sheriff MOH said as she went to pass a credit card across the counter.

"It's on me." Max shook his head, that charming smile of his that she used to know—but hadn't seen in a very long time—making an appearance. "My treat for the bride-to-be and all of you ladies."

"Ohhh," Miniskirt squealed, grabbing on to Max's forearm and leaning over to press a kiss to his cheek. "Thank you!" When she pulled back, there was a bright pink lip stain on his skin. "My name's Aubrey." She grinned at him.

"Max." He smiled back.

The sudden waves of jealousy pelting Caro were so forceful she was surprised she remained standing. She wanted to wipe Miniskirt's mark off his cheek. She wanted to rip the woman's hands off his arm. She wanted to throw that green drink right in his face . . . or in his lap. She hadn't decided.

But *why* was she jealous? She shouldn't care who Max flirted with. And yet . . .

It was a couple of seconds before Caro was able to unglue her tongue from the roof of her mouth, swallowing all those emotions back. Man, were they bitter.

"Coming right up," she said as she turned around, heading back for the kitchen. She was going to need a lot more ice cream . . . and maybe a couple of seconds of screaming into the freezer.

* * *

CARO WAS JEALOUS.

A lot of things had changed over the last fourteen years, but being able to read her wasn't one of them. Max didn't know what had possessed him to start flirting with Aubrey, but as the next hour went on, he didn't stop.

Maybe it was because deep down—*deep*, deep down—he knew there was still a part of him that was affected by Caro, and he wanted to see just how much she was still affected by him.

It was like pressing on a bruise to see if he still felt anything. And, as it turned out, he did.

Max had started a trend with his mudslide. After the order of nine for his new friends, the other party of girls who'd been drinking strawberry daiquiris switched their orders over to the green drink. Then a group of college students who were camping out at the lake showed up and joined in on the party.

He watched as Caro spent the next hour manning the blender. In between batches of the mudslides, she'd fill other patrons' orders,

Max being one of them. He probably should've called it an evening after that first drink, but he ordered himself a scotch and settled in.

Meanwhile, whenever Aubrey came up to the bar to talk to him, he'd get some serious side-eye from Caro. But he wasn't the only one flirting with strangers. Every time a guy came to the counter to order a drink, they'd flirt with Caro, and she'd flirt right back.

The man currently leaning against the bar was giving her a wide grin that showed off his overly bleached teeth. "What's your name, gorgeous?"

"Caroline." She smiled at him as she refilled his beer.

His eyes moved up and down her body. "You as sweet as the song says?"

"Even sweeter."

Max wondered, again, if she was seeing anyone. Another thought that pressed on the bruise.

He probably could've asked his earlier companions, but he hadn't wanted any more knowing smirks directed his way.

Shortly after placing that first milkshake order, Max had spotted Theo and Oscar sitting near the middle of the bar. When a space had freed up next to him, they'd moved down and had a drink. Max had spent more than a few long-ago summers hanging out with the two guys, and it had been nice to catch up, even if they were both watching how he and Caro interacted.

They'd left about ten minutes ago, both wishing him luck. But he didn't need luck. He'd be fine. He and Caro were capable of being civilized people in each other's presence. They were adults.

"Hey, sugar," a new guy with an Australian accent called out as he came up to the bar. "Can I get a refill of that grapefruit IPA?" He nodded to the tap as he set the pitcher down.

"Only if you keep talking to me with that accent. What are you doing all the way over here in little old Cruickshank?" she asked as she grabbed the pitcher and started filling it up.

The Aussie rested both of his hands flat on the bar, leaning in closer.

Max had no idea what the guy said to her because, at that *exact* moment, the drunk Braves fan who'd been yelling at the TV screen all night let out a rather loud bellow. He clearly took great exception to the Dodger who had just gotten a home run.

And he was still yelling when Caro's head fell back and she laughed at the ceiling. Max hadn't been able to hear that either, though maybe it was for the best. Her laugh had always done something funny to him.

He finished off the last of his scotch and set the empty glass on the counter. He should probably go.

Except Aussie was still talking to Caro, and he really didn't like it.

"Could I get another one of these?" Max called out to her.

Caro glanced over at him, her mouth still tilted with the smile she'd been giving the Aussie. God, her red lipstick was making him crazy.

"Sure." She nodded. "I need to go get another bottle. Be right back," she said as she pulled herself away.

The Aussie was watching the back of her, and it was no wonder, considering her jeans were molded to her ass.

Fuck, she looked good. Too good. Insanely good.

Yeah, he *really* needed to stop drinking.

"You need a refill." Aubrey's lazy drawl whispered in his ear as she slid into the seat next to his. It was something she'd been doing since she'd gotten there, splitting her time between the bachelorette party and him.

"Yeah, they've been pretty busy back there."

"It's because of all those mudslides. Thanks to you, I've found my new favorite drink."

"Is that so?" He turned in his seat, their knees softly bumping against each other.

"Mmm-hmm. I'll be dreaming about it for years to come." She tilted her head to the side as she slowly licked her lips.

It was a move meant to get Max thinking about her licking other things. It was sexy as hell . . . but why didn't it do anything for him?

And then Caro was in front of him again, that lemony scent of hers somehow making its way to him across the bar. Something that had been happening all night.

Yeah, he knew *exactly* why Aubrey wasn't doing anything for him.

"Your scotch," Caro said as she slid his drink in front of him, grabbing his empty glass in one easy move.

"Thank you. I'd also like a water and whatever Aubrey here would like to drink."

"Cranberry and vodka." She grabbed his biceps and squeezed. "Thanks, Max. I'll be right back." She let go before sliding off the barstool and heading for the bathroom.

"Don't you know she's just flirting with you to get free drinks?" Caro asked.

Yup, she was jealous. He pressed on that metaphorical bruise yet again.

"Why do you care?"

"I don't. I just didn't realize you'd decided to become a sugar daddy. You know she's probably ten years younger than you, right?"

"Why does it concern you, Caro?" He grabbed his scotch and took a satisfying sip. "It shouldn't matter to you who I flirt with. I'm a single guy, out for the evening, and I'm choosing to spend my time talking to a pretty girl."

"You're right." She nodded slowly as she filled a tall glass with ice and then grabbed the hose for water. "What you do doesn't matter to me."

Why did those words cut deeper than they should have? Why did he want it to matter to her? He didn't understand any of this. It made him confused and angry and stupid.

Stupid being the main reason he opened his mouth next.

"She's about the same age as girls I date anyways."

The lie had barely left his mouth when Caro set the glass on the bar. She slid it across—more than a little bit too hard—and it fell, ice and cold water rushing down onto his lap.

Chapter Six
What If I Never Get Over You?

It had been an accident. Caro hadn't meant to push the glass across the bar that hard.

Or had she? She'd stopped thinking properly after the last thing he'd said to her. Her ears had started ringing, while a jealousy unlike anything she'd experienced boiled over inside her chest.

There was just a moment of shocked silence before Max jumped up, and the sound from the bar hit Caro with force.

"What the hell, Caro!" Max got to his feet, the ice cubes in his lap hitting the floor.

"Whoops," she said as she reached for the empty glass on the bar.

"Whoops?" He grabbed the bottom of his shirt, wringing it out a little.

The move caused her to look down at the front of his jeans. It was a quick glance, but long enough to see that the material was molded to him in a rather indecent way.

Wasn't cold water supposed to cause shrinkage?

"Oh my gosh!" Aubrey cried out as she came up next to Max.

Perfect. She was back.

"Would you like me to cash you out?" Caro asked sweetly.

Max's lips tightened into a thin line, most likely so he wouldn't say anything else. He just nodded at her instead.

Caro headed for the register, knowing there were multiple sets of eyes on her. But she only caught two when she turned around. Gavin had the look of barely controlled mirth on his face and was biting his bottom lip, clearly trying to hold back a laugh. Meanwhile, Lilah's mouth was hanging open.

"Am I hallucinating? Or did you really just do that?"

"It was an accident," Caro said under her breath as she pulled up Max's tab.

"Well, accident or not, I think it had the opposite effect from what you would've liked." Lilah nodded in Max's direction.

Caro turned just enough to look over her shoulder. The sight that met her made her want to grab an entire bucket of ice water to throw at Max. Though that would probably be counterproductive.

He was still standing where she'd left him while Aubrey and three other girls from her bachelorette party were attempting to dry him off with napkins. Their hands were *all over* him.

Caro turned back to the register, taking a deep breath before letting it out through her nose.

"You always look like an angry dragon when you do that."

"Now is *not* the time for jokes." Caro hit the button to print Max's receipt.

"It wasn't a joke." Lilah held a pen out for Caro. "Now, try not to stab him with this. Okay?"

"Ha ha," Caro said sarcastically as she grabbed the pen from Lilah and headed back over to Max. It was then that she realized he was trying to get the girls to stop with their ministrations, but their hands were everywhere. It looked like he was trying to fight off an octopus.

"I'm really good, but thank you. No, it's okay, I promise. I got it."

"Here you go." She set the receipt and pen on the counter.

"Could I get some paper towels or something to dry him off?" Aubrey asked, dropping a wad of wet napkins on the counter.

"Sure." Caro tossed a clean rag over the counter before she turned around and headed for the bathroom. She locked herself in a stall, leaning back against it and taking a couple of deep, steadying breaths.

What was wrong with her? Why had that just happened? The intense feeling of jealousy was still ringing in her ears. It was so stupid. Their relationship was long over. They were practically strangers now.

It was a couple of minutes before she got herself together and came back out, and when she did, she couldn't stop the sinking feeling in her stomach. Aubrey along with the entire bachelorette party had left . . . and so had Max.

It was fine, she didn't care *what* he got up to. Didn't care *who* he slept with.

Except, apparently, she did care.

* * *

DING, DING, DING, DING . . .

The chimes of the antique grandfather clock filled the sitting room, signaling a new hour and a new day. It was midnight, and Max had been sprawled in Martin's worn leather chair since he'd gotten back to Ava's.

Well, he had stripped out of his wet clothes and taken a shower first. Then he'd headed downstairs and poured himself another glass of scotch. A *double* glass of scotch.

The chimes paused for a second before they started up again, counting the hour.

Ding. Caro had been jealous.

Ding. And so had he.

Ding. Was it past instincts lingering?

Ding. Or something more?

Ding. It wouldn't change anything if it was.

Ding. It wasn't like something was going to happen with them.

Ding. That door had been shut a long time ago.

Ding. Fourteen years ago.

Ding. And he wasn't opening that door again.

Ding. He couldn't.

Ding. Their end had been final.

Ding. Like death.

Max's eyes moved from the clock and over to the open double doors that led to Martin's office. An office that would never again feel the presence of one of the greatest men he'd ever known.

Max was pretty sure his father had been a great man too, but he barely remembered him. He'd been too young to have much more than flashes of memories. Snippets here and there. Not enough to really know a person. But he had a lifetime of memories with his grandfather.

It had been Martin who'd taught him how to throw a baseball, how to fish, how to drive. It was Martin who'd passed on his love for the Red Sox, his fashion sense in colorful suit jackets, his appreciation for scotch. It was Martin who'd taught him to be his own man.

It was Martin who'd had the biggest influence on who he'd become. But who *had* Max become?

Martin wouldn't have been proud of what Max had done tonight. Of what he'd said to Caro in the end. Yeah, he'd been pushing her, wanting to see if she was jealous, but he'd also told her a lie that had been cruel. He'd seen the hurt on her face before she'd pushed that glass across the bar.

He'd probably deserved it.

But he'd wanted to know. And now that he did, his thoughts were ricocheting around his skull, bouncing against each other and causing havoc in his brain.

Jealous or not, they weren't the same people anymore. At least he wasn't the same person he'd been before, the one she'd known. He wasn't the naive boy who'd believed love could conquer all. Who'd believed in her. Who'd believed in them. He'd stopped being that boy when everything had fallen apart.

The months before and after Rachel's death had been hard. Harder than anything he'd ever experienced in his life. The distance between them had grown slowly, like two creeping vines pulling apart two boulders. It seemed impossible, but it had happened.

He'd picked the University of North Carolina at Chapel Hill because of her. There was no way Caro would've been able to afford out-of-state tuition. And what he'd wanted more than anything was to be close to her. She'd been his priority.

But as the years had gone on, he'd stopped being hers. He'd understood in the beginning. Obviously. How does one not make their dying mother a priority? The thing was, Rachel had always been the rock of their family, and when she'd passed, Caro took on that responsibility. But in doing so, she'd pushed Max away. She insisted on taking care of everyone, yet she wouldn't let him take care of her.

She'd become everyone else's rock, but he couldn't be hers.

They'd talked daily, and then it had slowed to every other day. Then to every four days. Then to once a week. Sure, they'd texted, but it hadn't been the same. Nothing was the same. And then it felt like every time they did talk, they fought.

She was supposed to visit one weekend in April when she'd canceled at the last minute, just like she had every other time. Something had come up, and she couldn't make it. She promised she'd be there the next weekend. But the next weekend proved to be the final nail in the coffin of their relationship.

That was when Caro changed the plans—*their* plans—forever.

Max was going to the London School of Economics for the summer semester. The plan had been for Caro to go with him, to spend a couple of months in a foreign country. To visit art galleries and sketch to her heart's content. To go on an adventure with the love of her life. As Max's apartment had been paid for by Ava and Martin, Caro didn't have to worry about that, and she'd saved up more than enough money from all of her odd jobs around town. She'd gotten her passport, made a list of all the places she wanted to go. Ava and Martin had even bought her two brand-new suitcases.

But it was that weekend when she told him she wasn't going to London. It would've been the first summer they hadn't spent together since they'd met. And as it turned out, it would be the first of many summers, because not only did she tell him she wasn't going to London, but she wasn't joining him at Chapel Hill in the fall either. She wouldn't be joining him *anywhere* ever again.

"I can't do this anymore, Max. I can't be what you need me to be."

"We can make this work. It's us. This can't be the end. Not like this. I love you, Caro."

"I love you too, Max. But sometimes love isn't enough."

Everything had gone into slow motion, his chest cracking open at the reality. The thing he'd been dreading for months had finally arrived. It was over. *They* were over. She was done fighting. Done fighting for him. Done fighting for *them.* She made that very clear as she pulled the engagement ring from her finger and handed it back to him. Handed him back his heart.

He didn't know why he was reliving that moment again, like he was trying to figure out what had *really* happened. It didn't matter. None of it mattered. He wasn't in love with her anymore.

So then what was this feeling in his chest? A feeling that had been there since she'd fallen on him? Since she'd touched him? Since he'd touched her? A feeling he hadn't known in fourteen years.

It felt oddly like hope . . . and that filled him with dread.

* * *

CARO DREAMT OF Max that night. Warm summer smiles . . . her hand in his . . . his mouth on hers . . . him moving over her . . . him moving inside of her while she moaned his name.

She woke up sweaty and panting that morning, an ache in more than her heart. Once she caught her breath, she grabbed the pillow next to her and covered her face, letting out a good long scream.

All of this was so damn confusing she could barely see straight. Their relationship was done. *Long* over. Sure, she still found him attractive, as infuriating as that was, but she didn't have feelings for him anymore. So why, *why*, had she been so jealous last night?

Next time she saw him she was probably going to need to give him a better apology than *whoops*.

She pulled the pillow away and threw it next to her, looking over at Tibbett in his bed on the floor. He was staring at her with his sweet, sorrowful eyes. She really could've used some puppy snuggles last night, but as not all owners slept with their dogs, she tried to train them to sleep on their own.

Getting out of bed, she dropped down on the floor, the cushion of the rug helping her knees as she crawled over and lay down next to him.

"Why are men?" she asked as she pressed her face against his fur.

Tibbett licked her cheek.

"Well, there are some good males in the world. You being one of them," she told him as she started to scratch his chest, which she'd learned pretty quickly was his weak spot. His tail started to thump against the dog bed, and she laughed, stretching up to kiss him between the ears.

Caro smiled, the start of her day exponentially better already. That was the power of dogs. It was impossible for her not to get a little attached to her fosters, no matter how hard she tried, and, man, had she tried.

She'd started volunteering for Cruickshank Cats and Dogs Rescue in high school, and it was how she'd found her beloved Sweet Pea all those years ago. After Sweet Pea had died, she'd decided to start fostering . . . and hadn't stopped.

Her dogs were typically adopted within about a month, and

over the last three years, she'd found twenty-eight fosters forever homes. There were also the countless numbers she'd gotten adopted at the Saturday morning rescue booth she'd volunteered at for the last seventeen years, *and* the puppy/dog yoga class she did twice a month.

The rescue was one of her greatest passions, and there was no denying she was good at playing matchmaker with her four-legged friends . . . but there was also no denying that a little part of her broke every time she let one go.

Better a little part than a big part.

Caro could handle the little breaks. Pain in increments, dealt out over time. It was the big breaks that destroyed her, and she'd experienced more than her fair share over the years.

But there was no need to dwell on that . . . especially not with her current circumstances.

"You ready to start the day?" she asked Tibbett.

His answer was to roll over onto his back, wanting more chest scratches.

"Okay." Caro grinned, accommodating his demands. Like she'd do anything else. "You do know if we start the day, you'll get a cookie, though, right?"

At the word *cookie*, Tibbett rolled back over, getting up from his bed and heading for the door, his long ears flopping.

"We aren't quite there yet, Tibs. But you do need to go to the bathroom," she said as she pulled herself from the floor, following behind him.

There were three things Caro needed to get the day started: a hot shower, a cup of coffee, and a triple chocolate donut—okay, fine, *two* triple chocolate donuts—from Browned Butter. The little bell above the door rang as she and Tibbett stepped inside, the mouthwatering smell of freshly baked bread and pastries filling her lungs.

"Hey, Caro," Theo Taylor called out from behind the counter as he slid a full tray of tulip-shaped sugar cookies into the glass display case. Each and every one of them was decorated with brightly colored frosting.

"Hey, Theo." Caro gave him a tired smile.

"You okay?" he asked, his eyes focusing on her.

Being the focus of those blue eyes could make a person a little swoony, because Theo was a little swoony. The sexiness, plus his ability to make delicious pastries, made him one of Cruickshank's most eligible bachelors.

Well, most of the people who knew Theo thought that . . . One very big exception was Caro's little sister, Lucy.

Lucy and Theo were about two years apart, and since their mothers had been best friends, they'd grown up together from the very start. They'd gone to school together, had the same circle of friends, but Lucy and Theo had never been friends. *Never.*

To this day, Caro didn't understand where all the animosity between the two had come from, and she didn't bother to try. She was obviously on her sister's side, but she did adore Theo.

"I'll get through it." Caro shrugged a shoulder. He'd been at the bar last night, and though he'd missed the ice incident, he knew *exactly* why she wasn't okay.

"That doesn't sound very reassuring."

"Maybe I'll feel better after a little pick-me-up of carbs and sugar."

"Two triple chocolates?"

"You know me so well." She grinned.

"Do you want anything for Tibbett?" he asked as he bagged up both of her donuts.

There was a whole section of dog-friendly cookies. Though they were also big sellers for those who didn't have four legs.

"Yes, I promised him one this morning, and I need a couple of extras for the other dogs. I'll get three peanut butter and three sweet potato."

"Good choices." He nodded before he opened the case and popped them into a separate bag. "On the house," he said as he handed her the treats.

"No, Theo, that's not necessary."

"Yes, it is." The expression on his face made it very clear she wasn't going to win this. "Let someone take care of you for once."

"Thank you." Caro held the bag in the air before she and Tibbett turned and headed for the door.

When they stepped outside, Caro broke off a piece of a sweet potato cookie. Tibbett immediately sat, looking up at her with those damn sorrowful eyes that could melt anyone's soul.

"Good boy."

He leaned forward, gently taking the cookie from her hand.

"You'll get more at Dancing Donkey," she promised when he finished the bite.

At her words, he got back to his feet, leading the way with a very waggly tail.

Tibbett had been Caro's foster for the last three weeks, and he'd picked up on the routine pretty quickly, which was saying something, as no day was the same for Caro. Wednesdays she worked at the café, which was only four shops down from Browned Butter.

Dancing Donkey was one of many animal-friendly businesses in Cruickshank, not all that surprising, as Lorraine Belmont was the owner. Lorraine was the one responsible for starting Cruickshank Cats and Dogs Rescue eighteen years ago, and she'd gone a step further in making her shop animal friendly.

The café had two massive front windows that let in a lot of sunshine and brightened up the mint green walls. One had a display of coffee and merchandise; the other showed off a number of adoptable canines. There was a sturdy wooden pen that kept them contained, and on any given day it held three or four of the more well-behaved dogs from the rescue. Above them was a sign that read ADOPT ME.

Many, *many* dogs had found homes from that café.

When they walked in, there was a bit of a line at the counter. Coming in late in the morning meant she missed the early rush, but they were still pretty consistent with customers after nine. It was the time of day when the tourists started to venture out, and if they needed a caffeine fix, Dancing Donkey was the place to go.

Caro and Tibbett headed for the pen. There were two other dogs already in there: Rusty, a Lab mix with reddish brown fur, and Éclair, a beagle.

"Hello, babies," she said as she let Tibbett into the pen. She unclipped the leash from his harness before giving Rusty and Éclair head scratches. "I brought you all treats." Reaching into the bag, she grabbed the peanut butter ones, giving each of them a whole cookie . . . and Rusty the other half of the sweet potato as well.

"I saw that," someone called out from behind the counter.

Caro looked over to see Sasha Belmont at the espresso machine, steaming some milk. As Sasha was Lucy's best friend, she and Caro had also been incredibly close. Then again, the whole Belmont family was pretty much family. Always had been.

Sasha was grinning—like usual—and it made her natural beauty even more striking. She had freckled brown skin, a head full of curly hair that she showed off as much as possible, and golden brown eyes that were just as deadly as her brother's.

But *all* the Belmonts had those eyes.

"What?" Caro asked innocently as she made her way behind the counter. "He's bigger than the rest. He deserves a bigger treat."

"Uh-huh." But it was a moment later that her grin faltered, and she dropped her voice. "He deserves a bigger treat this morning, anyways. His adoption fell through."

"*Nooo.*" Caro put her purse in a cubby. "But he's *sooo* good."

"I know." She shook her head. "They were worried he was too big for their toddler, scared he'd knock her over. We'll find him a home, though."

"Yeah, we will." Caro looked over to the Lab, who was still happily munching on his cookie. He'd been Sasha's foster for the last couple of weeks, and all he wanted was a place to call home. Caro was pretty sure Sasha would have adopted the dog herself if she didn't already have two of her own, both of which had once been fosters.

Caro was the only person at the rescue who hadn't fallen victim to foster failure . . . yet.

"So where do you want me?"

"Register." She nodded over to where Gabby Mulligan was ringing up a customer. "She's got to get to class."

"What is it today?" Caro asked Gabby.

"Intro to Environmental Science." Gabby had been taking introductory courses at the college for the last two years, jumping around from subject to subject.

"That's quite a departure from last semester's French and women's studies."

"Yes, well, the professor is hot."

The woman at the counter had just taken a sip of her iced latte and simultaneously laughed, inhaling the coffee. She coughed, still laughing as Gabby leaned forward.

"Like, *really* hot," she emphasized. "And we do a hike at the end of the semester, and I can't wait to see what he looks like in shorts."

"I can't wait to hear all about it, Gabby." The woman laughed again, grinning as she shoved a couple of dollars into the tip jar.

"Knowing Gabby, I'm pretty sure it will be a story we *all* can't wait to hear."

"I'll keep everyone posted." Gabby winked as she stepped back from the cash register and started to untie the back of her apron. "See you tomorrow," she told Sasha as she grabbed her backpack from the cubby and headed for the door.

Caro took over the line while Sasha continued to fill the orders. It took about an hour to get through the rush, and once the last customer was out of the store, Caro went to the double sink and started helping Sasha with the dishes.

"Where's your mom?"

"She loaded up the roaster with Magic Morning Blend beans and then headed over to Asheville. A shelter over there is overrun with dogs, and they didn't have enough space, so she's getting some for the rescue to foster."

Not all the shelters in Asheville were no-kill, so if someone didn't take those dogs, there would be no second chances.

"Poor babies." Caro shook her head, looking over to the dogs, who were all peacefully napping in the sun. She wanted more than anything to find all of them homes.

"We will." Sasha gently bumped her hip into Caro's.

"What?" Caro asked turning back to Sasha.

"We'll find them all homes."

"Did I say that out loud?"

"No." Sasha grinned. "I just knew what you were thinking."

"Am I that easy to read?"

"Sometimes." She nodded.

Caro rolled her eyes as a loud beep filled the air, signaling that the beans in the roaster were done. "You get those. I'll finish up out here."

Sasha grabbed a towel from the rack, drying her hands as she headed through the swinging doors. Caro kept working, humming along to the Taylor Swift album that was playing from the speakers.

Once everything was drying, she checked the coffeepots. She'd just hit the start button to brew a fresh pot of Cruickshank Caramel Crunch when the bell chimed behind her. She turned to greet her new customer, and the good mood she'd been cultivating all morning disappeared.

Max was standing in front of her, looking just as confused as she felt.

"You've got to be kidding me," they both muttered in unison. It would've been funny under different circumstances, but there was no humor to be had between the pair of them. She was still thinking about the night before . . . and, it would seem, so was he.

"You work *here* too?" He pulled his sunglasses off and slid them on top of his head.

"Sure do."

"Right." His eyes narrowed like he was trying to figure something out, but then he shook his head like it didn't really matter. "Is it safe for me to be here? Or are you going to throw something else in my lap? Coffee is a little bit more dangerous than ice water."

"I don't know what you're talking about. Last night was an accident."

His mouth turned down in a frown. "Sure it was."

"If I did spill something on you, I'm sure your new friend would be more than happy to clean that up too."

"I'm sure Aubrey would. I'll ask her when I go back to her room, and I'll let you know."

So, he *had* slept with her, not that she cared. He could sleep with whoever he wanted. That sinking feeling in her stomach had nothing to do with him. It was just her donuts from earlier. Too much sugar.

"No need. I don't care." She placed her hands on the counter, doing her best to affect a posture of ease. "What do you want to drink, Max?"

He glanced up at the chalkboard above her, his eyes scanning over it for just a moment before he said, "A hazelnut latte, extra shot."

"Sure thing."

Caro let go of the counter and turned around. The faster she made him his drink, the faster he would get out of there. Max was still staring up at the sign when she slid the cup in front of him.

"That it?"

"No." He shook his head, his eyes still focused above her. "Aubrey wants a dirty chai with only one shot of espresso. Oh, and make it with oat milk."

The second Caro heard the order, she knew just how full of shit he was.

"Oh, does she?"

Max's eyes moved back to Caro as he nodded. "Yeah, it's her favorite, and she needs a little pick-me-up after last night."

"I just bet she does," Caro muttered, spinning the little screen in his direction so he could pay. Then she turned around to make the second order.

She was just finishing up when Sasha came out from the back with a box filled with bags of freshly roasted Magic Morning beans.

"Oh my God! Max?" Sasha almost squealed as she dropped the box on the counter before coming around, her arms wide open.

"Hey, Sash," he said as he pulled her into a hug.

Caro's jealousy was more intense than ever as she watched Sasha hug Max. Not that Sasha had ever had any romantic feelings for him; he'd always looked at her like a little sister, just like he had with Lucy. They were friends.

It was just that Sasha got to hug him, and Caro suddenly missed his hugs so much it hurt to breathe.

"I had no idea you were here." Sasha pulled back and gently punched Max in the arm.

"Just got in yesterday, and I'll be here through the end of June."

"Oh, really?" she asked, glancing over to Caro.

Caro had no idea what her expression looked like in that moment, but whatever it was, it made Sasha bite her bottom lip, hiding a smile. "It's good to see you, Max."

"You too, Sash. I should probably run, though. Don't want these to get cold," Max said as he reached for the two cups on the counter.

"You forgot the sprinkle of cinnamon," Caro said before she could stop herself.

His hands stilled, and he looked up. "What?"

"In Ava's order." Caro indicated one of the cups. "She always gets a dirty chai with one shot, oat milk, and a sprinkle of cinnamon. And you might as well take her these coffee beans too," she said as she grabbed two bags and dropped them into a brown paper bag. "She ordered them a couple of days ago."

If Caro hadn't known any better, she might have thought something like amusement flickered across Max's face, as if he found it funny that he'd been caught in a lie. He looped the handle of the bag around his wrist before he grabbed the two cups, turned around, and left.

Caro was still trying to figure out what that look had been about when Sasha's voice pulled her back to the moment.

"You knew he was here?"

"Yeah." She nodded before telling Sasha all about the day before.

"Seriously?" She gently whipped Caro's thigh with the towel in her hands. "I can't believe you didn't tell me he was back."

"I was trying not to think about it."

"I'm sure. You tell Lucy?"

Caro shook her head. "I haven't talked to her. I called her before my shift at Quigley's last night, but she didn't answer. She texted me later and said that she'd been driving all day and we'd talk later."

As Lucy hadn't had her big break yet, she paid the bills where she could. Just like Caro, she had a handful of jobs, from delivering flower arrangements to waitressing and dog walking. She was always busy.

"Well, it's going to be an interesting summer."

Caro let out a breath, turning back to the door that Max had walked through. "It's going to be something. That's for damn sure."

* * *

MAX'S MOOD HAD gone downhill from the moment he'd woken up that morning. First there'd been the massive hangover, then he'd discovered there was no coffee downstairs, which was why he'd gone to Dancing Donkey.

He hadn't expected to see Caro working behind the counter, but he was positive that Ava had known she'd be there when she'd sent him on his way that morning. Why did it feel like behind every door he opened was Caro, or a memory of her?

And, as if to prove the point, when he got home and pushed open the door to the kitchen, the scent of lemon hit him like a slap in the face. Sweet, tart, sugary goodness that made his mouth water and his stomach growl.

It smelled *just* like Caro.

It was the exact same scent that had filled his lungs when she'd fallen on him yesterday, the same scent that had his head turning toward her, his nose burying itself in her hair as he breathed her in. A reaction to her that had been beyond his control.

It was the same scent he'd caught hints of the night before at

Quigley's. Every time she'd been close enough, he hadn't been able to stop himself from taking a deep breath. He'd smelled it that morning too. Despite the aroma of coffee at the café, his nose had found Caro's lemony scent on the air. It was one of the reasons he'd tried so hard not to make eye contact with her while he'd been there. It had been too much for him.

And now that same scent was taking over Ava's kitchen, and he was surrounded by it.

Max looked around, finding his grandmother at the stove stirring a giant steaming pot. The counter was littered with measuring cups, wrappers that had once held sticks of butter, a canister of sugar, two whole cartons of eggshells, a zester, and a mound of squeezed lemons.

"What are you making?"

"Lemon curd. It's for the weekend market. How was Dancing Donkey?" she asked as she turned the burner down and looked over at him.

"How do you think?" He frowned, setting the bag of coffee beans on the counter before handing her the dirty chai she'd asked for.

"What do you mean?" she asked innocently.

Max raised his eyebrows at her. "You knew Caro was working there this morning, just like you knew she was working at Quigley's last night."

"I don't have her schedule memorized."

"Sure you don't." He didn't believe her for a second.

"Well, how was last night, then?"

He took a drag from his coffee cup, needing a little more caffeine before telling her. "She dumped a glass of ice water in my lap."

"*Sooo*, not good?"

"No, not good."

"Your pants are dry today, so there's that." She wasn't even trying to hide her smile now as she started to clean up the counter.

"One of the few things I've got going for me this morning." He set his coffee down before grabbing the bags of grounds and heading for the pantry. When he walked inside, he spotted two other bags on the shelf. "I thought you were out of coffee?" he said when he walked back into the kitchen.

"I found them after you left." She shrugged, barely waiting a second before switching back to the other topic. "So, what did you do last night?"

"How do you know *I* did something?"

Ava just raised her eyebrows.

Okay, fine, he had done something, but he wasn't going to admit it to his grandmother. He still didn't know why he'd been so bound and determined to make Caro jealous last night . . . or that morning. But as soon as she'd brought up Aubrey, he couldn't help himself.

He had to push on that bruise again.

"We just can't be around each other anymore." Max shook his head.

"You know it's been fourteen years, right?"

"I'm fully aware of how long it's been."

"Hmm." Ava grabbed her chai latte and took a drink. "So, what kept you up late last night?"

"I just couldn't sleep." He shrugged like it didn't matter.

"Did all of that scotch help?"

Max couldn't stop the smile that cracked his lips. "You never miss a thing."

"You couldn't get away with anything when you were fourteen, and you can't get away with it when you're thirty-four either."

"I wouldn't dream of trying."

"Hmm, there's still plenty of time left in the summer for you to prove that wrong."

"That there is." Max grabbed his cup from the counter, draining it before tossing it in the trash. "So how long do you plan on messing with us?"

"What are you talking about?"

"Come on, Ava. Not only did you know she was going to be here when I got in yesterday, but you set me up last night, and you did it again this morning."

"Fine," she agreed, though there was no guilt on her face at the admission. "I might've known. But I'm not *messing* with either of you, Max. Caro *lives* in Cruickshank, she *works* in Cruickshank; you're going to run into her while you're here, especially as she works *for me*. Caro is going to be around, and I need you to accept it."

He held up his hands in surrender. "I told you I accepted it yesterday."

"Then how did you get that ice water in your lap last night?"

Max didn't answer, he couldn't without lying.

"Look, Bean." She patted his arm. "I just think you two have some unfinished business you need to work out. And I've never in my life been good at not meddling, so I'm not sure why you think I'd stop now."

Max laughed. He couldn't help himself. "I don't know why you'd stop either."

"It's not like I think the two of you are getting back together."

"Well, that's good, because it isn't happening."

She kept talking as if he hadn't said anything. "But you two need to have some sort of conversation and move on. Make peace. Call a truce. *Something.* Like I said, it's been fourteen years, and life is too short to be this hurt about it."

"I'm not hurt about it." Not anymore. He'd gotten over it. He was fine. Sure, he'd avoided love since things ended with Caro, but that was just because he wasn't naive anymore. He knew better now. He knew that love wasn't enough.

Ava's eyebrows went high, not believing a word of it. "Then what are you?"

"I don't know." He shook his head.

"Well, figure it out." Ava patted his arm before she moved back to the pot of lemon curd.

Yeah, that was going to be a lot easier said than done.

Chapter Seven

Ghosts That We Knew

It was just after four when Caro finished her shift at Dancing Donkey. Her head was still a mess of thoughts that all revolved around Max, and there was only one person she wanted to talk to.

Swinging by Petal and Thorn—the floral shop/nursery where she worked a shift on Mondays—Caro picked out the prettiest flowers they had on hand. Purple irises, baby pink snapdragons, coral peonies, and yellow roses. She dropped Tibbett off at home—leaving him to chill with her dad's German shepherd, Leia—before she headed for her mom's old Jeep Wagoneer in the driveway. As her destination was about five miles outside of town, cranking up the old girl was a necessity.

Caro started the car, immediately rolling the windows down before popping a Dolly Parton mix CD into the player. The car was from 1991, and one of the very few modifications Caro had made was replacing the stereo system when it had crapped out ten years ago.

The guitar for "Jolene" started playing through the speakers as Caro pulled down the driveway and headed out of the neighborhood. It was one of those beautiful spring afternoons that Cruick-shank was famous for: seventy-two degrees, blue sky, birds chirping, flowers blooming.

It in no way reflected the wide range of emotions raging around in her head . . . and heart. Regret, pain, longing, sadness, anger . . . all tinged with a jealousy she didn't understand.

God, she was so confused. It was why she needed to talk to the wisest person she knew.

Her mother.

The last chords of "Nine to Five" had just finished playing through the speakers when Caro pulled into a spot at Caster Field Cemetery. Dolly Parton had always been one of Rachel's favorite artists, and Caro had a habit of playing Rachel's music whenever she was going to visit her. It had a way of putting Caro in the right mindset . . . of making her feel closer to her mother.

After rolling all the windows up, Caro grabbed the bag she'd packed at her dad's, along with the fresh flowers from the passenger seat. She headed for the path on the left, the one that went through the canopy of dogwood trees. A few petals of the flowers were falling and swirling in the breeze around her. It had been a long and cold winter, and the trees had bloomed late. The last of the bunch were now losing their blossoms, giving way to the green leaves of summer.

It wasn't a long walk to Rachel's grave, about a quarter of a mile and up a hill. It was right under a Summer Red maple, the new leaves still deep red, and it looked out onto the mountains. A perfect spot for her mother to rest.

"Hey, Mom," Caro said as she dropped to her knees in the grass, her fingers tracing the engraving on the light gray marble headstone.

RACHEL EVELYN BUCHANAN

She'd given both of her daughters the same middle name.

BELOVED DAUGHTER, WIFE, MOTHER, AND FRIEND

But she was so much more than all those things. Her mother had been absolutely *everything*. How could someone so full of life get taken so early? She'd been forty-six when she died.

Caro pulled the dead flowers out of the vase in front of the grave; they were the lilies her father brought when he'd visited a week ago. As Rachel had just as much of a green thumb as Ava—a trait they'd both nurtured in Caro—everyone who visited tried to keep fresh flowers on her grave as much as possible.

Caro spent the next couple of minutes changing everything out, putting the dead flowers in a plastic bag, and filling the vase with the fresh water she'd brought. She fixed a few of the sprigs of the snapdragons, making sure they were in the perfect spot, before she sat down in the grass, leaning back against the headstone. She fished out the metal thermos from her bag and did what she always did when she visited her mother: settled in and imagined a different world . . . one in which Rachel was still alive.

Caro always imagined her mother the way she'd been before she'd gotten sick. Just a few strands of gray in her dark brown hair, tiny patches of wrinkles at the corners of her mouth and eyes. This time, Caro pictured herself in her parents' kitchen, sunlight filling the room and a breeze coming through the open windows, gently blowing the yellow curtains back and forth. Her mother was wearing her favorite blue dress with red flowers, the same one that was at the back of Caro's closet and that she could never bring herself to wear.

"So, Max is back in town," imaginary Rachel said as she grabbed the vase of flowers from the counter and set it on the kitchen table. She didn't wait for a response before she turned and headed to the refrigerator, pulling out the pitcher of freshly brewed sweet tea.

"Yeah." Caro nodded as she adjusted the stem of the snapdragon that just wouldn't stay in place. "He came back yesterday, and he's going to be here for a few weeks."

Rachel glanced at her daughter before she poured them both a glass of tea. "A few weeks, huh? Summers always used to belong to the two of you."

"They used to, but they don't anymore."

"Not since you broke his heart?"

"Hey." Caro frowned. "I didn't walk out of that unscathed."

"I never said you did." Rachel shook her head as she sat down across from Caro, pushing one of the glasses of sweet tea toward her. "It's been fourteen years, though, so why do you look like it just happened yesterday?"

"Because after losing you, losing him was the most painful thing I've ever experienced. Seeing him always brings it all back."

"And unlike me, he's still here and you can't have him?"

"Yes." Caro groaned before dropping her head in her hands.

"Aw, Pumpkin." Rachel's hand was in Caro's hair, fingers gently running through the strands. "Look at me. Talk to me. Tell me what's going on in this beautiful mind of yours."

Caro pulled her head from her hands and looked at her mother. "It's just so complicated. There's a part of me that still wants him, except he's not the same Max. He's not *my* Max anymore."

"How do you know? You've barely been around him. He could be exactly the same Max. He could still be *your* Max."

"Well, that scares me even more."

"Why?" Rachel sat back in her chair, studying her daughter.

"Because I'll always love my Max. So it's easier to think he doesn't exist anymore." Caro's voice was barely a whisper, and it still hurt to say the words. They burned coming out of her mouth.

"Easier?" Rachel's eyes softened, sadness and pain making the blue so much bluer. "If there's anything I thought you knew, it was that life's not easy."

Caro looked down at the tea on the table, tracing through the condensation that had accumulated on the glass. "I've already learned so much the hard way, I just needed a break." Her voice cracked on the last word, the corners of her eyes burning and her vision blurring.

"I know. You've had to deal with way too much."

Caro swallowed hard before she looked back up at her mom. "I don't know what to do."

Rachel reached across the table, resting her hand on top of Caro's . . . It was cold, none of the warmth that she'd always remembered. "You'll figure it out. You always do."

"Promise?" Caro blinked, tears falling down her cheeks.

"I promise." Rachel nodded, her own eyes going watery.

"I miss you." Caro put her hand on top of her mom's.

"I miss you more." Rachel's smile was sad as she put her other hand on top of Caro's, completing the stack.

"I miss you most," Caro whispered.

She closed her eyes, taking a deep breath before letting it out in a rush. When she opened her eyes again, she was back in the cemetery, her hands clutching the cold thermos of sweet tea.

"I miss you most, Mom," she repeated, tears now streaming down her face. A breeze gently blew, and her hair moved around her shoulders. "I just need a sign of what to do next. Where to go from here. Give me a sign, Mom. Any sign," Caro begged as she looked out into the distance, seeing storm clouds heading toward Cruickshank.

* * *

THE STORM THAT Caro had spotted blew in that night, settling over the town and opening up with a blast. The thunder and lightning were so intense that it took no time at all for Tibbett to start whining. He was usually pretty chill, but he hated storms. Caro didn't last long before she broke her own rule and brought him onto the bed, wrapping him up in a blanket. He snuggled against her, finding comfort and calming down. Soon he was asleep, his soft snores just audible above the pounding rain.

"You trust me," she whispered as she gently ran his soft ears between her fingers. "I'll make sure you're safe."

As it turned out, Tibbett wasn't the only one who needed the contact. Caro was still more than a little raw after her visit to the graveyard, and she pressed her face against his warm fur, still thinking about her mother and what to do about Max.

You'll figure it out. You always do.

She didn't know what she was going to do, but she did know she couldn't handle this weird tension between them anymore. They were adults; they could be in the same room and not have it be awkward or painful.

But accomplishing that meant she was going to have to talk to Max.

She could do it. She was capable.

"I can do it," she whispered into the air.

At her voice, Tibbett moved his head, licking her cheek. Caro closed her eyes, breathing through the tightening feeling in her chest.

* * *

CARO WORKED A shift at Kathleen's Corner Bookstore on Thursdays, which was yet another place she brought her fosters. The owner, Hazel—Kathleen's great-granddaughter—had set up a comfy bed in the corner and an ADOPT ME sign above it.

Shipments arrived on Thursdays, and an extra set of hands in the shop was always helpful. It was good to have some busywork to do on a dark and gloomy day, something mindless like logging the new books into inventory and shelving them.

Though she'd had a late start that morning, because the second she'd walked in the building, she'd headed for the kids' corner, dismantling the display of her books.

Hazel's eyes had narrowed on Caro in confusion. "What are you doing?"

"Changing up the space a little. I thought a new display would be good."

"Without any of your own books?" Hazel's frown deepened. "You know, authors usually like their books to be front and center. You want to tell me what's up?"

There was no point dancing around the topic. Caro sighed, looking at the shop owner. "Max is back in town for the summer, and I don't want him to know."

Hazel's eyebrows went up. "You think no one is going to tell him?"

"I can't control if other people will or won't. But taking that down"—she pointed to the table—"is something I can control . . . and asking the people who might have an inclination to tell him not to." She looked at Hazel with a hopeful expression.

"I won't say anything." She shook her head. "Is that all that's bugging you today?"

"I don't know. Something feels . . . off." Caro absentmindedly rubbed at her chest. "I don't know if it's him being back in town, or . . . something else."

"You think it's the weather?"

"I'm sure that's part of it," Caro said as she looked out the windows to the dark gray sky and wet streets. At least the thunder and lightning had stopped.

"Well, I'm sure you'll figure out the other part." Hazel grabbed a stack of novels and headed for the fiction section.

Except Caro didn't need to figure it out. She already knew. It was Maximillian Abbott. Why was just *thinking* about how to talk to him scarier than anything she'd had to do in a really long time?

The bell above the door chimed, and Caro looked over as Sheila Connor walked in, her kids Ryan and Camille leading the way in a rush of bright blue and purple rain jackets.

"Hi, Ms. Caro!" they said as they beelined for the kids' section.

"Hi." She laughed. She knew both of the Connor kids very well. Ryan was best friends with her nephew Matthew.

"Slow down," Sheila called out to them as she set her umbrella in the stand by the door. She turned to Caro, letting out a sigh of exhaustion. "No school today. A tree fell and made a mess of the power lines. And they've been bouncing off the walls all morning. It would be fine if they could go outside, but that's not happening."

"Yeah, Lilah called me earlier. She's in the same predicament."

"I decided to bribe them with books and ice cream."

"That's a solid choice," Hazel said as she came out from behind one of the racks.

"I thought so." Sheila nodded. "Besides, their father always gets to be the fun parent. So, it's my turn today."

Both Hazel and Caro laughed.

"Well, your timing couldn't be more perfect. Your order of books came in, and I just unpacked them," Caro said as she moved behind the counter and found the stack.

"Mom?" Camille's soft voice called out, and they all turned to see her sitting on the floor with Tibbett's head in her lap. He was looking up at the seven-year-old in an adoring way that Caro had never seen from the dog before.

The sight of it took her breath away, the familiar tightness from last night squeezing her chest. And she knew, right then, that she was about to lose him.

She pulled a smile into place as she looked at Sheila and asked, "Just how much of the fun parent do you want to be?"

It took Camille and Ryan exactly twelve minutes to convince their mom to adopt the dog. Though the clincher had been when Tibbett climbed into Sheila's lap and licked her cheek. She'd melted. Cruickshank Cats and Dogs Rescue had a two-week trial period, but Caro knew the dog wasn't coming back. She'd found him his home. She told him as much when she pressed her face to his neck and whispered goodbye.

But knowing all this, knowing he'd finally found his people, didn't stop her from bursting into tears the second they left the bookstore.

"Oh, honey." Hazel pulled Caro into a hug, and she let the woman hold her while she cried.

What was wrong with her? Tibbett was the twenty-ninth foster Caro had found a home for, and she'd never been this sad before. Never felt like a part of herself had just walked out that door with the dog.

Why did it remind her of another time someone had walked away from her, taking part of her with him? Why was it that Max being here had opened the Pandora's box of her emotions? It wasn't like she hadn't seen him over the years. But what was different this time around?

She had no idea. But she knew she needed to figure out how to close that box again . . . and keep her heart safe.

* * *

MAX AND AVA spent all of Thursday morning and afternoon up in the attic. The rain tapped softly on the roof above them while Elton John played over the portable speaker that Ava carried with her from room to room. They'd been going through boxes and bins that hadn't been touched in years. There were old clothes, holiday decorations, books and magazines, toys, and a plethora of other things Ava and Martin hadn't been able to part with over the years.

As of now, Ava *still* wasn't able to get rid of a number of the things they'd gone through. He'd only been able to get her to throw out a bin of Christmas lights with half-working strands—

You just need to layer them to make a full strand.

—an old food processor that had stopped working in the eighties—

But that was a wedding gift from your great-aunt Muriel.

—and three entire boxes of yellowed tissue paper and wrinkled gift bags—

You can reuse all of that.

He'd also gotten her to donate some old bedding and towels, a set of mismatched dishes and silverware that she had no memory of, and a box of sports equipment that was beaten up but totally still useable.

Max had pulled out the three baseballs and two worn gloves to add to his own box of things to keep. They were the gloves Martin had used when he'd taught Landon how to play catch . . . the same gloves he'd used when he'd taught Max too. Max's box also included a stash of Martin's bow ties, a leather jacket that had belonged to his father, an old typewriter, and a wooden palette of Ava's that was covered in so many layers of paint that it looked like an art piece all by itself. He was going to frame it.

He was having a good time, going through things and listening to stories Ava had told him more times than he could count growing up . . . and hearing some he'd never known before. She talked about Landon and Martin, living in Boston and their time teaching at Harvard.

"Why do you have these flameless candles?" Max asked, opening a Tupperware container.

"I decorate with them for Halloween and Christmas. They're perfect for pumpkins and to put in the windows."

"Right." Max nodded as he closed the lid and grabbed another box that was full of VHS tapes. "Okay, now, these we can throw away."

Ava peered into the box before looking up at him, shaking her head emphatically. "Oh. No. We. Can't!"

"Do you really need old episodes of *M.A.S.H.*?" Max waved his hand over the box. "You know you can stream those somewhere."

"Those aren't old episodes of *M.A.S.H.*! Those are home videos that Martin recorded. He's in them, and so is your father, and you."

Max remembered some of those videos, but it had been a while since he'd seen them. He'd been so young when his father died that they were some of the only memories he had.

"Caro bought me this thing where you convert the tapes digitally. She's already converted a whole box of other tapes. The program is on Martin's computer. I was looking for these, but I hadn't found them yet. Can you take them downstairs and put them in his office?"

It was still Martin's office . . . *always* his office.

Max hesitated for just a moment before he nodded. "Yeah." He bent over and picked up the box before heading down two flights of stairs, taking his sweet time.

He'd been in his grandparents' house for over forty-eight hours at this point, and the only room he *still* hadn't gone in was Martin's office. It wasn't just the tapes in his arms that were full of memories.

Max set the box down just inside the room, lingering in the doorframe and looking around the space. The bookcase on the right wall was filled to bursting: hardbacks, paperbacks, leather-bound copies. There was an antique mantel clock in the middle, still seven minutes fast, like it had *always* been.

Why seven minutes? Max had asked him once.

Because it's more than five and less than ten, Martin had told him, like it was the most obvious answer in the world.

To this day, Max kept all his clocks and watches seven minutes fast. He was never late, and he always thought about his grandfather when he checked the time.

Max's gaze moved past the bay window that looked out to the front yard, and over to the two mahogany filing cabinets on the wall to the left. There were thirty or so framed photos sitting on top of the cabinets, all placed perfectly so that none was blocked by another.

Max had grown up staring at almost every single one of these pictures. He could close his eyes and see them, but they still drew him closer for a better look.

The biggest frame was antique silver. It held a picture of Ava and Martin on their wedding day almost sixty years ago. Ava had always been somewhat of a hippie, and she was wearing a long, lacy dress with white flowers in her blond hair. As for Martin, he had a Sean-Connery-circa-James-Bond thing going on, with his white tuxedo jacket and black bow tie.

That very same bow tie was in the box Max had saved for himself.

The next row was a timeline of Landon's life. One of him as a newborn baby, swaddled in a yellow lion-print blanket. Another when he was two or three, his dark blond hair ruffled as his bright blue eyes smiled up at the camera. He had the same hair color and eyes as Martin . . . the same hair color and eyes as Max.

There was a picture from when his father was six or seven. He was standing on a pier with Ava and Martin, all of them holding massive ice cream cones. Another with all of them wearing snowsuits outside the old brownstone in Boston, posing in front of three snowmen of varying sizes. Landon was probably in middle school then.

There were photos from each and every graduation: preschool, elementary school, middle school, high school, and college. Ava and Martin looking so damn proud as they stood by their son. The only one that was missing was from his PhD in engineering, because Landon had died two months before the ceremony.

There were a handful of pictures of Martin and Ava through the years on their many travels: Greece, Sydney, China, Russia, Italy, Brazil. They'd *lived* their life, had so many adventures together. Sure, Max had traveled for work, and he'd gone to many of those same places, but he was usually alone.

There was a picture of Landon carrying a two-year-old Max in a baby backpack as they hiked, Martin standing next to them looking like Gandalf. He was holding a hiking stick that looked like a staff and was sporting a beard, one that he'd decided to grow in his forties.

Three generations of Abbott men in one picture . . . and now Max was the only one left. He'd barely known a world with Landon in it. He didn't know everything he'd missed out on with his father. He was too young to remember. But he knew full well what he was missing now that Martin was gone. The only father he'd *really* known.

His eyes lingered on a picture of the two of them camping, a trip Max would remember for the rest of his life. He'd never forget those nights looking up at the ink-blue sky and searching for shooting stars, the taste of freshly caught trout cooked in a cast-iron skillet, the deep timbre of Martin's voice as he told him about life and love.

Love. It hadn't worked out for Max the way Martin had described it. But Martin had spent almost sixty years with the love of his life. He'd struck gold and thought everyone else could too. It wasn't like the man was naive; he'd experienced one of the greatest losses—having to bury a child—but he'd always believed there was way more good in life than bad.

There was always hope.

Max's gaze moved to the cluster of pictures to the right . . . the ones he'd been avoiding . . . the ones with him and Caro. There was one of the two of them wearing rain boots as they splashed through puddles. Another with them dressed as pirates as they poked their heads through the windows of the treehouse. One with them doing cartwheels in the backyard with Jeremy, Lilah, and Lucy.

Something weird and uneasy moved in his chest as he looked at the picture of them sitting on a park bench, Max's arm around Caro's shoulders as he pulled her in close and kissed her cheek. And that feeling only got worse as he focused on the frame that held a photo of the entire Buchanan family, along with Ava, Martin, and Max. They were all wearing matching Christmas pajamas as they ran around outside, trying to catch snowflakes on their tongues.

But the picture that made it just a little hard for him to breathe was the one of him and Caro on the night of her senior prom. Max was wearing a bright red tuxedo jacket that perfectly matched Caro's red dress. Her brown hair was curled, lying softly around her shoulders.

He remembered that night like it was yesterday. Dinner at Bernardine's, the little French bistro that had always been Caro's favorite. Walking hand in hand through downtown Cruickshank to the Duncan-Finley Barn—which was basically Cruickshank's rec center, a catchall for most town events. The barn had been filled with strands of lights, wrapped around every post, hanging from the rafters. Max held Caro close as they danced for hours, his hands on her hips, his lips at her ear, his nose in her hair, breathing in her citrus scent.

When it ended, they'd snuck into the loft above her parents' garage, a blow-up mattress and two bottles of champagne waiting for them. It hadn't been their first time—hell, it hadn't even been their hundredth—but there was something about making love to her that night that had changed him.

Max had loved Caro for most of his life, but that night he'd realized he was *in* love with her. A kind of love that was all-encompassing, the kind of love that transformed. He'd known beyond a shadow of a doubt that she was it. She belonged to him just as much as he belonged to her. He'd known he'd never be able to give himself to anyone else ever again.

And he'd been right about that last part.

Why did Martin still have those pictures of him and Caro?

That weird, uneasy feeling in his chest had morphed into something else, something that ached, and he realized his hand was outstretched, his fingers inching toward the frame that held the prom photo. He wanted to flip it facedown so that he wouldn't have to look at it. The second he touched the frame, he pulled back like he'd burned himself, unable to disrupt Martin's office from the way he'd left it.

This was his grandfather's space, and it had been his choice to have that picture up, even if Max didn't understand it. So instead, he turned around and walked out, realizing he was going to have to get over a lot of things if he was going into that room again.

He fisted his hands tightly before letting them go and shaking out his fingers. He needed to move. He needed to get out of the house. He needed to get some air.

He climbed to the second floor, calling up the stairs that led to the attic. "Ava? I'm going for a run."

Her head popped out of the open door, and she looked down at him, frowning. "It's raining."

"It's barely sprinkling now. I won't melt, I promise."

Her eyes narrowed, studying him. "Are you okay?"

His instinct was to say that he was fine, but that wasn't the truth. "That was the first time I've been in Martin's office since last year. I just need to clear my head a little bit."

"All right." She nodded slowly. "I might lie down and take a nap, anyways. But make sure to bring the flip phone. If it starts pouring again, I'll come pick you up."

"I will." He agreed before he headed to his room.

Less than five minutes later, Max opened the front door and stepped out onto the porch. The second he was outside, he took a deep breath, the cool, fresh air filling his lungs. Hopefully it would help clear his mind.

He stretched for a couple of minutes before he headed out, the light drizzle settling on his hair, skin, and clothes. It had been a while since he'd run in the rain, and it felt good as he made his way downtown.

Typically, when Max ran, he had music to push him along, something else to focus on besides his thoughts. That wasn't exactly possible now, what with the whole flip phone situation. But maybe no distractions was exactly what he needed, a way to force him to deal with . . . whatever he needed to deal with.

You know exactly *what you need to deal with*, a voice that sounded remarkably like Martin's said.

The pictures from the office were still filtering through his mind: his father, Martin, Caro. His past. That path was paved with pain. Some of it he'd dealt with—or thought he had—some of it he didn't know *how* to deal with.

Well, avoiding it isn't going to help. You need to face it straight on.

Max kept moving, picking up the pace as he took a left. Maybe it was Martin's voice still in his head, or maybe his feet were just carrying him down a path he'd traveled more times than he could count. He didn't know if it was muscle memory or instinct, but he was a good way down the road when he realized he'd turned onto Avondale Drive.

It was the street where the Buchanans lived. Where *Caro* lived.

Chapter Eight

Here You Come Again

Caro leaned back in the car seat, staring out the windshield as it slowly misted up with rain. The car was parked in the driveway, the engine off but the radio still playing. She had to finish out the song. She couldn't bring herself to stop Dolly in the middle of "I Will Always Love You."

The corners of her eyes pricked, and the tip of her nose burned. It was a sensation she'd grown accustomed to in the last twenty-four hours. It had started with visiting her mom, then getting Tibbett adopted, and now she was listening to a song she'd associated with Max ever since their breakup.

But he's not that Max anymore. He's not my Max.

He could be exactly the same Max, her mother's voice repeated in her head. *He could still be your Max.*

No, he couldn't. There was no *her* Max anymore. Just like she wasn't *his* Caro anymore. They were two different people, living two different lives. If anything had been clear to her in the last two days, it was that.

What if you're wrong?

It didn't matter if she was wrong, she couldn't go there again, *wouldn't* go there again. She was already dealing with too much. She couldn't handle more. Her heart was already hurting after opening it up even just a little bit to Tibbett.

She'd gone and let herself get attached to him, and now look at her. She was sitting in a car, listening to Dolly Parton, and crying. Her heart would shatter into a million pieces if she let anyone else in . . . especially Max.

God, why are you worrying about this? she asked herself as she ran her fingers under her eyes.

She still hadn't even gotten through the first hurdle of talking to him like a rational adult. And now she was concerned about falling in love with him again?

Caro really wanted to talk to Lucy. She missed her sister so fiercely that a fresh wave of tears filled her eyes. But after yet *another* unanswered phone call, she sent a text that said YOU BETTER call me tonight.

The last chords of the song filled the car, and Caro let out a breath, leaning her head back and blinking back the rest of the tears that threatened. She just needed a little help to get through this, that sign she'd asked her mom for the day before, *something* to push her in the right direction. But until then she needed to—

"Get it together, Buchanan," she said before she pulled the hood of her rain jacket over her head and got out of the car.

Caro headed for her apartment above the garage, but she heard a soft whine as she passed her mother's garden. She stopped and turned, her eyes scanning the rosebushes next to the Saint Francis statue. She was pretty sure the sound had come from right over there. Standing still, she listened and waited, and it was only another ten seconds or so before she heard the whine again. The bush shook a little bit, indicating exactly where it had come from.

There were plenty of critters in North Carolina—raccoons, possums, squirrels, skunks—but this wasn't a wild animal. Caro would have known that whine anywhere. It was a dog, and judging by the high pitch, it was probably a puppy.

Heading for the garden, she slipped her keys in the pocket of her rain jacket before squatting down. The bushes were a tangle of branches and thorns, but she found a spot where she could carefully push them apart. The second she did, her eyes landed on a puppy, soaking wet and covered in mud.

The thing couldn't have been more than ten pounds. It looked up at her with the saddest chocolate eyes she'd ever seen in her life. Even with the mud, she could see that its fur was reddish brown. There was string tied around its neck, and it was all tangled up in the sharp, prickly branches.

"Oh, sweetie," Caro said softly, slowly extending her hand. "I'm going to get you out of here."

The poor creature was clearly terrified, and as it cowered away from Caro's hand, it backed up into the thorns, crying out in pain. It tried to scramble away, the string around its neck getting tighter.

"I'm not going to hurt you," Caro whispered. "I just want to get you out of here." She reached in again, the back of her hand just close enough for the dog to lean forward and sniff. It was a few tentative seconds before it nudged her knuckles and licked her.

"Okay, that's progress." Caro slowly moved, her fingers extending to the dog's neck, giving it a little pet before trying to figure out the string situation. But it was no use; it was badly knotted and tangled. "We're going to have to try this another way." She gently moved the branches back in place, trying her best not to hit the dog with them.

"Caro?"

She would have known that deep, sexy voice anywhere, but it caught her so off guard that she yelped, falling backward right into the soggy, muddy grass. The sound of surprise wasn't the only one that filled the air—a high-pitched squeal came from the bushes.

"Crap." She scrambled back up, her shoes, legs, and hands now all covered in mud. "There's a puppy stuck in here, and I can't get it out. It's caught in the thorns and keeps hurting itself." Since she was already muddy, she knelt this time, her knees sinking into the wet, squishy grass. Then she gently pushed the branches back to find the puppy cowering worse than before.

"Jesus," Max breathed. "Your dad's tools still in the garage?"

"Yeah." She glanced up and got her first good look at him. He was wet from the rain, droplets on his skin and hair, and the fabric of his T-shirt clung to him in all the right places.

God, why did he look so good while she was covered in dirt? It was the second time the sound of his voice had her falling all over herself. It was so un-fucking-fair.

"The code still the same?"

"What?" She shook her head, trying to clear the fog from her brain. Damn his stupid too-handsome face.

An amused little smirk lifted the corners of Max's mouth, and something familiar filled Caro's chest.

Shit.

"The code to get into the garage—is it still your mom's birthday?"

"Oh, yes." Caro nodded.

"I'll be right back," he said before he turned around and jogged off.

Caro couldn't help but watch his running shorts clinging to the back of him too.

"Focus," she told herself as she turned to the puppy. There were much more pressing things at hand than Max's ass. "We're going to get you out of here."

We? Oh, no. No, no, no, no, no. There is no we. *There is Caro, and there is Max. Two totally and completely separate people. But there is no* we. *Not anymore.*

In less than a minute Max was back. "These should do the trick." He held up a pair of scissors as he dropped down next to her. "You keep those pushed back while I cut?"

"Yeah." She nodded, trying to focus on the thorny branches in her hands and not the feel of him next to her . . . the heat coming from his skin.

"It's okay, little one," he whispered to the puppy as he slowly reached his hand in, his arm brushing against Caro's, goose bumps popping up on her skin. Not that he would've noticed, but she was glad she was wearing a rain jacket.

The dog pressed its muddy little nose to Max's palm and sniffed. He waited a second before he gently ran his hand down its neck, sliding a finger under the string. Three expert snips later, and the dog was free.

Max wrapped his hands around the little dog's body, lifting it from the bushes. He took a quick peek at the belly—they both spotted that it was a girl—before pulling her against his chest, his shirt now covered in mud.

"We're going to get you inside, little lady, and get you warm and dry and fed," Max said as he cradled the shivering dog. She looked so tiny in his massive arms. He dropped one of his hands down, holding it out for Caro to grab. He sensed her hesitation, and his lips quirked up in a smile. "Come on, Caro, we're in this together now."

Reaching up, she put her hand in his and let him pull her from the ground.

Caro wasn't sure which part made her stomach somersault—was it the fact that Max was now saying *we*? Or that she'd gotten to touch his hand?

Both. It was definitely both.

* * *

MAX FOLLOWED BEHIND Caro as she led the way to the house. The back of her jean shorts was soaked through and covered in mud from when she fell, and as much as he tried not to look, he couldn't help himself. She'd always had a fantastic ass, and nothing had changed in that department. There were definitely a couple more inches to her curves now, and he couldn't stop the image that came to mind of relearning them.

As if the universe knew he needed some assistance staying in the moment, a tiny tongue moved across his jawline. He glanced down at the dog in his arms, looking into those sorrowful brown eyes.

"You're going to be okay," he told her as he scratched under her chin. Her answer was to give him another lick along his jaw.

Caro pulled the keys from her jacket pocket and unlocked the door, stepping in and moving away to let Max in. The side entrance to the Buchanan house led right into the mudroom and the kitchen beyond.

It had been a long time since Max had walked through that door, but as he looked around, it felt like it was only yesterday. The same plant hung in the window, the walls were still a light buttercream, the rack off to the side stacked with an assortment of shoes.

Some of those clearly belonged to people with much smaller feet. No doubt the grandkids, since Jeremy and Lilah had three. He'd met them at Martin's funeral last year. A glance at the refrigerator showed it covered in pictures from coloring books and paintings of handprints turned into animals.

The sound of nails clicking on the hardwood floors echoed down the hallway, and a second later, a German shepherd walked into the kitchen. She was a little on the smaller side for the breed, but intimidating, nonetheless. The puppy started to shake in Max's arms, and she let out a weird little barking yelp. She burrowed deeper into him, her face pushing into the warmth of his armpit.

"Leia, gentle," Caro said as the dog crossed over to them, heading for Max. Her wet nose pushed into his calf as she sniffed up his leg and to the dog in his arms. "She'll be good." She looked to Max. "She's going to want a pet from you, though."

Max adjusted the puppy before he moved one of his hands down, letting Leia sniff. She licked his knuckles before he scratched between her ears.

"Now, go sit. You can check the puppy out when she gets cleaned up," she told the dog, who sat back on her haunches, watching as her long, fluffy tail moved across the tile.

"Wow. I've never seen a dog listen like that before. Beau is good, but he isn't that good."

"Yeah, her previous owner was a retired cop who trained dogs. The rescue got her when he passed away," she told him as she pulled off her jacket. "I brought her home as a foster, and it took my father about four hours to decide to keep her. She wouldn't leave his side. Fastest adoption I've ever had." She hung her jacket up on the rack by the door before toeing off her shoes. "Truth be told, I think she trains the fosters better than I do."

Feet now bare—bright pink toenail polish visible—Caro walked over to the giant sink next to the washer and dryer and spun the faucet to turn the hot water on. Max's shoes weren't muddy like hers, but they were a little soggy from the rain, so he toed them off too, leaving them lined up on the mat next to hers.

There was something about the image of their shoes sitting next to each other that made his chest tighten. A longing for a life that hadn't happened? He turned away, not able to look at it anymore.

Caro moved her hand through the water, checking the temp before she glanced over at Max. "It's ready now. You can put her in." She nodded to the sink.

Max gently set her down, and the dog let out a low whine as she scurried to the corner, trying to climb up the side and get away from the stream of water.

"She's got a long body," Max said.

"Definitely part dachshund, if not all, and she's so skinny," Caro said as she eased the dog's front legs back down to the bottom of the sink.

The dog went to move again, but Max gently ran his fingers under her chin and tried to keep her still. She was small enough that he was pretty sure Caro could've managed bathing her on her own, but he was there, so he might as well help. Problem was, they were now standing so close together that their arms brushed. Skin to skin.

At the contact Caro's whole body froze. She paused for a moment before she cleared her throat and whispered, "Thank you." And then she reached for the shelf above them, grabbing a cup and filling it with water before slowly pouring it across the dog's back. The water ran black as more of the reddish brown fur became visible. "It's okay," Caro soothed. "I promise it's going to feel a lot better to get rid of all this mud."

It took a couple of cups before the water started to lighten up, and that was when they noticed the small stream of blood in the sink. Once the mud was washed away, Caro found some of the sources. There was a cut on the top of her front paw, another across her back where the string had been, and a third on her side.

"I think they're all shallow, but we'll take her to the vet for a better look."

"We?"

"Yeah. Didn't you say we were in this together now?"

"I did." He glanced over at her. "I just thought I'd have to fight you on it a little more."

"Yes, well, I'd prefer not to fight with you anymore." She turned, her head tilting back and her hazel-gray eyes meeting his.

It was the first time that afternoon that he'd gotten a good look at her face—hard not to when they were so close—and he realized something was wrong. Her eyes were puffy, a tinge of red around the irises. The tip of her nose was pink too, and her lips swollen. She'd been crying.

There was a tired sadness etched across her face, and Max wanted to make it go away.

"I'm sorry." He'd barely thought before speaking those words, but he meant them. "About the bar on Tuesday, and the café on Wednesday. I was a jerk."

Her eyes went wide, clearly surprised. She hesitated for just a moment before she nodded. "Thank you for saying that. Now make sure you have a hold on her. The soap is going to sting a little, and I'm sure she isn't going to like it."

Max got a good hold on the dog's front as Caro grabbed a bottle of shampoo, pouring some on her hands and lathering them together. The second she touched the spot on her back, the dog cried out in pain and struggled in Max's hands.

"It's okay," they both said at the same time.

It took a little bit for the dog to stop trying to escape and calm down, but Caro and Max continued to work together, Max maneuvering the dog around so Caro could get every spot. As long as he had his hands on the dog, she was good at staying still, but she did take a number of opportunities to shake her whole body, spraying soap and water all over the sides of the sink and his and Caro's arms.

Caro had just started washing behind the dog's ears when she asked the question he knew she'd been working up to. "So *why* were you being a jerk?"

Because the twenty-year-old boy who was in love with you still lives inside of me, and he wanted to see if you were as jealous as he was. But he couldn't tell her the truth . . . well, at least not *that* truth.

"I guess I just wanted to get a rise out you."

"Well, you did. That was apparent with the ice water incident."

"I thought that was an accident." He glanced over at the side of her face.

She was now rinsing the soap from the dog's head—being careful not to get any in its eyes—so she didn't turn to look at him. He still caught the grin that turned up the side of her mouth, though. "It was an on-purpose."

"An on-purpose?" He couldn't help but laugh.

"Yes, that's what we call it when my nephews and niece do something deliberately." She paused as she filled another cup with water and poured it across the dog's back, getting rid of the last of the suds. "I'm sorry about that, by the way." She turned the faucet off before looking up at him, her eyebrows raised high. "Though it clearly worked out for you and little Miss Miniskirt?"

"Aubrey? Yeah, not so much. I didn't go back to her room, by the way." He wasn't sure why he'd felt the need to tell her that . . . or the next words that fell out of his mouth. "And I was being more of an ass when I said she was the age of the women I usually dated. That was a lie."

"To get under my skin?"

"Yes."

"Good to know." If he hadn't known any better, he'd have thought there was a little more light in her eyes.

But why would telling her the truth have that effect? And why did he care?

He didn't have too long to think about that question before the puppy did a full-body shake. One so big that the water splashed all the way up to Max's face.

* * *

CARO'S HEAD WAS spinning a little as she grabbed a clean towel from the cabinet, scooping up the puppy from the sink and bringing the creature to her chest. Truth be told, her head had been spinning since Max had shown up fifteen minutes ago.

"I'd actually wanted to talk to you too," she said as she used a corner of the towel to dry the dog's head. "I'd really like it if we could be . . . good again . . . or something other than this weird tension."

"You mean, call a truce and act like adults?"

"Yes," she agreed. "That."

"Deal." He smiled as he leaned his hip against the sink, folding his arms across his chest. But a second later they were unfolding, and he was wrinkling his nose as he looked down at the mud that still clung to his shirt.

"You're going to need to change before we head to the vet." She nodded to the shirt.

"I'm not the only one." He pointed to her shorts. "You've got way more mud on you."

"Oh, believe me. I'm fully aware. There's nothing quite like the feeling of wet underwear." The second the words were out of her mouth, she knew her cheeks must be flaming pink. They definitely felt warmer. "I . . . I didn't mean it like that. I—"

"I knew what you meant." Max laughed, shaking his head.

"If . . . you . . . um . . . take your shirt off, you can hold her while I get you something to change into." And now her cheeks had to be bright red. "Just . . . so . . . you know . . . you don't get all of that mud on her again."

God, why was she acting this way? She'd seen Max with his shirt off more times than she could count. She'd seen him naked. Hell, he'd been *inside* of her.

And yet why did part of this feel new? Like she had a crush on someone she'd just met?

Max reached up, pulling the collar of his shirt away from his face and taking it off in one easy motion. Caro's breath caught in her lungs, her eyes going wide as she took in every inch of his biceps, chest, and abs.

Oh, sweet Lord. Max's body had always been amazing, but it was downright glorious now. There were so many dips and ridges that she wanted to trace, to learn. She swallowed hard, her throat suddenly very, very dry.

"Right." She swallowed again as she handed him the dog like it was a swaddled baby. "Okay." Giving herself a small moment of reprieve from the overwhelming hotness that was his body, she turned to the washer and dryer in the corner. She had a clean load in the dryer, and she opened the door, grabbing a pair of shorts, panties, and a T-shirt.

When she turned back around, Max's focus was on the clothes in her hand, zeroing in on the scrap of blue that was her thong. There was a heat in his eyes that had her heart beating faster.

"I'll just go . . . and change . . . and then get you some clothes."

Max cleared his throat, some color now on his own cheeks. "I just need a shirt. My shorts are already dry."

"Okay." She nodded, taking a few steps back, still looking at his bared chest and arms before she turned and almost walked right into Leia. The dog was still patiently waiting and watching in the doorway, but she moved from her spot, giving Caro enough space to get through.

She couldn't get away fast enough.

What the hell was that?

She reached up, brushing her fingers across her flushed cheeks. It wasn't like the mudroom was very big, but it had felt positively minuscule with him standing there wearing no shirt and holding a puppy. It was an image worthy of a calendar.

The last twenty minutes might've been the weirdest of her life. How did everything feel familiar, but at the same time *so* different?

She might not have an answer now, but considering their new truce, she had a feeling she was going to find out.

* * *

THE NEXT HOUR was the shortest Max had experienced since he'd been in Cruickshank. Maybe it was because they were so busy . . . or maybe it was because he was with Caro.

They got the puppy to drink some water, and even though the bowl wasn't very big, she still managed to fall into it, requiring another toweling off.

Caro called the vet and made an appointment with Oscar. Meanwhile, Max supervised Leia meeting the puppy. She cried and whined, trying to hide behind Max's feet, but when the German shepherd licked her face, she calmed down.

The next task was food. Caro scrambled some eggs—making a couple for Leia too—and once they cooled, she hand-fed the dog. Wanting to get closer to Caro and the food, the pup tried to crawl out of Max's lap, but he managed to hold her in place.

"We have to go slow, little one," Caro told the puppy as she held her palm out with another piece of egg. Even in her eagerness to eat, she was still pretty gentle as she nibbled the bites out of Caro's hand.

"We should name her," Max said.

Caro looked up at him, hesitation on her face.

"What?"

"I just . . . I don't usually name the dogs. They usually have one from the shelters where we get them, or if they're strays, Lorraine or Sasha names them."

"And why don't you?" Max asked as he readjusted his grip on the squirming pup.

"One of my stupid rules for trying not to get attached."

"Does it work?"

"Nope." She shook her head. "It feels like each one is getting worse."

"What do you mean?"

She made a sad little frown as she held out her hand with another bit of egg. "Tibbett got adopted today. The basset hound I had at your grandmother's."

"Ahh." He nodded. "Is that why you were crying?"

Her frown deepened. "How did you know I'd been crying?"

"Come on, Caro." Max shook his head. "I know we don't know each other like we used to, but I can still tell when you're upset."

She sighed before relenting. "I was working at Kathleen's Corner today, and the second his new owners walked him out of the building I burst into tears. Hazel sent me home."

"Well, maybe it was meant to be. If Tibbett hadn't gotten adopted and you hadn't come home early, you wouldn't have found her," Max said as he scratched between the dog's ears. She wiggled more in his lap, her long body stretching out across his thighs.

"That's true." Her eyebrows bunched together in thought.

"What?"

"Just thinking about the timing of things. What were you doing over here, anyways?"

"I wanted to go for a run, and before I realized it, I found myself down this street. I knew I needed to apologize. Maybe my feet just took me in this direction."

"Yeah." Caro nodded, feeding the dog the last bit of eggs. "Maybe."

"So what's the next step with her? After the vet?"

"I'm going to check the missing pet database. See if anyone listed her as lost on there. But she might be chipped too. They'll scan her."

"There's a missing pet database?"

"Yeah, all of the rescues, shelters, and vets within a hundred-mile radius have access to it. I created it a couple of years ago."

"Impressive."

"Thanks." She shrugged like it was no big deal. "It's got a lot of people reunited with their animals."

"So, if she's not on the website and she isn't chipped, are you going to foster her?"

"Most likely. And with the rescue, we always hold found dogs for at least two weeks before putting them up for adoption."

"So she needs a name."

Caro sighed, pushing the empty plate back on the table. "You're right. She does."

"What was that again?"

"I agreed she needs a name?"

"No." He shook his head. "The other part."

"The part where I said you're right?"

"There it is." He grinned.

Caro rolled her eyes but let out a laugh that did funny things to his chest. "Did you have any suggestions in mind?" she asked.

Max looked down at the dog, scratching a spot on her side that was away from her cuts. "What about something like Kiki, or Gigi, or Zuzu."

"I'm sensing a pattern here."

"Hey, those are fun names."

Caro smiled, holding up her hands in surrender. "I'm not saying they aren't. They just all are the same two letters repeated."

"Okay, what were you thinking? And you can't tell me you don't have any ideas, even if you weren't saying them out loud." Max was still scratching the dog's side, and he must've found her spot, because she slowly started to roll over, giving him more access to her belly.

"Maybe it's because I've been listening to her the last day, but Dolly."

"Oh, that's a good name." Max nodded slowly. "I just imagine a dog named Dolly to be blond, like a golden retriever. Or a poodle with curly hair."

"Okay, fair point. What about Rosie? Since we found her in the rosebushes?"

"I like that, it's just . . ."

"It still doesn't fit." Caro looked down at the dog, who was now kicking her legs in the air as Max continued to scratch her belly. Her eyes were closed in ecstasy, her little tongue lolling. "I feel like a boy name that's short for a girl name would be cute. Like Lou, or Joey, or George."

"What about Frankie?" Max asked. "She was under the Saint Francis statue. Frankie could be short for Frances."

"Oh my gosh. Frankie! *That's* perfect for her."

"See? We got there in the end." Max held his palm in the air, and Caro gave him a high five.

There was a familiarity in the simple gesture, and though it was just for a second that their hands touched, the warmth of her skin lingered against his palm. He couldn't stop himself from closing his hand and holding on to it for a moment longer.

"Okay." He cleared his throat. "So, what now?"

Caro glanced at her Apple Watch. "Her appointment is at two, so we should probably go."

"Sounds good." Max nodded as they both stood. At the movement, Leia got up from her spot next to them, looking eager to join.

"You can play with her when we get back." Caro scratched the top of Leia's head. "Leia needs to go out before we leave, and Frankie here"—she reached up to the dog in Max's arms—"needs to try too. There's a slip-collar leash at my place, and I need to get some clean shoes."

They all headed for the door—Caro holding Frankie while Max slipped on his own sneakers and a jacket that she handed him— before going outside.

It was raining again, the light mist from earlier replaced with a steady drizzle. Caro pulled the hood of her jacket up as she ran up the path and over to her place. Max and Frankie stayed underneath the overhang, and his eyes automatically went to the little loft apartment above the detached garage. An ache he wasn't prepared for spread from his heart and out to his chest, going down his arms.

Caro had moved up there the summer after she graduated high school. She might have been staying in Cruickshank to help take care of her mom, but she'd still wanted a little independence, and it was a move that had greatly benefited Max. That summer—the last summer they'd had together—he'd pretty much lived in that loft. Every night he'd gone to sleep tangled up with her.

A wet, snuffling nose pushed into his thigh, and Max looked down to see Leia in front of him. Not wanting to mess with the rain for longer than she had to, she'd made quick work of her bathroom break. Max opened the door, and Leia didn't even hesitate before heading back into the house.

Caro was barely gone three minutes and then she was coming back down the stairs, an umbrella in one hand and a green leash in the other. She joined him underneath the overhang and slipped the leash over Frankie's head.

"Let's see if she'll go," she said as he set the dog on the ground. She popped the umbrella—the noise and sudden movement making Frankie jump—before she stepped out onto the path.

Frankie didn't move.

"Come on," Caro said as she gently tugged on the leash. "I'm sure you have to potty."

Frankie just dug her heels in.

Max laughed as he stepped around them, pulling his hood up and heading for the grass. He squatted down, clapping his hands between his thighs. "Come on, Frankie," he called. "It's okay out here. Just a little wet."

The dog looked from Max to Caro and back to Max before she slowly moved her little legs and stepped off the path. Caro kept the umbrella over her as they headed to the grass.

Max stood, taking a step back as the dog followed, and they

continued on that way for a couple of minutes before she finally squatted.

"Well, that was a production." Caro shook her head. "I think Frankie is a bit of a drama queen."

"Good thing she's cute."

"Good thing." Caro laughed as she handed him the leash. "Let me go grab a towel and lock up."

She was back in a flash, and Max scooped Frankie up before heading for the old Jeep. "I can't believe you still have this," he said as he settled into the passenger seat.

It was yet another space that held way too many memories. Rachel had driven them around in this when they were kids, and when he and Caro had started to drive, they'd taken it out on many dates . . . and fooled around in the back seat more times than he could count.

He wondered if she was thinking about those times . . . but if she was, she didn't let on.

"She's still going strong," Caro said as she patted the steering wheel. She started the engine, and the music cut on. The opening chords to "Here You Come Again" filling the car.

"See? Dolly." Caro gestured to the stereo before she backed out of the drive.

"I do. Anything in particular inspire you to play her?"

"I went to visit my mom yesterday." She glanced over at Max as she made a right onto the street.

A sad smile turned up the corners of his mouth. "I always think of your mom when I listen to Dolly too."

"She was her favorite."

It was weird to think Rachel's death had impacted him more than his own father's, but it had. She'd been like a mother to him, up there with Ava, and more so than the woman who'd given birth to him.

The handful of times he'd been in town, he'd always visited her grave. He hadn't gone yet, but that was because he'd have to visit another grave too.

"I need to go see her . . . and Martin. I don't know if I'm ready, though," Max said as he rubbed his finger between Frankie's ears. Petting her seemed to help calm the range of painful emotions that moved through his chest.

Or maybe it was finally talking about how he'd been feeling for the last few days. Or, hell, the last year. Truce or not, things weren't perfect with Caro. And they might not know each other all that well anymore, but she understood this. Understood his loss better than anyone, besides Ava.

"It's okay if you're not."

"That's why I had to go for a run." He'd started talking, and now he couldn't stop. "I went into his office for the first time, and it was just . . . all too much."

Caro pulled to a stop in front of a red light. "Max." She whispered his name, and he turned to look at her. There was a softness in her expression that squeezed at his heart. "Don't force it. You'll figure it out in your own time." She reached over and grabbed his forearm, and just like earlier, the place where their skin touched burned.

The inside of the car suddenly felt very warm as they looked at each other. Neither moved until a loud honk from the car behind them made Caro pull her hand away and turn back to the road.

Chapter Nine

From the Beginning

"Well, there's no microchip," Oscar said as he set the scanner down on the table next to the puppy. "And I'm hesitant to think Frankie has someone who is looking for her . . . or they aren't looking very hard."

"Why's that?" Max asked, his brow furrowing like it always did when he was upset about something.

He wasn't the only one who could still read the other's emotions.

"Well, judging by her teeth," Oscar said as he gently pushed the puppy's lips back, "I think she's four or five months old. But based off her paws, she's too small for her age. She should probably be five pounds heavier. My best guess is that she's been on her own for a week or two, maybe more, but she hasn't been getting proper nutrition for a while. She's been able to find food, but she's malnourished too. Poor thing hasn't been taken care of."

"Is she going to be okay?" Max asked.

Caro was *very* concerned about the dog herself, but there was something about seeing Max so worried after such a short time with the pup. It was sweet.

"Yes." Oscar nodded as he shone a light in her eyes. "Once she gets a little meat on her, and some medicine, Frankie will be all good."

"Well, she didn't have any problem eating when I fed her earlier. I made her a scrambled egg after her bath, and she was inhaling it. I had to feed her by hand so she'd slow down."

"It never takes you long to get them eating out of your hand." Oscar looked up from his exam and grinned at Caro.

"No kidding," Max muttered under his breath.

Both Caro and Oscar turned to him, and by his expression, it was clear Max hadn't meant to say that out loud. If she hadn't known any better, she'd have thought there was a small blush creeping up into his cheeks.

Maybe it was just a trick of the light.

Oscar laughed, shaking his head. "Well, I'm glad to see you're getting along. The tension between the two of you at the bar the other night was so thick it would've taken a chainsaw to cut through it."

"Yes, well, we've moved past that," Caro said.

"Sure you have." Oscar laughed again. "So, what's your plan for Frankie?" He gently scratched under the dog's chin, and she closed her eyes in pleasure.

"I'm for sure going to foster her until she's better. I haven't had a puppy in a while, though." She typically got older dogs, but there had been a few puppies over the last couple of years. "It's going to be interesting."

"Seems like a theme. There are *a lot* of interesting things going on this summer." Oscar waggled his eyebrows as he looked between her and Max.

Subtle, Oscar, very subtle.

* * *

THIRTY MINUTES LATER, Max, Caro, and Frankie headed for the exit. Oscar had given Frankie all her first shots and tested her for heartworms, then given Caro some medicine for an ear infection and a topical cream for the wounds on her back and paw.

Caro now had the dog zipped up in the front of her jacket, her head burrowed under Caro's chin. Max wasn't a betting man, but if he had been, he'd have said that dog was going to burrow its way into her heart in no time at all.

"Don't we need to pay?" he asked as Caro walked right past the receptionist's desk.

"It's already paid for." She shook her head. "When it comes to animals with the rescue, there's a fund."

"You must have some generous donors."

"Just one *very* generous donor."

"Ava?"

"Well, it was Ava *and* Martin." Caro nodded as she pushed the front door open, and they stepped out under the awning. The rain was still coming down in a steady drizzle. "Want to go to the pet shop before we head back? It's just around the corner, and Frankie needs a new leash and collar."

"Yeah, I'll put these in the car"—he held up the bag of meds—"and grab your umbrella."

Caro pulled the keys out of her pocket, handing them over to Max. Their fingers brushed, and the electricity they'd been passing back and forth all day sparked between them. And for what felt like the hundredth time, Max forced himself to pull away.

He headed out into the rain, and he was pretty sure that if there had still been lightning in the sky, he would've attracted it like a freaking rod.

This feeling was absolutely insane. Now he remembered exactly why he'd stayed away from her for so long—he couldn't help himself when it came to Caro. He'd never been able to. Distance had been his only saving grace, and he had no idea what he was going to do now.

A minute later, as they both huddled underneath the umbrella and made their way to the main street, he realized he wanted to knock down the next barrier.

He wanted to know her again.

"Can I ask you something?" He glanced over at her.

"Yes."

"*Why* haven't you adopted a dog since Sweet Pea?" She was silent for a moment too long, and Max glanced over at her. "You don't have to answer if you don't want to."

"It's not that." She shook her head. "Sweet Pea was my mom's. One of the last tethers I had to her. And when she died . . . well, it felt like I'd lost my mom all over again."

"That makes sense."

"It's been easier to . . . not get attached. Or to at least *try* and not get attached."

He had the impression she was talking about more than just dogs, and as much as he wanted to push on that topic, it felt like *too* much for whatever this newfound thing between them was.

Besides, the flip phone in his pocket started making a trilling noise. He pulled it out, glancing at the front, Home flashing on the little screen.

"Sorry, it's Ava." He should've called her earlier, but he hadn't wanted to wake her up from her nap. Popping the front open with his thumb, he put the speaker to his ear.

"Hey, Ava."

"Where are you? I thought you'd be home by now."

"I'm with Caro. We found a puppy and just got finished up at the vet. Oscar checked her out."

There was a beat of silence on the other line. "You found a puppy? With Caro?"

"Yes."

"And everyone's still breathing? No bones have been broken?"

"You're hilarious. I'll be back in less than an hour."

"Okay. I can't wait to hear all about your afternoon." The grin in her voice was evident, and he knew he was going to get interrogated the *second* he walked in the door. "Have fun, Bean."

"Bye." He rolled his eyes as he flipped the phone shut, sliding it back in his pocket. "Sorry about that," he apologized again as he turned to her.

Her eyebrows were bunched together in confusion as she looked up at him.

"What?"

"Why are you using Martin's old flip phone?"

"How did you know it was his?"

"First, because of that ringtone. I can't even count the number of times I had to call that thing to figure out where he'd left it."

"I can only imagine." Max laughed, thinking about his grandfather. It wasn't that Martin had been an absentminded professor; he just had no use for cell phones. "I'm using it because I made a bet with Ava. She wasn't a very big fan of how much I was working the first day. She seemed to think it interfered with being on vacation."

"Well, yes, working on your vacation is counterintuitive."

"So if I gave it up for a week and only used this, she said she'd make me her pineapple coconut whipped dream cake."

"Ohhh," Caro moaned, and the noise traveled right down Max's spine. "I haven't had that in years."

"That's just more incentive for you to be nice to me. I might share."

"In that case, next time I have the urge to throw water on you, I'll keep that cake in mind."

"Please do."

Caro laughed again, and it was yet another sound that vibrated in his bones. *God*, how he'd missed it.

You've missed her. Again, it was Martin's voice speaking in Max's head, and his grandfather was starting to sound a little exasperated.

"So, how's not working going for you?" she asked as they paused, waiting for the cars to pass before crossing the street.

"Well, it's only been about two days. I'm still getting used to it, though I'm not completely off the grid. Ava let me make an amendment, so I can call my assistant, Edward, in the morning. I'm not too worried; he can handle everything—he's been able to for years. The man needs a promotion when I get back to New York."

It would be one of the last things he'd make sure to do before heading off to England. *England.* Why was that thought suddenly accompanied by a sinking feeling in his chest?

Just as he was trying to push that thought to the back of his mind, something came along and did it for him.

As they turned another corner, a massive five-story brick building came into view. Max didn't need to spot the FOR SALE sign to know that it was vacant. There were boards in the windows, and the grass in front was tall and weedy, the flowers that had died in the winter still planted in the ground.

"What happened to the Kincaid Spring Factory?" He paused when they were across from it, and Caro stopped at his side.

"A company in Asheville bought them out about five years ago or so. They own the building too, but just haven't been able to sell it. It would take a lot to fix up, so they were talking about tearing it down and selling the land."

"What?" Max looked over at her in horror. "They can't tear it down! That building is probably two hundred years old. And the architecture is amazing, it's Italianate Victorian. Look how ornate that brickwork is, and those arches are a work of art. And then there are the windows, which in and of themselves are amazing—"

"Hey, Max, calm down." Caro held up one of her hands in surrender. "I didn't say I supported it, and neither does most of the town. *Because* it's a historical building, they have to get the majority of the Cruickshank City Council to approve, and they won't do it."

"Well, I guess that's something." He stared up at the building, and the wheels in his head started turning . . . the wheels that had made him millions . . . the wheels that had made him a success.

* * *

MAX PUSHED A cart down the aisle of Whiskers and Wags pet shop while Caro followed behind him, trying very hard not to look at his ass in those shorts.

Okay, maybe not *very* hard.

She was still slightly thrown by the events of the last few hours. They'd gone from this awkward weird tension between them to . . .

friends? Maybe it was the whole Frankie rescue mission that had forced things to change.

Or maybe it was just inevitable that they'd find their way to . . . whatever this was.

"I just really think she'd look better in the turquoise, over the purple," Max said as he held two collars in the air.

He'd vetoed all but those two choices. Apparently, he had an eye for million-dollar properties . . . and dog fashion.

"Is that so?" Caro asked as she adjusted Frankie in her arms. "What do you think?" She held the dog close to the collars. She hesitated for a second before nudging the turquoise.

"See? Frankie agrees. And her leash should be that bright pink one."

"Since you're so certain about all of this, I relent." Caro grinned, shaking her head.

"And I'm paying."

"You'll get no argument from me there."

"Good." He nodded. "Because we aren't done yet."

It was another twenty minutes before they were at the register, Frankie getting a brand-new bed, fluffy pink blanket, and an assortment of toys. She now had a rainbow pastel dragon, a blue narwhal, and a purple platypus.

"You know I'm just fostering her, right?" Caro asked as he pulled out his credit card.

"Yeah," he said, his mouth forming a little smirk in the left corner.

"What's that look?"

"It's nothing. You can give the stuff to her new family or keep it.

Your choice. But she gets to enjoy it now. She deserves to be spoiled a little." He scratched under her chin. "Or a lot."

Caro couldn't argue with that last part. Frankie deserved to be spoiled beyond reason.

Max grabbed the bags before they went outside and headed the few blocks back to the car. The rain had stopped while they'd been in the pet store, and since they no longer needed to huddle under the umbrella, there was more space between them as they walked by the Kincaid factory again. Max was intently staring at it, and Caro waited until they passed before speaking.

"So, what is it with that building that's got you so obsessed?"

He turned to her, his eyebrows furrowed. "How do you know I'm obsessed?"

"I guess it's the same reason that you knew I was upset earlier. Some things haven't changed. I know the look on your face when you get obsessive."

Mainly because that look used to be directed at her more often than not.

"Cruickshank doesn't have any hotels, at least not within the city limits. And I think that building might make the perfect location for a boutique hotel."

An unexpected little bubble of hope filled her chest. If his company bought the factory, would that mean he'd have to visit? Come here more often?

Except, what did it matter if Max was in Cruickshank more often? The two of them might be getting along at the moment, but nothing else had changed. The little bubble popped, and she didn't want to look too closely at why it had formed in the first place.

Why had one afternoon with him messed with her head so much?

"You want me to drive?" Max asked when they got back to the car. "She looks pretty comfortable." He nodded to the now sleeping bundle in Caro's jacket.

"Do you want me to drop you off?"

"And risk Ava interrogating both of us at the same time? Hard pass."

"You're right. She'll be so much worse if we're together."

"She'll be unbearable. Besides, I never finished my run, and it's not raining anymore." He gestured to the sky.

"Well, I'd hate to disturb her from her comfortable position," Caro said as she looked down at Frankie, unable to stop the smile that curved her lips. The dog was so adorable it was stupid. "You drive."

She rounded the car and got in the passenger seat. As she settled in, she couldn't help but think about how right it felt to see him in the driver's seat. There were so many memories of Max in that car. Of him leaning over the center console, his palm moving to the back of her head, his fingers in her hair as he pulled her in close for a kiss. Of him stretching her out on the back seat, his hands moving under her dress.

The man used to have magic hands that could make her fall apart in absolutely no time at all. She wondered if they still could.

Jesus Christ, she needed to get a grip on herself. The second Max had the car started, she turned the vents to blow on her.

"You okay?"

"Yeah. Frankie is a little heater." It wasn't a lie—the dog was hot—but that wasn't the main reason her cheeks were flushed. "So, what's the first step you have to take with the warehouse?" she asked, trying to focus on something else besides his hands. But they were now gripping the steering wheel, turning it with ease.

"I'll have my assistant get the building plans and do an assessment to see if I'm right about it being a good property to turn into a hotel."

"Have you ever been wrong? With your first instinct?"

Max glanced over as he made a right, his eyes focusing on her. "Nope." He shook his head before he turned back to the road. "I always know from the beginning."

It had only been a second, but there was something about that look that made her think he was talking about more than building assessments.

He'd always told her he'd known the moment they'd met that she'd altered the course of his life. At the age of six he hadn't understood what it was; he'd just known there'd been a shift. A new path had opened up.

But as Caro had learned the hard way, sometimes those paths weren't permanent. Life threw curveballs at you.

Curveballs. The last couple of days had been full of them. And as they pulled up to her father's house, another curveball was waiting. A familiar black SUV was parked in the driveway.

"No way," Caro whispered, the corners of her eyes starting to burn as they filled with tears. The image of the car blurred, and she blinked, needing to make sure she wasn't hallucinating.

Lucy was home, and judging by the small U-Haul attached to the back of her car, she wasn't leaving anytime soon.

A second later her sister walked out of the house. She was wearing jeans and a purple raincoat, her dark brown hair piled up in a messy bun on the top of her head. She was heading for her

SUV, but she paused when she spotted the Jeep Wagoneer in the driveway, her eyes narrowing in confusion and her head tilting to the side.

"Is that Lucy?" Max asked, parking and turning the engine off.

"Yes," Caro said as she unzipped her jacket and pulled a sleeping Frankie from her chest. "Can you take her for a second?" She didn't even wait for him to answer before she passed the dog over the console to Max.

Then Caro was out of the car, slamming the door behind her as she ran across the driveway. "Are you really here?" she asked, pulling Lucy into a hug. As soon she had her arms around her sister, the tears started to flow freely.

"I'm really here," Lucy said as she hugged Caro back, her grip just as fierce.

Caro held on to her sister for a good few moments before she pulled back. Lucy was smiling as she wiped the tears from under Caro's eyes. She'd never been as much of a crier as Caro, but her own hazel eyes were a little misty.

Lucy's hazel wasn't the same as Caro's; her eyes were more green than gray. That's how most of their features were, similar but with slight differences. Both sisters were short, but Lucy proudly had an inch on Caro, which she liked to bring up often. They both had dark brown hair, but where Caro's had a reddish tint to it, Lucy's was chestnut. And while they both had curves, Lucy had more, as she was a size twelve. The only things that were the same were the pert noses that they'd gotten from their mother.

"Is this why you haven't answered any of my phone calls?" Caro asked as she grabbed Lucy's arms.

"I told you I was driving." Lucy grinned in that smartass way of hers.

"Not across the country. Did Dad or Jeremy know? Or Sasha?"

"No, they didn't know." Lucy shook her head. "I'll explain everything. I swear. But first things first, is that who I think it is in our driveway holding an adorable puppy?"

Caro let go of Lucy's arms and turned to see Max standing next to the car, Frankie looking up at him adoringly as he scratched under her chin. She turned back to her sister, who was now full-on grinning.

"Looks like we both have some explaining to do." Lucy waggled her eyebrows.

"You'd know all about it if you'd answered your phone calls."

"I was driving. Safety first."

"Yes, well, next time you drive across the country, I'd like a little heads-up."

Pain and sadness flickered across Lucy's face. "There isn't going to be a next time, Caro."

Caro grabbed her sister's arm again. "Luce?"

"Later." She shook her head. "I promise."

"Okay." Caro dropped her hand as Lucy moved around her. "Maximillian Abbott!"

"Hey, kiddo. Long time no see," he said as he pulled her into a one-armed hug.

"How many times have I told you *not* to call me kiddo?"

"And how many times did I ever listen?"

Lucy rolled her eyes, lightly punching his arm. "You're supposed to be in New York."

"And you're supposed to be in Los Angeles."

"Well, looks like we're both full of surprises. Who's this?" she asked as Frankie sniffed her hand before she scratched the dog's head.

"Frankie. Caro and I found her in your mom's rose garden a couple of hours ago. The afternoon turned into a bit of a rescue mission."

"Oh, really? I can't wait to hear all about it." She looked between Max and Caro, clearly trying to figure out what was going on.

Well, she could join the fucking club.

"I should probably get going. Ava's waiting for me, and I'm sure we'll have time to catch up later," he said as he handed Frankie to Lucy.

"Will we?" she asked, adjusting the dog in her arms.

"I'd imagine, as I'm going to be in town for the next six weeks."

"Six weeks," Lucy repeated slowly, again looking between him and Caro. "Interesting."

"Bye, Frankie." He scratched under the dog's chin one more time. "Kiddo." He ruffled the bun on Lucy's head.

"Hey!"

Lucy moved out from under his hand, and Max grinned as he took a step back. But his grin faltered as he looked over at Caro, something unsure in his expression.

"Bye, Caroline. I'll see you tomorrow at Ava's."

"Us," Lucy corrected. "You'll see *us* tomorrow, but can you not tell Ava? I want to surprise her."

"Will do." He turned and jogged out of the driveway.

Once he was out of earshot, Lucy let out a low whistle. "Damn, that man has aged like a fine wine."

"He's okay."

Lucy very slowly—and dramatically—turned to Caro. "*O-kay?*"

"I mean, his muscles are, like, a little bit bigger. But besides that, he looks pretty much the same as always."

Lucy tipped her head back and started laughing, a full belly laugh. "Oh, Caro, you're trying so hard, aren't you?"

"Trying so hard to what?"

"To act like you're fine with him being in town."

"I *am* fine. Now, tell me what happened." Caro indicated the SUV and U-Haul. She knew that Lucy had been struggling a little the last couple of months, but not pick-up-her-life-and-drive-across-the-US struggling. In fact, she'd *just* started dating a guy who she'd had a massive crush on. Every time she'd talked about Scott, she'd sounded almost giddy.

Or as giddy as it was possible for Lucy to sound.

Lucy took a deep breath before letting it out in a rush. "So many things."

"What happened with Scott?"

"We are no longer. We weren't meant to be, much like Los Angeles and I weren't meant to be. I wasn't cut out for it. Not the city. Not the environment. Not the people. The last few months have been . . ." She trailed off, shaking her head. "Awful."

"Oh, Luce." Caro grabbed her sister's arm. "Why didn't you tell me?"

"I wasn't ready to admit it, but I am now. I'm going to be thirty years old next year, I have a college degree that I haven't used for a day since I graduated, a bank account that has never seen four figures, and I'm barely making it. All of you have had to help me out financially whenever *any* crisis hits. I just . . . I feel like I've failed."

"You have *not* failed." Caro tightened her grip on Lucy's arm. "Failing would have been not trying at all."

"I don't know." Lucy shook her head. "I was waiting tables, delivering flowers, walking dogs, and getting every other possible part-time job while I went on audition after audition or gig after gig, and nothing ever turned into anything. I just . . . I'm done. I needed to get away. I needed to come home."

Caro had a feeling there was more to this story, more that Lucy wasn't ready to talk about. But she needed to know one thing before she moved on.

"Are you okay?"

Lucy took a deep breath, letting it out through her nose, her shoulders slumping in what looked like relief. "I am now."

"Good." Caro pulled Lucy in for another hug, this one not as tight, as Frankie was between them. "Now let's get you unloaded and settled."

"The only thing I've brought inside is my very cranky cat. She's great at flying, but turns out she hates thirty-four-hour road trips."

"Oh, I completely forgot that Estee would be here."

"Yes, well, good luck getting any attention from her. Leia is currently consoling her." Leia was the kind of dog that adopted all creatures—two-legged and four-legged—into her pack. She and Estee had always gotten along. "And we have to introduce her to Frankie," she said as she nuzzled the dog.

"You know," Caro said as they all headed for the house, "if you'd told me, I would have flown out there and driven with you."

"I know you would've, that's why I didn't tell you. Caroline, I know you think you still need to take care of me, but you don't."

"Lucy, I will *always* want to take care of you, just like you're always going to want to take care of me. That's how family works. Or it's how *this* family works. Accept it." She looked over at her sister before playfully bumping their shoulders together.

Lucy bumped back. "Fine, I accept it."

"You better." Caro wrapped her arm around Lucy, bringing her in close as they walked up the path.

Caro would have been lying if she'd said she wasn't worried about Lucy. They were four years apart, but that big-sister instinct had been born the second Caro had held her all those years ago.

There was nothing Caro wouldn't do for Lucy. She would always protect her, even if she didn't know what she was protecting her from.

Chapter Ten

So, So, So Many Signs

The next hour was busy, but busy was good. Focusing on getting Lucy settled in meant she didn't have to think about this new, weird, complicated feeling she had about Max.

First up were the animals.

Poor Frankie had been through a roller coaster that day and didn't know what to do upon meeting the dark gray Scottish fold with orange eyes and a need for mischief. She was a lot more unsure of Estee than she had been about Leia, and would slowly sneak up, and then run away when the cat looked at her sideways.

It was Leia—not surprisingly—who ended up bringing them all together by starting to play with one of the many toys scattered around the house. After running around the kitchen island in circles, they all needed a good long nap. They created a fur pile on the large dog bed in the living room—Estee stretched out on Leia's back, and Frankie curled up between Leia's front paws.

With all the pets asleep, it only took a couple of trips to unpack Lucy's car. The U-Haul would obviously have to wait for another day.

Once that was done, it was time for phone calls. Thursdays were family dinner night, and their dad always came home early so he could prep whatever fancy dinner he'd decided on for that week, but it was usually after five when everyone else showed up.

"I'm going to call Lilah and tell her she should come over early. The power was out at the school, and she's been home with the kids all day. I'm guessing you want to surprise them too?"

"Obviously."

Jeremy and Lilah owned a house less than a block away, so it was barely ten minutes later when Lilah, Matthew, Christopher, Emilia, and Angus the schnauzer got there. The second they saw Lucy, *all* of them screamed in delight and tackled her, bringing her down to the living room floor in a tickle wrestling match. It riled up the animals again, Angus the rowdiest of all.

When it was finally settled, everyone laughing and gasping for breath, Emilia snuggled into Lucy's side and whispered, "I've missed you," into her aunt's neck.

Lucy's eyes immediately got soft and watery as she wrapped her arms around Emilia and whispered right back, "I've missed you too."

It was Sasha who arrived next. Lucy had called, knowing full well her best friend wouldn't be very happy if she wasn't involved in that evening's homecoming. She'd even brought fresh focaccia, tomatoes, and mozzarella for a hearty appetizer, as there were two extra mouths for Wes to feed. Though that wasn't typically a problem, as he usually cooked too much anyway.

Their dad got home around four thirty, the kitchen door slamming shut as he called out, "Where is she?"

"In here," Lucy called back as she slipped Emilia from her lap and stood.

Wes's hurried footsteps echoed down the hall. He came to an

abrupt stop on the threshold, the look of pure happiness on his face enough to make Caro's eyes fill with tears for what felt like the hundredth time that day. And the second Wes pulled Lucy into his arms and softly said, "My babies are all home," those tears began freely streaming down her face.

He held on to Lucy for a good long while, and when he pulled back, there were tears in his beard. It wasn't just Caro who couldn't handle seeing their dad cry: Lucy was wiping her fingers under her own eyes.

"Come on, Dad. I saw you a few months ago. You act like I haven't been home for years."

"You haven't *lived* here for years. I'm just happy you're back." He leaned down and pressed a kiss to her forehead before he stepped away. Then he spotted the bundle of fur snuggled up in Matthew's lap.

"Who's this?" he asked as he walked over, stopping to give Estee some attention where she lounged on the back of the couch before he crouched down to pet Frankie. The dog immediately rolled over, exposing her belly.

"That's Frankie. The dog Caro rescued with Max today," Lucy answered.

"Max? You failed to mention that part," Lilah said.

Wes looked over at Caro, his eyebrows raised high. He was well aware Max was back in town, but besides her mentioning it to him last night, they hadn't really discussed it.

Rachel had been the pusher, whereas Wes had never forced his kids to talk about topics they didn't want to discuss. He'd always been of the mind that if they wanted to tell him, he'd know. But after Rachel's death, it had proven to be somewhat detrimental to his kids . . . especially Lucy.

"Yes, it's been a busy day for Caro. She got Tibbett adopted and found a foster all within an hour of each other. We're going to have plenty to talk about tonight," Lilah said.

"We sure are." Sasha grinned.

"I'm going to wash up and change before I start dinner. I'm a little dusty from today." Wes was an electrician, and some days he got a little dirtier than others. He was currently working on a development on the other side of town, the same one her brother's construction company was contracted for.

"We'll all be in to help," Lucy said.

Wes gave her one last smile before he headed down the hall to his room. The second he was out of earshot, Lilah rounded on Caro. "So Max, huh?"

"Who's Max?" Emilia asked.

"Aunt Caro's ex-boyfriend," Lucy answered.

Emilia's big blue eyes went wide. She was the only one of Jeremy and Lilah's kids who had gotten Rachel's eyes. "You had a boyfriend?"

Okay, fine, so it had been a long time since Caro had dated. But Emilia acting like this was the most shocking piece of news she'd ever learned really wasn't helping.

"It was a long time ago," Sasha told Emilia.

"A long, long, *long* time ago." Lucy piled on.

"Thanks." Caro frowned. "Can we move on from this?"

"Sure." Lilah grinned before she looked to her kids. "You guys helping, coloring, or do you want to watch a movie?"

"Movie," Matthew and Christopher said in unison. "And can I hold Frankie?" Matthew asked Caro.

"Absolutely." Caro grabbed the remote and turned on the TV.

"What about you, Emilia?"

"I want to help Papa cook with Aunt Lucy."

"Good." Lucy bent down and picked Emilia up, the little girl wrapping her arms around Lucy's neck, before heading for the kitchen.

* * *

THE MENU FOR the night was pesto gnocchi with pancetta, summer squash salad, and strawberry shortcake. The kitchen became loud and busy in no time with everyone prepping and cooking. CCR's "Born on the Bayou" played through the Bluetooth speaker in the corner, accompanied by the sizzle of pancetta as Wes pushed it around the pan with a spatula.

Caro and Lilah sat at the center island cutting up veggies while Lucy helped Emilia with the herbs. Sasha had set up the appetizer, a big plate of the caprese sitting next to the focaccia that everyone was snacking on.

It was just after five when Jeremy opened the door to the mudroom and walked into the kitchen, looking around for the new arrival.

"No. Shit," he said as he pulled Lucy into a hug and spun her around.

"Daddy! Swear jar!" Emilia called out from the stool at the sink, where she was washing basil.

"Dang it." Jeremy grinned as he set Lucy down. "She always catches me." Unlike Caro and Lucy, Jeremy had inherited height from their father. He was six foot two, lean and muscular, and had just as much of his thick, dark brown hair on his face as he had on his head.

"Mama." Emilia tugged on Lilah's shirt. "I'm all done with the herbs. Can I watch the movie with Matthew and Christopher?"

"Yes, baby," Lilah said as she lifted her from the stool and set her on the floor.

Emilia went to her father, hugging his leg before letting go and running for the living room.

"Walk," Jeremy called out, and her little legs slowed. "Well, what's going on?" he asked as he headed for the fridge to grab a beer for himself and Wes. Lilah nudged her empty wineglass forward. Jeremy took the hint and grabbed the bottle, refilling everyone.

Now that everyone was there, Lucy told them what was going on with her homecoming. It was pretty much what she'd told Caro earlier. But judging by the way Lilah was studying Lucy and the uncertainty in Sasha's eyes, she knew she wasn't the only one who thought there was more to the story.

"You know we've always got your back? Right?" Jeremy asked Lucy as he hooked his arm around her neck and pulled her in close to press a kiss to her temple.

"No matter what," Caro added.

"I do know that." Lucy gave them a soft, sad smile.

"There's nothing wrong with taking a little time to regroup," Lilah told her.

"Well, you guys are all stuck with me for a while as I do just that."

"Good," Sasha said. "Because we've all missed you."

"We have," Wes agreed.

"So, now that *that's* out of the way." Lucy turned her focus on Caro. "Can we *please* talk about the fact that Max is back in town and that Caro spent the day with him rescuing a dog?"

"It wasn't the day. It was just the afternoon." Caro frowned at her sister.

"Okay." Lucy shrugged. "The *afternoon*."

Caro couldn't even be annoyed that Lucy had moved the spotlight to her, mainly because Lucy had a huge grin on her mouth.

"Yeah, I want to know about this too. I've been anxiously awaiting an update after the bar incident," Jeremy said.

"What bar incident?" Lucy leaned against the counter as she reached for another piece of bread.

"When Caro dumped a glass of ice-cold water in Max's lap because he was flirting with a twentysomething blonde," Sasha answered.

"Caro did what, now?" Wes asked, no longer playing bystander on this particular topic.

"I didn't *dump* a glass of water in his lap. I . . . knocked it over because he was being an ass. But we've since made up, and everything is fine."

"*Fine?*" Jeremy asked.

"It looked more than *fine* this afternoon." Lucy mimicked Jeremy's drawl on the word.

"Well, *he* looks more than *fine* these days," Lilah added.

"Hey!" Jeremy turned to his wife in mock outrage.

"You know I only have eyes for you, baby." She patted him on the chest. "But I'm not blind."

"None of us are." Sasha shook her head.

"Okay, can we not with all of this?" Caro glanced around at her family. "All I can tell you is we've somehow gotten to the point where we can be in the same room again and it isn't awkward as all hell. That's it."

"Yeah." Lucy grinned. "I don't believe that for a second. Apparently, I came home at *exactly* the right time."

"I don't know what you think is going to happen." Caro shook her head. "Whatever Max and I had was in the past. He's moved on, and so have I."

"Okay." Jeremy took a slow sip of his beer. "We taking bets on this?"

"How much?" Wes asked.

"Dad!" Caro put her hand over her heart. "Et tu, Brute?"

"Twenty bucks?" Lilah asked.

"That sounds good," Lucy added.

"Are the terms how long is it going to take before their past becomes present?" Jeremy asked.

"Oh, please." Lucy looked to her brother, shaking her head. "We all know this a bet on when they're going to have sex."

"Can. We. Not!" Caro's face went bright red as she glanced over at her father.

"Yeah." Jeremy shook his head. "I don't really need to know about that either."

"Come on. I'm not naive enough to think my *adult* children aren't having sex. There's proof of it in my living room." Wes pointed to where all three of his grandchildren were.

"You guys are all the absolute worst."

"So, whoever is closest to the date? In either direction?" Sasha confirmed, and everyone nodded. "I'm picking two weeks from today, so that's the first of June."

"Hmm." Jeremy looked thoughtful. "The sixth."

"I'm going June fifteenth," Wes said.

"A week from today." Lucy threw her guess in.

Lilah looked at Caro, her eyes narrowing as she studied her for a moment. "May twenty-ninth."

"You all suck. You know that?" Caro frowned at everyone.

"You're not going to make your own bet?" Jeremy asked.

Caro's frown deepened as she took a sip of her wine. No, she wasn't going to play along . . . mainly because there was a part of her that felt like their past had already become present.

She just wasn't going to tell *any* of them that.

* * *

THE STEADY HUM of the running dishwasher and CCR's "Have You Ever Seen the Rain" were the only sounds in the kitchen as Caro, Lucy, Lilah, and Sasha sat down at the kitchen table, all of them with fresh glasses of wine. Leia, Estee, and Frankie were all asleep on the bed by the kitchen table, full from their own dinners. And Jeremy and Wes had taken the grandkids home to tuck them in and read bedtime stories.

"Frankie is really cute," Sasha said as she settled in her seat. "She's really lucky you found her."

Caro looked over at the dog, her little head using Leia's paw as a pillow. "You know, I've been wondering about the timing of all of it."

"What do you mean?" Lucy asked.

Caro turned back to the table, her eyebrows furrowed in thought. "Well, Max pointed out that if Tibbett hadn't gotten adopted, I wouldn't have come home early, and I wouldn't have found her. Also, the fact that Max was running by at the exact same time."

"I'll take it one further," Lilah said. "If the storm hadn't hit and the school hadn't lost power, then the Connors wouldn't have come to the bookstore to adopt Tibbett in the first place."

Caro's mouth fell open, and she pulled in a startled breath.

"What?" Sasha asked.

"I . . . I went and saw Mom yesterday, mainly to talk to her about Max. And when I asked her for a sign, I saw the storm in the distance."

"So does that mean that your mom sent you Frankie at the *exact* right time to force you and Max together again?" Sasha asked.

"Sounds like something she would do." Lilah grinned as she took a sip of wine.

"Well, if she's a gift from your mom, I think you're going to have to keep her." Sasha pointed to the dog. "Good thing you have two weeks to figure that out."

Caro looked over at Frankie, a tightness squeezing at her heart. Was she ready to have a dog again? Was she ready for any of the things that had been happening?

"What do you think?" Caro turned to Lucy, who'd gone oddly quiet.

Lucy tilted her head to the side, a sad smile on her mouth. "I don't know." She shrugged. "I don't believe in signs like that anymore."

"You don't?" Sasha frowned.

"When did you become a skeptic?" Lilah asked.

Caro gently kicked her sister under the table. "I don't think Frankie was the only thing Mom sent me. You showed up almost *exactly* twenty-four hours later."

"Yes, well, I don't think that was a sign so much as me having to get away from my shithead boyfriend." Lucy's expression transformed, going from sad to angry. The change wasn't because of what Caro had just said, but something she was battling. Something she'd been holding back for the last couple of hours.

The energy around the table shifted, the three women all leaning forward, their eyes focused on Lucy. They'd all known there was something more to this story, and now that Lucy had opened that door, they were going to get answers.

"What did Scott do?" Lilah asked in her don't-mess-with-me tone.

"Yeah. Lucy, what happened?" Caro demanded.

Lucy took another sip of her wine before setting her glass on the table. She took a deep breath, letting it out on a frustrated sigh. "I'm going to tell you everything, because I *need* you guys to know exactly why I'm back."

"What you told us earlier isn't the reason?" Sasha asked.

"It's part of it, but there's more. More that Dad and Jeremy can't know. Circle of trust?"

Caro's stomach bottomed out at those three words.

When Rachel died, the family she'd left behind had all dealt with the loss in different ways. Wes had drowned in his grief, Jeremy had been an angry asshole, Lucy had withdrawn from everyone, and Caro distracted herself by trying to fix everyone and everything. Rachel's death had left a big hole for a lot of people, and Caro had spread herself out so thin trying to patch that hole. She'd missed things. Big things.

It was what had started the rift with Max . . . but he wasn't the only one she'd messed up with.

Lucy had always worn clothes that were too big for her, trying de her body when she'd developed faster than her friends, and then when she'd started to gain weight. It also worked when she'd started to lose weight.

Caro still didn't know *how* she hadn't noticed. Not until things had gotten really bad. Not until Lucy had lost forty pounds in the span of three months. The bulimia had started when their mother was still alive, when she was so sick and they'd all known it was just a matter of time before she was gone. Lucy couldn't control Rachel's death, but she could control her own body.

Sasha was the one who'd figured it out, and she'd told Caro and Lilah. It was the three of them who sat Lucy down. That was when the circle of trust had been formed. Whatever was said in it didn't leave.

Besides Dr. Bloom—the therapist Caro had found for Lucy—the people at that table were the only ones who knew about what had happened. And while the circle of trust had been invoked by all of them for many different reasons over the years, Caro had a feeling about why it was being invoked now.

"Circle of trust." The three women nodded.

"But before I tell you, you all have to *promise* me that you aren't going to treat me with kid gloves the next few weeks."

"We won't treat you like you're fragile, but if we see something, you know we're going to say something," Lilah said.

"Lilah." Lucy patted her hand. "I have never in my life worried about you not saying something."

Lilah's eyes narrowed, but there was a small quirk to her mouth. "Good."

"Okay." Lucy took another deep breath and let it out in a rush. "What I said about LA and it not being the environment for me was the truth. I loved it in the beginning, but it started to bec toxic—or it probably always was. It was just slowly poisoning me, and it took me years to finally figure it out. I can't tell you how many times I heard that I wasn't the right look, or the right sound, or the right anything. Years of it. But I knew someone would see it one day, figure out how good I was. Now I just wonder if I was delusional."

"You are *not* delusional," Sasha said fiercely.

Lucy smiled at her. "Anyways, I could take it. I could handle whatever they said. These people didn't know me. So what did their opinion matter?"

"They don't matter," Caro agreed.

"Problem was, I found someone whose opinion I *thought* mattered."

"What did that bastard do?" Lilah repeated the question.

"Our relationship was great in the beginning." Lucy shook her head. "He was sweet and thoughtful. When I was with him, things were good. I was happy. So happy it made me forget how unhappy I'd been. But then things started to change, and it was so subtle that I didn't notice at first. We'd go to the gym together and he'd get me to do ten more minutes on the treadmill, but he was so encouraging with it. Like, *You can do this.* And then we'd go out to eat, and he started to ask, *Are you sure you want that?* It didn't take long before he just started ordering for me. He ate whatever the hell he wanted, but I always had grilled chicken and salad."

"I'm sorry, he started to do what?" Caro asked.

"He'd get to the restaurant before me and order before I even got there. But that wasn't even the worst of it. He started to point stuff out on my body. He'd pinch my side, or my stomach, or my thigh and tell me I needed to work on that."

"He. Did. What?" Lilah was practically seething.

Lucy closed her eyes, shaking her head. And when she opened them, there was moisture gathering at the corners. "I have done so much work to get where I'm at." Her voice was thick now. "Both physically and mentally. And I love my body. I love how I look. He was making me doubt everything, so much so that the last time I was with him, I got sick."

"You threw up?"

"Yes." She nodded, blinking as a tear slid down her cheek. She wiped it away, but now more were falling from both eyes. "That's the first time I've ever been so upset that I've involuntarily thrown up. I had no control of it whatsoever. It was then that I knew I was done. I started packing that night. So here I am."

"Luce, I'm so proud of you it's ridiculous," Caro said as her own eyes filled with tears.

"You are?"

"We all are." Lilah grabbed Lucy's hand. "You realized what was happening, and you pulled yourself out. That's amazing, and don't you ever fucking forget it."

"Damn straight." Sasha agreed before she rubbed her hands to-gether, looking between Caro and Lilah. "So, which one of us is booking the flights to LA so we can remove that scumbag's balls from his body?"

"He's not worth you going to jail." Lucy gave Sasha a small smile.

"No, but you're worth it," Sasha said.

"Yeah, she is." Caro got up from the table, coming up next to Lucy and pressing a kiss to the top of her head. "We got you, now and always."

"Now and always," Sasha and Lilah echoed.

"I'm really glad I'm home." Lucy gave them all a watery smile.

"So are we," Caro said.

"And the last thing, to alleviate your worries even more—because I know you all have them—I will be going to see Dr. Bloom again, just until I'm really in a good headspace. I already have an appointment for next week."

"Well, I feel like that settles everything." Lilah nodded.

"Yes, so can we get back to more fun topics? Like Caro and Max?" Lucy asked.

"How long am I going to have to be the topic of conversation?" Caro asked as she sat back down and grabbed her wine.

"A while, I'm pretty sure," Sasha said.

"At least until he leaves." Lucy grinned.

Caro let out another sigh, but she wasn't going to complain. Lucy was smiling again.

Chapter Eleven

Friends to Lovers. Lovers to Friends.

Caro woke with a puppy curled up in the blankets next to her. She hadn't even attempted to make Frankie sleep in a crate or on the floor. One look at those sweet brown eyes, and she'd been a goner. Besides, Caro needed a little snuggling after everything that had happened with Lucy.

Caro knew her sister would be okay. One, because Lucy was strong. But two, because of the strength that would always be at her back in the form of her, Lilah, and Sasha. They knew what had happened, and they'd all be there if Lucy needed anything.

Her sister wasn't alone.

And Caro had also appreciated not being alone that night. Turned out, Frankie was a burrower, into both blankets *and* hearts. The second Caro had put her on the bed, the dog had found her way under the covers and stayed there until morning.

Caro pulled the quilt up, looking for the little ball of fur.

"Good morning." One pet to her side, and Frankie rolled onto her back, exposing her entire belly. "How'd you sleep? All warm and toasty?"

Frankie wiggled around, her paws flailing in the air as she moved her head back and forth, playfully biting at Caro's fingers.

"Is that so?" Caro laughed, that same joy the dog inspired yesterday filling her chest again.

Caro let Frankie play for a little bit before she scooped her up and took her outside. She knew the short span of a puppy bladder, and she really didn't want an accident in her bed.

She took a deep breath of the crisp morning air. Friday had dawned bright and beautiful, the storm long gone, not a cloud in the clear blue sky. If the weather was any indication of the day to come, it was going to be good. At least, she hoped so, since she'd be spending several hours with Max.

They'd made so much progress the day before, and she just wanted to keep going in a positive direction with him. But not the direction her family thought.

That wasn't a possibility.

Yes, she was still attracted to him. How could she not be? And the few times they'd touched, she thought her skin was going to burst into flames. But that had always been the case. And sure, yesterday afternoon had made her remember a feeling she hadn't experienced for fourteen years. But none of it changed the facts.

They didn't live in the same place. They'd become different people over the years.

But are we really that different? And why does being with him feel the same?

Caro shook her head, pulling herself back to the moment. "Come on," she said as she lifted Frankie from the grass and climbed the stairs. "Let's get ready for whatever this is."

About forty minutes later, Caro, Lucy, and Frankie were slowly heading down Alexander Avenue. *Slowly* being the key word.

Frankie was proving just how much she didn't like a leash. She kept trying to get it in her mouth, biting at the air around her and spinning in circles. The second she got a chance, she chewed on the bright pink nylon. She also zigzagged back and forth on the sidewalk, getting under Caro's and Lucy's feet.

The real problem was, the more Frankie dragged her paws, the longer it took Caro to get to her second cup of coffee.

"Okay, that's enough practice for now." Caro scooped Frankie into her arms, and the dog gave her cheek a nice big lick. "Thank you, Frankie," she said as she stretched her shoulder up and wiped her face against her T-shirt.

"You're going to need a much bigger caffeine boost for puppy training," Lucy said as they turned the corner. She was looking even better that morning; no doubt a good night's sleep in a safe place had done wonders.

"Yes, that and a carb boost," Caro agreed as her stomach growled, the smell of fresh pastries from Browned Butter filling the air.

"Umm, about that." Lucy eyed the glass doors warily as they stopped in front of the shop. "I don't know if I should go in there. Maybe you should just get my order, and I'll stay out here with Frankie."

"You scared of Theo?" Caro asked, adjusting Frankie in her arms.

Lucy's head snapped over to Caro, her pouty lips in a deep frown. "I'm not scared of anyone, especially Theo Taylor."

"Then why do you want to hide outside? Shouldn't you just rip the Band-Aid off?"

"This isn't going to be ripping-a-Band-Aid-off kind of pain; this is going to be getting-your-bikini-area-waxed pain."

"You're going to be here for a while. How do you plan on avoiding him?"

"I hadn't thought it out yet."

"Also, your best friends are his best friends."

"Ugh, fine. Let's get this over with." Lucy reached for the door handle.

The little bell above the door rang, signaling a new customer as they walked in. It was just after nine o'clock, and there was a bit of a line, the morning rush still going strong. Caro peeked over to the register to see who was running it and spotted the blond head of Juliet Taylor, Theo's mother. Lucy's shoulders relaxed next to Caro's.

"You think she's going to be any easier on you?" Caro whispered. "She's going to go full-on mama bear when she finds out what you did."

Juliet had been like a sister to their mother, and as such, she treated the Buchanan kids like her own.

"I don't doubt it," Lucy agreed before her eyes darted back to the counter. "Shit," she whispered as her entire body stiffened.

Caro turned to see Theo coming through the door to the kitchen, a tray filled with croissants in his hands. His eyes came up, looking over the line before his feet slowed to a stop and his entire body stilled. It was very clear by his frown that he'd just spotted Lucy. The anger that flashed through his eyes was obvious, even from this distance.

If looks could kill, Lucy would have been six feet under. While Caro still had that instinct to protect her sister, she knew whatever this was with Theo was Lucy's battle to fight. It always had been.

Besides, they'd all promised no kid gloves last night, so she was going to act like she usually did when it came to those two.

"I think he's happy to see you," Caro whispered out of the side of her mouth.

"Shut up," Lucy snapped back.

Theo looked away, continuing to the pastry display and opening the case. Once the croissants were in place, he headed for the register, tapping his mother on the shoulder and pointing over to the line.

Juliet's eyes went huge the second they landed on Lucy. "Excuse me?!" she all but shouted, making some of the people in line jump and look around. "Lucy Evelyn Buchanan. What are you doing here?"

"She middle-named you. You *are* in trouble."

"Shut up," Lucy repeated, this time elbowing Caro in the ribs. The move jostled Frankie a little bit, and the dog squirmed in Caro's arms. "Sorry, Frankie." She patted the dog's head. "But she deserved it."

Juliet moved out from behind the counter and crossed the space in a few quick steps, throwing her arms around Lucy and hauling her in for a hug. "How long are you visiting?"

"I'm not visiting. I'm moving back for a bit."

Lucy hadn't said it very loudly, but her voice carried to where Theo was listening from his spot at the cash register. His entire body tensed, a feat considering he was already so rigid he was in danger of snapping in two.

Juliet's blue eyes filled with concern as they searched Lucy's face for answers. "You let me know if you need anything. You understand? Anything."

"Yes, ma'am."

"Okay, baby." She gave Lucy another hug. She let go, then leaned in and pressed a kiss to Caro's cheek. "It looks like a lot of things are happening around here lately. It's going to be fun to watch. See you later, loves." She winked before she headed back to the counter.

"That went better than expected."

"We still aren't done," Lucy said under her breath as the line moved again and they were standing in front of Theo.

"Hello." Even under his thick beard, Caro saw his jaw tic. He managed to pull a smile into place, but there wasn't an ounce of warmth in it.

"Theo." Lucy said his name a bit hard.

"The usual?" he asked Caro.

"It's actually going to be a dozen donuts today, a box of croissants, four sweet potato cookies, and four peanut butter cookies."

Theo typed the order into the iPad in front of him as Caro named the donuts she wanted. "And you?" he asked, not even looking up.

"Cookies and cream, and strawberry shortcake."

"Coming right up." He still didn't glance at her as he flipped the screen toward them, then walked off.

"Oh," Lucy said under her breath. "He's making you pay today."

"Hey, he doesn't *always* give me free donuts. Just when he's in a good mood . . . which is never when you're around."

"Isn't that the truth."

* * *

MAX STARED DOWN at ten crates of strawberries, each filled to the brim. They'd been delivered the day before and kept in the cool garage until Ava could get to them today. Or, really, until *they* could get to them.

He was now very much a part of that day's project: strawberry jam. They'd be making it, jarring it, and labeling it, all for the Saturday market the following morning.

He was a big fan of strawberry jam but more the eating-it part. Producing it was a lengthy, messy process, and they were making *a lot*. It was going to be a long day, not helped by the fact that his sleep had been restless. Full of dreams of tangled limbs, soft brown hair twisted in his fingers, citrus-scented skin, breathy sighs across parted lips . . .

When he'd woken up, he thought he'd just been dreaming about that prom night from all those years ago. Memories stirred up from the pictures in Martin's office and made all the more real by the afternoon spent with her. Except Caro's hair was shorter in the dream, the length it was now, just past her shoulder blades. She smelled of lemon—not the orange of long ago—the scent that had been haunting him since he'd gotten to Cruickshank. And her mouth had been painted the bright red she'd been wearing at Quigley's the other night.

It wasn't all that surprising that Caro had been at the forefront of his brain, since Ava had wanted a full blow-by-blow breakdown of the day before. He'd thought giving in to her questioning was his best option, because maybe she'd let up.

But he'd been wrong.

"So are you guys friends again?" she pressed.

"We're *friendly*. Can't you just be happy with that?"

"Hmph," she'd huffed as she took her coffee outside and went to water her flowers. She wasn't satisfied with that response, judging by the frown she was still wearing thirty minutes later when she asked him to get the strawberries.

Max grabbed the closest crate and headed for the kitchen. He'd just set the last one on the island when the heavy wooden door swung open and there stood Caro, holding a bag from Browned Butter and a carrier of coffee cups.

Her hair was pulled up in her signature messy bun, and she was wearing a pink sweater, with black shorts that hugged her curves. There was a small smile on her face.

She was still so unbelievably beautiful.

"Hey."

"Hey," he repeated, his own lips twitching at the corners. "Did you bring Frankie?"

"Yeah." She pointed behind her at the door. "Ava took her from me. She's fussing over Lucy now. I thought I'd give them a moment." Her eyes moved to the crates, and she let out a soft sigh. "Well, we're going to be busy today. Good thing I brought some fuel." She held up the bag and drink carrier. "Caffeine and carbs."

"Bless you." He stepped forward, taking the coffees from her.

"I got you a hazelnut latte, like you ordered the other day."

"Thanks." He set the carrier on the counter, spotting his name on one of the paper cups. Caro set the massive bag from Browned Butter next to it, then reached across him to grab her coffee.

The scent of lemon filled his nose and lungs. It took everything in him not to turn to her, to grab her and press his face to her neck. But then she was taking a step back, just out of reach.

Always out of reach these days.

He brought the cup of coffee to his nose, taking a deep breath that would hopefully clear his head. But as Caro dug through the bag filled with pastries, he knew there would be no hope for a clear head today.

"Donuts," she said as she popped open the first box.

Max groaned as he looked inside, spotting half a dozen of the triple chocolate. The donut that had always been their favorite. A soft and airy chocolate donut, filled with whipped milk chocolate, and covered in rich, dark ganache.

It was perfection.

Max hadn't made his way into the bakery since he'd been back in town, mainly because if he had, he would've ordered a whole dozen of these and eaten them all by himself. He'd already had a veggie omelet for breakfast, but he'd never been one to resist these donuts . . . so why start now?

They reached into the box at the exact same moment, laughing as they both went for the biggest one. Max got there first, and Caro relented, picking the second biggest.

"Cheers," she said as she bumped her donut to his.

Max hesitated for just a second, watching as Caro bit into hers. She closed her eyes and made a soft groan of satisfaction. That sound was a hook behind Max's navel, jerking up.

Fuuuuuuuuccccckkkk.

Everything about it was a sweet torment, so he joined in, taking a bite from his own donut. It was exactly as perfect as he remembered.

"So, how was Ava when you got home yesterday?" Caro asked before she took another bite, seemingly oblivious to Max's inner turmoil. Her tongue darted out to lick some chocolate from the side of her lip.

Focus, man. Focus.

"Oh, you know, a full-on grilling that's continued this morning."

"Something to look forward to. At least she's distracted with Lucy for a bit."

"Well, when she is no longer distracted, just know that she hasn't been satisfied with what I told her at all. I explained we were good now, but she wants us to be friends again."

Caro laughed. "We haven't been friends since I was twelve and you were thirteen . . ."

She trailed off, both of them apparently remembering when he'd pulled her behind the oak tree in the backyard and kissed her for the first time.

He could still hear the little catch in her throat right before he'd pressed his mouth to hers. Neither of them had known what they were doing, but it didn't take long for them to figure it out.

God, he wanted to kiss her again, to taste her chocolate-flavored mouth . . .

"Do you think it's possible?" Caro asked. "For us to be friends again."

He didn't know, but he was saved from having to answer because the door behind them swung open. Ava led the group, still holding Frankie, with Lucy and Beau following behind.

"You knew Lucy was back yesterday, and you didn't tell me?" Ava narrowed her eyes on Max, a frown in place. "You said you told me the whole story."

"I told you about finding Frankie." He indicated the dog. "Lucy wasn't part of that, and she asked me not to tell you."

"Yes, well. If you left that part out, I'm just wondering what else you left out."

Max rolled his eyes. "None of it. Here," he said as he grabbed the cup labeled *chai* from the carrier. "Maybe this will make you less cranky about it." He held the drink out, giving Frankie a little scratch on the head. The dog licked his hand, flailing a little bit in Ava's arms.

"I'm not cranky." Ava adjusted Frankie before she grabbed the drink, looking down at the name written in black marker on the other side. "Who's Aubrey?"

It was super unfortunate that Max had just taken a sip of his own coffee, because he inhaled it down the wrong pipe. Caro was laughing as he coughed, trying to breathe properly again.

"You're hilarious." Max frowned.

"Thanks, I think so too." She turned to Ava. "It's just an inside joke between Max and me."

Ava's eyes narrowed as she looked between them, studying them. And then she gave a small nod. For whatever reason, that answer seemed to satisfy her.

God, his grandmother was an enigma half the time. It drove him crazy, but he wouldn't take her any other way.

They spent the next couple of minutes munching on donuts while Ava told them the game plan and what everyone's task was for the afternoon. It came as absolutely no surprise that he and Caro were both given the job of cutting the tops off the strawberries. They set up matching stations at the center island and got to work.

He knew perfectly well what Ava was doing, but he'd naively thought she'd let up after the progress they'd made the day before. But no, she was doubling down, trying even harder to force them together. Maybe so they *could* be friends?

But he wasn't sure if it was possible. He'd always want Caro in a way that was more than friendly. And the more time he was with her, the more he knew how true that was.

Knowing all that didn't change how much he enjoyed working next to her that day. How he'd catch a sly look on her face whenever she said something clever. But she'd always been funny, had always had the ability to make him laugh harder than anyone ever could. Just like he'd once had the same ability with her.

There was a joy being around her. One he hadn't known in years. One he'd barely remembered was possible. One he'd tried to forget.

But there was no forgetting it as he went to bed that night. He thought about her laugh for hours, which was probably what caused him to dream about her mouth.

* * *

THERE WAS NO time for Max to get a break from whatever these feelings were with Caro. He was in for yet another many hours working right alongside her at the Saturday market the following morning.

From mid-spring through early fall, the Cruickshank Market happened every Saturday morning. The Sweeny Park pavilion was right next to the Duncan-Finley Barn, and both were already lined with vendors who were setting up their booths and tables for the day.

Local farmers were there with their fresh fruits, vegetables, honeys, and jams. Craftspeople had come with all their wares: quilts, woodworking, wind chimes, art, jewelry, and a variety of other things that Max couldn't get a good look at from where he was walking. There was a lady who was selling incense, another who had all-natural soaps and lotions, and even a guy who made hand-knotted hammocks.

People were already walking around with fresh cups of coffee from Dancing Donkey in one hand and a hot pastry from Browned Butter in the other, watching and waiting as the booths were set up.

A vendor with pre-bagged caramel popcorn and a continuous turnover of freshly popped kettle corn was expertly stationed next to the Cruickshank Community Arts drink stand. Just looking at the treats made Max thirsty. The beverage booth would have a consistent line once the late morning sun started to warm things up. Their freshly squeezed lemonade was irresistible. If Max hadn't been doing everything in his power to avoid lemons, he'd have gotten a cup . . . or two . . . or three.

There was always a team or organization from Mount Mac-Callion High School running the car wash. That morning it was the drama club pulling out the hoses and setting up the signs. On the opposite side of the park, two guys were playing guitar while a group of thirty or so people were finishing up a yoga class under a cluster of dogwood trees.

Max's eyes lingered in that direction, knowing that Caro was over there. She'd mentioned that she and Lucy would be taking the class before heading over to join them. The group was too far away to really see, but he was almost positive she and Lucy were in the back right corner.

But he pulled his gaze away, focusing on his and Ava's destination, the booth in the back corner of the pavilion: Cruickshank Cats and Dogs Rescue. There were a dozen or so crates with dogs ranging in size from a tiny Chihuahua to a massive Great Dane. A pen of seven puppies sat next to a crate with an orange tabby cat and her three kittens.

"So, someone donates something for the rescue to sell every week?" Max asked as he set the box with strawberry jam down.

"Usually a couple of people. Mary Laird always makes her apple butter when it's in season, and Robyn Bryant has a pepper jelly that is just"—she made a chef's kiss in the air—"especially with a little cream cheese on some freshly toasted bread. It's amazing. I have some at home, but I'll need to get another jar if she has some today."

"As I live and breathe. Maximillian Abbott," a voice said from behind them.

Max turned around to see Lorraine Taylor in bright purple overalls, her hands resting on her curvy hips.

"Get over here and give me a hug." She swiped her long black braids over her shoulder, holding her arms out wide.

"Hi, Lorraine." Max smiled as he walked into her open arms.

She gave him a tight squeeze before letting go, her hands moving to his biceps as she looked him up and down. "You're looking good, Max."

"So are you," he said, giving her a slow, easy grin. Just like all her children, she had the same dusting of freckles across her brown cheeks and nose, and those golden brown eyes.

"Are you flirting with me?" She let go, lightly smacking him on both arms as she laughed, shaking her head. "Is he flirting with me?" she repeated, turning to Ava.

"It appears that way." Ava nodded.

"You know I'm twice your age, right?"

"You still look as beautiful as I remember. And I'm still very much single."

"You're ridiculous." Lorraine shook her head at him, her mouth forming a smirk. "Anyways, you going to help your grandmother sell our wares?"

"That's the plan. If there's a lull, I want to walk around for a little bit. It's been about ten years since I've been to one of these," he said as he glanced at all the activity around them.

"That's too long, Max."

"I know. I won't let it be that long again."

"You better not. You've been missed," she said as she lightly squeezed his arm. "Now, help me set up." Lorraine moved around him to the back of the tables, where a couple of neon green Tupperware containers were stacked. She popped the lid off the container at the top of the stack before pulling out a long white vinyl roll. "This banner needs to be put up along the front. There's a hook attached to the top right corner of the table."

"Got it," Max said as he moved to one end while Lorraine went to the other. Max looped the metal grommet onto the hook that had been screwed into the table before taking a step back and looking at the sign.

CRUICKSHANK CATS AND DOGS RESCUE was drawn out in a rainbow of colors, each shade blending into the next. Different cartoon cats and dogs were drawn all around. Some were in front, some on top of the letters, some peeking out from behind.

He'd seen so many of these doodles over the years that there was no doubt in his mind who'd done it. "This is Caro's work."

"It is," Lorraine said next to him. "She's done all our art. We did a refresh a couple of years ago, and it's made all the difference in the world."

"She always was really talented."

"In so many ways. She and Lucy are almost finished with yoga. Good thing too. It's going to be a busy day." Lorraine looked around to where the class was at.

"I'm going to get the rest of the stuff from the car." Max pointed to the parking lot. They'd had to drive instead of walk because of the amount of stuff they had to bring. There were two more boxes of strawberry jam and another of lemon curd that needed to be unloaded.

When he came back with the last of it, Caro and Lucy had joined the group.

Caro's hair was pulled back in a braid, a handful of tendrils falling down around her face. She was wearing a simple white tank top that was tied up in the middle, exposing her belly button. But his real focus was on her yoga pants, which had lacy mesh side panels running all the way up to the waist band.

Is she wearing underwear?

Oh, good God. If there was absolutely any chance of him surviving this, he really, *really* needed to not be thinking about her underwear, or lack thereof. His brain very unhelpfully flashed back to the other day when he'd spotted the scrap of blue lace that she'd pulled from the dryer.

"Hey," Caro said, giving him that smile that drove him crazy.

"Hey." Despite all the uncertainty that swirled around them, he couldn't help but smile back.

"Long time no see," Lucy said as she bumped her shoulder against his. "I thought we made more than this yesterday." She indicated the jars.

"Oh, this isn't even half of it," Max said, setting the box down behind the table. "I think you guys are going to be selling strawberry jam all summer."

"Oh, no we won't." Lorraine shook her head. "That along with the lemon curd will be gone by the end of the afternoon. Mark my words. The people here don't mess around with the stuff your grandmother makes. Which is why I will be buying mine right now," she said as she snatched four jars from the table. Two of the curd and two of the jam.

Max laughed as he moved to help Ava finish lining up the jars.

"Caro, Max was impressed with your banner," Lorraine said, her light and casual air fooling no one. "Knew it was your work immediately."

Good God, she was just as bad as Ava.

Caro glanced over at him, but the expression on her face wasn't pleasure. She looked uncertain . . . worried. "Thanks," she said slowly.

"You're welcome?" His words came out like a question. Wanting to move past whatever this awkward moment was, he pointed to a box that was labeled BOOKS. "Do you want me to put these out?"

"No," Caro said a bit too loudly. "We don't need those."

Lorraine and Ava looked over at her, frowning, but it was Lorraine who spoke. "We're focusing on the jars today."

"Gotcha." Max nodded, but he didn't miss Caro pushing the box to the side before stacking something else on top of it.

Chapter Twelve
A Stroll Down Memory Lane

Max snapped the book in his hands shut, leaning back in his chair and letting out a long sigh of frustration.

He and Ava had gotten back from the market about an hour ago, and after a quick lunch she'd headed upstairs for a nap, while he'd headed to the sunroom with a book. That was thirty minutes ago, and he still hadn't made it past the first two pages.

His mind kept wandering back to Caro, and chocolate donuts, and yoga pants, and underwear, and her skin on his, and her laugh. Loud, and sweet, and uncontrollable.

He remembered pinning her beneath him countless times while he tickled her sides, her body moving under him, her hair a mess, her laughter wild and breathless. But his favorite part had always been when he let her take over, flipping them so she was on top, her legs straddling his hips while her hands explored every inch of his chest . . . and stomach . . . and . . . and . . .

Yeah, he needed to do something to occupy his head and his hands, and reading just wasn't going to cut it. Taking an afternoon siesta like Ava was out of the question. Unless it was a power nap on a plane, or he needed to fight off jet lag, Max could not remember the last time he'd deliberately lain down in the middle of the day. It had to be more than five years. Maybe ten. And there was no chance he'd be able to quiet his brain enough to fall asleep that afternoon.

He was tired, though; the morning and afternoon at the market had been long. They had in fact sold out of *all* the jarred jams, jellies, and curds. Not only had it been a lot of work running the table, but he'd also had to talk to a lot of people.

There were a number of Cruickshank residents that Max knew, having spent so many summers there. And as soon as they spotted him, they'd made their way over to the table for a chat. It had been a lot, to say the least.

Pulling himself up from the chair, Max headed into the den. He thought about going upstairs to the attic and starting on some more boxes, but his eyes caught on the open double doors to Martin's office. His feet faltered before he turned and headed in that direction.

While he and Caro were on good terms now, that problem wasn't *exactly* fixed, but it was what it was. Now he needed to conquer the other thing that was haunting him. And if anything was going to take his mind off Caro, it was Martin's office.

Max hesitated on the threshold for just a second before rounding the desk and taking a seat. He'd been holding his breath since he walked into the room, and he let it out in a rush, reaching forward and running his hands along the ledge of the desk. The smooth mahogany wood was still as shiny as it had always been.

An old blue and black mug with an illustration of the solar system, reading, GALAXY'S GREATEST GRANDPA—a gift Max had given Martin the very first Christmas he'd spent in this house—was filled with the same brand of black, blue, and red pens that Max was partial to and had started buying Martin years ago. The same ones that rolled onto the page smoothly and never smudged. A gold letter opener sat beside it, MARTIN HAWTHORNE ABBOTT engraved on the handle. A blue and green Tiffany lamp sat on one corner while an antique miniature globe sat on the other.

It had been almost a year since Martin had sat in this chair, yet Max could still feel his presence. Hard not to when the man had been behind the desk almost daily, writing book after book for the last fifty years of his life.

Max wasn't sure where to begin until his eyes landed on the box of tapes he'd brought in the other day. Watching old home videos would definitely be diving into the deep end. But he might as well get it over with.

There was a fairly new iMac on the desk, and when Max hit the button on the trackpad, the screen came to life, the little cursor in the password box blinking expectantly.

"Well, shit," Max mumbled, tapping the top of the desk as he thought for a second.

Martin had an excellent memory—and was an absolute wizard when it came to trivia—but passwords wouldn't have been his forte. He would've considered that useless knowledge. Plus, he'd never been big on technology. Just look at the flip phone he'd been using.

The record player in the den had been used more often than the Bluetooth speaker. He'd never read an eBook in his life. Hell, he'd never even owned a digital watch. The only reason he'd gone from using a typewriter to a computer was because it sped up the writing process.

There was only one mode of advancing technology Martin had readily embraced, and that was photography and video. He always had the newest camera or video recorder, eager to capture the moment, to put the memory on film. He'd been sentimental in the best way.

So, he *was* capable of change; he'd just refused it where he didn't want it, and memorizing passwords was definitely something he didn't want. Which meant that said passwords would've been easily accessible for him and Ava to find.

Scooting the chair back, Max opened the top center drawer to find a half-used yellow legal pad. Martin's neat and tiny cursive jumped off the page, a checklist with more than half the entries scratched off:

~~Batteries for the smoke alarm~~
~~Beau's meds from vet~~
~~Order Ava's canning supplies~~
~~Pick up book order (7-28)~~
~~Dinner for Caro's new deal (7-31)~~
Max's birthday present
Talk with Carlton about next book (8-5)
Book plane tickets for New York (9-17 to 9-24)
Tickets for Sox vs. Yankees with Max (9-19)

Ava and Martin had been planning on visiting Max for his birthday last year, but Martin had died on August 2. He'd gone into the hospital with some chest pain, and he'd never come out. Max had been at work when Ava called him, and the second she said his name, he'd known. He'd known that the man who raised him was gone.

None of those things at the end of the list had happened. In fact, when September 20 rolled around, Max hadn't celebrated at all. He'd sat in his apartment drowning himself in a bottle of scotch, and not stopping until he couldn't think anymore.

He couldn't process it then, and he hadn't let himself process it for the last year. If he was busy, he didn't need to think. It was a tried-and-true defense mechanism, one that he'd perfected over the years. It meant he wouldn't have to think about the fact that his dad had died, or that he had a mother and stepfather who never really thought about him. He'd used it after Rachel died . . . and after he and Caro broke up.

But he had to face the truth now.

Max scanned the list again, his finger tracing over *Dinner for Caro's new deal.*

He had no clue what that was about and made a note to ask Ava later. But almost immediately, he scratched it off his mental to-do list. He hadn't asked Ava about anything Caro-related since their breakup. If he wanted to know, he had to ask Caro.

That moment back at the market flashed through his mind when she'd very deliberately stopped him from opening one of the boxes.

She was hiding something, didn't want *him* to know something. It wasn't like he could be upset about it. She didn't owe him anything. And he was keeping some important information to himself as well.

They'd talked about his work the other day; it would've only made sense to tell her about his new position. But there was too much history with him and her and London. Her decision to not go with him all those years ago was part of what ended their relationship.

Some things were just better not discussed . . . and maybe whatever she'd been hiding was one of them.

Setting the legal pad to the side, Max dug farther into the drawer, spotting a little black bound notebook. He pulled it out, sliding the elastic off, and when he flipped to the first page, he grinned. All the passwords were neatly listed, and the first one was for the computer.

A couple of clicks later, and he found the folder labeled MARTIN'S VIDEOS. Everything was named and dated, but one in particular caught his eye: *Max's first summer in Boston.* He double-clicked, and the screen went from black to a scene in Ava and Martin's old brownstone.

Billy Joel's "Tell Her About It" was playing in the background, and a much younger Ava was sitting on the floor with a baby Max, toys spread out on the elaborate multicolored rug. He was just under a year old and focused on the blocks, stacking them higher and higher.

"I think he's going to be an architect." Martin's disembodied voice came from somewhere behind the camera as the frame adjusted.

"He sure does love to build stuff," another voice said, one that Max hadn't heard very often in his life, but one that he knew nonetheless.

His father.

Something in Max's chest squeezed tightly at hearing those voices, just a moment of pain before it let go.

"Yes, he definitely loves to create things." Ava nodded right before Max's little fist swung wildly and the tower came tumbling down. "And then destroy them," she added as Max let out a shriek of laughter. "Now, quit messing with that camera and get down here."

"I'm just making sure it's lined up properly," Landon said. The frame moved a little bit to the left. It was at that moment that the song ended, that side of the record now done.

"Let me fix Billy." There was movement to the right of the screen, his grandfather walking around the sofa to the record player in the background.

The track changed to "Uptown Girl" and Martin came back into view, sitting a few feet away from Ava. A second later, Landon moved around the camera and took a seat next to Martin. He too had a thick beard, though it wasn't nearly as long as the one Martin was sporting.

Baby Max reached out for his father, but Landon was too far away. Determined as ever, Max's little legs shifted beneath him, and he lunged forward, crawling toward Landon. When he got to his father, he grabbed on to Landon's legs and pulled himself up into a standing position.

"He's never done that!" Landon cried out excitedly. "He's been crawling like crazy, but he hasn't stood up yet. Good job, Bean!"

Baby Max, still on his legs, turned toward his grandfather, reaching out. Martin held his hands out and Max grabbed them, bouncing up and down before plopping onto his butt. But he was only on the ground for a second before Martin scooped him up, giving him a kiss on the cheek. Baby Max giggled hysterically at the feel of his grandfather's bearded face.

He longed for a past he didn't remember, but as much as it hurt to watch, he couldn't take his eyes off the screen as the video cut from scene to scene.

He watched as a baby Max ate a bowl of ice cream . . . or, more accurately, swam in it. Saw a clip of him snuggled up next to Ava and Martin's old Lab, Legolas. And a whole montage of him learning to walk over a number of weeks.

It was a good thirty minutes before a wet nose pushed into Max's knee, pulling his focus from the screen.

"Hey, bud." Max paused the video before scratching Beau's head; the dog's fluffy tail wagged excitedly.

"We thought we'd see what you were up to."

Max looked up to find Ava in the doorway, her own sad expression on her face. She must've caught the tail end of Martin reading Max *The Velveteen Rabbit*.

"I found the videos. I don't remember ever watching these before." He waved to the screen with his free hand, the other one still petting Beau. "It's been a while since I've seen Dad."

Ava came into the room, rounding the desk and leaning her hip against the side. Her eyes settled on the screen, where a grinning Landon held Max in the air like he was an airplane.

"They were in a box that was mislabeled during the move. Martin found them a few years ago, we had weeks of movie nights watching them." She smiled wistfully, her eyes going from the screen to Max. "He had to pull out all of these devices and wires to hook it up to the television. Took him hours, but he would not be stopped."

Beau flopped down on the floor, no longer needing pets but content to just lie between him and Ava.

"I bet." Max's smile turned sad. "Dad looked so young."

"He *was* young." Ava nodded slowly. "It's one of life's great trag-edies that you didn't really know him."

"It's really fucking unfair is what it is," Max qualified.

Ava let out a little laugh. "It is that, for sure." She took a deep breath and let it out on a huff. "He was in his second year of the PhD program that summer." She waved to the computer. "Your mom was nose deep in med school, and they were both so busy they couldn't see straight. That was the first summer we got you, the first of many." She grinned. "He took the train up every week-end to see you. He wanted you so badly. Never forget that."

His father had wanted him. His mother, not so much. Max knew he was an accident. Sure, his parents had been married, but Vanessa had wanted to wait until after they were both out of school before having kids. When she'd gotten pregnant, Landon had vowed to make it work.

His dad had loved him. He might not have had a lot of time with Landon, but he did know that. Ava and Martin had made sure of it.

"Would it make you sad to watch them again?" Max looked up at his grandmother.

"Yes." She gave him that sad smile again. "But we should watch them anyway. Maybe after dinner?"

"That sounds good."

Ava reached up, her fingers running through Max's hair affec-tionately. "I'm really proud of you."

"What? For finally coming in here?"

Her hand moved to the side of his head, tracing his temple be-fore resting it on his shoulder and gently squeezing. "Yes, and for making up with Caro. Burying the hatchet."

"Oh." He dipped his chin, breaking their eye contact. "That." He didn't think he'd buried anything. What he'd actually done was *unbury* things. *A lot* of things.

Ava's fingers went to his jaw, pushing his head back up so she could look into his eyes. "And I'm just proud of you in general, Bean. And so was Martin. And your father would've been. You were always a good kid."

"Not in the end. I stopped coming here." He waved around them.

"That didn't mean we didn't see you every year." She dropped her hand to his, patting it. "You made time for us. I don't know many people who have a grandson who flies them out to Europe to stay in five-star establishments, eat the best food, and go on the best tours."

All of that was true, yes. Max *had* always seen them, multiple times a year. Whether they visited him in New York for the holidays or he had them join him on a business trip. But, as he was usually working during those times, it felt more like *they* had made time for *him*, and not the other way around. And once Max went into self-preservation mode after Martin's death, he'd pulled away from Ava when she'd needed him most.

"Yeah, I guess." The words hung in the air before Max shook his head, knowing it wasn't true. "I should've done more. Visited more. Called more."

"Max, you can't change the past, all you can do is learn from it. You want to go back in time, but you can't. What you *can* do is take the time you have now."

She was right. She usually was. Though he didn't always like to tell her so. There were a lot of things he wished he could do over, but as that wasn't a possibility, he'd just have to learn from the choices he'd made.

"Always so wise." He looked up at her.

"Just listen to me, kid. You'll get far."

"I've already gotten far because of you."

"Thanks." Her mouth split into a grin.

"So, what's up next for the day?"

"Dinner." She pushed her hip off the desk and stood straight, Beau pulling himself up from the floor at her movement. "I want to do this slow-roasted salmon, but you have to marinate it for a little bit. And I thought we could do stuffed baked artichokes, and those take a bit to prepare."

"Sounds delicious."

"Perfect. I'll start pulling everything out while you make us a refreshing summer drink."

"What do you want?"

"Surprise me," she said as she practically skipped into the kitchen, Beau trailing behind like the constant shadow he was.

Max went into the den, feeling a tightness in his chest when he spotted the same multicolored rug and record player from the old home video. "Hey," he called out. "What are your thoughts on some Billy Joel in vinyl?"

"I only have good thoughts about Billy Joel, in vinyl or otherwise."

He grinned, heading for the record player.

* * *

MAX SPENT THE better part of Sunday in Martin's office. It took him exactly one cup of coffee to learn the program to transfer the tapes to the computer. It had to be playing while it recorded, so he had them on in the background while he started going through the filing cabinets.

Ava joined him after lunch, helping him sort stuff into either the keep pile or the destroy pile. The destroy pile was four times larger.

"I don't think you need this receipt from 1972 for a hardware store in Boston." Max held the little piece of paper in the air.

"You never know, we might need to return that hammer," Ava joked.

"I'm pretty sure they're no longer in business."

"Well, then maybe we can let that one go."

They worked throughout the afternoon, only stopping when it was time for dinner. That night they watched a couple of the home videos. Max saw his father graduate from college, a book reading of Martin's on Martha's Vineyard, and an art show of Ava's in New York. They skipped the one of Landon and Vanessa's wedding— Max wasn't up for it—and moved on to a whole series from a week-long vacation at a beach house down on the Gulf Coast. Max had been about two years old, and his mother was noticeably absent from the trip.

As Max went up to his room that night, he felt . . . unsettled. Like something was missing. He told himself the feeling was because of his day in Martin's office, combined with the videos. And though it might have been partly that, it wasn't the root cause.

Sunday was the first day he'd been in town that he hadn't seen Caro. He paused as he walked by the framed pictures in his room. Her pictures of Cruickshank.

Was this as far as she'd gotten? She'd wanted to travel. See works of art from all over the world.

It had always been her dream to be an artist. Well, she'd always *been* an artist, but had dreamt of making a career out of her art. The fact that she hadn't was disappointing; he just wasn't sure if he was disappointed for her . . . or in her.

And why did he care? What she'd done—or hadn't done—with her life was none of his business. It didn't change the fact that he couldn't stop the instinct of wanting more for her.

But he was just going to have to keep it to himself. Just another thing to add to the ever-growing list.

* * *

PETAL AND THORN had gotten a shipment of plants, so Caro was pretty busy with her hands in the dirt for most of the morning. Frankie had come with her, and she stayed in the little pen Caro had set up, alternating between playing with the purple platypus Max had bought her and napping.

Evie and Vera—the owners of the shop—were also inclined to pick up the pup for snuggles in between helping customers and making floral arrangements, getting a hit of that sweet, sweet puppy breath. They were dog moms to one of Caro's former fosters, a golden retriever named Marigold, with long blond hair and three legs. Their daughter, Abigail, had just turned eight and had been begging for a dog, and Marigold had been the perfect fit.

Marigold had played with Frankie off and on but was currently stretched out in a patch of sun in front of the window, snoring away.

Caro had just finished adding soil and watering the last of the plants when the bell above the door rang. "I'll be right with you," she called out over her shoulder as she washed her hands. As Evie and Vera had left to make some deliveries and get lunch, Caro was the only one in the shop.

When she turned around, she found Max standing at the counter, grinning and shaking his head as he pushed his sunglasses off his nose and onto the top of his head. He had a canvas tote bag looped over his shoulder and a cup of coffee from Dancing Donkey.

"Of course you're here." His jaw and cheeks were dusted with scruff, like he hadn't shaved the last two days.

It had been a long time since she hadn't seen him clean-shaven, and it made her a little light-headed. That or she was hungry. Maybe both.

"Every Monday." She shook her head, trying to clear it. "What are *you* doing here?"

"Ava sent me to pick up her seed order."

Caro's eyebrows bunched together in confusion. "I told her I was bringing those tomorrow."

"Yes, well, that wouldn't have given her an opportunity to force us to interact *today*."

"What do you mean?"

Max laughed. "She's been doing this since I got here. It's why she didn't tell you I was coming last Tuesday, when she knew you'd be at the house. She was also the person who suggested that I go to Quigley's that night. She hid the coffee on Wednesday morning so I'd have to go to Dancing Donkey. At this point I'd be surprised if she wasn't responsible for planting Frankie."

At the dog's name, a loud squeaky bark filled the air. Apparently, Max's voice had awoken her from her slumber.

He leaned over the counter, spotting the dog, who was currently trying to climb the little pen, her long body stretching up.

"She clearly wants to see you." Caro scooped the dog up and handed her over to him. The dog wiggled in his arms, desperate to lick his face.

"Hello, Frankie girl," he said as he kissed the top of her head. She was like this *every time* he held her.

Caro understood perfectly. She'd be squirming in delight if he were holding her too.

The bell chimed again, and Evie and Vera walked in, each holding a checkered yellow-and-teal to-go cup from Frenchy Fries.

"Hey, Max!" Vera stopped next to him, giving Frankie a little scratch under the chin. "Can you tell Ava we've already eaten a whole jar of the strawberry jam? It's one of her best. We're going to have to buy more on Saturday."

"I'll tell her as soon as she gets back. She's teaching her art class today. She gave me a list of errands to do while she was gone." He pulled a piece of paper out of his pocket with his free hand and waved it in the air.

"What else is on there?" Caro asked as she snatched it from him. She had no idea what had possessed her to do it, and as their fingers brushed, there was that weird little flip low in her belly.

She hadn't felt it in such a long time . . . that is, until these last few days with Max. She wasn't the only one who was affected either: their gazes met at the brief touch, and the blue of his eyes got darker.

Caro cleared her throat, trying to refocus as she looked down at the piece of paper, reading Ava's loopy handwriting:

~~Post office: mail packages~~
Vet: pick up Beau's meds
~~Dancing Donkey: order coffee beans~~
Kathleen's Corner: drop off book order (see
    attached)
Petal and Thorn: pick up seeds
Browned Butter: get two loaves of bread (your
    choice)
Cheese Wheel & Wine: pick up cheese order and
    get a bottle of wine for dinner
Meat Market: pick up fish for tonight and
    something else for tomorrow
Groceries: half & half, yogurt, butter, grapes,
    limes, and mushrooms

"Looks like she's keeping you busy. I thought you were on vacation?" Caro glanced up and found those blue eyes still on her.

"She knows I don't do well with idle time."

"Yes, well, half of these things I already do for her regularly, as I work at the places."

"How many jobs do you have around here, anyways?" he asked, studying her, a slight frown on his mouth.

"Including working for Ava?" She waved the list around before handing it back to him. "Five."

Everyone knew Caro actually had six jobs, if she counted her books . . . but he'd said *around here*. Her eyes met Evie's and Vera's. They were standing a few feet behind him, and they had both raised their eyebrows at the lie.

She'd told them she didn't want him to know about her books. Judging by their frowns, they didn't understand her decision, but they respected it.

"With five jobs, it looks like you know plenty about not being idle," Max said.

"She does." Vera nodded, a mischievous light in her eyes. "In fact, she very rarely ever takes time off."

"Yeah." Evie grinned, cottoning on to her wife's tone. "You know what, Caro? You should take the rest of the day. You've already finished up with the plants. We're all good here. Maybe you and Max should go to lunch, *both* of you enjoy an afternoon." She turned to him, holding up her cup. "You should go to Frenchy Fries. They have the Parmesan herb today, and you know you have to eat them when they're piping hot. Otherwise, they just aren't as good."

"You two are about as subtle as Ava." Caro shook her head.

"What?" they said in unison.

"Would you like to go to lunch with me?" Max asked casually enough, but when she turned back to him, she caught the glimmer of hope in his eyes.

"Yes." Caro nodded, because she really, really would.

* * *

MAX HADN'T MINDED Vera and Evie's setup one little bit. In fact he'd been grateful for it. And it wasn't just them—Ava had known exactly what she was doing when she gave him that list this morning. He might've even thanked her for it if she wouldn't have been smug about it.

It was another one of those perfect late spring afternoons in Cruickshank: seventy-two degrees, clear blue skies, birds chirping, and a light wind carrying through the blooming trees around them. It couldn't have been more different from the last time Max and Caro walked through downtown, sheltered under an umbrella in the rain.

He wished he could walk that close to her today. Feel her skin on his . . .

"Well, Frankie's doing better on a leash," Max said, looking down at the dog in front of them, trying to distract himself from the sweet lemon scent on the air.

"She's a work in progress, for sure," Caro said as she pulled on the pink leash, guiding Frankie around a metal trash can. "I've been taking her when my dad walks Leia, so that's helped a little."

"Still no word on where she came from?"

Caro's hand tightened on the leash before she looked up at him, a frown pulling down her lips. "Nope, and I hope it stays that way. Wherever she came from, I have a feeling those people don't deserve her."

And he had a feeling she was right.

Frenchy Fries was on the same street as the Kincaid Spring Factory, and they both glanced at it as they walked by.

"*So*," she said the word slowly. "Anything happening with that?" She pointed toward the building.

"I talked to my assistant about it on Friday. Asked him to get all the building plans and specs. They were in my inbox this morning."

"And? Do you still think it's a viable project? For your company?"

"I do."

"What's your next step?"

"I have to put a proposal together to pitch to my boss. However, per my bet with Ava, I'm not really allowed to start working on it until Wednesday. She did approve of it when I told her about it, though. But once I've officially won my pineapple coconut whipped dream cake, I'll research the town, get tourism numbers, look into the hotels outside of Cruickshank."

"That makes sense." She nodded. "And how long does that usually take you?"

"Typically?" He glanced over at her. "A project like this would take me a few days, but I'll only be working on it when Ava is busy with something else. I can't interfere with the taskmaster."

"No." She smiled. "That would be dangerous. If there is anything I've learned over the years working for Ava, it's that."

"Can I ask you a question?"

"Yeah."

"I ask this with no judgment, just genuine curiosity, but why do you have all of these part-time jobs?" He'd been wondering why she worked at Quigley's and Dancing Donkey, but now that he knew about all these other places, he couldn't help himself.

"Well, I work at Petal and Thorn because the plants and flowers make me feel closer to my mom. I work at Dancing Donkey because it's a link to the rescue and I enjoy working with Sasha and Lorraine. They're family. Just like the Quigleys are. That bar is one of my homes, and I love it there. As for Kathleen's, books make my soul happy, even if it's just one day a week. And Ava's—well, despite her being the taskmaster, I love her and I love that house. There are a lot of good memories there . . . of my mom . . . of Martin . . . and some of you." She bumped her shoulder against his. "I love all of those jobs, and as opposed to giving one up"—she shrugged—"I choose them all."

Max wasn't sure why . . . Actually, he knew *exactly* why, but he found it hard to say anything after that last part. She still thought about him. It shouldn't have been that surprising, as he still thought about her, no matter how hard he'd tried not to.

They walked past the last two storefronts in silence before they were standing in front of the yellow-and-teal-striped awning of Frenchy Fries. The front of the café featured tall windows framed with white, showing off the inside, which was filled with more yellow and teal.

"You want me to go in and order while you grab us a seat?" He pointed to the courtyard across the road. It didn't belong to the café but was where a lot of people would bring their food if they wanted to eat outside.

"Sure." Caro reached for her wallet.

"No." Max shook his head. "I'm paying."

"That's not necessary."

"Yes, it is. I asked you to lunch, I'm paying for it. Just tell me what you want."

Her pretty lips bunched together, a stubborn set he knew so well. She studied him for a second before her mouth relaxed and she let out a sigh. She knew she wasn't going to win this one.

"Fine. I'd like the grilled cheese with Brie, apple, and fig jam. A large lemonade. And the herb Parmesan fries."

"Done." Max nodded as he headed inside.

There were a couple of people in line in front of him, but it moved quickly enough. Ten minutes later, he was crossing the street with their food.

Caro had found a spot in the back corner, snagging one of the few wrought-iron tables that was free. Ivy climbed the brick walls behind her, and she was looking down at the book in her hands,

Frankie sitting at her feet, her brown eyes watching everything around them.

"What are you reading?" Max asked as he set everything down on the table.

She looked up, closing the book, and he saw the cover. It had an intricate pattern of swirls around a blade. "Just a book about a fairy war . . . with a lot of sex."

"My favorite." He grinned.

"What did you get?"

"Same as you, it sounded too good." He'd even gotten a lemonade, unable to resist the temptation any longer.

"Where are your fries?" She pulled one of the bags toward her, ripping the top half off.

"We're sharing those." He nodded to where her hand had disappeared into the bag before sliding her sandwich in front of her. "I ordered an extra-large."

"Are you sure it's going to be enough?" she teased, grinning at him.

He couldn't stop his eyes from lingering on her mouth. Suddenly very thirsty, he took a sip of the tart-sweet lemonade . . . and he was pretty sure his head was going to explode. He was a fucking masochist.

Caro unwrapped her sandwich just as Max did. "Cheers." She held up one half, and Max bumped a corner of his against it. It was the same thing she'd done with the donut, the same thing they'd always done when they shared a meal.

"Cheers," he said before they both took a bite.

Caro let out a little moan as she chewed. "It's perfect."

It was indeed . . . The sandwich wasn't half bad either.

"Every time I eat this, I think of this restaurant in Toulouse. It was right on the Garonne."

"You went to France?" Max couldn't hide his surprise as he reached for a French fry.

"It was seven years ago now. Sasha, Lucy, Lilah, and I back-packed through Europe for two months that summer."

"So you did go?"

He'd wanted to travel with her, to go places, just the two of them, and *really* experience the world. But they'd never had the chance. There were lots of things that had never happened, though. Lots of missed adventures.

"Yeah." She nodded, giving him a small, wistful smile. "Lucy and Sasha had just graduated from college, and Lilah used it as an extended bachelorette party."

"A two-month bachelorette party? How did Jeremy feel about that?"

"Well, he didn't get much say in the matter as they were broken up at the time."

Max choked on his lemonade. "They weren't even engaged?"

"Nope." Caro grinned. "That was probably the third time they'd broken up, and she knew it was going to be the last. He proposed the night we got back, and they were married four months later."

"Seriously?"

"Jeremy wasn't messing around anymore. They wasted no time, as was evidenced by the fact that Matthew was born seven months after the wedding. Lilah couldn't drink at the reception."

"I'm bummed I missed that."

"Me too." The smile on her mouth got smaller, and Max wished he hadn't said it.

"So where did you go in Europe?" he asked, leading them away from a path that might be dangerous.

He didn't want to rehash how they'd fallen apart. Didn't want to talk about the fact that she'd walked away without fighting. He couldn't do it and not get upset. Couldn't do it and not lose his fucking mind.

Caro took another bite of her sandwich before she launched into her trip, telling him how they'd flown into Spain before going to France, Italy, Switzerland, Germany, the Netherlands, and finishing up with London, Scotland, and Ireland.

But her travels hadn't ended there. She'd spent a week camping in the Grand Canyon with her dad; had driven down the California coast with Lucy; gone to Yellowstone National Park with Jeremy; Boston with Ava and Martin; Miami, Austin, Saint Louis, New Orleans, and so many other cities, always with someone else in tow. Someone to enjoy it with.

He'd been wrong to think she hadn't gone anywhere, that her life had never expanded beyond Cruickshank. How was it that he'd been disappointed to think she hadn't . . . and he was still disappointed to learn she had?

It was because he hadn't been a part of it.

"Did you ever go to New York again?"

She'd gone up once before with Rachel and Ava to see him. Caro's birthday was October 23, and the only thing she'd wanted when she turned sixteen was to spend it with Max. They'd flown up on a Thursday, and he'd spent the next three days showing her all his favorite places, everywhere he'd ever told her about.

His grandmother and Rachel had let them do their own thing that Sunday, and he'd snuck her into his parents' empty apartment and made love to her in his own bed. They'd lost their virginities to each other the summer before, and while they were still figuring things out in those days, they'd been rather enthusiastic about it.

"Yeah." She nodded slowly. "I went with Lucy after she graduated from high school. Just the two of us. We went to a Broadway show almost every night."

After Lucy graduated . . . That would've been three years after they broke up. He'd just graduated from Columbia and was back in New York from his months at the London School of Economics.

"That it?"

"No." Caro shook her head. "I've been up a few other times. They were never as fun as that first time with you, though."

"Yes, well, no one does New York better than me." He shook his head, smiling, trying to move past whatever this weird feeling was in his chest. Knowing she'd been there and he hadn't seen her made him feel some kind of way he didn't understand.

And apparently she knew it, even though he was trying to hide it.

"If I'm being one hundred percent honest with you, it was weird being there and not telling you. I wanted to call you, Max. I wanted to see you. But after everything, I didn't think you wanted to see me. I knew you'd moved on, and I didn't want to complicate things."

"You *knew* I moved on?" He raised his eyebrows. "I thought Ava and Martin didn't tell you things about me."

"They didn't." She shook her head as she grabbed another fry. "But you are googleable, and sometimes a girl gets curious about her ex. I know about your big important job, Max, from your tower in the Manhattan sky."

"Actually, I won't be in Manhattan for much longer." He had no idea *why* that truth had just escaped his lips. Maybe because she'd revealed a number of things to him that afternoon. She hadn't said it outright, but she'd missed him.

Just like he'd missed her.

"You won't?"

"No, I actually just got a promotion. I'm moving to London."

"You are?" Her mouth turned up in a smile, but her eyes said something else.

"I was just promoted to the head of the real assets division in London."

"Will that pop up when I google you tonight?" She was still smiling, trying to make a joke to cover what he could have sworn looked a little like disappointment.

"Probably." Max nodded. "They made the official announcement last week. Right before I came here."

"Well, congratulations. I always knew you were meant for bigger things."

Bigger than what? Bigger than you? But he couldn't ask. Couldn't let himself go down any path that involved those questions. And it seemed like Caro didn't want to either, as she steered them back to safer waters.

"So, what about you?" Caro asked, taking another bite of her sandwich. "Where have all of your travels taken you? Probably a lot of places with your job."

Max told her about everywhere he'd gone to in Europe, and Caro's eyes lit up when they compared stories about where they'd both been. He told her about South Africa, Egypt, and Madagascar. His favorite spot in Singapore. How much he'd loved Australia and New Zealand. And how he'd visited every country in South America.

But it was just a distraction for both of them to not think about what he *knew* was on both of their minds . . . a different life . . . one where'd they'd ended up together.

Chapter Thirteen

The Trouble with Wanting

Caro spent the rest of the afternoon with Max, crossing stuff off her own to-do list while helping him with his. It was the least she could do, considering he'd bought her lunch.

Or that was just the excuse she told herself.

Even with everything she'd found out at lunch, she still wanted to be around him. She couldn't help it. Growing up, they'd never really been able to stay away from each other, until they'd had to. Now that the door was open again, Caro was going to use it for as long as she could. She knew that when he left at the end of the summer, this brief glimpse into the past was going to be gone.

How could it not be when he was picking up his entire life and moving to London . . . not that that affected her at all. She was fine. Everything was fine.

Except it really, *really* wasn't. Because why—for the love of God—did her chest ache whenever she thought about it?

"You have any good book recs?" Max asked as they wandered up and down the aisles of Kathleen's Corner. "I tried to read something the other day, but I couldn't get into it."

"What was it about?" Caro asked as she tried to focus on something—*anything*—other than the fact that he'd be an entire ocean away.

"Inflation trends."

She wrinkled her nose. "Sounds . . . riveting."

Max laughed. "Exactly. Maybe I should read something for fun, since I'm on vacation and all."

"I think that's a good idea." Caro nodded as she rounded one of the book stacks, Max following behind her with Frankie in his arms.

"Do you want one with fairies?" she asked, glancing over her shoulder.

"Maybe not fairies . . ." He shook his head. "But fantasy sounds good."

"How about some Greek gods?" she asked as she pulled out a book with a black and gold cover. "I read this last year and couldn't put it down."

"I've seen this one before." He took it from her and scanned the cover copy. "Okay," he said after a moment or two. "I'm sold."

Caro led him to the register, doing her best to keep him from looking at the kids' section. She might've dismantled the display, but her books were still over there. Things might've been moved since last Thursday, and she couldn't get close enough to investigate.

But Hazel took Ava's book order quickly before ringing him up, and they were out the door not long after.

They made their way through the rest of Ava's list, getting everything she'd asked for. Theo and Juliet were clearly surprised to see them come into Browned Butter together, and while both of them smirked, neither said anything as they filled Max's and Caro's orders.

Since Mondays were girls' night—and since Lucy was back in town and they should *really* celebrate her return—Caro decided to get two bottles of wine and a selection of cheeses and meats for the charcuterie board she was going to put together. With the baguette she'd bought at Browned Butter, she just needed some olives and fruit from the grocery store, and she'd be good to go.

"What do you think about this one?" Max asked as he held a toothpick in the air, a white chunk of cheese on the end.

Caro leaned forward, wrapping her lips around the toothpick before pulling back. Her eyes met his, and by the surprise in his expression, she realized he'd meant to hand it to her, not for her to practically eat it out of his hand.

God, the more time she spent with him, the more she fell into old patterns. It was becoming more and more complicated, and she didn't know what to do about it.

But as none of this was permanent, maybe she didn't need to figure it out so much as just learn to deal with it.

It was just too bad for her that she had no idea how.

* * *

CARO WAS NONE the wiser about what to do as the week progressed. Tuesday had them again working side by side at Ava's. Everyone was in the attic, including Lucy, as she'd be helping with the cleaning and downsizing for the rest of the summer.

They stayed at it through the morning and afternoon—June Carter and Johnny Cash playing through Ava's trusty Bluetooth speaker—sorting through books, old gardening magazines, and furniture that hadn't been used in years.

Max was in and out, carrying the stuff that had been deemed disposable or donatable downstairs. It was good to have him around for the task because the boxes with the magazines were *very* heavy, and Caro didn't even want to think about navigating the stairs with a bulky piece of furniture. Max had much bigger muscles than any of them. Much, *much* bigger.

She'd been unable to resist stealing a few glances at them as they flexed, which happened whenever he picked anything up.

He'd taken fourteen loads down so far. She knew because she'd paid attention to each and every one of them. And Lucy had smirked at her every single time, knowing exactly what Caro was staring at.

On Wednesday morning, Max came into Dancing Donkey, a little out of breath from his run, the fabric of his shirt clinging to his chest. He ordered his hazelnut latte—iced this time—and Ava's dirty chai and then he was out the door, leaving her light-headed in his wake.

Caro was working her shift at Kathleen's Corner on Thursday when Max walked in after lunch, requesting another recommendation, as he'd already finished the book he'd bought the other day. Caro grabbed one by the same author, handing it to him with a smile.

"Maybe I should get two books," he said. "Just in case I finish this before next Thursday."

Every day that Caro saw him, she knew she was falling deeper and deeper into . . . whatever this was with Max. Not that either of them had talked about it. No, they were staunchly ignoring it. The lingering touches, the longing stares. But that torture was *nothing* compared to what happened on Friday.

When she and Lucy had shown up that morning, Ava sent Caro outside to let Max know they were there. What Ava had *conveniently* left out was that Max was swimming laps. He'd spotted her as he neared the side of the pool where she stood, standing up in the shallow end and revealing every single muscle on his chest, his skin glistening with water.

Jesus Christ. If this was how she was going to die, what a way to go . . .

She'd stopped breathing when he got out of the water, barely able to mumble out that she'd see him inside before she headed for the house. She glared at Ava when she came in, her cheeks on fire.

"What?" Ava asked innocently.

Caro said nothing as she walked to the refrigerator, sticking her head inside and hoping the blast of cold air would help with her flaming skin.

Lucy and Ava both burst out laughing. Well, at least it was funny for someone.

Friday night she found Max sitting at the bar at Quigley's, Theo on one side and Oscar on the other. They stayed until closing, all of them nursing their glasses of scotch. Despite the late hour, Max was at the Saturday morning market bright and early, ready to help Ava and Caro sell out the rest of the strawberry jam.

It was taking everything in Caro to focus as they set up that morning, because she kept getting distracted by his beard. She'd tracked the progress of it and was pretty sure he hadn't shaved all week, since he was now sporting enough facial hair to make her shiver every time she looked at him.

He'd never had a beard when they'd been together, just a little bit of scruff sometimes. It looked good. Too good. Illegally good.

Great, just great. So it was going to be Ava, Caro, Max, and Max's stupid, sexy beard all working together . . . like one big happy family.

But she was given a small distraction when Lorraine introduced her to the newest foster dog: a black and white English bulldog and Dalmatian mix named Domino. As there'd been an influx of rescues brought in the last couple of weeks, she'd told Lorraine she'd take another. She wasn't used to having more than one, but Lucy was around to help, so she figured the two of them could handle it.

"She's precious," Caro said as she dropped to the ground and the dog ran up to her, waggling her butt the whole way. She crawled into Caro's lap within seconds, licking her face with exuberant enthusiasm.

"Where did you get her?" Lucy asked, sitting down on the ground next to Caro. Domino immediately jumped into her lap, showing just as much affection.

"Same shelter I got the dogs from last week. They brought her in, and all she would do was sit in the corner shaking. Wouldn't eat either. I got her home last night, and she was a completely different dog."

"So she doesn't do well with cages," Caro said as the dog flopped back onto her. "Good to know."

She looked up to find Max watching her, a gleam in his eye. "Are they all putty in her hands?" he asked Lorraine.

The woman grinned. "Every single one of them." It hadn't been meant for Caro to hear, but she didn't miss it when Lorraine followed it up with "You should know that better than anyone, Max."

Caro kept her eyes down, focusing on Domino. She didn't think she could handle seeing whatever expression was on his face . . . and didn't want him to see hers.

Mainly because she was the one who'd become putty in the last couple of weeks, and it was his hands that she was wishing for.

* * *

SUNDAY CAME AND went without Caro seeing Max, just like the Sunday before. They were the only days that she hadn't seen him at all since he'd been in town.

She'd attempted to keep herself busy working on some sketches for her next book, and while it had helped a little, she still felt restless.

It was a feeling that was still lingering in her chest when Monday dawned, dark and gloomy. The clouds had rolled in sometime that night, and the heavy rain woke her early that morning. So early that she, Frankie, and Domino were all loaded up in the Wagoneer and headed for Petal and Thorn an hour before her shift started.

That day's shipment of plants was almost double what it had been the week before, and she got to work getting them unboxed and watered. An entire box of heartleaf philodendron had overgrown their containers, and she had to repot them. It was therapeutic to sink her fingers into the soil and get lost in the task.

Her fingernails were almost black by the end of it, the dirt wedged so far under that she had to scrub for a while to get it all out. When she looked down at her hands, she decided she needed a manicure, and she had the time, as she was leaving the shop an hour earlier than usual. But she would much rather have spent another afternoon with Max.

Since Ava would be in Asheville teaching her art class, he'd be all alone at the house that afternoon.

Or she was pretty sure he would be. Maybe he needed company . . . and they did have the plant he'd ordered for Ava last week. Maybe she should stop by and see him. While she could *technically* drop it off tomorrow, it was $350, an expensive variety that she should really get to him as soon as possible.

It wouldn't hurt to take it to him today, and maybe stare at his beard for a little bit while she did so.

Caro swung by her dad's house first, dropping Frankie and Domino off. Domino might not need a crate, but Frankie couldn't be left to her own devices. She had absolutely no problem settling herself into her little doggy bed and curling up in the blankets for a cozy afternoon nap.

It was still raining as Caro headed for Ava's, a heavier downpour than it had been all day. As she needed both hands to get the plant inside, there would be no umbrella. Pulling the hood of her rain jacket on, she zipped all the zips and snapped all the snaps.

"Why did I decide to do this, again?" she asked herself as she headed for the door, the rain already soaking into her shoes.

She hit the doorbell once, waiting the longest minute of her life before hitting it again. She should've called. Maybe he wasn't there. But Ava had driven to Asheville, and where would he have gone without a car in this weather?

Pulling her keys out of her pocket, Caro found the one to Ava's house and let herself in.

"Max?" she called out as she stepped into the entryway. But Beau was the only one at the door, his fluffy tail wagging. "Is he here?" she asked the dog. He just rubbed his face against her leg.

The lights in the hallway and living room were on, and she heard a voice coming from somewhere in the house. Setting the plant down on the table in the entryway, Caro kicked off her wet shoes and pulled off her jacket, hanging it up on the hook.

"Max?" she called out again.

There was still no answer as she and Beau headed for the kitchen. Her feet faltered, coming to a standstill as she again heard that voice, realizing it was coming from Martin's office. It was a voice she hadn't heard in years, one that had her heart in her throat.

"Okay, so now that the cookies are cooled, we have to roll them. First, we sift the powdered sugar into the bowl."

"Like this?" a child's voice asked.

"Yes, *exactly* like that, Pumpkin."

Without a conscious thought, Caro started moving toward Martin's office, toward the voice that had just cracked her chest wide open. As she rounded the desk, the computer came into view, and there was her mom, right there on the screen.

She was in Ava and Martin's kitchen with Max and Caro standing on either side of her, each boosted up by a chair. They were probably seven and eight, and all three of them were wearing aprons, but Max and Caro were also sporting white chef's hats.

Rachel's brown hair—the exact shade as Caro's—was pulled back in a ponytail. She was wearing the blue dress with red flowers. The same one Caro had imagined her wearing the last time she'd gone to the graveyard, when she'd asked her for a sign.

Rachel glanced up at the camera and smiled, and Caro forgot how to breathe.

There were photos and videos of her mother, ones that Caro had looked at and watched more times than she could possibly count, but she'd never seen this one. She didn't remember this moment, and watching it now was like getting a piece of her mom back.

"Okay," Rachel said, "now for the next step. You have to check if the powdered sugar is fluffy enough, and you do it just like this," she said as she dipped her finger into the sugar before bumping it on Caro's and Max's noses in turn.

Caro giggled before she stuck her fingers in the sugar and rubbed it on her mother's cheek. Max looked unsure for just a moment before he followed suit, his fingers leaving a track of white across Rachel's other cheek.

"Does that pass the check?" she asked.

They both nodded, grinning.

Rachel poured a little bit of the sugar into the bowls in front of Max and Caro. "Okay, so now we take the cookies and roll them in here, very gently." Max and Caro followed her lead, slowly rolling them around in the sugar before placing them on the trays in neat rows.

Caro watched, unable to take her eyes off the screen as each and every cookie was rolled in sugar and put on the tray.

"Now, go get Martin and Ava so we can taste them," Rachel told Max and Caro.

She helped each of them down from their chairs, and they ran out of frame and into the study. It wasn't even fifteen seconds later before they were back, Caro holding Martin's hand and Max tugging on Ava's. All five of them bit into a cookie, Martin and Ava saying how delicious they were before the screen went black, the video over.

"Caro?"

She turned to find Max in the doorway, his expression full of concern. And that was when she realized tears were streaming down her face.

"Come here." Max moved toward her.

Caro didn't even hesitate. She walked right into his arms, finding that safe place she used to call home.

* * *

CARO WAS SOBBING into Max's chest, her tears soaking his shirt, warming his skin. She was in his arms, something he'd wanted for so fucking long. He hadn't exactly wanted her to be crying when it happened, but he couldn't deny how good it felt to be holding her again.

His hands were at her back, rubbing up and down and trying to soothe her in any way possible. He knew she was hurting. Hell, he was hurting after seeing Rachel on the screen.

It wasn't the first video he'd seen of her. He'd discovered the set of tapes yesterday and had been converting them all afternoon while doing stuff around Martin's office. Caro must've just gotten here, because he'd only been in the garage for about five minutes looking for a screwdriver to tighten a loose hinge on one of the doors to the bookcase.

When he'd walked back into the sitting room, he'd seen Caro standing in Martin's office, staring at the screen like she'd seen a ghost.

And she had.

Seeing videos with Rachel in them had thrown him for a loop, but as he'd watched Caro—sadness and pain clear in the way she stood, her shoulders shaking, the sound of her gasping for air through her tears—something in him had broken.

He wanted to tell her it was going to be okay. But things hadn't been okay since Rachel died. He'd known that then, and he still knew it now.

So all he could do was try to be her safe harbor, a safe place to land.

"I've got you, Caro," he whispered into her hair. "I'm here."

"It hurts." Her voice cracked. "It's so fucking unfair."

"I know."

"I just want her back so much. I miss her."

"I know," he repeated. "Believe me, I know." He knew because he missed Rachel too, and he missed his father, and Martin . . . and he missed Caro.

Except Caro wasn't dead; she was in his arms. Warm, and breathing, and *very* much alive. But she wasn't his, no matter how much he wished she was. Before he even realized he was doing it, he pressed a kiss to her temple.

Caro stilled in his arms, her head coming up from his chest. Her hazel-gray eyes were red rimmed, her lips slightly swollen and parted. Her breathing was still uneven, but not from the choking sobs that had overtaken her moments ago.

No, this was something else entirely. Her hand was fisted in his shirt, and she tugged—*hard*—pulling him down to her.

Max wouldn't have been able to stop the kiss if he'd tried, but he didn't try, not even a little bit. His mouth landed on hers, her lips softer than he remembered, her mouth sweeter. She opened for him just like she always had, no hesitancy, no resistance.

His hands moved, one going to the back of her head, and the

other to the small of her back, bracing her against him as he deepened the kiss. Caro moaned into his mouth, the sound reverberating throughout his entire body.

God, he needed more of her. He *needed* everything.

The last time Max had kissed Caro, he hadn't known it was the end. He'd thought about that fact more than he'd like to admit. He'd also thought about what he'd give for one final kiss. And now, with his lips on Caro's, he knew the answer.

He'd *give* anything.

The pent-up need wasn't just coming from him either. There was an all-consuming hunger on both sides, as Caro kissed him just as fiercely, her hands at his waist, moving around, her fingernails digging through the fabric of his shirt as she clawed her way up his back.

And then her arms were wrapped around his neck, trying to get enough leverage to pull herself up his body. He was almost a foot taller than her, and the angle wasn't giving her what she needed. What *they* needed, which was for her to be fully against him.

Max lifted her, pulling her legs around his waist as he backed her up against the wall. His hands were on her ass, and he couldn't stop the groan that vibrated through his chest when he squeezed. But it was nothing compared to the sound he made when she started to move against him, pressing into his erection.

"Fuck, Caro." He groaned, pulling his mouth away and resting his forehead against hers, their uneven breaths mixing in the space between. "Tell me you want this. Tell me you want me as much as I want you."

"Take me to bed, Max."

He squeezed her ass one last time before letting go, another groan escaping his lips when she slid down his body. And then he was grabbing her hand and leading her out of the den and up the stairs. The second they were on the landing, he was pulling her against him again, his mouth on hers as he backed her down the hallway to his bedroom.

Chapter Fourteen

Home

They were doing this. They were *really* doing this, after fourteen *long* years.

Fourteen years. God, the last time she'd had sex with Max she'd been nineteen. Things had been tighter, firmer, higher, smaller. Doubt crept into her mind. She couldn't stop it. What if he got her naked and was disappointed?

Caro ripped her mouth away from Max's, looking up at him with concern.

"Please don't tell me you've changed your mind. I beg you."

"No." She shook her head, letting out a little awkward laugh. "I just—I didn't shave my legs today. I don't even remember the last time I did." Had it been Saturday . . . or maybe Friday?

Max's forehead wrinkled in confusion. "What?"

"I don't know what your expectations are here. Things have changed since we were last together. *I've* changed." She indicated her body.

"So have I."

"Yes." Caro nodded, reaching for his biceps and giving them a good squeeze. "But unlike you, my changes haven't been for the better." Like the fact that she'd been a size four last time she'd been with Max. These days she was a size eight.

Max's confused expression changed to one of incredulity. "Caro, are you serious right now? The very last thing I'm thinking about is if you shaved your legs or anything else that's changed with your body."

"Then what *are* you thinking about?"

"What kind of underwear you're wearing."

"I . . . What?"

Max's hands moved from her waist to her hips, his palms running over the fabric of her shorts. "Just to be clear, I don't care if it's lace, silk, cotton, boyshorts, bikini, or a thong. Because they're about to be on my bedroom floor." His fingers moved back up, tracing over the top of her shorts and sending shivers down her spine as he reached for the snap and pulled down the zipper.

Caro swallowed hard. "If you had to guess?" she asked breathlessly.

"You always liked things with lace." He moved to the side, his mouth on the shell of her ear, tracing it with his tongue. "And I did see that thong of yours the other day." Max gently bit into her earlobe before he dropped to his knees in front of her. His fingers hooked in the sides of her shorts before he pulled them down, revealing black lace.

They were cheeky briefs, and once her legs were clear, Max turned her around, getting a look at her from behind.

"Damn," he whispered.

Caro gasped as he bit her right butt cheek. She hadn't even caught her breath before he was on his feet, spinning her back around. His hands tangled in the hem of her T-shirt as he pulled it over her head. He licked his lips as he looked her up and down, his fingers traveling down one side of the hem of her black bra before going back up the other side. The heat in his blue eyes was enough to wipe away all those stupid doubts from moments before.

"You're fucking perfect, Caro," he said as he leaned down to kiss her again, his hands wrapped around her waist, his fingers digging into her skin, rough and possessing.

"I want to see you," she said against his mouth. "I want to feel you against me, Max."

He broke the kiss again, moving back far enough to pull his shirt over his head. She hadn't been this close to him in over a decade, and she'd been dying to touch him for weeks. So she did now, her fingers walking over his abs. She wanted to count them with her tongue.

Soon, very soon.

He reached for the front of his jeans, but Caro pushed his hands away, her fingers making quick work of the button and zipper. When she pulled them down his hips, she found boxer briefs, his erection straining against the soft gray cotton. Caro lightly traced over the outline.

Max's groan filled the room, and before she knew it, he was kicking free of his jeans and pushing her down onto the bed. He crawled on top of her, pulling her up until her head hit the pillows. And then he was kissing her again, his tongue thrusting into her mouth as his hips moved between her legs. His hands were at the top of her head, pulling out the messy bun and fanning her hair out around her.

He pulled back, looking at her unraveling beneath him. "I want to taste every part of you." He leaned down, his mouth trailing across her neck, his lips pressing kisses along her collarbone before dragging his teeth against the skin of her chest.

His hands moved to the back of her bra, and she arched, giving him better access. He had it undone with an easy flick of his fingers, pulling it away and tossing it behind him. And then his lips were on her breast, sucking her nipple deep into his mouth.

Caro's entire body bucked beneath him, feeling the jolt of pleasure in her bones.

"Max." Her hands were on his head, her fingers twisting in his hair as she held him to her. His tongue rasped across her sensitive flesh over, and over, and over again before he moved to her other breast, repeating the process.

All this time and he still knew *exactly* where to touch her, how to drive her absolutely insane.

His mouth was moving down now, dragging across her belly, his teeth nipping at the delicate fabric of her underwear. He sat up on his knees, his fingers hooking in the fabric at the sides before he pulled them down her legs. His eyes darkened as he looked at the apex of her thighs and the thatch of brown curls. He licked his lips and Caro was pretty sure her entire body was going to spontaneously combust, right then and there.

"Let's see how much you want me," he said as he ran his hand over her, gently slipping a finger inside.

Caro gasped as Max groaned, and then he was sliding in another finger.

"It would seem a lot." He nodded, satisfied.

And then his hand disappeared, and he was lowering himself back onto the bed, pulling her legs over his shoulders as he settled in.

"Oh, God." Caro's back arched off the bed at the first moment of contact, her eyes closing as she pressed her head into the pillows.

Max's hands tightened on her thighs, guiding her as she started to move against his mouth. She couldn't help herself. The scrape of his beard on her sensitive skin, his lips sucking, his tongue licking.

It was *too* much. It was *too* good. It was beyond what she could handle . . . and yet . . . and yet she wanted more. She wanted everything. And he gave it. God, did he give it.

The orgasm inside of her built, higher and higher until she went right over the edge. Her hands fisted in the blanket as she writhed beneath him, screaming his name. He brought her down slowly, dragging out every moment of pleasure until she melted into the bed, heart pounding, breaths ragged.

Opening her eyes was a slow process, but when she was finally able to, Max was pressing a kiss to the inside of her thigh. He sat up, wiping his mouth with the back of his hand, his eyes filled with a dark desire that wasn't in any way satiated.

Caro's stomach flipped, her heartbeat somehow becoming even more erratic.

Yeah, she'd never been over this man. Not for a second. And she never, ever would be over him. Not for as long as she lived.

* * *

MAX'S EYES SLOWLY moved over Caro's body, taking in her flushed skin, the uneven movement of her chest as she tried to catch her breath, her slightly swollen lips, her dazed eyes, and her hair spread out beneath her. He'd never forget how she looked in this moment.

It was true she had changed, but in an amazing way. Her hips were curvier, her breasts fuller, and her ass? Well, he'd very much enjoyed taking a bite out of it.

"You're fucking perfect, Caro." Max repeated his words from

earlier. Apparently, she wasn't aware, so he was going to tell her as many times as he had to.

"Come here." Her hands lifted, reaching for him, but Max pulled away. He knew that if he went down, he wasn't coming back up.

"Give me a second. I need to grab a condom." He shifted out from between her legs, a task that took much more willpower than he'd been prepared for.

Caro dropped her hands to the bed. "Hurry."

Max didn't need to be told twice. He practically ran to the bathroom, grabbing his toiletry kit from the counter. When he unzipped the side pocket, he found four condoms.

"Okay, I can work with this." He nodded as he headed back into the bedroom.

Caro was still spread out on the bed, surrounded by white pillows and the fluffy duvet. He needed to be inside of her like he needed his next breath.

Ripping one of the condoms off, he tossed the other three onto the nightstand. But before he could do anything about his boxers, Caro was sitting up and reaching for him.

"No." She swatted his hands away. "It's my turn."

She knelt on the bed in front of him, grabbing his hips and pulling him close. Her breasts were pushed up against his chest, her mouth on his as one of her hands slid beneath the elastic. And then her fingers were wrapped around his cock, stroking him as her other hand worked the fabric down his hips.

"Jesus Christ, Caro." Max groaned as her thumb swiped over the tip.

She let go of him, the absence of her touch almost causing him physical pain. But then she was pushing his boxers the rest of the way down his legs until he could kick them off.

"Give me that." She took the condom from his hand, bringing the wrapper to her mouth and ripping it open with her teeth. And then her hands were on his cock again, rolling the condom down the length of him.

Her arms wrapped around his neck as she pulled him in close, her tongue thrusting into his mouth as he palmed her ass and ground into her.

"Fuck me, Max," she whispered against his lips.

He pushed her back onto the bed, one hand holding her against him, while the other one braced their fall. And then he was settling himself between her thighs, reaching between them, and lining his cock up to her entrance.

Max pulled his mouth from hers, and when he looked down into her face, he found her eyes already on his. This had always been one of his favorite parts, watching her as he slid inside of her body. It had been so long, and he wanted the moment to last forever.

It was a slow push, her body opening to him as her lips parted on a soft gasp, just like they always did.

You're home.

"Max." Caro's hand moved to his head, her fingers threading in his hair. "Don't be gentle," she said as her legs wrapped around his waist.

"I won't." He reached up, grabbing her hand and pressing it above her head, their fingers twining together. His other hand moved beneath her hip, holding on to her as he pulled back just enough before thrusting inside of her again.

They moved together, neither of them gentle. Caro pulled at his hair, bit at his lip, dug her heels into his back. There was something about it that felt . . . the same. They knew exactly what the other wanted. What the other needed. They found their rhythm, found each other.

But, at the same time, *something* was different. Maybe it was because of the years apart. Maybe the want was greater. The need deeper. All Max knew was that he never wanted to let go again, and his hold on her tightened. His hand at her waist flexed, his fingers digging into her flesh. She gasped against his mouth, her own grip on him becoming stronger as her kiss somehow became even more fierce.

He'd never found another partner like her, one who matched him in every way. And being with her again made him realize he never would.

You're home.

That thought kept repeating in his head.

Fuck.

"Max." Caro moaned his name. "I'm so close. Touch me." Her words were a plea, and he'd *never* been one to deny her. Not here, not like this.

He moved his hand between their bodies. As soon as he pressed his fingers to her clit, she started to move against him harder.

"Yes," she moaned against his mouth.

"Come on, baby. Come for me."

It was just a couple more thrusts before she was clutching his shoulders, her fingers digging into his back as she tightened around him, sending him into his own climax.

Max moved through it, pumping his hips through his release, his mouth at her throat as he groaned her name into her sweet lemon-scented skin. He knew then and there that scent would haunt him for the rest of his life.

And he was perfectly okay with it.

* * *

"So that happened . . ." Max said as he stared up at the ceiling. It was the first thing either of them had said. Until then, the only sound in the room had been their breathing and the rain that was still coming down outside, hitting the roof and windows.

Caro was sprawled across his chest, and she laughed at his words, her breath moving across his skin.

He had absolutely no idea how much time had passed as they lay in bed, contemplating what had just happened. He didn't know exactly what was going on in Caro's head, but he was definitely thinking about the fact that they'd just had sex.

Incredible sex.

"Is it going to happen again?" Caro asked.

Max rolled onto his side, adjusting their bodies so her head rested on his arm and he could look into her hazel-gray eyes. "God, I hope so." He slid his hand down her bare hip, his fingers tightening as he pulled her against him.

Her lips parted at the contact, inhaling a tiny gasp of air. Max followed it, pressing his mouth to hers, his tongue sliding between her lips to find hers. One of Caro's hands was pressed against his chest, the other on his biceps, and he felt all ten of her nails bite into his skin. But then they released, and she pulled back, looking up into his face.

There was doubt in her eyes now . . . worry. "What are we doing, Max?"

"I don't know exactly." He shook his head, brushing a strand of hair out of her face and tucking it behind her ear. "But summers were always ours, Caro. Why not take this one too?" His finger traced the shell of that ear as he slowly brought his hand down the side of her face. She shivered against him. "No complications or rules, just us."

"Just sex?" She frowned.

"I don't think it will ever be *just sex* between us."

"And doesn't that make it complicated?"

"I guess it does." His fingers were on her jaw now, his thumb tracing over her lips. "All I know is that I want you, Caro. I've always wanted you. And if we get one more summer together, I want to take it."

"I want to take it too."

"Then that's what we do."

Neither of them said *and deal with the consequences later*, but they both heard those unspoken words. And as Caro leaned in and pressed her mouth to his again, he knew she didn't want to address them at the moment either.

Though, even if they *had* wanted to discuss it, they wouldn't have been able to. Her hand was just drifting down his stomach, inches away from its intended goal when a door downstairs shut and Ava called out.

"Max? Caro?"

Beau had been curled up on one of the blankets that had fallen to the floor, and he took off at Ava's voice, his paws skittering on the hardwood floors.

"*Shhhhit.*" Max groaned as he pulled away from Caro.

A horrified laugh escaped her as she almost fell out of bed.

"What time is it? I thought she had her classes until three on Mondays."

"She does," Max whispered as he crossed to his bedroom door. "Be right down," he called out, grabbing their clothes from the hallway before shutting the door.

When he turned around, it was to find Caro putting her bra back on. "I can't find my underwear."

"No time," he said as he tossed her shorts and shirt across the bed. "I'll find them later." He grabbed his own pants, not even bothering with his underwear as he pulled them on.

"How are we playing this?" she asked as she snatched her shirt from the bed, practically diving into it.

"We were in the attic?" he suggested as he shoved his arms into his shirt.

"Doing what?" She spotted her hair tie at the foot of the bed and grabbed it, frantically gathering her hair up into a messy bun.

"Uhhh." His brain was not working. *Think, man. Think!* "I wanted to show you . . . umm . . . the old board games up there."

"Seriously?" She frowned at him.

"What? We used to play them when we were kids. It could've been some nostalgic thing between us. She'll love it."

"Okay, it's all we got," she said as she walked past him, heading for the door. Max couldn't help himself, he grabbed her arm, tugging her in to his chest as he pressed one last kiss to her mouth.

She was grinning when he pulled back. "Even if we get caught, it was worth it."

"I mean, it's not like she can ground us . . . We're adults now." And yet he felt like he was a teenager again, getting caught fooling around with Caro.

Something that had happened on many, *many* occasions.

"She might." She laughed, taking a deep breath as she opened the door and stepped out into the hallway. She glanced over her shoulder at him and mouthed, *Coast is clear*, before she headed for the stairs.

They were about halfway down when he noticed the tag sticking out from the back of her shirt. She'd put it on inside out. And there was no time to warn her, as Ava was walking down the hallway right toward them.

Maybe she wouldn't notice . . . Fat fucking chance. Ava was already studying them as she neared, her overly perceptive eyes moving back and forth.

"You're home early," Max said as casually as he could . . . too casually.

Ava's eyes narrowed even more. "My nude model didn't show up. He had car trouble. We couldn't exactly substitute him with a fruit bowl. Bananas only go so far. I didn't realize you were coming over today, Caro."

"I, um, well, Max ordered a plant." She indicated the table by the front door.

"A plant?" Ava repeated.

"Yes." The plant. *The plant!* "I ordered one of those fancy monsteras for you. There was a spot in your sunroom where I thought it would go perfectly."

"I see." She nodded slowly. "And what were you guys doing upstairs?"

"I told Caro about the board games I'd found, the ones we used to play."

"So you went upstairs and decided to play naked Twister?"

Well, so much for that plan.

"I wasn't born yesterday. You two have sex written all over your faces. And your shirt is on inside out." She pointed to Caro.

Caro glanced over at her shoulder, seeing the seam. "Dammit."

"What did I tell you when you got here, Max? You couldn't get anything by me when you two were sneaking around as horny teenagers, and you can't do it as horny adults."

"*Okay*, can we not?" Caro shook her head, her cheeks getting redder and redder by the second.

"Just as long as you two used protection."

"Jesus Christ, Ava." Max groaned as he ran his hand across his face. Was this really happening right now?

"What?" She grinned. "Safety first."

Caro cleared her throat before she looked between the two of them. "I'm, um, going to go now. I'll, uh, see you two tomorrow." She spared Max one last look, a half smile turning up her lips before she headed for the door.

"Bye, Caro," Ava called out.

Once she was outside, Max turned to his grandmother, who was still smirking. "Was that necessary?"

"I think so." She nodded. "Looks like you two made some progress."

"Progress that we aren't discussing."

"Why?"

Max let out a sigh. "Because you aren't going to like it. I am fully aware of everything you've done so far to force us together. But it doesn't mean we're getting *back* together."

"Well, we will just see about that, now, won't we?" She turned around and headed for the kitchen. "I could use some help getting dinner prepped," she called out over her shoulder as if the matter was settled.

Well, at least it was settled for someone.

* * *

GIRLS' NIGHT ALWAYS consisted of Caro, Lilah, and Sasha—and Lucy, now that she was back in town. The host rotated every week, and this Monday it was Lilah's turn. Caro was the last one to arrive; Sasha's bright green hatchback was already in the driveway. Sasha and Lucy had driven together as they'd spent the day scouring job listings to find Lucy something more permanent than the shifts she'd picked up at Dancing Donkey and Quigley's.

Caro let herself into the house, bypassing Matthew, Christopher, and Emilia, who were all watching a movie in the living room.

"They're all in the kitchen." Matthew pointed, not even taking his eyes from the screen.

Something with lemon and garlic was baking in the oven, a salad already made on the counter. Lilah was chopping up a watermelon, Lucy opening a bottle of wine, Sasha putting some sort of chocolate tort in the fridge, and Jeremy taking a sip of his beer. "I slept with Max," Caro announced the second she set foot inside the room.

Everyone stilled as they looked over at her. Well, everyone except for Jeremy, who spit his beer out.

"What the hell, Caro?" he said when he could speak.

"Finally!" Lucy threw one of her hands in the air.

"I *knew* it!" Lilah dropped the knife on the cutting board.

"What?" Caro looked to her. "What do you mean, *you knew it*?"

"Today's the twenty-ninth." She grinned. "I won the bet."

"I don't know why we even bother going against her." Sasha shook her head at Lilah. "She always wins."

"Was it good?" Lucy asked.

"Of course it was good." Lilah waved at Caro's face. "She's still flushed."

"You know I'm still in the room?" Jeremy asked.

"Oh, don't act so scandalized." Lucy threw the cork at him. "You were the one who started the bet on when they were going to bang."

"I wasn't intending it to be a banging bet!"

"Well, it is." Lilah glanced at him before looking back to Caro. "So was it good? How many times?"

"Just the once. Ava came home early."

"Cockblocked by Ava." Sasha tut-tutted.

"Everyone can still see me? Right? I haven't gone invisible?" Jeremy waved his arms around.

"You can leave the kitchen whenever you want." Lucy smiled at him sweetly.

"I'm going to go watch the movie with the kids. Holler at me if you need anything."

"Hey, babe," Lilah called out to him. "Did you forget something?"

He leaned in and kissed her.

"Nope, that's not it." She shook her head. "Though appreciated."

"What?" His brows furrowed.

"My twenty bucks."

"Do you want it in cash?" He smiled as he leaned against the counter. "Or would you prefer to exchange it for something else?"

"Hmm. Let me think about it."

"See? This is why you can't complain about hearing about Caro's sex life." Lucy waved her hand back and forth between the two of them. "You two are the absolute worst."

"Yeah, we are." Jeremy playfully slapped Lilah's butt, winking at her before heading for the living room with his beer.

"Okay." Lilah looked to the stove. "Everything is done, and the chicken needs thirty more minutes. So wine"—she pointed to Lucy, who was still holding the newly opened bottle—"and porch"—she pointed to the back door. "I'll meet you guys out there. I just need to go grab something," she said before heading for her and Jeremy's bedroom.

Lucy divided the bottle between four glasses, before picking up two and heading outside, Caro and Sasha grabbing their own and following. It was still raining, and the soft taps on the metal roof created a nice ambiance with the twinkle lights strung up around them. The sun hadn't set yet, but the sky was dark enough with those gray storm clouds that the lights glowed.

They all settled into their usual spots on the overstuffed sofas and chairs as Lilah came outside, tossing a wrapped box at Caro. "I got you a present."

Caro pulled the paper off to reveal a box of condoms. A *large* box of condoms.

Sasha choked on her wine, while Lucy's head fell back and she laughed at the ceiling.

"You're hilarious," Caro deadpanned as she balled the wrapping up and threw it at Lilah.

She caught it in the air, setting it on the table next to her. "If you don't want them, I can take them back." She smiled sweetly.

"No, I'll keep them," Caro said just a bit too quickly, her mouth splitting into a grin.

All four of them burst out laughing before Lucy pointed at Caro and said, "Start from the beginning."

So Caro did. They'd all known about her Monday with him last week; it had been one of the topics of conversation of that girls' night. But she hadn't told them how everything had escalated the last few days. How all the time she'd spent with him had left her wanting *more*.

"When I got to Ava's, I couldn't find him, but I heard a voice in the office, so I followed it." Her voice got a little tight at this part, unable to hold back the emotion as she looked to Lucy. "It was Mom."

"What?"

"Ava has these video tapes that Martin made. I'd been converting them, and Max took over last week. He must've found some with Mom on them."

"What was she doing? In the video?" Lucy asked, voice a little bit hoarse.

"She was baking, with Max and me. I was probably seven. I don't remember it at all. Anyways, I lost it. And then he was there, and he was holding me. Everything hurt so much that I couldn't breathe. He kissed the side of my head, and . . . and then I was kissing him."

"Jesus," Sasha whispered as she took a sip of wine.

"I was hurting . . . and then I wasn't. He made me forget."

"Or he took away the pain," Lucy said. There was something about her expression that had Caro's eyes narrowing on her sister. It was like she was desperate for the same thing.

"I don't know what it was," she said, shaking her head slowly. "Either way, things escalated very quickly. He had me up against the wall, and he was telling me how much he wanted me." The deep timbre of his voice was still in her ear, the scratch of his beard still on her skin. She'd never wanted anything more in that moment.

God, she still wanted him now. Once hadn't been nearly enough.

"*Je-sus*," Sasha said again, this time enunciating the syllables.

"Well, how did it compare?" Lilah asked.

"It was the same . . . but different." She paused, still trying to figure it out. "I don't know how that's possible . . . but it was."

"It makes sense to me." Lilah nodded. "You guys *know* each other, but at the same time, you've changed."

"Did you guys have time to talk? About whatever this is? Before Ava showed up?" Lucy asked.

"Not a lot." She took a deep breath and sighed, taking a sip of her wine. "He basically said summers were always ours, and he wanted to have one more with me."

"*One* more?" Lilah frowned. "Meaning there won't be another?"

"I don't know how there can be." Caro shook her head. "He's moving to London, and I live here." She waved her hand around them.

"What about long distance? You guys did it before," Lucy pressed.

"Yeah, when the endgame was us being together. But long distance didn't work when we were four hours apart. Now there'd be a whole ocean between us. Besides, I don't know that he wants anything more than this summer."

"Do you want more?" Sasha asked.

"We had sex once. I don't think this is the time for me to think about *more*." More sex? Yes. Anything beyond that? No.

"So what? You're just going to let the summer play out?" Lilah's eyes narrowed, studying. Assessing. "No plan? That's very un-Caro-like."

"Well, maybe I need to be a little un-Caro-like for a bit. I mean, hell, I had two orgasms this afternoon, and I'm so tense about all of this, I can't see straight. Shouldn't I be more relaxed than this?" Caro asked.

The long bath she'd taken hadn't worked either. Or the manicure. Or the meditating.

"Two?!" Lucy exclaimed. "You said you only had sex with him once."

"It was only once. He just . . . took care of me first. Like I said, not everything was different."

"*Jesus. Christ.* I need a boyfriend." Sasha shook her head as she took a sip of her wine, her own sexual frustration clear in every word.

Everyone couldn't help but laugh.

"Well, no matter what happens with the two of you, I promise not to get in the way this time," Lucy said.

"What are you talking about?" Caro asked.

"Come on, everyone here knows that I'm the reason you two broke up."

"We do?" Lilah's eyebrows bunched together, her mouth going tight.

"Yeah, we do?" Caro repeated.

"Come on, Caro." Lucy's eyes went sad as she looked at her sister. "It was only after you found out about me that the two of you broke up."

"Luce, you had nothing to do with my breakup with Max. I was the one who shut him out. I was the one who pulled away. I was the one who decided our fate. He and I were already on the way out the door."

"Well, I was the one who shut the door behind you."

"No, you weren't." Caro shook her head as she leaned closer to her sister. "Luce, after Mom died, everything was falling apart for all of us. My heart was so broken I didn't know how to be *me* anymore. And I knew Max would never stop fighting for me, which meant that he'd keep sacrificing what he wanted for me. He'd already picked Chapel Hill because of me, and I wasn't going. And I feared he wouldn't go to London without me. So I made the choice for us. You need to stop blaming yourself for something that you had no part of. Do you understand me?"

Lucy didn't say anything; her only response was a small nod of the head.

"Does he know all of that?" Sasha asked.

"No, I never told him." Caro sat back in her seat again, her eyes lingering on Lucy.

"Maybe you should," Lilah said. "Just like you should tell him about *The Adventures of Pumpkin and Bean*."

Caro moved her focus to her friend. "I can't tell him about the books."

"Why?" Lucy asked.

"Because then he'll know that I was still in love with him eight years ago."

"And what's wrong with that?" Sasha waved her wineglass in the air.

"Because then he'll figure out that she's still in love with him now," Lilah answered for her.

"I'm not in love with him." Caro shook her head, taking a sip of wine to wash away the bitter taste that had just filled her mouth.

"Okay." Lilah made a face that said she didn't believe a word of it.

It was just too bad for Caro that she didn't believe what she was saying either.

"I'm not."

"Okay," Lilah repeated. "I'll drop it." She held her hands up in surrender.

"Will you?"

"For now." Her friend grinned. "You guys want to make another bet?"

"No. More. Bets." Caro shook her head as everyone laughed.

Sasha, thankfully, changed the subject and started telling them all about the guy she'd been chatting with on one of her dating apps. Caro knew she'd done it because she'd taken mercy on her. She listened as Sasha talked, but her eyes drifted over to her sister.

While Lucy might've acknowledged what Caro had said about her breakup with Max—and how it hadn't been Lucy's fault at all— she feared her sister didn't believe it.

Apparently, both of them were refusing to acknowledge the truth that evening.

Chapter Fifteen

Contentment and Hope

It was taking everything in Max to sit still and watch TV that evening. He hadn't been this restless since the first night he was in Cruickshank. Ava wasn't helping matters either. She wasn't saying anything about Caro specifically, just random remarks here and there while giving him annoying, knowing looks.

It was driving him crazy.

"One would think you'd be less agitated, given your afternoon." She paused the show they were watching and looked over at him.

"I'm not agitated."

"You're fidgeting with your watch. A clear sign of agitation with you."

Max had indeed started flicking the clasp open and closed again. "I've just been cooped up in the house all day." He would've gone for a run, but it had been raining most of the evening. All he'd been able to do was take a cold shower, and that hadn't helped even a little bit. He'd tried to distract himself by working on the proposal for the Kincaid project, but he couldn't focus for the life of him.

There was something pent up inside him. Something that had only gotten worse after his afternoon with Caro. He'd gotten a taste of her, and it hadn't been enough.

It would *never* be enough.

"Mmm-hmm." Ava frowned at him before turning back to the TV and unpausing the show.

After that first night, she'd figured out how much he hated home improvement shows, so they were now working their way through old seasons of *The Amazing Race*, a TV show where people traveled the world with a partner.

He thought about the places Caro had told him she'd visited last week. He'd been to some of those same cities, seen some of those same things. But as he thought about them now, he pictured them through her eyes and not what he'd seen with his own.

Why did he feel like he'd missed out somehow? Not just on *really* experiencing these places . . . but on seeing them with her. Like he'd lost something. Something he'd *never* be able to get back, no matter how much he tried.

"You know," Ava said after a moment, "I believe you mess with your watch when you think you're wasting time."

Max glanced back down at his wrist, where he'd started flipping the clasp open and closed again. And then he looked over at his grandmother, shaking his head. "I don't think I'm wasting time with you."

She smiled at him, reaching over and patting his hand. "That's sweet, but we both know you want to see Caro. So why don't you? It's late, and I'm tired anyways. And you know it's going to be a busy day tomorrow."

"It's a busy day here *every* day."

"Well, life's too short to just sit around twiddling your thumbs."

"Have you ever twiddled your thumbs?"

Ava thought for a second before she nodded. "One time back in the seventies. It was boring, I vowed to never do it again."

Max laughed, shaking his head.

"There it is." She pointed to his smile before she got up, stretching her lower back. Beau looked over at her, getting to his feet and trotting to the doggy door, just like he did every night. The dog knew the routine like the back of his paw.

"Now, be off with you"—Ava waved her hand toward the front door—"and go see Caro. Just make sure to be back by ten."

Max glanced down at his watch. "By ten? It's almost nine now." That wasn't nearly enough time for him to do all the things he wanted to do with her . . . and to her.

"I meant ten tomorrow." She smiled before she headed for the stairs. "Night, Bean."

He was out the door less than five minutes later, heading down the street toward Caro's house. The skies were still cloudy, and he wasn't sure if it was just a lull in the rain or it was done for the night. There was a bit of a chill in the air, and his rain jacket gave just enough protection from the light breeze.

The streetlights glowed in the dark as Max made his way through town, closer and closer to her. Except she wasn't at her house when he got there. He couldn't see any lights on in her loft above the garage, and the Jeep Wagoneer was missing from the drive.

"*Dammit.*" He'd forgotten that Mondays were girls' night.

"Max?"

He turned around to see Caro's father standing by the trash cans, tossing a white bag inside. "Hey, Mr. Buchanan."

"Mr. Buchanan? You haven't called me that since you were a kid. I prefer Wes."

"Wes," Max corrected as he made his way across the yard. "I was looking for Caro, but I guess she isn't back yet."

"Yeah, it's apparently a late girls' night. She's usually home before nine." He paused, his eyes narrowing on Max before he said, "I haven't really gotten to talk to you since you've been back in town. You want to come in and have a beer . . . or a glass of whiskey?"

"Whiskey would be great."

"Perfect," Wes said as he held the screen door open.

The second Max walked inside, the scurrying of many canine feet across the tile floor greeted his ears. Leia, followed closely by Domino, and then Frankie with her little legs. The dogs surrounded him.

"Hello," he told them all as he petted each in turn.

"You'd think I didn't give them any attention. We've all been lying on the sofa watching baseball for the last hour," Wes said as he went to wash his hands.

"Who's playing?"

"Braves versus the Sox. Sox are up by two runs. Want to watch?"

"Yeah." Max nodded. He was usually pretty good about following Boston's season, but as Ava wasn't a huge baseball fan, he hadn't subjected her to watching games.

"Good, I'll get the drinks while you give them all a treat. They're in the Wookiee cookie jar." He pointed over to the shelf. "Frankie gets one broken in half. And try to get them to sit."

"A Wookiee cookie jar. Very clever." Wes had always loved Star Wars. He'd been the one to introduce the franchise to Max when he was a kid. He and Caro used to pretend the treehouse at his grandparents was the *Millennium Falcon*. He was always Han, and she was always Leia . . . but a Jedi version of Leia.

"Caro got it for me for Father's Day a couple of years ago."

"She was always the best gift giver." Max pulled the head off the Wookiee and grabbed a handful of treats. "Sit," he told the dogs as he turned around.

Leia was already sitting, watching Max intently. Domino was doing a weird little fidgety dance, sitting down for a second before standing back up. And Frankie, well, she'd rolled onto her back as usual.

"I guess that will have to do." Wes laughed.

Once the dogs had all run off with their treats, Wes handed Max a short glass with a generous two fingers of the amber liquid.

"To your good health." Max held his glass in the air.

"May we drink one together in ten years' time, and a few in between," Wes said as he clinked his glass to Max's before they both took a sip. "It's good to see you again, son." He clapped his free hand on Max's shoulder.

Wes had always called Max son. *Always.* He'd claimed Max more than his stepfather ever had.

"You too, Wes." Max nodded, a tightness in his chest as they headed to the living room.

* * *

IT WAS AFTER ten when Caro and Lucy pulled into their father's driveway and saw the house still lit up from the inside.

"I guess it's a good game if he's up this late," Lucy said as they got out of the car and headed up the path to the door.

They kicked off their shoes in the mudroom, hanging up their coats and dropping their purses on the counter as they headed through the kitchen. Caro was just on the threshold of the hallway when she heard a voice that was not her father's.

Max.

"Come on. Come on! *Come on!*" Another second, and he yelled. *"Home run!"*

Caro stopped, her heart pounding in her chest as she grabbed Lucy's arm. She turned to her sister, her eyes going wide. Lucy was wearing her own surprised expression, but a moment later it turned sly.

"Looks like he wants another round," she whispered.

"You're the worst."

"I'm the best, and you know it," she said before she pulled her arm from Caro's grasp and walked into the living room. "Max! What are *you* doing here?" There was absolutely nothing subtle in her question.

Caro took a deep breath, letting it out in a rush before following Lucy. The sight that greeted her made her already-pounding heart stutter before picking up speed again.

Her father was sitting on the reclining leather sofa with his feet propped up. Leia was stretched out next to him with her head in his lap, Estee lying on the headrest above him. Max was on the love seat, Frankie in his lap, while a snoring Domino was asleep next to him. None of the animals had moved when Caro and Lucy walked in; the only one who had even opened an eye was Leia. But she closed it again a second later and went back to sleep.

"Hi." Max stood up, setting Frankie back down on the sofa. His blue eyes focused on her with such intensity that there was no doubt in her mind as to *exactly* why he was there.

"I found him outside a little while ago. We've been watching baseball and drinking whiskey," Wes said as he held his almost-empty glass in the air.

"How's the game going?" Lucy asked as she made her way over to the sofa and took Max's seat, putting Frankie in her lap. The dog spun around twice before settling back down.

"Very good. They're tied and in their second extra inning."

"Excellent. I'll stay up and watch with you, since Max is about to leave. Aren't you, Max?" She grinned up at him with knowing eyes.

"I know it's late, but I was hoping we could talk." He hadn't taken his eyes off Caro since she'd walked into the room.

"Yeah." Lucy made a shooing motion. "Go talk."

"I need to get Frankie and Domino first," Caro said, looking at the dogs. Frankie was already asleep again, and Domino hadn't moved at all. It sounded like she was just snoring louder.

"I got them tonight. Don't worry," Lucy said, waving her hand again. "Now begone, the both of you." She winked at Max.

There was a light flush already creeping into Caro's cheeks, both from the intense way Max was looking at her and the implication of Lucy's offer to take the dogs . . . all night.

Max grabbed the short glass from the side table before he crossed over to her. "Hey, you," he said again so only she could hear.

Why did those two little words have her stomach doing somersaults?

"Hey." She didn't know why she did it, but she held out her hand, reaching for him across the couple of feet between them.

He didn't even hesitate to grab it.

Caro took a step back, heading for the kitchen, but she turned when her father called out.

"Pumpkin? Tell Lilah I'll give her twenty bucks when I see her on Thursday. Since she won the bet and all. Right down to the day and everything."

Caro had no doubt the heat in her cheeks was a full-on red now.

"Thanks for that, Dad."

"Anytime." He grinned.

Caro glanced at Max, his eyebrows raised high.

"I'll tell you in a second." She shook her head as she pulled his hand, leading him out of the room.

She turned to him in the kitchen, and he brought the glass of whiskey to his mouth, taking a fairly big sip before holding it out to her. Caro took it, downing the last of the amber liquid.

It warmed her throat and belly as she set the glass in the sink. They quickly put their shoes on and then she was grabbing his hand again and pulling him out the door.

"Okay? What was that?"

"My family made a bet on us."

"Having sex?" A horrified laugh escaped his lips.

"I believe the wording was somewhere along the lines of *When our past becomes the present*, but essentially."

"And Lilah got it down to the day?" he asked, sounding impressed.

"She did indeed."

"So, she's *still* weirdly psychic. Good to know."

"You have no idea." Caro shook her head.

They'd just gotten to the top of the stairs, and she let go of his hand. Something in the air shifted around them as she fumbled with her keys, a process made more difficult as Max crowded in behind her, his palms on her hips and his face incredibly close to her neck.

"I haven't stopped thinking about you since you left," he whispered, his lips brushing across her skin. And then he did the thing, the thing that had always driven her out of her mind, he ran his nose along the slope of her neck. Her knees almost buckled.

Caro finally got the key in the hole, twisting it in the lock before she turned in Max's arms. Her back was against the door as she looked at him, his mouth mere inches from hers.

"I haven't stopped thinking about you either." She grabbed the front of his shirt, pulling him to her.

There was nothing subtle in the kiss, no buildup at all. The second his mouth was on hers, it was all-consuming. He groaned as his tongue found hers, and Caro's arms wrapped around his shoulders, trying to pull herself higher to change the angle, to deepen the kiss.

To deepen everything.

It's not love, it's not love, it's not love. It's just lust. Mind-bending, knee-weakening lust.

"I need you inside of me." She'd barely gotten the words out before Max was reaching behind her, finding the handle, and pushing the door open.

He held her to him as he walked her backward into the house and closed the door. They barely broke the kiss as they kicked off their shoes and Caro dropped her purse on the coffee table.

She'd left a small lamp on in the living room, enough for the soft glow to give a little light in the loft. Enough for them to make their way through the space without tripping on anything.

They wasted absolutely zero time divesting each other of their clothes. His T-shirt hit the ground, followed by her shorts. Max pulled Caro's shirt off, her hands only leaving the front of his pants long enough for him to get the fabric off her arms and over her head. The second he had her bra off, his head dropped to her breasts, sucking a nipple into his mouth before dragging his teeth across the sensitive flesh. He backed her up until she hit the wall, and then he was kneeling in front of her.

Max looked up at her, the heat in his blue eyes so intense she was surprised her legs didn't melt right out from beneath her.

"I need to taste you again." His fingers hooked in the sides of her panties—this time light pink lace—and he pulled them down. He lifted one of her legs up—her thigh resting on his shoulder as he spread her—and then devoured her.

"Max." Caro's head fell back against the wall, a moan filling the air around them as her fingers dove into his hair. She held him to her, her nails raking against his scalp.

It took him *very* little time to get the orgasm building, and she was a goner when he slid two fingers inside of her. He didn't stop, riding out every last crest and wave, slowly bringing her back down.

Her leg was still over his shoulder when she finally caught her breath enough to open her eyes. The smile on his mouth was so satisfied she thought she might come again. He kissed the inside of her thigh before pulling it from his shoulder, setting her foot back on the floor, and standing up.

"I plan on making you do that many, *many* times," he said before his mouth covered hers and he was pulling her down onto the bed. He fell onto his back, taking the impact with her sprawled across his chest.

"This feels familiar." Caro grinned.

"Except this time, you didn't fall on me from the top of a ladder."

She ran her fingers across his jaw, the tips rasping across the scruff of his beard. "Clearly it was a sign."

More signs. So many of them.

"Of what?"

"That we were going to end up here eventually."

"Apparently we were." He smiled as he palmed the back of her head, his fingers sliding into her hair before he kissed her again. They were long, slow kisses as his other hand moved up and down her back in lazy, mind-melting strokes. She started to move against him, unable to help herself. Max flexed his hips up, his erection pressing into her. "Caro, I want you to ride me."

She smiled against his mouth, her legs moving so she could straddle him. She braced herself against his chest as she sat up, settling herself right on his cock. It was straining through the fabric of his boxer briefs.

"Do you? What if I want to do a little exploring first? You've gotten your turn."

He moved his arms up, his hands going behind his head, every muscle in his biceps flexing with the movement. "Explore away."

"Some of these are new." She traced over the ridges and dips on his pecs and arms.

"Some are." He nodded, his eyes tracking her slow progress.

"Some of these are too." She moved to his stomach, walking her fingers down his abs one by one. "I wouldn't have thought you'd have a lot of free time to work out, being Mr. Bigshot and all."

"I *don't* have a lot of free time." He pulled in an uneven breath, his nostrils flaring. "But I run."

"That you do." She grinned, sitting back a little as she toyed with the elastic of his boxer briefs. He went for a run every morning, and he always took a couple of laps in front of wherever she was working that day. She somehow always caught him just as he ran by the window.

"I also have a weight-lifting bench in my apartment and an exercise bike in my office at work."

She hooked her fingers in the fabric and pulled down. Max's cock sprang free, his breathing just a little more uneven as he continued to watch her. His Adam's apple bobbed as he swallowed hard.

"Sounds exhausting." She ran a finger from the base to the tip, his entire body shuddering beneath her.

"Yes, well— Jesus Christ, Caro!" Max groaned as his body arched off the bed. Apparently, he hadn't been ready for her to lean down and wrap her mouth around him.

He'd made her fall apart mere minutes ago, and she wanted to return the favor. She took him deeper into her mouth, before slowly— ever so slowly—dragging her tongue up and swirling it over the broad head.

Out of the corner of her eye, she saw his hands fisting in the blanket, his chest heaving for breath. She was only able to get in a few more strokes before he was pulling her away from him. By the look in his eyes, she knew he'd been on the verge. And as much as she wanted the satisfaction of making him come apart with her mouth, she needed him inside of her.

"Shit." He shook his head, the desperation in his expression clear. "I didn't bring any condoms. *Please*, tell me you have some."

"I don't." She shook her head.

Panic filled Max's eyes, and a wicked smile pulled her lips up.

"Or I didn't until a couple of hours ago." Caro gave Max another long stroke with her hand—his nostrils flaring again as he pulled a sharp breath into his lungs—before she got out of bed. "Apparently Lilah knows all." She grabbed the box from her purse, holding it up in the air.

Max had propped himself up on his elbows, watching her, and his face filled with relief as he saw the box of condoms.

"God bless Lilah and her weird psychic powers. I'm going to have to thank her later. Many, *many* times."

Caro laughed as she grabbed one, setting the rest of the box on the nightstand.

"Does she like flowers or chocolate?" he asked as he pulled his boxers the rest of the way down his legs, kicking them off the side of the bed.

"Both." She crawled on top of him again and made very quick work with the condom.

"Done." But that was the last word he got out as she palmed his cock, lining him up with her entrance, and slowly slid down. He held on to her thighs, his fingers pressing in hard.

"How do you want this, Max?" She braced herself on his chest as she started to move over him. "Slow and steady?" She raised her eyebrows. "Or fast and rough?"

He grinned, one of his hands leaving her hip and moving up. His fingers slid into her hair as he pulled her mouth to his. "Slow and steady," he breathed against her lips before kissing her, his tongue finding hers, moving against it in the same leisurely, unhurried pace as their bodies.

He kissed her as if they had all night . . .

Because they did.

* * *

SOFT MORNING SUNSHINE was coming through the windows when Max opened his eyes that morning. For just a second, he thought he was dreaming, because it was a dream he'd had more times than he could count over the last fourteen years.

He was in bed with Caro, her naked body pressed up against his. She was still asleep, her head on his chest and her arm wrapped around his waist.

Except he wasn't dreaming. This was real. *She* was real. Her breath on his skin was real. The warmth of her. The weight of her. The lemon scent that surrounded him.

He smiled, a contentedness he hadn't felt in a long time settling over him. He hadn't felt this way since the last time he'd been in this little loft apartment.

It seemed smaller now, not that it had ever been very large. It wasn't even four hundred square feet. Hell, his apartment in Manhattan was about four times bigger. The entirety of this place could fit into his bedroom alone. Well, maybe the bedroom *and* bathroom.

But the smallness of the loft didn't make him feel claustrophobic. It was cozy . . . comforting . . . safe. A number of things were different about the space, but for him, it still felt familiar.

Maybe because it still felt like Caro.

The floral rug in the living room was brighter than the one that had been there before. The squishy dark teal sofa was more comfortable than the old mustard yellow one she'd had back in the day. It was covered in fluffy pillows and soft throws. An assortment of plants were set up everywhere, most of them occupying a window-sill or hanging close by. There were way more art pieces and pho-tographs covering the walls, which were the same soft yellow he'd helped her paint all those years ago. The blond hardwood floors were a little bit more scratched and worn than before, but familiar all the same.

The queen bed was no longer on low legs but propped up on a platform of drawers that pulled out from both sides, and it had a new tufted, royal blue velvet headboard. The nightstands were now a matching set, and the old dresser in the corner had been sanded and repainted.

Her tiny kitchen was still all black and white, except for the pops of turquoise that had been added here and there. The bath-room was the biggest change, as it had been completely gutted and remodeled, an antique white tub *just* fitting in against the back wall. Caro had always loved her baths.

The space felt lived in, a much warmer place to be than his cold, sterile apartment. In the four years that he'd lived there, it had never felt like home. Nor had the apartment he'd had before that . . . or the one before that . . . or the one before that. Maybe that was why Max had no qualms about leaving for England.

Well, he'd *had* no qualms about leaving New York for England . . .

His arms tightened around Caro, pulling her closer to him. She stirred against his chest, and he looked down, watching her eyes slowly blink open.

"Morning." He smiled, running his fingers down the side of her face and tracing her cheek.

"Morning." Her voice was soft and husky. "What time is it?"

"Almost eight."

"What time did we even go to bed last night?" She stretched, her body moving against his as her hand slid over his abdomen.

"After two."

"Less than six hours of sleep." She groaned, burying her face in his chest. "It's going to be a long day." There would no doubt be some extensive project at Ava's. But when they were done with that, Caro was going to have to pull a shift at Quigley's.

"I'm sorry." He kissed the top of her head. "We should've stopped after that second round last night." When he'd pulled her ankles over his shoulders.

She looked back up at him, her brows furrowed and her lips in a pout. "No, we shouldn't have. I regret nothing." Her mouth transformed into a wicked smile, and her hand moved farther down his abs, the sheet twitching. "In fact, I think we should try round three again," she whispered in his ear before she bit down on his earlobe. "See if we can perfect it."

Max didn't even hesitate. He had Caro facedown on the mattress, pulling her hips up in the air in a matter of seconds. She was laughing, no doubt because of how fast he'd moved. But her laughter turned to moans as he slid deep inside of her again.

* * *

It was 9:56 when Caro and Max opened Ava's front door, each carrying two cups of coffee from Dancing Donkey. There were voices and clattering pans coming from the kitchen. Lucy was already here, having texted that morning to say she was bringing Frankie and Domino over.

Max turned to Caro, his eyebrows lifted. "United front?"

"If we divide, they conquer."

"Then let's go," he said before he leaned down, pressing a kiss to the top of her head. It was such a small gesture, and yet it sent a wave of pleasure throughout her body.

When they walked into the kitchen, they found Ava and Lucy already working, the center island covered in baking supplies: flour, sugar, butter, eggs, heavy cream, and about a dozen other ingredients.

"Good morning." Caro set the coffees down before scooping up Frankie. The dog had practically sprinted over the second they'd crossed the threshold. She'd left Beau and Domino in the middle of a tug-of-war over a stuffed giraffe.

"Good morning to you too," Ava said, looking both Caro and Max over.

"How was she last night?" Caro asked Lucy as she pressed a kiss to Frankie's soft little head. The dog returned the gesture by licking her in the face.

Caro had very much enjoyed her companion in bed, but last night was the first since she'd found Frankie that the dog hadn't slept with her. She'd missed the pup being burrowed next to her.

"The best. She just snuggled up with Estee and passed out."

"She does love to snuggle." Max handed Ava her chai latte before scratching Frankie under the chin. The dog wiggled in Caro's arms, clearly wanting to give Max some love as well. He set his own coffee on the counter as Caro passed the dog over. He pulled her in to his chest, getting a good lick on the beard.

"You guys got an early start," Max said as he looked over the ingredients on the counter.

"Yes, well, not all of us had late nights." Lucy waggled her eyebrows.

"O-kay." Caro frowned at her sister. "Do you want the coffee I brought you or not?"

"I want it."

"Then no harassment," Caro said, sliding the cup across the counter.

"I'll try." Lucy grabbed her coffee.

Ava was glancing between Max and Caro, a smirk on her face. But she mercifully didn't say anything. "Well, since you won our little bet about not working that first week and using Martin's flip phone, I figured it was time I make you that pineapple coconut whipped dream cake."

"I told you I would win."

"I should've known better." She shook her head. "You don't usually back down from a challenge. It's that stubborn streak that you have. I don't know where you got it."

Lucy inhaled her coffee, choking on it.

Ava looked over at her. "What?"

"Nothing." She bit her bottom lip, trying so hard to hide her smile. Everyone in that room knew *exactly* where Max had gotten his stubborn streak.

"Uh-huh." Ava's eyes narrowed on Lucy for just a second before she turned her overly assessing gaze back to Max and Caro. "You look less . . . agitated this morning."

There it was.

Lucy choked on her coffee again.

"All right, everyone is fully aware that Caro and I spent the night together. And we aren't discussing it beyond that."

"Okay," Lucy and Ava said in unison, but by the mischievous looks on both of their faces, Caro knew that Max's little line in the sand was going to be ignored.

Judging by the frown on Max's face, he knew it too. "Anyways, what's today's project?"

"Well, Lucy and I have got this under control, though we're making two, so we're going to be busy for a bit."

"Two?" Max asked.

Ava pointed a measuring cup at him. "They aren't both for you. You just get the one, and everyone else has to share one."

"Sounds fair to me." He grinned.

"Since you two are getting along so well now"—Ava waved the measuring cup, this time at the two of them—"I figured you and Caro could work in the attic together. Maybe go through those games you showed her yesterday. We'll join you when we're done here."

Caro let out an awkward little cough, nodding. "Sounds good." She turned to Max, who was staring at his grandmother like he had no idea what to do with her.

No one did.

He sighed, setting Frankie down on the ground. She scampered back over to Beau and Domino, who were now wrestling, the giraffe forgotten. Beau let Frankie into the mix, being gentler with her as she jumped on him.

"You going to keep an eye on Frankie for me?" Caro asked Beau.

His answer was to lick Frankie in the face.

"Let's go." Caro grabbed Max's wrist and pulled him from the kitchen. She turned to him as the door swung shut behind them. "That wasn't too bad."

"Yes, well, I think she's waiting for when we least expect it to pounce with the interrogation."

He kissed her before they headed down the hallway. As they passed the sitting room, Caro's eyes caught on Martin's office. "Hey." She grabbed Max's wrist again. "I . . . I meant to ask about the video yesterday. The one of my mom. We got a little sidetracked before I could."

"Just a little."

"Are there more?"

"Yeah." He nodded. "I converted a lot of them yesterday. I'm sure there are more in that box, though."

"Do you think you could copy the ones you have onto a disc? I want to show my family. I know they'd like to see her too."

"Come on, let's set it up before we go upstairs." He grabbed her hand, their fingers twining together as he led her into the room.

Her hand in his had caused a wave of pleasure to run through her body. But it was nothing compared to the practical tsunami when he sat down in the leather chair and pulled her into his lap, his arms coming around her as he reached for the mouse and keyboard.

When the computer lit up, he typed in the password, and a document filled the screen.

The Kincaid.

"Is this your proposal?" She hadn't asked him about it since their afternoon together the previous week.

"No." He shook his head, his chin brushing against her shoulder. "This is . . . something else."

She looked over at him, their faces so close together. "What do you mean, something else?"

"These are *my* ideas for the remodel. What I would do."

"Can I see it?" She didn't try to hide the excitement in her eyes.

"Yeah. It's not finished, though."

"That's okay." She turned to the screen as he started clicking through it. Blueprints of the current building popped up, before being replaced by one with a different design.

"See, stairs would go here." He trailed his nose up the slope of her neck until his mouth was at her ear, his voice vibrating across her skin as he pointed to the screen. "They'd lead up to the next level and the first floor of rooms. And the top floor"—his finger moved up and to the right—"would be where the bar and restaurant would go. You'd get a view of the city, and the mountains beyond."

He explained his ideas on each slide, his lips brushing against her ear the whole time. She shifted in his lap, turning so she could get a better look at his face.

"You got all of that from the blueprints?"

"Well, and the walkthrough I went on with the broker last week."

"Why didn't you tell me you went on a walkthrough?" She playfully pushed on his shoulder.

"I don't know. Maybe because whenever I'm around you, I get distracted by your mouth."

"Oh, is that it?" She rolled her eyes but grinned at him.

"Yeah." He tipped her chin up and kissed her. "That's it."

It was a minute before they pulled apart and she pointed toward the screen again. "You've done a lot of work on that."

"Yeah, it's been a good way to pass the time when Ava takes her afternoon naps or when she goes to bed and I'm not tired yet."

"So," she said slowly, a bubble of hope that he might be staying in Cruickshank longer filling her chest. "You're pursuing this? Your company might buy the building? Turn it into a hotel?"

He nodded. "My boss likes what I've sent to her so far. So I think so."

"You've already talked to your boss about it?"

"Yeah, she thought it had a lot of potential, but she wants to see more."

"More than that?" She gestured to the screen behind her.

He hesitated for just a moment before he shook his head. "No one is going to see that."

"I don't understand."

"I only find the buildings, Caro. Typically, I'm working for a specific client, and once they buy it, they take over. Or if it's something that I've found on my own, Bergen and Hennings buys it and usually sells it for a pretty high profit margin. I have nothing to do with the remodels."

And just like that, the bubble of hope in her chest popped. His words might as well have been a tiny pin through her heart. She'd thought maybe, just maybe, she could get more time with him before he moved to London. Or maybe he'd have to visit again sometime soon. It took *everything* in her to keep her disappointment under control. "So, all of these ideas you have?" She gestured at the screen. "They won't happen?"

"No." He shook his head, studying her face. "They won't."

"Then why put so much work into that?"

"Every time I find a building, I always have ideas of what *I* would do if given the chance. And, I don't know, I was doing it for me. I wanted to put my ideas onto paper, so to speak."

He shrugged like it was no big deal, except she felt like it was.

"What's that look?"

"It just doesn't sound easy, seeing potential in something, then handing it over to someone else. Walking away."

"It's never easy to walk away." He shook his head, his blue eyes going just a little bit sad. And she knew he wasn't just talking about the job anymore. "It's going to be harder this time than it usually is. I'm more attached."

She couldn't say anything, her throat constricting painfully. Instead, she nodded slowly.

"Caro?" His voice was so soft.

She cleared her throat, turning back to the computer. She couldn't look at the expression on his face any longer. "Let's copy those videos of my mom." She somehow kept her voice even.

She'd known from the very beginning that he wasn't staying. And she'd known yesterday when they'd fallen into bed together. Sex or no, nothing had changed.

But then why, *why*, did it feel like something had? That there'd been a shift? That maybe there was a possibility for that something *more* that she'd been trying so hard not to think about.

Maybe she was the only one who felt different.

It's not love, she reminded herself for what felt like the hundredth time. *Not anymore.*

Chapter Sixteen

One That I Want

Ava and Lucy didn't join Max and Caro in the attic until after lunch.

He wanted that time alone with Caro, craved it, but he knew he was just making it harder for himself. For her. For them.

He would've needed to be blind to miss that moment in the office, the hope that had flared in her eyes before he'd told her the reality, that he wouldn't have anything to do with the Kincaid project if it was bought.

And it appeared that neither of them wanted to dwell in that truth, as they both chose to ignore it while they worked together in the attic. The hours were full of conversation as each filled the other in on the last fourteen years.

She told him about finishing her degree at the college in Asheville, the one she was only supposed to go to for a year before joining him . . . though neither of them brought up that part. She told him about her nephews and niece, and how happy she'd been to see her best friend settled down with her brother. She talked a lot about

Martin and Ava. He had his own memories with them over those years, but he'd missed out on a lot, and it was bittersweet.

Max told Caro about graduating from Chapel Hill. About getting into Columbia and moving back to New York, about how the city had felt different after his mother and stepfather's home had ceased to become his in every way.

Not that it had ever really felt like home—that had always been the Victorian house in Cruickshank.

He told her about his first job, how he'd climbed the ranks before getting recruited to Bergen and Hennings. How he'd made his own space in the company, made himself an asset. She asked about his promotion, but neither of them discussed London. In fact, they hadn't brought up the city at all. Max didn't want to talk about that summer she was supposed to join him there, or the semester he'd spent in grad school. There was too much baggage, and he didn't want to unpack it.

And, apparently, neither did she.

He chose not to overanalyze exactly why. Instead, he kissed Caro before she and Lucy left that afternoon, promising to see her later that night at Quigley's.

* * *

MAX SHOWED UP at the bar a little after nine. Theo and Oscar joined him for a beer before they headed out around eleven, but he stayed until twelve, when Gavin, Lilah, and Lucy shooed him and Caro out the door, saying they had the last hour covered. When they got back to her dad's house, they collected Frankie and Domino before heading for the loft.

Max had Caro naked and against the wall within minutes, and both collapsed onto the sofa afterward to catch their breath. He'd sent half of his cake home with Caro that afternoon, and they enjoyed a rather large slice in her bed, with Caro wearing Max's shirt as she straddled him, feeding both of them bites.

It was a struggle to get out of bed on Wednesday morning, not because they were tired, but because they couldn't let go of each other. Eventually, Max and Frankie went back to Ava's for breakfast while Caro headed to work at Dancing Donkey with Domino. Around two, Max and Frankie showed up at the shop, his laptop in a bag over his shoulder.

"Hey, you," Caro said as she rounded the corner to give him a kiss. "I didn't know I'd be seeing you this afternoon."

"I thought I'd come work and get a little hit of caffeine."

"Or a little hit of Caro?" Sasha asked as she wiped down the espresso machine.

"Definitely the latter." Lorraine looked over from where she was refilling the coffee maker.

Caro rolled her eyes, but she didn't hide her own smile as she gave him another kiss. She was happy he'd come to see her, which in turn made him happy.

You're just getting in deeper and deeper, man.

"Yes, well, seeing Caro was the main draw, but Ava and Beau were trying to take a nap, and Frankie refused to let them sleep."

"That sounds about right," Caro said as she scooped the dog out of his arms, pulling her close and pressing a kiss to her head.

Max could tell that Caro was getting more and more attached to Frankie, just as Frankie was getting attached to Caro.

The dog had become Caro's shadow. She might like to go off and play—especially when there were other dogs around—but she always had to know *exactly* where Caro was at all times. And if she didn't, she'd walk around whining until she found her.

She'd told him that she didn't typically sleep with her fosters, but Frankie slept next to them every night. Well, next to Caro, specifically. The dog was either on the pillow by Caro's head or curled up next to her stomach, always wrapped up in the pink blanket that he'd bought.

He would've felt bad for Domino, but she very much liked to sprawl out on her own bed on the floor, much like she was doing right now on the other side of the pen with all the other fosters.

Tomorrow would be two weeks from when they'd found Frankie, which meant that the rescue would need to list her as an adoptable dog.

Caro hadn't brought up the topic of keeping Frankie, and if she was anything like she used to be, he knew she'd have to come to the conclusion of keeping the dog all on her own. She'd always been that way. He worried that her fear of being hurt again was getting in the way of her happiness. He understood that better than anyone . . . mainly because he had the exact same fucking problem.

"Do you want the usual?" Sasha asked him.

"Nah, I think a cold brew, and with the hazelnut please."

"Got it." She nodded.

"I thought Ava banned you from working?" Lorraine asked as he set up a workstation near one of the windows.

"She didn't ban me." Max shook his head. "She wanted me to learn to relax a little. Which I have. But she actually approves of this project."

"Oh, really?" Lorraine asked.

He told them about the Kincaid factory, and Sasha's eyebrows rose. "That would be a great property for a hotel. You're going to need to talk to the Cruickshank City Council."

"I *am* talking to them at Tuesday's meeting. So the proposal needs to be done by then."

"You are?" Caro looked over at him, her face neutral, impassive.

"I talked to Clifford Cally this morning. He gave me the six thirty time slot."

"Good, I'm sure you'll kill it." She'd been excited to hear about the Kincaid before, but not after their conversation yesterday.

She was holding back, and he hated it. But there was nothing for him to do. This couldn't be permanent.

It was just one last summer . . .

Lorraine was looking between him and Caro, and he knew she was studying them, trying to figure out what was going on. Apparently, she couldn't figure it out—couldn't figure them out—so she moved her focus just to Caro, who was still holding Frankie.

"So, what are we doing with this dog?" she asked, clearly wanting to settle something that afternoon.

"What do you mean?" Caro looked up.

Lorraine shook her head, giving Caro a somewhat pitying smile. "Honey, you know what tomorrow is just as much as we all do." She waved her hand around to indicate Max and Sasha. "Are we keeping Frankie, or what?"

We. It made Max smile. That's how everything was with them, a group effort. Family by choice. And if Caro kept Frankie, Frankie would be part of that family.

Caro bit at the corner of her lip before letting it go, her mouth forming a small smile. "I don't think I can give her up."

"Thank God, you finally figured it out." Sasha sounded beyond exasperated. "Welcome to two weeks ago."

"Shut up." Caro shook her head before she pressed another kiss between Frankie's ears. "You're mine," she whispered to the dog. "You're home now. You're not going anywhere."

She'd figured it out, figured out that she couldn't let go of the dog. Relief washed through him, but it was short-lived. As he watched her, that familiar tightness started to take over his chest, the tightness that happened whenever he thought about the fact that he wasn't staying.

It had never been part of the plan, but none of this stuff with Caro had been part of the plan. Not wanting to be around her all the time. Not sleeping with her. Not falling in love with her again . . .

No, no, it wasn't love. He'd be an idiot to fall in love with Caro again . . . but, he'd never been very smart when it came to her.

* * *

THE NEXT FEW days went by in a flash, May quickly turning into June. Max found himself staying at Caro's loft every night. He'd only been in Cruickshank for three weeks, not even a whole month, and everything had changed so much.

Though he might not be sleeping at Ava's, he made a point to spend as much time with her as before. He was always back at her place for breakfast, and he spent pretty much every day doing whatever task she assigned him. Caro showed up more often than her usual Tuesdays and Fridays, popping in for lunch or dinner between her many jobs.

Lucy was coming over regularly too, helping wherever she could. Between the four of them, they made a lot of progress on the house;

the attic was now cleared of everything that needed to be thrown away or donated.

It had been the biggest beast to tackle, and they'd done it.

When he wasn't working on a new project with Ava—and when he couldn't be with Caro—he continued his proposal for the Kincaid project, both the official one and the unofficial.

He'd had a good vibe after his meeting with the city council on Tuesday, especially with Caro and Ava sitting in the front row of the town hall.

There was absolutely nothing neutral about Caro's expression this time. Both she and Ava beamed at him throughout his whole pitch. Max knew he was good at his job—he'd never faltered in his confidence there—but there was something about the pride in their eyes that made him feel some sort of way that he wasn't used to.

Maybe because his mother and stepfather had never looked at him that way. Not once. Not ever.

As he presented the proposal, it became clear to him—in a way that was much more obvious than he'd even realized—just how attached to Cruickshank he really was. To the people. To Ava. To Caro. To the friends he'd never forgotten over the last fourteen years.

There was no answer from the council when they left that night. The seven members wanted to take a few days to look things over, do their own research, come back with any issues they might have.

But answer or no, everyone gathered at Quigley's that night to cheer his success. Jeremy, Oscar, Theo, Sasha, Wes, and even Lorraine and Juliet stopped by. Lucy, Gavin, and Lilah were all working, pushing drinks across the counter as every new person showed up. They all wanted to celebrate what he was trying to do, celebrate *him*.

It made Max feel like he was part of a community again. Part of Cruickshank, with these people he'd grown up with, these people he cared about. It made him feel like he was part of *Caro's* life again, like he was *home*. A feeling that became even more real when she invited him and Ava to join their family dinner night on Thursday.

Max immediately got suckered into coloring with Emilia. But how was he supposed to say no when she looked up at him with those blue eyes? Eyes that were *so* much like Rachel's.

"I didn't know you were this good with kids," Ava whispered as she passed him a purple crayon so he could color his dragon.

"I didn't either." He shook his head.

"I'm pretty sure she has a crush on him," Lilah said just loud enough for Max to hear. "I bet she likes his beard."

"Well, she can just get in line." Caro looked over at him, giving him a wicked grin.

He'd stopped shaving because he was on vacation . . . and he'd been a little inspired when he'd seen that first video of Martin and his father, both sporting beards of their own. He hadn't expected the added benefit of Caro's appreciation. She'd told him just how big a fan she was, especially when she felt it brushing against the insides of her thighs.

"Are you Aunt Caro's boyfriend again?" Emilia asked Max, those blue, blue eyes focused on him. God, why did it feel like *Rachel* was the one who was asking him that question and not the three-year-old in front of him?

The kitchen went silent around them. Well, silent except for the pop and sizzle of the fish Wes was frying in the cast-iron skillet.

"Yeah," Lucy asked, smirking at Max. "What are you now?"

"We're, um . . ." He turned to Caro for help, but her face had gone neutral, not giving a thing away. Either because she didn't want him to know what she was thinking or she didn't know herself.

"Friends," Max finally said to Emilia. "Your aunt Caro and I are friends."

Wasn't that what Ava had wanted them to be? The problem was, it wasn't true. Not even friends with benefits would've been an accurate description. Whatever this was, it was more than friendship. It always had been, but it had morphed over the last week and a half. Gotten even *more* complicated. What the *more* was, he didn't know.

Actually, that was a lie too. He knew exactly what it was, even if he refused to admit it to himself. No matter how much he'd tried not to open his heart back up to her, he hadn't been able to stop it from happening. So now he was just living in denial.

Denial of his feelings. Denial of the future. And as the two of them hadn't discussed anything—apparently neither of them wanted to broach the subject—he'd thought he'd be able to stay in that denial and continue on with whatever this *not* friendship was. But he'd been wrong. So, very, *very* wrong. And he wasn't the only one who knew it either.

"No, you're not." Matthew looked up from his own coloring book, frowning. His expression clearly said that Max wasn't fooling anyone. "We all saw you two kissing outside, and friends don't kiss."

How old was this kid again? Six?

Max glanced at Lilah, and she must've seen the desperation in his eyes and taken pity on him. "Sometimes relationships are complicated, Matthew. Now drop it."

The stern look on Lilah's face was one that brooked no argument. Matthew frowned at his mother before he returned to coloring his pirate ship.

Thank you, Max mouthed to her.

"You're welcome. And, Max, along with flowers and chocolate, I also enjoy shoes."

"Noted."

Max had indeed thanked Lilah for that box of condoms. He'd sent her an extra-large bouquet of flowers, along with chocolates shipped from his favorite shop in New York. He'd gotten some for Caro too, though it ended up being a present for both of them the night she'd opened the box.

God, every night with her was incredible.

His eyes moved to her, where she was leaning back against the counter, laughing at something Lilah had just whispered in her ear. When she glanced over at him, that mischievous glint was back in her eyes, promising another unforgettable evening.

He found himself imagining a lifetime of nights with her. It was a dangerous fantasy, for his head . . . and his heart. But what if it could all become a reality? What if he could have all the nights? Days? Weeks? Months? Years? What if she wanted that too? What if they both let every guard down? Let the other one in without reservations?

Could he do it? Could he try?

Would he survive it if it didn't work out again?

When he looked back to the table, he found Ava watching him, those ever-assessing eyes studying him.

"What?" he asked as he reached for the green crayon.

"Oh, nothing." She smiled, shaking her head.

And she wasn't the only one who was watching him that night. Jeremy had an eye on him for most of the evening. Hell, he'd been paying close attention for weeks now. After dinner, Jeremy pulled Max outside to watch the kids. They stood on the sidewalk enjoying their beers as Matthew, Christopher, and Emilia rode their bikes up and down the driveway.

"So, you and Caro are *friends*, huh?"

Max looked over at him, even more unsure of what to say to Jeremy than to Emilia. "I don't know what we are." He shook his head.

"Look." Jeremy affectionately slapped his hand down on Max's shoulder, shaking it a little. "It's not that I want to ask you what your intentions are with my sister, but . . . I mean . . . What *are* your intentions? Are you guys just, like, fooling around for the summer?"

"When it comes to Caro, *fooling around* has never been in my vocabulary."

"I didn't think so." Jeremy dropped his hand. "I know that you two broke up after our mom died, and her death for sure changed Caro. It changed all of us. But losing you was a different loss for her. She's never been the same, Max."

"What do you mean?"

"Your relationship was always so . . . *intense*, even from the start. Like worlds colliding or something. God, I remember that first summer, and when you had to leave, she cried for days. You would've thought you'd died and were never coming back. And she was like that every year. This deep sadness that would linger around her for months and months until you came back. And that's how it's felt for the last fourteen years. Well, until the last few weeks when the two of you became *friends* again." Jeremy smirked as he emphasized the word.

Max laughed, shaking his head.

"You know, being friends isn't a bad thing. My wife is my best friend, but she's also so much more. And I think that might be the case with you and Caro. But what do I know?" He shrugged before taking a sip of his beer.

"It would appear much more than me, man." Max sighed.

"Well." Jeremy slapped him on the back again. "You'll figure it out. Just try not to hurt each other in the process."

"I won't," Max promised. He never wanted to hurt her again. But was that even possible at this point? When they were in this deep?

When are you going to see it, Max? Martin's voice asked in his head. *When are you going to* finally *see the truth? See what this really is? When are you going to admit how you really feel?*

He didn't know, but God, he hoped it wouldn't be too late when he figured it out.

* * *

Sunday was Ava's birthday, and *everyone* was there to celebrate. It was her first without Martin, and they all wanted to distract her from that fact, something that she wasn't blind to.

Caro knew Ava was grateful for it.

All the Buchanans, Quigleys, Taylors, and Belmonts were invited, and it was a bit of a packed house.

There were three rib roasts cooking on the grill outside, manned by Wes, Desmond Quigley, and Isaac Taylor. The three patriarchs had taken up the task, while the other men came and went with beers in their hands, checking on the progress.

Theo and Jeremy were in the kitchen, in charge of roasting pounds of potatoes in the brick oven. Meanwhile, Lorraine and Nari

Quigley were ready to start frying up the brussels sprouts. Ever the bartenders, Lilah and Gavin went around the kitchen and back-yard making sure everyone had a drink. Lucy, Sasha, and Juliet Taylor were manning the appetizers.

Max was in charge of the ambiance, rotating the records on the player and keeping the music just loud enough for it to flow into the kitchen and through the open sitting room doors. They'd lis-tened to Elton John, Queen, Neil Diamond, and Tina Turner.

Beau and Frankie were the only dogs running around, taking turns playing with the kids and each other. Domino had been adopted the day before at the Saturday market and, while Caro was sad to see the funny little dog go, saying goodbye hadn't hurt as much as when Tibbett had been adopted. She had still shed a few tears when Domino walked off with her new owners, but it had helped that she hadn't gone home to an empty house at the end of the day. Frankie had been there—her new permanent addition—and so had Max.

Though *he* wasn't as permanent. That thought rattled around in her head as she looked over at him. He was sitting at the dining room table playing Go Fish with Matthew, Christopher, and Os-car. Emilia was on his lap, pointing at the cards he held in front of them; he was letting her pick which one she wanted.

Her chest filled with that bittersweet sensation—loving the mo-ment, but knowing it was short-lived—because she wanted so much more than this summer with him. God, she wanted everything.

"Want to take a walk with me outside?" An arm slid through Ca-ro's, and she looked over to see Ava at her side, a soft, warm smile on her face. "We haven't had a lot of time, just you and me, in a while."

They hadn't. In fact, she could count on one hand how many

times they'd been alone in a room together since Max had been back in town.

"Absolutely." Caro nodded, and Lilah filled up both of their glasses with blackberry and peach sangria—peaches that Max had picked from the trees a couple of days ago—before they headed for the sunroom and out onto the back patio. Beau and Frankie followed behind them, taking off into the yard the second they cleared the door.

The trio of dads all looked up, Wes waving tongs in the air in acknowledgment while continuing his debate with Isaac and Desmond about the best way to make ribs.

"It sure is a beautiful day," Ava said as they walked down the path sipping their sangria, blooming red dahlias on either side of them.

"Did you bring me out here to talk about the weather?"

"No." Ava looked over at her, grinning. "I did not. I want to know about you and Max."

Caro had had a feeling this was going to be about him. She took a deep breath, her focus on the path in front of her. "There is no me and Max."

"You sure about that?" Ava asked as they turned, heading for the peach trees at the back of the property.

"He's leaving in two weeks and then moving to London. And the Kincaid getting approved or not, he wouldn't be coming to visit more often." He'd already told her that he had nothing to do with the remodels.

"Have you asked him if he would come back?"

"No."

"Have the two of you talked about the future at all?"

"No," Caro repeated, shaking her head. They'd talked about the past—both of them deliberately not touching on certain topics, like their breakup—and the present. There was no talk beyond that summer . . . beyond the next two weeks.

"And why not?"

"Because there is no future with us." The admission hurt, that same bittersweet feeling from earlier intensifying, overflowing in her chest.

Ava pulled on Caro's arm, making her turn. "Bullshit." Her no-nonsense tone was more forceful than usual.

Caro's eyes went wide. "Excuse me?" she asked on a nervous laugh.

"You heard me, it's bullshit. You don't talk about the future. Do you talk about *anything*?" She narrowed her eyes, frowning. "Or are you two just having sex?"

Apparently Ava wasn't beating around any bushes today. At the blunt question, another burst of awkward laughter escaped Caro's mouth. "We talk."

Ava let out a sigh, shaking her head. "Come here." She pulled Caro over to the wooden bench under the peach trees, where two cardinals were jumping around from branch to branch.

They took a seat, setting their glasses of sangria down on the wide arms. When Caro turned, Ava grabbed one of her hands, holding on tight. "What do *you* want?"

"I don't know." Caro shook her head.

"Bullshit."

"You're feisty today."

"I'm feisty *every* day." Her mouth twitched with that smile again before it turned a little sad, serious. "Are you happy, Caro? Truly happy?"

"I . . ." She hesitated, not because she didn't want to tell Ava the truth, but because she didn't know. "Something's missing. Something's *been* missing." Max had been missing. Caro didn't say it, but Ava could see it in her expression.

"You never let yourself move on from him. Did you? No matter how much you told yourself that you had?"

"No, I didn't." Caro shook her head. She'd dated over the years, but nothing that had ever become *something* more. Because none of those men had been Max.

"You're in love with him, Caro."

"I am," Caro admitted. She couldn't lie, not to Ava and not about this. Those two words burned in her throat, that same feeling at the corners of her eyes. She'd given her heart to him a long time ago, and she'd never gotten it back.

"I'm guessing you haven't told him *that* either. Just like you haven't told him about the books."

"No, I haven't told him I love him." She hadn't admitted it out loud to anyone, not even Lucy or Lilah. "As for the books, those are proof . . . proof of what I *feel* for him. I don't know if he feels the same way."

"Do you think it's a coincidence that Max never got married? Do you know that he's never had a *truly* serious relationship?"

"We haven't talked about our other relationships."

"Of course you haven't." Ava rolled her eyes. "Max never moved on either, Caro. I see the way he looks at you, the way you look at him. The way you were *just* looking at him." She waved to the house with her free hand. "You two love each other."

"You know it's not as simple as that. I live here. He's moving to London."

"And you wouldn't move for him? He wouldn't move for you?

Logistically, this is the same problem you would've had fourteen years ago. What was the plan then?"

"The plan was for us to be together."

"And why can't that be the plan now?"

Caro didn't say anything, just looked at Ava. She knew her fear was obvious in her eyes.

"You can't let this fear drive you away." Ava's hand tightened on Caro's. "There is *nothing* easy about love. Having it, or losing it. And I know that full well."

Ava didn't say *better than you*, but Caro knew that was the truth. She'd buried her only child almost thirty years ago. That was something a parent should *never* have to do.

"I know you do." Caro shook her head. "But what if you're wrong? What if he doesn't feel the same way? Or what if he does and it isn't enough?"

She'd said it herself all those years ago: sometimes love wasn't enough.

"Then you tried and you *know*. Isn't trying and failing worse than *not* trying and never knowing?" Ava gently cupped the side of Caro's face. "You are braver than you will ever know, Caro. So I'm going to ask you again, *what do you want?*"

"I want Max," she said without hesitation.

"Then get him." Ava leaned in, her smile brighter than ever. "And you *know* where to start."

* * *

THE POP AND sizzle of oil filled the kitchen as Caro and Ava walked back in. Nari and Lorraine had started on the brussels sprouts, meaning dinner was almost ready.

Caro made a beeline for Lucy, Lilah, and Sasha, an idea for how to try to get Max back already taking root in her head.

She grabbed Lucy's hand before ushering them all out into the hallway. "I need your help."

"Are we murdering someone, or getting rid of a body?" Sasha asked.

"You have *got* to stop with the true crime podcasts." Lucy shook her head.

"Never." Sasha grinned.

"Well, I know you're ride or die, Sasha, but the dying is not part of it. At least not today."

"Then what is?" Lilah asked.

"It . . . it's Max."

"*Yes.*" Lucy drew out the word.

"What about him?" Sasha's smile grew as she bounced on her feet.

Caro hesitated for just a second, looking between them all. "I'm still in love with him."

"Fucking finally," Lucy said.

"I knew it." Sasha was now beaming.

"Has that ever been up for debate?" Lilah asked. "I told you this weeks ago."

"Yes, yes." Caro waved her hand in the air. "Everyone else figured it out before I was willing to admit it to myself. *I get it.*"

"What do you want us to do?" Lilah asked.

"Yeah." Sasha nodded. "What's your plan?"

"We'll make it happen." Lucy's hand was still in Caro's, and she squeezed tight.

* * *

MAX SAT BACK in his chair, sticking the four of hearts into his hand and studying the other cards he was holding. He grabbed the ace of spades and discarded it on top of the pile.

"Just what I needed," Ava said as she reached across the table and snatched it up.

Max groaned. He'd been feeding her cards all night.

It was almost ten, and the majority of the guests had left after the massive tiramisu that Theo and Juliet had made. As Ava was turning eighty-five, they'd opted for just the two candles, one in the shape of an eight, and the other a five. Ava had closed her eyes, making a wish before blowing out the flame.

He'd been the one she looked at when she opened her eyes, and he had a feeling whatever that wish was, it had been about him. But that was where her benevolence had ended, because as soon as they'd pulled out the three decks of cards, she became ruthless.

There were ten of them gathered around the table: Ava, Max, Caro, Lucy, Jeremy, Lilah, Wes, Lorraine, Sasha, and Theo.

They'd been playing Rummy for the last two-ish hours, and Ava was the only one at the table who didn't have points in the middle triple digits. In fact, they were on their last hand, and she still hadn't cracked one hundred, going out hand after hand after hand.

"You aren't allowed to sit on that side of Ava next time we play," Lilah said to Max.

"Believe me, I am *not* doing this on purpose."

"Sure, you aren't." Lorraine shook her head. "You two are in cahoots over there."

"Cahoots?" Ava raised her eyebrows as she discarded the nine of spades.

"Yes, cahoots." Lucy nodded, ignoring the nine and drawing from the pile. She took one look at the card and dropped the six of hearts.

"Unlike Lucy over here who has helped me not at all." Theo shook his head as he picked up the six.

Max was a little surprised that Theo had stayed, as he'd pretty much avoided Lucy like the plague since she'd returned to town. They'd both been working in the kitchen that day, but they'd stayed on opposite ends, ignoring each other.

"You just picked up my discard." Lucy pointed to his hand.

"Yes, well, you're bound to accidentally give me something." Theo shrugged as he dropped the three of hearts.

Lucy just rolled her eyes.

Caro was sitting to Max's right, and he felt her leg lightly bouncing against his. He put his hand on her knee and squeezed. "You okay?"

She looked over at him, biting her lip. "Yes." There was a secret smile on her mouth, and he desperately wanted to lean forward and kiss it. But since there was a table full of people around him, he resisted the urge.

As much fun as he was having playing cards with everyone, he couldn't wait to get Caro alone. It had been such a busy day, and other than waking up together that morning, they hadn't had any time to themselves.

He always wanted time for just the two of them, but it felt like it was getting worse as the clock was counting down to the end of the summer. The less time they had, the more he wanted to be spending it with Caro.

They made their way around the table a few more times—Ava picking up each and every one of Max's discards—before she put all her cards on the table.

"And that"—she grinned as she folded her hands—"is how it's done."

"There is no beating her," Jeremy said as he started adding his points.

"There never was." Wes shook his head.

Once the cards were put away, everyone tucked their chairs under the table, wishing Ava happy birthday one more time before they left.

"Do you need any help?" Lilah waved to the few cups scattered around the kitchen.

"Nah, we got it." Caro shook her head. "Go enjoy the rest of your child-free evening." Desmond and Nari had left earlier, taking the kids for a night at Grandma and Grandpa's.

"Oh, we will." Jeremy waggled his eyebrows.

"Hush." Lilah lightly hit him in the shoulder. "Call me tomorrow." She gave Caro a mischievous smile before she grabbed Jeremy's hand and headed for the door.

"I got Frankie," Lucy said as she scooped the sleeping puppy up from the dog bed in the corner, where she was snuggled with Beau. "See you in the morning." She kissed Ava on the head.

"I sure will." Ava nodded.

Ava had her art classes at the college, and as Lucy had some stuff she needed to do in Asheville, they were going to make the twenty-minute drive together and have lunch between Ava's classes. Not only did Lucy have an appointment with Dr. Bloom—she'd been going weekly since she'd been back in town—but she was meeting up with one of her old music teachers to discuss a potential job for the summer.

Lucy was still working shifts at Quigley's and Dancing Donkey, but Caro knew how much she wanted to be doing *something* with music. Things might not have panned out in LA, but it was still her passion.

"See you tomorrow too." Lucy winked at Caro.

"What was that?" Max looked over at Caro.

"Nothing." She shook her head. "Ava, Max and I are going to finish up down here and then be in the backyard for a bit."

"We are?" Max asked, studying her face. That same nervous bouncing energy from earlier was radiating off her.

"We are." Caro nodded.

The corner of Ava's mouth pulled up in a little smile. "Well, just make sure to lock up back there." She pointed to the mudroom. "I'll get the front door."

"Okay," Caro said before she gave Ava a hug.

Max could've sworn he heard Ava whisper, *Good girl*, to Caro before she let go and pulled Max into a hug.

"Good night, Bean." She kissed his cheek.

"Night, Ava."

"What are we doing outside?" Max asked as he opened the dishwasher and loaded the last of the cups.

"You'll see," Caro said, wiping down the table and setting the bouquet of hydrangeas back in the center. "Can you grab a bottle of wine?"

"This is getting more interesting. White or red?" He headed for the bar in the sitting room, letting his hand slide across the small of her back as he passed.

He felt the shiver that ran down her spine. "White."

He was back a minute later, the cork already out of the bottle of her favorite sauvignon blanc. He made to grab two wineglasses from the cabinet, but she shook her head. "No glasses." She grabbed the bottle, taking a swig before handing it back to him.

"More and more interesting," he said as he took a drink too.

"Just you wait." She turned off all the lights and held out her hand. He didn't hesitate to grab it, letting her lead him to the mudroom. Beau passed them on the way, pushing through the doggy door and heading upstairs to Ava.

"You can lock it. We aren't coming back inside."

Max grabbed his keys from his pocket, locking up, and then Caro was pulling him out into the middle of the backyard, right toward the oak tree with the treehouse.

When they were underneath it, she turned to him, her palm sliding up his chest to the back of his neck. She barely tugged before he was lowering his head and she was stretching up, their mouths meeting in the middle.

She tasted like the wine. Crisp and citrusy. The kiss was slow at first, languid, but the fire inside of him blazed. His hand moved to her back, lowering until it was at her ass, tugging her against him. She gasped, pulling back to look up into his face.

"What are we doing, Caro?" He needed to know how long he had to wait to get inside of her.

"Going up there." She pointed above them.

Max looked up at the treehouse, seeing that the door in the floor above the stairs was already open. "Seriously?" He still hadn't gone up there since he'd been back.

"Yeah." The smile on her face was so perfect it made his chest tighten. "I'll go up first, and then you can pass me that." She nodded to the bottle of wine in his hand.

Caro turned to the ladder, pulling herself up one rung at a time. She was wearing a short red and white summer dress, and he couldn't help but look.

"That lace drives me out of my mind, Caroline," he whispered as he spotted her underwear. There wasn't a lot of light out there, but he could tell it was white.

"Don't worry," she called over her shoulder. "I won't be wearing it for very long."

"No, you won't." He took another drink of the wine.

Once she disappeared inside, her hand shot out for the bottle, and then he followed her up. When his head cleared the hole in the floor, he couldn't make out too much in the dark, just Caro standing in front of him and a pile of something off to the left.

When Martin and Wes had built this thing twenty-six years ago, they'd made the ceiling just high enough for them to be able to stand inside in case they needed to come up and fix anything. But since Max was taller than both men—and he couldn't see where the roof was—he stood slowly, stepping off to the side and flipping the door shut. He had a pretty good idea of what was going to happen up here, and once things got started, he really didn't want either of them falling through.

"We doing this in the dark?" Max pulled Caro to him, her body flush against his.

"No." She shook her head. "But I want to toast first." The bottle of wine was in her hands again. "To the past becoming the present." She tipped the bottle back, taking a sip before passing it to him.

"To the past becoming the present," Max repeated before taking a sip of his own.

All of a sudden the space was lit up with flameless candles—the same ones he'd found in the attic earlier in the summer. The pile on the floor that he'd been unable to make out was a pallet of blankets and pillows.

"When did you do this?" Max let out a little laugh as he looked back to Caro. She had a remote in her hand, and she set it down on the ledge next to them.

"I didn't." She shook her head as she grabbed the wine from him, putting it on the ledge too. "Lucy, Lilah, and Sasha did."

"When?"

"After dinner." She wrapped her arms around his neck, pressing her body to his. "When you and Ava took Beau and Frankie on a walk."

"Of course."

Caro had practically shoved them all out the door, telling him the only way to stop Ava from cleaning up was to get her out of the house. She'd said they weren't allowed back for thirty minutes.

"It's perfect." He leaned down, covering her mouth with his, his hands going to her thighs, slipping under the hem of her dress and pushing up. He pressed his fingers into her bare skin, kneading until he got to her ass and squeezed.

She moaned before pulling back, her eyes dazed. "Max, wait, I need to tell you something first."

Something about the look in her eyes made his heart pick up its pace. "What's that?"

"I love you."

He'd been waiting fourteen years to hear her say those words again, and he could've sworn his heart stopped beating, because it felt like the entire world had stopped spinning. But then it started again, spinning so fast he wasn't sure how he was still standing.

"Caro," he whispered, moving his hand to the side of her face and cradling her head. She leaned into his touch, her eyes not leaving his as he *finally* said it out loud. "I love you too. I will *always* love you."

The relief in her expression was so profound it took his breath away. But it was nothing compared to when she stretched up against him, her lips so close to his that they brushed when she spoke.

"Show me." She barely had the words out before his mouth was on hers, their tongues twisting together.

Caro loved him. He didn't care about anything else. There was a desperation that was crawling out of his chest. A desperation that had been there since everything had fallen apart all those years ago. A desperation to be inside of her, to show her *exactly* how he felt. Like he couldn't survive without her. Couldn't survive a life without touching or tasting her. Without feeling her heart beating against his. Without waking up with her scent in his lungs.

She was all he wanted. All he'd *ever* wanted.

His hands were under her dress, pulling it up her body. Her fingers tangled in the hem of his shirt, and the second they were both free and clear, he kissed her again. And then he was working on the back of her bra while she fumbled with the button and zipper on his jeans.

It didn't take them very long to strip each other down, and then Max was laying Caro on the piles of pillows, settling himself between her thighs. Her hair was spread out all around her head, her skin glowed, and the lights were dancing in her hazel eyes.

"You're so beautiful, Caro. So beautiful it takes my breath away."

"So are you." She reached up, cradling the side of his face. "Max, I don't want anything between us tonight." Her other hand moved between their bodies, lining his cock up with her entrance.

She was showing him her love too.

"I don't either." He grabbed the hand at his face, lacing their fingers together as he stretched it up and above their heads. "Caroline," he whispered as he barely brushed his lips along one cheek and then the other. He moved his free hand to her hip, holding on to her. "I love you." He told her again as he pressed into her.

Caro gasped, her entire body arching into him. Nails bit into his skin, the sharp pressure so much more pleasure than pain. She dragged a hand down his back, and the moan that escaped his throat vibrated throughout his entire body. His hand tightened on her thigh as he started to move, slowly thrusting into her before pulling back.

He had no idea how long they moved together. It could've been minutes, or hours, or days. Time ceased to exist.

She *loved* him.

He knew she was close, but he wasn't ready to be done. He wanted to stay in this moment longer. Wanted to stay there forever.

But as she moaned his name, her core starting to tighten around him, he let himself go over the edge with her. Let her drag him down. The pleasure was so intense he thought he might've blacked out, and it took him more than a few seconds to return to consciousness. Caro's arms were wrapped around him, her legs bracing his thighs. Max was holding on to her, his chest pressed against hers, his mouth at her neck as he tried to catch his breath.

His fingers on her thigh tightened, digging into her skin, refusing to let go of the moment. He never wanted to let go. But he never *had* wanted to let go.

"I love you, Max," Caro whispered as she rubbed her hands up and down his back. "I love you. I love you. I love you."

There was no going back this time . . . no leaving her again.

Chapter Seventeen
Tightrope

Caro woke to the sound of cardinals singing. She slowly opened her eyes to find Max asleep next to her, his head on the same pillow, his face inches from her own. They were still in the treehouse, buried under the blankets they'd made love on for hours the night before.

Made love. He *loved* her.

Her lips curled into a smile as she slid her hand down his chest. He let out a groan, pressing into her.

"Max," she whispered. "We have to get up."

"But do we?" His eyes slowly blinked open.

"Yes, because I inconveniently have to be at work by eight."

Max groaned, burying his face in her neck as he wrapped his arms around her. "Can't we just stay up here all day?"

"I don't want last night to be over either."

He ran his nose along the slope of her neck before he pulled back to look into her face. "Well, it won't be."

"It won't?" Caro sat up, the blanket falling from her shoulders and pooling around her hips. She was wearing his T-shirt and nothing else.

"No." He shook his head as he slid his palm along her bare thigh. "We're doing this again."

They hadn't discussed that last night, but she'd known it just as much as he did. "We are," she agreed, feeling her smile overtake her face. "But we need to talk about it. Figure everything out."

"I thought we figured it out last night. I love you. You love me." He grinned, squeezing her thigh.

"Max." She laughed, lightly punching his arm. "That wasn't figuring everything out. Where are we going to live?"

"Here."

"In this treehouse?" She waved a hand around them.

"No." He sat up, his hand going to the back of her head as he pulled her mouth to his, the kiss long and deep. "In Cruickshank," he whispered against her lips. "It's you and me, Caro. Until the end this time."

Her stomach was doing that uncontrollable somersault thing.

"Until the end." She nodded, her palms going flat on his chest as she moved her fingers back and forth across his skin. "So, dinner tonight? Just you and me?"

He might think that everything was good and settled, but she still had one more thing to tell him. She couldn't keep her books secret for a second longer. In fact, she was so excited to finally tell him she could barely stand it. But that reveal needed to be done with more time than she had.

A lot more time. She knew he was going to have questions, and she had a lot of explaining to do.

"I thought Mondays were girls' night," Max said as he covered her hand, pressing it to his heart.

"They are, but they'll understand. I think they might even encourage it."

"Well, that's evident." Max gestured at the treehouse. "So, your place tonight?"

"Yes. Four o'clock. We'll go grocery shopping and cook together."

"Perfect. Now that that's settled." He wrapped his arms around her, pulling her down on top of him. "We don't have to leave last night *yet*," he said as he rolled her to her back, settling between her thighs.

* * *

THE SECOND THEY walked through the mudroom door, the telltale smell of coffee filled the air.

"Well, good morning." Ava grinned as she set her newspaper down on the table. "Did you two have a slumber party in the treehouse?"

"Something like that," Max said.

Caro's cheeks went pink, but she smiled back. "Morning, Ava."

"Morning, my dear. You staying for coffee and breakfast?"

Caro glanced down at her Apple Watch, checking the time. "I'm afraid I can't do either."

"I'll make you a cup to go." Max squeezed her hand.

"Thanks." She stretched up, pressing a kiss to his cheek.

"You're welcome." He let go and headed for the coffee maker.

"So, how did you sleep?" Caro asked Ava.

"Okay. But I probably could've gotten a little more. I woke up with a headache. My guess is the sangria . . . and the shouting during Rummy."

Max glanced over at her as he poured the coffee. "If I remember correctly, you were the one doing the shouting."

"Oh, that's right. That was me," she said as if she'd only just remembered.

Max finished making Caro's coffee, twisting on the lid to the travel mug before handing it to her.

She kissed his lips as she whispered, "I love you."

They'd told each other that more times than he could count last night, both of them apparently making up for lost time.

Max moved his mouth to her ear. "I love you too, Caroline."

She was smiling as she pulled back from him, not taking her eyes from his as she walked backward. "See you at four."

"At four," he repeated.

"Bye, Ava," Caro said as she pressed a kiss to her head before walking out of the kitchen.

As soon as the front door closed, Ava asked, "Did I hear an *L*-word from the both of you just now?"

"You might've." Max leaned back against the counter.

"And?" She waved her hands in the air, signaling that she clearly needed more.

"We're back together."

"I *knew* it." She stood up from the table, crossing over to him and throwing her arms around him. "I'm so happy."

Max hugged her back, unable to stop the smile that turned up his mouth.

"So, what's next?" Ava asked as she pulled back.

"Well, you'll be happy to know that we're talking tonight to figure it *all* out, but the short of it for now is I'm going to move to Cruickshank."

"Good." She cupped the side of his face as she looked up at him. "You figured it out. Took you long enough," she said as she dropped her hand and not so gently punched him in the chest.

"Ow." He flinched. "What was that for?"

"You really made me work for it, Max. Both of you did. The two of you truly boggle the mind with your stubbornness." She shook her head before she punched him again.

"*Hey!*" He moved away from her, rubbing at the spot on his chest. "We got there in the end. Be happy about that."

"Oh, I am. Especially now that you'll be coming home. To *your* home." She waved her hands around them, indicating the Victorian.

"What?"

"I was never selling, Max. I was just trying to get this place ready for you."

"What?" he repeated.

"*This* is your home. And Caro is your destiny. And if I have anything to say about it, you're finally going to get your dream career with that hotel."

"Did you plan that part of this too?" He wouldn't have been surprised at this point.

"No, that was all you, kid." She grinned. "But as soon as you started working on it, I knew this one was different. I've heard about so many of these projects, been there when you landed some of these deals, seen them before and after the remodels, and you've never talked about *any* of them with as much excitement as you have this building. I know it's made you happy, something you haven't been in a long time."

"It was that obvious?"

"Yes. It's had me very worried."

"You don't need to worry about me."

A burst of laughter escaped Ava's lips, and she shook her head. "I will worry about you until I take my last breath, and most likely even after that. Max, these last couple of weeks there's been a light back in your eyes that I haven't seen in years. It's clearest when Caro's around, but it's also when you're around everyone else. When you're having a beer with the boys, or when you're playing with Beau, or holding Frankie, or coloring with Emilia, or going back and forth with Lucy and Lilah and Sasha."

"I've also been happier when I'm around you."

"Yes, well, that's obvious." She put her hand to her chest. "I'm a delight."

"You are that." He smiled.

Ava moved toward him again, her hand up, and he held his arms up in protection. "I'm not going to hit you again." She swatted his hands away as she placed her palm over his heart. "I just wanted you to know how important this thing is. And how sometimes it might get hurt, battered and bruised, but it's stronger than you will ever know. *You* are stronger than you will ever know. And you and Caro? Well, the two of you together are a force that can't be broken. Do you understand me?"

"I understand."

"Good. I love you, Bean. Now and always." Ava smiled up at him, taking a deep breath before letting out a contented sigh. Like she'd said all she needed to say.

* * *

MAX SPENT THE morning and afternoon working on his proposal for the Kincaid project, not the one he'd done to buy it, but the one that was his vision for what to do with it. Now that he knew what he wanted—Caro, Cruickshank, the Kincaid—he had to set his plan in motion.

And his next step was showing his boss *exactly* what he envisioned.

The phone sitting on the desk next to him started ringing, *his* phone. He'd stopped using Martin's flip phone after he'd won the bet, but he'd continued the routine of keeping its use to a minimum. He was texting Caro way more than he was using it for business of any kind.

His assistant's name was on the screen, and he accepted the call, pressing the speaker button.

"What's going on, Edward?"

"Hey, Max. Mrs. Bergen wanted to see the Kincaid presentation, but when I looked at the one I had, it was from a few days before your meeting with the council. And as I know you, I know you were editing until the last minute."

"Sure thing, I'll forward it over right now."

The phone ringing followed by Max talking had woken Beau up from where he'd been sleeping on his dog bed. He had a good long stretch before he trotted over to Max, tail wagging.

Max looked at the clock, seeing that it was just after one, which meant it was time for their afternoon walk, a routine they'd started the last couple of weeks.

"Is there anything else going on?" Max asked as he pulled up the file.

Beau sat up on his hind legs, waving his front paws in the air before falling forward onto Max. He petted Beau's head, mouthing, *Give me a minute*, before looking back to the computer. Beau didn't seem to understand his request and instead started nudging his nose under Max's arm.

"No. I just sent you an email with more apartment listings in London," Edward said as it popped up in his inbox. "And I should have another batch of places in a couple of days."

"Hey, Edward, hold off on the apartment hunt. I'm also going to need you to schedule a meeting with Mrs. Bergen for sometime this week."

Edward paused on the other line. "Uh, okay. I can do that. Anything else?"

Max wasn't going to elaborate about what was going on. He needed to talk to Adrienne first.

"That's it," he said as he added the file to the email. The task was a little more complicated than usual because Beau had fully lodged his head under Max's armpit. "I've got to go. My grandmother's dog is demanding we go for a walk. I'll talk to you tomorrow."

"Have a good one," Edward said before the phone screen blinked and the call disconnected.

Max hit the send button on the email before turning to Beau. "All right, man." Max ruffled the dog's head before he stood up. "Go get your leash."

Beau tore off for the front door. Max couldn't help but grin as he followed behind him.

There was a peace in his chest as he and Beau headed for downtown. He knew he was making the right choices. Knew *this* was where he was supposed to be. And that Caro was who he was supposed to be with.

Max had brought Beau's ball, so they spent a good half hour playing fetch at the park, both of them getting thirsty. As he'd had a long night and was pretty sure he was in for another, he headed to Dancing Donkey for a little pick-me-up. Plus, they made a blended drink for dogs that Beau went crazy for.

They even served it in a dog bowl.

"Well, look who it is." Lorraine smiled as he walked in.

"You know Caro's not working today, right?" Sasha asked him.

"Hey, I come here when she's not working."

"Sure you do. You have a nice night?" she asked innocently.

"The best."

"Excellent. Now, what can I get you?"

Max ordered his and Beau's drinks and gave Lorraine a kiss on the cheek before heading for a table near the window. He put Beau's bowl on the ground, settling into his seat and taking a sip of his iced latte as he looked out the window.

Normally, this would be a time when he'd pull out his phone and mindlessly check his email, or the stocks, or the news. But it didn't have the same pull on him as it used to. The only thing he was waiting to hear about was the decision the Cruickshank City Council had made about the proposal, but that wasn't until tomorrow night.

He took another sip of his coffee, his focus moving to the table next to him as a mother and daughter walked over to it. The little girl was probably seven or eight, with hazel eyes and her dark brown hair in pigtails. For just a second, he saw Caro at that age. Except this little girl's eyes were more brown than gray, her hair just a little bit lighter, and freckles across her nose and cheeks.

She looked a lot like her mother, who set a backpack down on one of the chairs. "Camille, sit here with Tibbett while I go get our drinks."

It was then that Max noticed the dog who was at the girl's feet, and he immediately recognized the basset hound Caro had been fostering when he first came to town. Beau was so excited to see his old friend that he moved closer to the basset hound, licking his cheek.

Camille smiled at the dogs before she took a seat, reaching for the backpack and unzipping it. She pulled out a book, settling in to read while she waited for her mother. But she'd only flipped open the cover when her backpack overbalanced and spilled out onto the floor, scattering its contents everywhere.

"Oh no," she gasped as she made a dive for them.

Beau and Tibbett got startled by the movement, both of them scurrying away. Problem was, Tibbett's leash was still in the girl's hand, and he pulled her right off her chair.

Max moved to catch her before she hit the ground, his own drink flying in the air before hitting the floor, his foot landing in the bowl of Beau's drink. Somehow he was the only one covered in the coffee.

"My books!" the little girl cried out as she made to rescue them from the puddle that was quickly racing toward them.

Max grabbed as many of them as he could, and when he stood, his eyes landed on the one at the very top.

His breath caught in his throat as he stared at the cover. He'd never seen the two cartoon children on the cover before, but as had been proven time and time again, he'd have known Caro's art *anywhere*. His eyes slowly moved up to the title, and he couldn't breathe at all anymore.

The Adventures of Pumpkin and Bean by C. E. Buchanan.

Caro had written a children's book. A book about *them*. How had he never known this? How had no one told him? How had Ava not told him?

Caro doesn't ask about you, Max, just like you don't ask about her.

He hadn't asked. He hadn't asked about anything that had to do with her because it was too fucking painful. But *how* had no one else told him? How in all the weeks that he'd been in Cruickshank had it *never* been mentioned that there was a book about *them*?

And how, *how* had Caro not told him? What the hell had last night been? Weren't they putting it all out on the line? He had.

"Max, are you okay?" Sasha was standing in front of him, a towel in her hands.

Nope. No, he was not okay. He was nowhere close to okay.

"What is this?" He flipped the top book so Sasha could see, and her eyes went wide. *Shit*, she mouthed.

"That's one of Ms. Caro's books," a soft voice said from somewhere around Max's elbow.

Camille held out her hands for the stack of books that he'd rescued from the coffee spill. He handed them over before looking to the mom, who had a grateful expression on her face.

"Thank you for catching her." The mom was now back at the table, holding on to Tibbett's leash. "I'm sorry about your coffee. I can buy you another one."

"No, that's okay." Max shook his head as he looked back to Camille, pointing to the books in her hands. "You said *one of* Ms. Caro's books? There are more?"

"Yeah." Camille's head bobbed up and down. "She has five, and the sixth one is coming out this fall. She promised me an early copy when she gets it."

"She's written *six* books?" The shock in his voice wasn't surprise that she'd been able to write six books, but because he'd had no clue. "And they're all about Pumpkin and Bean?"

"Yes, but the first one is my favorite." Camille held it up. "They go on a pirate ship and make friends with a bright orange octopus named—"

"Oswald," Max said before she could finish. He hadn't thought about Oswald the Orange Octopus in longer than he could remember.

Camille frowned, her little eyebrows bunching together. "How do you know about Oswald?"

"Because." Lorraine had joined the group, and she let out a sigh, like the cat was out of the bag. "Max *is* Bean."

"*What?* You're Bean?" Camille's mouth dropped open, her eyes going wide. "Does that mean that Ms. Caro is Pumpkin?" she asked Lorraine.

"She is." Lorraine nodded.

"How has she never told me?" Camille asked.

"That's a question I have too," Max said to Camille.

"Wait, you're Max?" the mom asked, glancing between him and Beau, who'd wandered back to his side and was now lapping up what remained in his dog bowl. "Max Abbott? You're Ava's grandson?"

"I am."

Something clicked behind her eyes as she put everything together.

Well, at least someone had figured something out, because Max sure as shit hadn't.

"Are you going to read them?" Camille asked, looking up at him with those sweet, innocent eyes.

"Yeah," he said, trying to keep his emotions in check as he talked to the little girl. It was very, very hard. "That's exactly what I'm going to do."

"Max," Lorraine warned. "Talk to Caro before you get upset."

"*Before* I get upset? There is no before. How has she not told me about these books?"

"Max." Sasha just shook her head, apparently unable to say anything else.

God, he'd woken up that morning knowing exactly what he wanted. Been so confident and sure of everything.

"I've got to go." He shook his head, grabbing Beau's leash before heading for the door. He had to get out of there.

The rug had just completely gotten pulled out from under him. If Caro had kept this from him, what else didn't he know?

* * *

CARO'S APPLE WATCH was buzzing against her wrist again. Sasha had already called twice, but as Caro had her hands covered in soil, she hadn't been able to answer the phone. She headed for the sink, washing the dirt off as her phone started ringing for the fourth time.

Clearly it was an emergency.

"Sash, what's going on?" Caro said as she put the phone to her ear.

"Max knows about the books," Sasha said so fast that Caro almost missed it.

"What?" No, no, no, no, no. She was going to tell him tonight. She was *hours* away from him knowing *everything*. "How?"

"He came to get a drink at Dancing Donkey, and the Connors were here, and Camille had your book. He knew it was yours the second he saw it."

"Oh God. Was he upset?"

"Yeah," Sasha said softly. "He really was. He left, but I don't know where he went. Probably back to Ava's."

"Shit. Shit, shit, shit."

"I'm so sorry, Caro."

God, her chest was suddenly so tight she couldn't breathe. And that stupid prickling feeling was at the corner of her eyes. *Calm down, calm down, calm down. Figure out what you're going to do.*

"You can get through this, Caro. Just tell him everything, and it will all be okay. You guys have come this far . . . You can work past this."

"Yeah. We can." Though she wasn't sure if she was trying to convince herself more or her friend. "Thanks for calling me, Sash." The words came out on a whisper.

"It's going to be okay," Sasha repeated, but as Caro hung up the phone, she didn't know that it was. All she did know was that she had to get to Max.

* * *

CARO PULLED UP to Ava's house less than ten minutes later and then she was climbing the steps with Frankie in her arms. She didn't even bother to knock or ring the doorbell, and just let herself in the front door.

"Max!" she called out as she set Frankie down. The dog immediately took off in search of Beau. "Max!" she screamed again as she set her purse and keys on the table by the door.

He didn't answer, but she heard noise coming from the floor above, so she headed for the stairs. His bedroom door was open, and when she walked in, he was emerging from the bathroom, pulling a shirt over his head. The second his face cleared the fabric, she caught sight of his expression, and she knew it wasn't good.

"Max, I can explain."

"That's good." He nodded, his mouth so tight she wondered how he was even able to speak. "Because I don't fucking understand. *How* have you written a series of children's books about *us*, and never told me?"

"I was going to tell you tonight."

"Why didn't you tell me eight years ago?" He threw his arms in the air. "When you wrote the damn book?"

"I tried to!"

His arms dropped, confusion filling his eyes. "What?"

"I went to New York, Max. I went to get you back. It was after the book was published. I was going to tell you all about it." She swallowed hard, trying to push through the pain from that day, but it didn't work. "I was going to tell you what a mistake I made when I broke up with you, when I walked away. I was going to tell you how I'd never stopped loving you. And that book was supposed to be a love letter to you."

"Then why didn't you tell me?"

She took a breath, trying to steady herself. "There was a café just down the street from the apartment where you lived at the time. The bottom floor was the coffee shop, and the top floor was the bookstore."

"Bookside." He nodded slowly.

"I went there the morning that I was going to tell you. I was trying to work up the courage. I'd gone over exactly what I was going to say more times than I could count, but the closer I got, the more I couldn't remember." Her eyes were starting to get watery.

"I didn't want to screw it up again. But there was also this fear that you might not feel the same way about me."

"So, what, you just never came to find me?" His face tightened again, his jaw ticcing under his beard.

She blinked, a tear tracking down her cheek as she shook her head. "You came and found me."

"What?"

"You know, I still think about the timing of that day. How was it that you'd walk in there when I was there?"

"You're telling me that you came to New York to tell me you were still in love with me, and I walked into the same café you were at, and you *still* didn't say anything?"

"You weren't alone. There was some beautiful blonde on your arm. She was leaning in to your side, and you went to whisper something in her ear." She felt like she was back there, seeing it all over again. Her *heart* breaking all over again. "You trailed your nose along the slope of her neck. The thing you always did to *me*. Something in me died, seeing you do it to someone else. I'd been terrified that you might've moved on, and there it was, proof that you had. So I left." She wiped the tears from her cheeks, but it was no use; more were falling.

Max let out a breath, his shoulders slumping. "Caro, I don't even remember who that was."

"You'd still moved on."

"No! I hadn't!" he all but shouted as he closed the distance between them and grabbed her shoulders. His grip wasn't hard, just strong enough to hold on. "You want to know why I did that? The thing I always did to you? Because I was always *looking* for you. *Looking* for some part of you *anywhere* else. And I always came up short. Each and every time. Caro, you were all I ever wanted. And I was right there, and you walked away again." He let go of her shoulders, his hands dropping away from her body.

Why did it feel like he was letting go of her?

"Max, I'm sorry."

"You should've told me then."

"I know. I know. But I'm telling you now. I love you. I have always loved you. I *will* always love you."

"I don't know that I can believe that."

"Why?" The word was barely more than a whisper.

"Because you walk away when things get hard. You pushed me away after your mom died. Things got hard, and you stopped fighting. And now I'm finding out that eight years ago you came to find me, to tell me that you wrote a book about us, and when you see me with someone else, you assume I've moved on and immediately run. Again, not fighting."

"How was I supposed to know it wasn't a serious relationship?"

"Exactly, Caro. How were you supposed to know if you didn't talk to me? We've lost fourteen years, eight of them over someone who didn't mean anything to me. Jesus Christ, Caro." He shook his head as he ran his hands through his hair. "What are we doing now? How do I know that when things get hard now, you aren't just going to bail again?"

"I love you, Max," she told him again.

He just shook his head. "You were the one that said love isn't always enough."

"That's not fair. I was nineteen. I fucked up. But I'm here now. I'm fighting now."

"Are you? I've put it all out on the line with you the last couple of weeks. I'm moving back here to be with you. I've told you every-thing, no secrets. I know we didn't talk about the future, because we were both delusional, but we'd discussed everything else." His phone started ringing from the dresser next to him. But he didn't look away from her as he kept talking. "And you leave *this* out?"

"No, we didn't, Max. We didn't talk about everything." Caro shook her head as her Apple Watch started vibrating against her wrist. Her phone was still in her purse, but she could hear it down-stairs. "We didn't talk about London, and me never going to Cha-pel Hill. We never talked about the fact that I didn't choose you when you always chose me. We didn't talk about our breakup. We didn't talk about the end of us."

"Then let's talk about it now. Where do you want to start?"

Her wrist had stopped vibrating with the call, but it buzzed again with a text. She figured it was probably Sasha, concerned about everything with Max. But if she was going to focus on this conversation, she needed to get rid of the distraction. When she flipped her wrist to silence her watch and her phone, she saw a text from Lucy that had been sent to her and Max.

Call me now. It's Ava.

And then Max's phone was ringing again. "Is that Lucy?" Caro pointed to his phone. "Something's wrong with Ava."

Max's hand shot out for the dresser, and he grabbed the phone, barely looking at the screen before he tapped it and turned it on speaker. "Luce, what's going on with Ava?"

"Max, thank God." Lucy's voice was choked, like she could barely get the words out. "She collapsed after her last class. We're headed to the hospital now."

"Caro's with me. We're on our way." His hand was suddenly

stretched out for hers. She didn't even think twice before she reached out and grabbed it. Their fingers twined together as he led her down the stairs.

Ten seconds, it had taken less than ten seconds for the car crash that was her life to become a full-on train wreck. That had been his first instinct, to reach out for her. It was the only thing that was keeping her from completely falling apart.

Beau and Frankie were playing with a toy in the hallway. They both looked up when they saw Max and Caro.

"Shit. We need to do something about Frankie."

"She'll be fine in the house. The doggy door is shut. I didn't open it up when Beau and I got home. Come on." He grabbed the keys Caro had left on the table and pulled her out the door.

The hospital was just on the other side of the Asheville city limits, typically only a fifteen-minute drive from Cruickshank. Max made it there in ten, neither of them speaking, his hands gripping the steering wheel, his knuckles getting whiter and whiter.

This couldn't be happening. It wasn't Ava's time yet. Caro still needed her. Max still needed her. So did Lucy, and Lorraine, and everyone who'd been in that kitchen last night celebrating her birthday. They all needed her.

Caro's hand was in Max's again as he led her through the hospital. God, she hoped he wouldn't let go. Not now. Not ever.

How had everything fallen apart so spectacularly? This morning everything had been perfect. Max loved her. She loved him. They'd figured it out. They were going to be together. Now she wasn't sure if that was a reality anymore. That alone could have broken her. But now . . .

What if she lost both of them?

She couldn't think about it. Couldn't let herself go down that path. It was too much to bear. The desperation in her chest started clawing, ripping at everything. The closer they got, the less she could breathe.

The only time in her life that Caro had felt more helpless was when her mom had died. She had prayed to God to save her. He hadn't listened then. Would he listen now?

Please, please don't take her. Don't do this to Max. Don't do this to me. I can't lose anyone else. I can't. I can't. I can't. It's too much. This is too much.

Caro spotted Lucy in the waiting room the second they walked through the door. Their eyes met, Lucy's mascara smeared under her eyes, eyes filled with pain and sadness.

One look, and Caro knew immediately that her prayers had gone unanswered.

Tears were falling down Lucy's face as she whispered, "Ava's gone."

Caro's hand tightened in Max's, holding on to him as everything came crashing down around them.

Chapter Eighteen
Hold You Dear

The doctors said the stroke had been catastrophic. One moment Ava had been there, and the next, she was gone.

For the second night in a row, Ava's kitchen was packed, full of the same people as the night before, plus a few extra. Casseroles, salads, sandwich trays, and various other plates of food covered the kitchen island and counters. There were clusters of friends in every corner, all of them talking about the incredible woman they'd just lost.

More chairs had been dragged around the table, every seat occupied except for one. The one Ava always sat in.

Ava was gone.

She'd left him. The last member of his family. Well, the last member who actually cared about him. Max didn't count his mother. Hell, she hadn't even called him since he'd given her assistant the news hours ago. He'd have been surprised if she even acknowledged the woman who'd been more of a mother than she'd ever been. The woman who'd *actually* raised him. The woman who'd loved him without condition. The woman who'd never have chosen to leave him.

He'd known Ava wasn't going to live forever. Life didn't work that way. Death was inevitable. He'd just thought he'd have more time. God, he'd wasted so much of it.

"Max?" Caro's hand tightened in his, pulling him from his thoughts.

They hadn't resolved anything from earlier, the rest of their fight postponed. It had been pushed to the back burner. He'd been so angry with her—he still was, to be honest. That was twice that she'd walked away from him . . . that she hadn't fought for them. Would she this time? She'd been his anchor the last couple of hours, barely leaving his side.

Would she stay there this time? Or would she bail again?

He stared at her for a second, so grateful she was there. She was still so beautiful, even with her red nose and her hazel eyes lined with sadness.

"Are you hungry?" she asked.

"Not really, but I should eat something." Max looked down at the glass of scotch in front of him, the one Wes and Jeremy kept re-filling. They'd stationed themselves close, Wes sitting at the corner next to him, with Jeremy on Wes's other side.

He'd been wrong. He did still have family. The Buchanans were his family. *Caro* was his family. But he'd lost them all once before. Was he going to lose them again?

He leaned his forehead against hers, needing to feel more of her against him. He inhaled deeply, her lemony scent filling his lungs. She was the only thing that was holding him together. The only thing that was stopping him from crumbling. He hadn't cried yet. Some part of his brain still refused to accept the reality.

He also had the feeling that if he started, he wouldn't stop.

"I'll be right back." She pulled away, pressing a kiss to his cheek before she handed him Frankie, who had been asleep in her lap. She pushed back her chair and headed over to Lilah and Lucy, who were manning the food.

Lucy had not sat down all evening, needing to stay busy to deal with her grief.

She'd been with Ava in those last moments, showing up at the end of her last art class and sitting at the back of the room, waiting for it to wrap up. She'd seen Ava clutch her head before leaning over her desk and collapsing onto the floor. She'd held Ava's hand until the ambulance arrived. Lucy hadn't left Ava's side.

Max *hated* that Lucy had been the one who had to go through it. If he could've sheltered her from that pain, he would've. But at the same time, he was *so* grateful Ava hadn't been alone. That she'd had someone she loved next to her. Maybe that had made leaving just a little bit easier.

He hoped so, because being the one she'd left behind sure wasn't easy.

A wet nose pressed into Max's arm, and he looked down to find Beau. He reached out, petting his head. The dog was having a rough go of it. He knew something was wrong but didn't understand why Ava wasn't home yet. He'd searched the house more times than Max could count, going through each floor, looking in every room. When he couldn't find her, he went outside and searched the entire backyard. When that didn't work, he waited by the front door, jumping up every time it opened.

But it was never Ava. She would never walk through it again.

She was gone. Just like his father. Just like Rachel. Just like Martin.

God, he still hadn't even dealt with Martin's death. Still hadn't been able to bring himself to visit his grandfather's grave, and now he had to bury his grandmother too.

It was bullshit. Such unbelievable bullshit.

It was incredible that he'd woken up that morning thinking he had everything figured out. And now *nothing* was figured out. Everything had been completely turned upside down. It felt like everything was slipping through his fingers. His *life* was slipping through his fingers, and he was just trying to hold on.

But he wasn't sure if he was going to be able to.

He wanted Caro. He wanted her more than anything. He *loved* her more than anything.

Sometimes love isn't enough.

Would it be this time? He didn't know, but he was going to find out.

* * *

CONSCIOUSNESS WAS SLOW to set in the following morning. Caro opened her eyes, blinking through the fog in her brain. It took her a second to remember the day before, to remember why there was a lingering ache in her chest, to remember that Ava was gone.

That ache turned into a pain that had her body folding in on itself. *Everything* hurt so fucking much, and her head was pounding. There'd been too much crying and too much wine. It had been after midnight when she and Max had made their way upstairs, neither of them saying anything as they got into bed. She'd cried herself to sleep, him holding her the entire time.

There were still so many things unspoken between them, and it was killing her. She wanted to fix it. Wanted to fix them. But how could she do that now? What was the point in fixing the roof when the walls were crumbling down around them?

Max still hadn't cried. Was he holding himself back? Trying to protect himself from her? He'd told her his fear when they'd been fighting: she ran when things got tough. Did he think she was going to run now?

She rolled over, finding the spot next to her empty. The sheets were cold. At her movement, Beau stirred at her feet, belly-crawling up the bed and stretching out against her.

Caro wrapped her arms around him, burying her face in his neck. "I know, bud," she whispered into his fur. "We're going to get through it together."

She lay there with him for a good couple of minutes, giving him some much needed love and comfort—and getting some from him in return—before she pulled herself out of bed. She'd slept in one of Max's too-large T-shirts, the hem dropping down to her thighs. She was going to need to go home and pack a bag to bring back here.

She had no idea what the next couple of days would bring, with him, with her, with *them*. There was Ava's funeral to plan, calls to be made, things to do. But she needed some coffee before she could even think about any of it.

Beau followed behind her when she headed down the back stairs toward the kitchen. The scent of coffee filled her nose as she stepped onto the rough tile floor. Max was sitting at the table, Frankie chewing on a toy at his feet. He was staring at the folded newspaper that sat in front of Ava's chair. The same chair she'd been sitting in the morning before. The very last place Caro had seen her. The last place she'd *ever* see her.

She'd still been alive twenty-four hours ago. Her breath filling that kitchen, breaths that would be some of her last.

Caro swallowed hard, that ache in her chest intensifying. *Don't cry. Don't cry. Don't cry.* If she started again, she wasn't going to stop. And she knew that Max needed her. She wasn't running again, and she was going to show him that she could be his rock. That they could be each other's.

"Hey." Max's voice pulled her out of her own head, and he stood from the table, crossing to her and wrapping his arms around her. He pressed his nose to her throat and inhaled deeply.

When he moved back, she looked into his tired and lined face. "When did you get up?"

"I came down here around five. Frankie came with me."

"I think she likes you better than me." Caro frowned between him and the dog.

"Not possible." He shook his head. "Let me get you some coffee." He kissed the top of her head before he moved over to the coffee maker, apparently needing something to do.

He'd done the same thing yesterday morning when she'd been so full of hope for the future. But now? She wasn't sure what she felt except for bone-crushing grief and fear. Fear of not getting this right with him again.

He filled both of their cups before pointing toward the sunroom. "Want to sit out there with me?"

"Yeah." She nodded, letting him lead the way.

Bright, clear sunshine streamed into the room. How could it be so beautiful outside when everything inside of her was dark and gray?

They settled into the sofa, neither of them saying anything as they sipped their coffee.

It was Max who finally broke the silence a few moments later. "I'm going to go to the funeral home at nine."

"I'm going with you."

"You don't need to." He shook his head. "There's not going to be that much planning. After Martin's death last year, I know she got everything sorted."

Caro set her mug on the table, taking his and doing the same. Then she grabbed his hand and turned to him, her knee brushing against his thigh as she folded her leg on the sofa. "I'm going with you," she repeated. "Don't argue with me. I'm going to win."

A very small smile uplifted the corner of his mouth. "Okay. I won't argue with you." God, he looked so tired. She gently ran her fingers down the side of his face. He leaned into her touch.

"Max, I know we still haven't fixed us, and I doubt that's going to happen today or tomorrow, because everything sucks, but I'm not going anywhere this time. I love you, and we are going to get through this. Together. There's no other option."

"Promise?" It was a plea, one that broke her heart because she knew he was searching for any ounce of hope.

"I swear it."

His eyes shut hard, a tear falling out. And when he opened them, there were more in his beautiful blue eyes. A sob escaped his chest before he dropped his head into Caro's lap, finally letting go.

And she held him through it all. Just like she always would.

* * *

MAX HAD BEEN right—the funeral was pretty much planned down to the letter. Ava had it all figured out. The casket, the plot, the church, the dress, the food. She wanted Lucy to sing "What a Wonderful World," Caro to do the flowers, and for him to do the eulogy.

The funeral would be on Saturday, giving anyone who needed to fly in enough time to get to town. He knew there would be some people from Harvard, and others from all over the United States, but if it was anything like Martin's funeral, most of Cruickshank was going to want to be there.

Ava and Martin had established a big life down here, and people had loved them dearly.

When they left the funeral home, Caro headed for Petal and Thorn to order the flowers while Max needed to go see Ava's lawyer. He'd had a voicemail on his phone that there was something that needed to be given to him immediately.

Even with everything he and Caro had discussed, there was still so much that needed to be said. He just didn't know what it was yet. There was a restlessness in Max that he needed to burn off, that he had to get out so he didn't go crazy.

Staying busy had always been his defense mechanism, but there was nothing to stay busy with at the moment. He could go for a run . . . or maybe a walk was the better option. He'd have been surprised if he'd gotten four hours of sleep the night before, and a run might be pushing it. He was already walking to the lawyer's office; he'd just take the roundabout way . . . the way that brought him to the opposite side of town from where he needed to be . . . the way that had him standing in front of the Kincaid.

He stared up at the building, Ava's words from yesterday in his head.

I knew this one was different.

So had he. The second he'd seen it empty and abandoned, something had changed in him.

You've never talked about any of them with as much excitement as you have this building.

Because none of them had ever excited him as much. This felt like his . . . maybe because Cruickshank was his home.

I know it's made you happy, something you haven't been in a long time.

God, he'd been so close, so close to having everything line up in a perfect little row. Except life wasn't perfect. It was messy and complicated, and sometimes the people you loved messed up . . .

Caro had promised she wasn't going anywhere this time, and as he stared at that building, he knew beyond any shadow of a doubt—no matter how much he'd been hurt in the past—there was no walking away for him either.

You've always known that, Max, Ava's voice said in his head.

A small smile lifted his mouth. Lately his consciousness had sounded like Martin. Apparently Ava was joining the mix now. Well, she'd never been one to stay silent; he'd have been surprised if she started now.

And he had a feeling that whatever was waiting for him at the law office was just one more thing she wanted to tell him.

* * *

MAX STARED DOWN at the yellow envelope on the table. He'd gotten it from Ava's lawyer about an hour ago and hadn't been able to bring himself to open it. It was flat, save for a square bulge at the bottom.

"You need another coffee?"

Max looked up to see Lorraine standing in front of him before glancing down to see his empty coffee cup.

When had he finished it?

"No." He shook his head. It was already buzzing; the last thing he needed was more caffeine.

"Well, then do you need help opening that envelope?" She pointed to the table.

"I think I got it."

Lorraine looked at him, resting her hands on her hips. "Whatever's in there, it's important."

"I know." Max nodded. "That's why I'm scared to open it."

"Ava would never give you more than you could handle."

"She'd push it to the limit, though."

"She always did." Lorraine squeezed his shoulder before she grabbed the empty cup and headed back to the counter.

But before Max could reach for the envelope, his phone started buzzing against the table. He saw the name on the screen and picked it up. "Mrs. Bergen."

"Maximillian Abbott, exactly *how* many times do I have to tell you to call me Adrienne?"

"At least one more time."

"Well, it better be many more times." He could hear the smile in her voice, but it turned somber a moment later. "Edward told me about Ava. I was very sorry to hear it. I always enjoyed her when I saw her."

Adrienne had spent time with both of his grandparents over

the years. She'd gone to dinners with them in New York, and when they'd come on trips with him to Europe, she'd always made a point of taking them to the best restaurants.

Hell, his boss had made more of an effort with Ava and Martin than his own mother had. And he still hadn't heard from her, almost twenty-four hours after Ava's death. It didn't surprise him, and at this point in his life, he was mostly numb to it.

"Thank you." Max couldn't help but bow his head at her words.

"You know if there's anything I can do, it's done."

"I know that." He nodded as if she could see him. "And there is actually something I wanted to talk to you about."

"I'm guessing it might have to do with the very extensive remodel plan you accidentally sent me on the Kincaid."

Max froze in his seat. "What?" How had he done that? He thought back to the conversation he'd had with Edward yesterday, when he'd been resending the file, and how Beau had distracted him, just wanting to go on his walk.

"I haven't seen anything like that from you before," Adrienne went on. "I was impressed."

"I just had a few ideas."

"I'd say there were more than a few." She paused for a second, taking a breath. "Is this where you tell me you aren't taking the promotion in London?"

"Yes."

"I thought so." He could tell she was smiling again. "You know, I talked to Edward yesterday about the Kincaid, about your plan . . . and about how you'd been acting the last couple of weeks. He said he had a feeling too, based on something he'd sensed since you'd gone down to Cruickshank."

"And what was that?" Of course Edward had known something was up. That man had worked with him for the last four years, and he'd usually figured out what Max needed before Max did.

"He said you sounded happy. Something he'd never heard you sound before. Max, I knew you weren't happy in New York. I was hoping a change of scenery would help you. And clearly it did. I just had the wrong location."

Max couldn't say anything. He was thinking about the last conversation he'd had with Ava, the one where she'd questioned his happiness.

It was all she'd wanted for him. All she'd *ever* wanted for him. And she apparently wasn't the only person who'd thought he was drowning. Adrienne had noticed . . . even Edward.

"Don't get me wrong," she went on. "You were more than qualified to take over the London office. I've known from the jump that you were an asset to this company. So tell me, what do *you* want?"

"I want to take over the Kincaid. I want to be in charge of the remodel from start to finish, and I want to run it."

"That's what I thought," Adrienne said. "It's a good thing the council approved the project."

Max sat up straighter in his chair. "They did?"

"They were going to tell you tonight, but considering Ava's death, they contacted us. We're in the process of finalizing the contract with the seller. So, it's yours . . . Well, it's *ours*. But you know what I mean."

"I do."

"I guess I'll just have to be happy with the fact that we didn't lose you completely."

"About that. Once the Kincaid is up and running, I wouldn't be opposed to taking on some consulting jobs here or there."

"I like the sound of that. I'll work on a deal. And by the way, Edward asked if he could go down there and help during the remodel process. He apparently would like a change of scenery himself."

"Seriously?"

"Seriously. You've inspired loyalty in a number of people, Max. Me included."

"Thank you."

"No thank-yous necessary. I'll talk to you sometime next week when things have settled down."

"Yeah." Max swallowed hard, still at a loss for words. "Next week."

He hung up the phone, setting it on the table and staring at it.

How had that just happened? His exact plan, wrapped up in a tiny little bow and handed to him.

You weren't handed this, Max, Ava told him. *You worked for it. You know you did. You put everything into motion . . . even if some of it was by accident.*

He let out a little laugh, thinking about that email again. Even if Beau hadn't interfered, it was what he would've asked for. It was what he would've told Adrienne he wanted.

And what else do you want?

Caro.

He'd spent so many years working hard so he didn't have to think about how unhappy he was. About how much he missed her. And then he'd come to Cruickshank, come back to Caro, and everything had fit again.

Ava had known. She'd *always* known it was about Caro for him. She'd told him so that morning after Quigley's, after he'd drowned himself in a bottle of scotch because he'd realized he'd never stopped loving her. No matter how much he'd told himself he had. No matter how much he'd tried to deny it in those weeks after.

I just think you two have some unfinished business you need to work out. And I've never in my life been good at not meddling, so I'm not sure why you think I'd stop now.

No, she hadn't been good at not meddling. He eyed the envelope in front of him, knowing that whatever else was in there was going to be some push toward Caro. This would've been her backup plan, the failsafe, just in case he hadn't come down that summer to figure it all out . . .

Max squeezed his fists a couple of times before releasing them. He reached for the envelope, prying up the two metal tabs and lifting the flap.

He slipped his hand inside, feeling nothing until he got to the bulge at the back. He had a feeling he knew what it was, and his suspicions were confirmed the second his fingers touched the velvet. He pulled the box out, taking a steadying breath before he flipped it open.

There, nestled in the purple satin, was Caro's engagement ring. The round stone in the middle gleamed in the light above him, the halo of tiny diamonds giving off a little sparkle themselves.

It had been fourteen years since he'd seen it, and the intricate white gold setting was still pristine.

The ring had once belonged to Ava's mother—Max's great-grandmother—Violet, designed by his great-grandfather Bertram. She'd worn it every day for sixty-two years after he slipped it on her finger. That was what Max had thought would be the case when he'd slipped it on Caro's fourteen years ago.

He pulled the ring out of the box, finding the tiny inscription on the inside. *To a lifetime of adventures.*

His mind flashed to the books . . . the books Caro had written. *The Adventures of Pumpkin and Bean.*

Besides that quick look at the cover yesterday—and the little that Camille had told him—he didn't know anything about them. Didn't know what she'd written about *them.*

She'd said that first one was supposed to be a love letter . . . Were they all?

It was then that Max noticed the folded purple Post-it stuck to the inside of the box. He opened it up to find Ava's looping handwriting and her last words to him.

Go get her.

Chapter Nineteen

Won't Back Down

Caro got back to Ava's a little after two, dropping her bag and heading for the kitchen to let Beau and Frankie out.

Beau's hunt for Ava was slowing, like maybe he was starting to understand. Every time she'd left, Ava had always told him *exactly* when she'd be back. Whether it was an hour, a day, or a week, she'd kiss him on the head and tell him how long she'd be gone. Caro knew she'd told Beau she'd be back by dinner yesterday. And she wasn't.

People might say dogs couldn't comprehend something like that. But Beau did. Beau knew.

He walked to the middle of the yard, lying down between the flower beds, like he knew this was where she was. Caro spent a good thirty minutes trying to coax him inside, but he wouldn't move. So she let him stay, heading inside with Frankie.

And now Caro couldn't sit still. Something felt weird. She'd been in that house without Ava before, but knowing she'd never be back made it feel . . . empty. And Max not being there made Caro uneasy.

Or maybe that uneasiness was just the last twenty-four hours.

She couldn't stop thinking, couldn't turn her brain off. God, she just wanted to fix it. Make Max see how *in this* she was with him. The good and the bad. It was all them now.

Maybe cleaning would help her figure it out, and she knew exactly what to try to tackle. The refrigerator was a mess, all of the food from last night shoved in where it could fit.

Frankie had followed her around the kitchen for a bit before giving up and pulling a toy onto the dog bed in the corner. She was now asleep so soundly it was going to take something major to wake her up.

It was just as Caro snapped the lid on the Tupperware container that something else clicked into place. She'd figured out exactly what she needed to do, and her realization couldn't have come at a more perfect time. The front door opened and closed, the echo of it vibrating through the house a second before she heard his voice.

"Caro?"

"I'm in the kitchen, Max!" she called out, setting the container in the fridge before moving to the sink to wash her hands.

She didn't even have time to dry them before the door swung open and Max walked in. There was determination radiating from every part of him—his expression, the set of his shoulders, how he walked. He had a brown bag from Kathleen's Corner Bookstore in his hand, and he set it on the counter before he grabbed her face, leaned down, and covered her mouth with his.

The kiss was just as determined as the rest of him, his lips parting hers with fierce demand, their tongues twisting. She grabbed the front of his shirt, holding on to him as he kissed her harder. It was a good minute before he pulled back, looking down at her as he tried to catch his breath.

"What was that?" she asked.

"You never stopped loving me." It wasn't a question; he knew it. "All those years."

"Never." She shook her head. "Not for a second."

"Good, because I never stopped loving you." Max kissed her again before he let go of her.

Her hands fell away from his chest, the fabric wet and bunched from where she'd gripped it. "Max?" She looked up at him confused. Her brain wasn't working properly after those kisses.

He reached for the bag, pulling out five books . . . five children's books . . . five of *her* books. He grabbed the top one before he put the others on the counter. "I still don't understand how no one told me about these."

"Not everyone knows those are about us . . ." She pointed to the book in his hands. "Not everyone knows that you're Bean. And the people who do—" She gave a small shrug of the shoulders. "I asked them not to say anything."

"Because you didn't want me to know about this?" He flipped the cover of the book open to the dedication page. She didn't need to look over. She knew exactly what it said.

To M.
I'll always wish for more adventures.

"You said it was a love letter," he said as he set the book down next to them.

"It *is* a love letter. I wanted you to see, see how much I still loved you. How much I'd always love you." Her voice cracked on those last words, and dammit, she was crying again. But she wasn't going to hold back, wasn't going to hold back with him ever again. "Max, when my mom died, everything fell apart. I didn't know how to fix us."

"Well, it wasn't *your* job to fix us. It was *our* job."

"I know. But I was barely holding myself together." She put her hand on her chest. "And I . . . I felt like I was keeping you back. You always picked me, Max. Always. And I'd stopped picking you for a while. I thought it was hurting you. So I made the decision for us. I thought in letting you go I *was* choosing you. But I was wrong. I made a mistake, one that I have lived with every day for the last fourteen years. And then I did it again eight years ago. I chose for us. I didn't tell you the truth. If I could go back in time and change it, I would. I'd find a way."

"You know, a very wise woman told me we can't change the past. But we can learn from it. We might not be able to go back in time, but we *can* take the time we have now to do it right."

"I think I know that wise woman."

"And I think she was talking about you when she told me that. I can't lose you again, Caro."

"I can't lose you either, Max." Caro moved her hands to the front of his chest, and she could feel his heart beating under her palms. "But I also can't let you sacrifice more for me."

Something like doubt flickered across his face. "What do you mean?"

"I've been so selfish. Yesterday morning, you said you'd move here, and I never even asked you if that was what you wanted. You said it, and I went with it. I love Cruickshank, but I want you more. You're more important to me, and if you want a life outside of here, I'll go, Max. I'll move to London so you can take that job."

"You want to move to London with me?"

"I'll move anywhere with you. New York, Australia, Singapore, Brazil, South Africa. I don't care, I'll go."

"Anywhere?" He smiled.

"Anywhere."

"And what if I told you *this* is where I want to be? That I want to be in Cruickshank, with you, for the rest of my life."

"You promise?" Her hands fisted in the fabric of his shirt again, holding on so tight she didn't know if she'd ever let go. But she wasn't letting go. Not of him. Not ever again.

"I swear."

"And you won't feel like you're settling, that you're giving up on your dream job?"

"No." He shook his head. "Especially as I'm about to *get* my dream job."

"What do you mean?"

"I'm getting the Kincaid, Caro. It's mine. And so are you."

Caro pulled in a shaky breath, her eyes blurring as she blinked, tears now running down her face. "And you're mine."

Max ran his thumbs under her eyes as he leaned in, resting his forehead against hers. "I am. You don't have to wish for more adventures anymore, Caro." He indicated the book that was still open next to them. "We're going to get them."

And then he was kissing her, pushing her back against the counter as he wrapped his arms around her, holding her close. So close. Like he would never let go again.

It was a minute before he pulled back, and Caro buried her face against his chest, breathing in deep. Herby, lightly spicy, a little salty, and all him.

And he was all *hers.* This was where she was *always* supposed to be. With him.

* * *

MAX HAD NO idea how long they stood there, holding each other, his hands slowly going up and down her back, his mouth at her neck, his nose moving back and forth across her skin. It was the first time he'd felt a moment of peace since Ava had died.

"I wish she knew," Max whispered. "Wish she knew that we'd figured it all out."

Caro pulled her face from his chest and looked up at him. "She didn't know?"

"Well, I told her I was moving back. And while she knew I wanted the Kincaid, she doesn't know that I got it. I just wish she knew that it all worked out, and that it was because of her."

Caro's face fell, her own sadness clear. But it was only there for a second before it transformed, her eyes going bright. "I have an idea." She grabbed his hand, pulling him across the kitchen so fast he could barely keep up with her. "Frankie." She nudged the dog bed as they passed. "Let's go outside." Frankie lifted her head, spotted them heading for the mudroom, and scampered off the bed, now leading the way.

The puppy hadn't moved once since he'd gotten home. She'd slept through the world righting itself as Caro and Max had *finally* and *truly* found their way back to each other.

Caro pushed through the door, the warmth from the sun hitting her skin. It was still shining just as brightly as it had been that morning. The day couldn't have been more beautiful, as if Ava wouldn't have it any other way.

"We can still tell her." Caro pulled him to the middle of the yard and stopped when they got to a spot surrounded by flowers.

"What do you mean we can still tell her?"

"Beau came out here when I got home, and he won't come back inside," she said as she pointed to where the dog was lying a few feet away. "I think he knows Ava is in her garden." She grabbed Max's other hand and looked up at him. "So let's tell her."

"You're serious?" Max had barely gotten the question out when a red cardinal landed on the tree next to them.

Caro spotted it too, her grin growing. "Ava, you will be happy to know that Max and I are *officially* back together. Something that was helped along by your meddling."

"Ava, meddle? No." Max shook his head, and the bird puffed up its feathers, twittering madly. "Okay, okay, I got the Kincaid." He looked back to Caro as a light breeze blew around them, her hair ruffling around her shoulders. "And I got the girl. Caro and I are getting married."

Her lips parted, and she pulled in a startled breath. "We are?"

"God, I hope so." Max let go of her right hand to reach into his pocket and pull out a familiar blue velvet box. "Ava left me something," he said as he popped it open.

Caro stared down at the engagement ring that had once been hers and then she looked back up at him, letting out another unsteady breath.

"I know the timing isn't perfect, and that we're both grieving, and that we will be for a while to come. But if yesterday taught me anything, if the last year has taught me anything, it's that time is precious, and I'm not wasting another second of it. Not with you. We might've gotten delayed a little bit, but I still want that lifetime of adventures."

"I want that with you too, Max."

"Good. Marry me."

He'd barely gotten *me* out when she said, "Yes."

There were tears streaming down her face again as he pulled the ring from the box and slid it onto her finger. And then her arms were around his neck and he was kissing her like his life depended on it.

"This is it this time," he whispered. "Though I'd propose to you for the rest of my life if I had to."

She laughed, shaking her head. "You won't have to propose again, Max. This is it. I promise."

The cardinal on the tree next to them took off, flying by their heads. Caro and Max watched as it passed over Beau before lifting into the air, joining another one that was passing by. The dog still hadn't moved from the grass, not even when Frankie started pulling on his ears.

The happiness that had been swelling inside Max dimmed for just a moment. "Is he going to be okay?"

"Yeah," Caro said slowly as she turned back to face him. "It's going to take him some time, but we'll get him through it. We'll get *each other* through it."

"From here on out," Max agreed, leaning in and sealing his promise with a kiss. The breeze blew around them again, the flowers and trees all moving as if they agreed.

Epilogue

A Life of Adventures

Caro closed the door of the greenhouse behind her before she headed up the path and back to the house. The sun was sitting low in the sky, painting the yard in golden yellows, burnt oranges, and deep reds. Ava's gardens were full to bursting with blooming fall flowers, red celosia, purple asters, bright yellow daisies, and the orange chrysanthemums that she'd insisted on planting all those months ago.

They deserve a chance to bloom just like everyone else. Caro pictured Ava the way she'd been in the garden that day, dirt on her cheeks and a smile on her face.

Yes, everything did deserve a chance to bloom.

Even after I'm gone, it means part of me will still be here.

Well, Ava would always be there. In that garden, in that house, in Caro's heart.

The new owners will get to see her in all of her fall glory.

Did she and Max count as *new* owners? This house had *always* been home to both of them, but they'd never been the owners before now.

Well, technically only Max was the owner, as Ava had left him the old Victorian. But once they were married, it would be both of theirs, and that was not too far off. The wedding was going to be next summer, which made sense, as summers had always belonged to them.

Though now *every* time of year would belong to them. Winter, spring, summer, and fall. And what a glorious fall they were having. The leaves on the dogwoods had all turned orange and red, Max's favorite part of the season.

Beau, Frankie, and their new foster, Cooper, were running around, the fallen leaves on the ground crunching under their paws. They'd all followed Caro outside when she'd gone to the greenhouse, needing to get more Swiss chard, rosemary, and thyme for the soup Max was making.

Frankie started barking as she got down low in the grass, ready to pounce as Cooper ran by her. Beau had been circling both of them, but when he spotted Caro, he made a beeline toward her. He'd gotten better in the months since Ava's death, but it was clear how much he still missed her. He came out to the gardens daily, sometimes lying down in the grass for hours.

Those weeks after Ava's death, he'd made a habit of going into her closet, often pulling down one of her sweaters before curling up on top. But that had stopped when they'd cleaned out the room, something that had been painful beyond words for both Caro and Max.

But they'd gotten through it together, just like they'd promised.

"Hey, bud," Caro said as Beau sniffed at the greens she'd cut. "Those aren't for you." She moved them away from his nose, and he nudged her elbow. She reached down with her free hand, scratching his head. "Go corral Frankie and Cooper and bring them inside." She pointed to the two dogs, who were now wrestling.

Beau took off toward them, and the three dogs made it back to the house just before Caro. When she walked into the kitchen, she found it empty, the lid back on the pot and the burner turned down low.

"Max?" she called out as she set the herbs and chard on the counter.

"In here." His voice floated in from the sitting room, and she followed, rounding the corner.

Max's back was to her as he moved the arm over the record player. The second the song started, her mouth split into a grin. Dolly Parton and Kenny Rogers were singing "Islands in the Stream."

He turned to her, his hands outstretched and a smile on that too-handsome bearded face of his. "Dance with me."

Caro didn't even hesitate. She was across the room in an instant. Max wrapped one arm around her back, his other hand grabbing her left and lifting it between them. He rubbed his thumb across the band of the ring on her finger, and then he pressed a kiss to it, just like he did *whenever* he held her left hand.

His lips brushed against her temple as he started to move them around the room. "I'm going to dance with you for the rest of my life, Caroline," he whispered.

"You better, Maximillian," she said as she pressed her head against his chest, right over his heart.

A heart that was hers, just as hers belonged to him.

Acknowledgments

This book has been a labor of love, and I wouldn't have been able to finish it without the help and wisdom of three people: Sarah E. Younger, my absolutely amazing agent and friend. This first decade working with you has been fan-freaking-tastic, and I can't wait to see what happens over the next ten years. You helped me develop this story from a teeny, tiny seed. Thank you for the many (*many*) brainstorming sessions. I wouldn't have discovered Caro and Max without you. Also, thanks for pushing me to watch *Ted Lasso*.

Next on my list is Nicole Fischer, my editor, who fought for me and fought for this book. Your patience is something that can't be measured. This story has been almost three years in the making. I was at a Christmas market in 2019 when I received a phone call from my agent. She told me my name had come up with an editor, an editor I'd been wanting to work with for years. It was a full-circle moment for me when the person who read my first novel as an intern became my editor for this one. I'm still unbelievably thrilled at how this all turned out.

The third person is Jessica Lemmon. I don't know that I would've gotten through the pandemic without our weekly FaceTime-and-wine date nights. Date nights that have continued for more than two years. Thank you for helping me get through more roadblocks than I can count. Don't worry, I've finally gotten past the mudslide scene, and we won't speak of it again.

I'd be remiss to not thank Nikki Rushbrook, my ever-loyal beta reader. I always know my books are in trusted hands when I give them to you.

To my parents for your continued love and support of this dream of mine.

To my dog, Teddy. I know people always say that when you get a rescue dog, you aren't the one rescuing them, they're rescuing you. It's true. You've had my heart since I brought you home in 2017. Your fuzzy little face in the window when I pull into the driveway every day is my favorite thing in this world. Your unconditional love has changed me in so many ways.

And last, but certainly not least, thank you to everyone at Avon and HarperCollins. I'm so grateful for everyone who has put time and effort into *Dog Days Forever*.

About the author

About the book

Insights,
Interviews
& More...

Meet Shannon Richard

Gloria Widener

SHANNON RICHARD lives in Tallahassee, Florida, with her adorable rescue dog, Teddy—not that she's biased or anything. She enjoys experimenting with new recipes in the kitchen or perfecting old ones, typically with a glass of sauvignon blanc in hand. She feels no shame about the amount of reality TV she indulges in, listens to entirely too many podcasts, and is now a plant lady. ∾

Behind the Book

The initial seed that sprouted this story came from the idea that dogs can change our lives . . . so I want to tell you about the dogs who have changed mine.

My father joined the US Air Force when he was eighteen and met my mother two years later. After they got married, they moved around from base to base as my father climbed the ranks, living in and out of the United States. They had my brothers, then I rounded out the bunch when they were stationed in the Philippines. But there was still something missing from those early family pictures.

The deal was that when we finally moved stateside again, we could get a dog. I was almost two when we moved to Tacoma, Washington, and that was when we got Prancer, our Airedale terrier. She was always more attached to my father and my brother Jonathan, but she was the protector of our house. That role continued when we moved to Florida a year later.

I was in the second grade when Belle, a reddish brown cocker spaniel with the sweetest eyes and the softest ears, came into our lives. She was my inspiration for Sweet Pea, a dog who appears as only a memory in the pages of *Dog Days Forever* but one with a lasting impact on Caroline Buchanan. We had Belle for ▸

3

only five years before she died of cancer, leaving behind a hole that would never fully be filled.

It was about a year after we lost Belle that I found Chloe and Caleb—also cocker spaniels. They were siblings from the same litter. Chloe was white and tan, with freckles on her nose. She quickly became the alpha and was obsessed with chasing tennis balls. Caleb was black and white and had the disposition of a grumpy Eeyore. Sad and moody, he was still a good dog. Although we got Caleb neutered, we'd always planned on breeding Chloe, and she had a litter of puppies when I was in eleventh grade. She went into labor around ten o'clock at night, a couple of days before Christmas. Six hours later, she had five healthy puppies. She was a vigilant mama, and it was only a few hours after giving birth when she went to get her sixth baby, adding it to her brood in the playpen. That sixth baby was, of course, her tennis ball.

We were going to keep only one puppy . . . that was what my mom and I had promised my father. We kept two.

Cody and Chase became part of the family—we had a thing for *C* names at this point. Cody was the one I picked out, the last born in the litter and all white except for a black spot on his butt. He was just as ball-obsessed as his mother and loved a good cuddle.

Chase was my mother's shadow for fourteen years. I've never met a gentler dog in my life, and an old soul from the start. I went off to college a year and a half later, but all four of those dogs were always mine.

It was 2008—and my senior year at Florida State University—when I told my five other roommates that we should get a puppy. There were four of us who wanted a dog, and we all knew that when we graduated at the end of the year, only one was going to keep him. Cooper—again with the *C* names—was a black and brown dachshund who loved to burrow under the blankets and had the ability to find any scrap of food that was left out. My dear, dear friend Kaitie was the one who got him. He was there when she got married to her husband, Stephen, in 2012, and when she had her daughter, Amelia, a year later. He was a formative member of their family.

What with Frankie being a dachshund, I wanted to give Cooper a little shout-out in *Dog Days Forever*, so I wrote him into the epilogue as Caro and Max's new foster. The epilogue was completed months before Cooper passed away in May 2022. I'd forgotten about that part of the story until I got edits back from my publisher. While it was bittersweet to read, I'm really happy that he's part of this book.

I have had the best dogs throughout ▶

my life, but the one who's changed my life the most is Teddy. I bought my house in 2016, the first time I was on my own. I knew I wanted to adopt a rescue and had been looking at the local shelters and rescue organizations in town for months. It was in February 2017 that I came across a listing for a four-and-a-half-year-old mixed terrier who'd been surrendered multiple times. When I saw his picture—looked at his sad brown eyes and little bearded face—I had a feeling he was mine, a feeling that was cemented when I went to meet him. He crawled into my lap and stole my heart.

I've often said that adopting Teddy was the best decision I've ever made. The thing is, every dog that I've chosen has been one of my best decisions. I'm just lucky that they always chose me back.

Also, I have to mention my parents' current dogs, who I love dearly. Boomer is a chocolate-brown cocker spaniel— yes, I know another one—who snores something fierce but is truly lovable. And then there is hot-mess express Callie, an all-white terrier mix with pink paws. I found her at Tallahassee Big Dog Rescue—the same rescue where I got Teddy. We were told she was almost full grown at twenty-one pounds . . .

She's close to sixty pounds now. ᕙ

Callie and Boomer

Cooper

Behind the Book *(continued)*

Chase, Chloe, Cody, and Caleb

Teddy

Behind the Book *(continued)*

Teddy

Teddy

Behind the Book *(continued)*

Teddy

Reading Group Guide

1. Caro rescues and fosters dogs but never actually adopts any of them, until she finds Frankie. Have you ever fostered a pet? Did you end up keeping it? Or have you ever adopted a rescue pet? If you don't have a pet, would you ever get one? If so, what type?

2. Caro believes Frankie is a sign from her late mother. Do you believe in signs? Do you believe that loved ones watch over you after they pass?

3. Max has stayed away from Cruickshank for years, rarely returning to his grandparents' house because it reminds him of Caro and his broken heart. Have you ever avoided a person or place because the memories were too difficult to face?

4. Do you think Caro made the right choice to end things with Max when they were younger? Do you think they would have lasted if they'd worked through their issues all those years ago? What are your feelings on second-chance love stories? Have you ever rekindled a relationship after years apart? ▶

5. The book is set in a fictional town in North Carolina, full of locals who all know one another, family-owned businesses, and picturesque landscapes. Did the description of Cruickshank make you want to visit somewhere similar? Would you ever live in such a place? Do you prefer a small, cozy town like Cruickshank or a big, bustling city like New York?

6. Why do you think Caro works so many odd jobs? If you could pick any job of Caro's, which would you choose and why?

7. The book hints at a secret, volatile history between Lucy and Theo— did you pick up on that? Well, you are in luck. Lucy's story is coming soon! It will contain more puppies, delicious baked goods, and lots of cozy canine cuddles around the Christmas tree. But before you read it, do you have any theories on what might have happened between her and Theo? Why do you think they can't stand each other? ∾

Discover great authors, exclusive offers, and more at hc.com.